A SONG TO DROWN THE WORLD

ROWENA SPRING

EDGE SCIENCE FICTION AND FANTASY PUBLISHING
An Imprint of HADES PUBLICATIONS, INC.
CALGARY

A Song to Drown the World

Copyright © 2025 by Rowena Spring

This is a work of fiction. Names, characters, places, and incidents are the products of the author's imagination or are used fictitiously and are not to be construed as real. Any resemblance to actual events, locales, organizations, or persons, living or dead, is entirely coincidental.

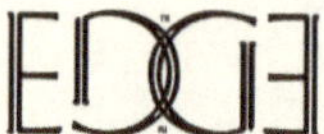

EDGE SCIENCE FICTION AND FANTASY PUBLISHING
An Imprint of HADES PUBLICATIONS, INC.
P.O. Box 1414, Calgary, Alberta, T2P 2L6, Canada

The EDGE Team:
Producer: Brian Hades
Assistant to the Publisher: Ella Beaumont
Edited by: Ella Beaumont
Cover Art: Jamie Ty
Book Design: Mark Steele

ISBN: 9781770532540

EDGE Science Fiction and Fantasy Publishing and Hades Publications, Inc. acknowledges the ongoing support of the Alberta Foundation for the Arts and the Canada Council for the Arts for our publishing programme.

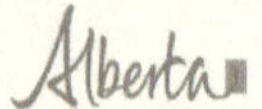

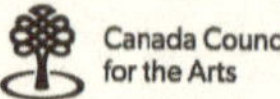

Library and Archives Canada Cataloguing in Publication
Title: A song to drown the world / Rowena Spring.
Names: Spring, Rowena, author.
Description: First edition.
Identifiers: Canadiana (print) 20250211661 | Canadiana (ebook) 20250215020 | ISBN 9781770532557 (hardcover) | ISBN 9781770532540 (softcover) | ISBN 9781770532533 (EPUB)
Subjects: LCGFT: Fantasy fiction. | LCGFT: Novels.
Classification: LCC PS8637.P765 S66 2025 | DDC C813/.6—dc23

FIRST EDITION
(20250823)
Printed in USA
www.edgewebsite.com

Publisher's Note:

Picture this: a woman alone on a cliff, the ocean her only companion. Her voice can summon tempests and shape tides, a power both divine and damning. Her name is Marguerite, a seawitch forged by storms and abandoned by humanity. But her story does not end at the edge of the water.

Imagine her now in a place where her magic falters—where the ocean is silent, the desert unrelenting, and the sands hold secrets older than time. Betrayed by a mentor and exiled to a realm that resists her every strength, Marguerite must navigate a landscape of brutal beauty and unexpected alliances. She will meet a wanderer whose kindness disarms her, a sister whose presence stirs something unfamiliar, and a force beneath the dunes that could consume them all.

This is her journey—a battle not just for survival but for redemption, for love, for the discovery of who she is without the tides to define her. Step into A Song to Drown the World, where magic sings in whispers, and the desert hums with danger. Witness Marguerite's transformation as she dares to belong. And when you close the final page, ask yourself: could you survive the silence?

Brian Hades, publisher

Dedication

For Xena, always

Overture

She was born in the heart of the greatest ice storm her small village had ever known. That was what they said, anyway. She had her doubts. It was far, far too poetic. Marguerite did not trust poetry.

She was an odd child. Her skin too pale, her eyes too dark, her hair silver even in the cradle, and her body too cold. She didn't speak for the first five years of her life (so they said. Marguerite wasn't sure. She thought maybe no one listened). On her fifth birthday, she sang down her first storm (so they said. It was three days after, actually. More poetry).

It wasn't much of a storm, not really. Not compared to the storms she would call later. And banish. She would learn that, too, in time. But not as soon as she should have.

It battered the village for half a day, before vanishing as quickly as it had come. She had stopped singing some time before. Had, in fact, slept the most innocent sleep she had ever had during the end of it.

They had wanted to kill her. She didn't think it was mercy that spared her life. It was fear. It was knowing that the storm had come from the ocean, that the rain tasted of salt and loss, and that if the ocean loved her that much, it would not forgive her killers.

Seawitch, they whispered. It had been many years since one had graced their coast. They still knew the stories, told them around the fire when the rain battered the shutters. They told them during her first storm.

Seawitches were lonesome creatures, they agreed, and anyway, her parents were afraid of her and would no longer have her in the house. It was a shame. They had tried so very long and so very hard to have a baby. Perhaps, whispered the villagers, they had prayed to the wrong gods and that's why Marguerite was what she was. They were subtly shunned after that, Marguerite would later suspect. She never knew. She never spoke to her parents again. She wouldn't know them now if she met them in the street.

That was a lie. She would know them because they would turn and run.

They built her a cottage on a cliff and carried her up in a litter. They told her it was to honor her, that this was a special, sacred place, fit only for a woman of her gifts (over one storm-drenched night, she had become a woman, though she had still felt so very, very young). And then they left.

She spent the next thirteen years alone. They left food, trying to time it for when she slept. Sometimes she woke and tried to catch them, but they were too fast for her child's legs and by the time she could have caught them, she had long given up caring. There were books, too, and cloth, and once a flute. She learned to cook and to sew. She favored long dresses because they were easier to stitch together than pants. Sometimes she went shirtless. It was cold, there, in that little northern place, but it didn't bother her. She wasn't sure if she was born frozen or if the ice entered her soul when her people left her. She stopped wondering in her second year alone. There were things that mattered more. She began to forget the girl she might have been.

Mostly, she sang.

She learned how to build to a crescendo that would cause a wave so high she could almost touch it from her cliff. She learned the precise series of notes that would calm a sea to glass. She spent entire days raising and lowering the tides. She sang a fog that surrounded her cottage and, when she decided she liked it, sang a song that ensured it would never leave. She learned to read the ocean, to understand it, and then, to be like it. Her moods became changeable, as violent and unpredictable as the sea. In turn, the sea became her mirror, became capricious and wild.

She saw brown pods far away on the sea sometimes and she delighted in sending wave after wave at them until they vanished or until their bright white pennants hung in tatters. She did not know what she was doing but that did not excuse her; she would not have cared if she had.

Mama Bella came when she drowned her third fleet.

"They call you a goddess, you know," she said. The first voice other than her own that Marguerite had heard in thirteen years. The first spoken words since she had ceased to do anything but sing six years ago.

"I don't hold with that," Mama Bella continued. "Girls ought to be girls and not goddesses." She smiled. Marguerite did not understand what it meant. She had thought, perhaps, it was a threat like the way the wolves she saw sometimes bared their teeth at a rival. If she had ever been smiled at before, she had long ago forgotten it. "I don't hold with girls drowning innocent sailors, either. It's time someone took you in hand. Past time. They should have called me during your first storm."

"I have myself in hand," Marguerite sang because this was her place, her world, and she was master of it, and ocean music was the only way she knew how to communicate anymore. And then she sang an older, deeper song, an angry song, a drowning song. The wind whipped up, pulling at Mama Bella's braids and tugging at the pleats in her skirt. Marguerite's dress remained hanging down neatly.

Mama Bella smiled and winked and whistled. It was a bright, cheery tune, at odds with the somber surroundings. The wind died and the sun came out from the clouds. Marguerite had kept her cliff shrouded in fog for years. She had forgotten the sun. It beamed down and struck her face. She blinked and turned away, rubbing her eyes.

Mama Bella stepped around so they could look at each other.

"I can teach you to do that," she said. "You taught yourself to sing down a storm. I can teach you to sing up a sunny day." She held out her hand. The sun, now that it wasn't hurting her eyes, was a gentle presence on her back. The world looked different when it was lit up. No one had ever come to find her before.

She placed her small, cold hand in Mama Bella's strong, hot one.

She discovered that she had, in fact, missed the warmth.

Chapter One

Marguerite was angry. She cradled that emotion, held it close, fuelled it with every wrong that had ever been dealt her, and refused to let it go. Anger was familiar and had always been her ally. (She had heard others say that anger was a knife with a blade for the hilt. She had always thought their problem was that they did not know how to wield it.) She would have summoned the ocean and sung a song to drown the world but, well — that was the problem, wasn't it?

She looked out across a landscape both terrifyingly strange and disturbingly familiar. The horizon undulated. The wind blew her hair out of her face. Her eyes and cheeks stung. But the undulation was sand, not water, the wind a harsh, dry breeze, not the cool, wet tempests she had conjured so often, and her face stung from sand, not salt. She blinked and then rubbed her eyes. She had never minded the salt getting into her eyes — salt was meant to be in eyes, escaped only when things were dire — but she did not like the feeling of grit and earth. She did not like this place, what Mama Bella had called a desert.

One year she had been Mama Bella's apprentice, one year of learning from her. Less of magic than she had expected, more of bread-baking and plant-tending and all the other little sundries that she supposed her parents should have taught her. And then one day, Mama Bella had told her she was finished. That she had learned all she was going to from the safety of Mama Bella's home.

Mama Bella had told her that she would be sent elsewhere for a year, that she would have to learn and grow on her own. And at the end of the year, Mama Bella would "revisit" whether Marguerite could be allowed to wander freely.

She had had high hopes when Mama Bella showed her the door. It was ornate, the ancient wood inlaid with delicate metal strips in a design that had reminded her of a wave. It had been a long time since she had sung to an ocean that belonged to her and she had hoped that the lesson Mama Bella wanted her to learn was hidden in the water.

Her tongue felt odd. It was, she discovered with some surprise, stuck to the roof of her mouth. That had never happened before. She unstuck it consciously. Her mouth felt dry and empty, and tasted of rust. That had never happened either.

She didn't like this place. She didn't want to be here. She turned, skirts whirling around her like sea froth, and put her hand to the door handle. She pulled. It didn't give, of course. Mama Bella had told her that if she learned as she was supposed to, it would unseal in a year and Mama Bella always spoke the truth. Mama Bella was too powerful not to; everything she said became true by her speaking it. Marguerite knew this, but she was angry and the anger told her that she, too, was powerful. She pulled again, grabbing the handle with both hands and yanking, though it burned her skin. It did not move.

She would sing then, a song of power, a song to bend the world to her will. If she could tame an ocean, she could tame a single door. She opened her mouth and drew in her breath, as she had a hundred thousand times before. It stung. It had never stung before. She coughed, surprised, and found black grit in her hand. She tried to start a vibrato and the sound stuck in her throat, her tongue like a leaden lump in her mouth, refusing to move.

She swallowed, like glass shards sliding down her throat, and forced out a single note, as soft and wavering as a puff of smoke. A note that could not even have quieted a lapping wave, if there had been waves to quiet.

Her mouth tasted bitter. She did not know if it was dryness or defeat. She had never before tasted either. It would have been wise to sit then, to take stock, to calm herself, to look through the provisions that Mama Bella had given her, to drink a little before trying to sing again. Instead, Marguerite collapsed like a wave onto the sand and began to cry. It was, as the saying went, a storm of weeping. In Marguerite's case, this was usually a literal phrase. It chafed her bitterly that in this place it was only a metaphor. More poetry. She had not liked it when it romanticized her; she did not like it when it mocked her either.

She stopped crying quickly, not because she was done being upset (she would not be done with *that* for quite some time), but because her body was wiser than her mind and had already begun to adapt to the harsh surroundings it now found itself in. She dried her eyes with the edge of her skirt, a thick black piece of cloth that Mama Bella had told her was foolish but which she had worn anyway. There was sand on the hem and it rubbed into her eyes. She had been here only a few minutes and was already heartily sick of sand.

Yet she was stuck, at least for the moment. Neither anger nor sorrow had done her any good. She breathed in, carefully, letting in as little hot air as possible to not parch her lungs, and took stock of herself and her surroundings. She had not changed: hair still too silver, skin still too pale and too cold. If she knew more about the desert sun, that would have worried her, but Marguerite had lived far too much of her life shrouded in mist and she did not understand what brightness did to unusually pale women. Everything about her surroundings had changed. The desert — sand. In every direction, sand. Yellows and browns and reds in the sky. Marguerite had once built herself a world of greys and blues and soft lines. The desert's harshness disturbed her. There was a shimmer in the distance that looked almost like water, but she understood that the air on the horizon lied. If there had truly been water there, it would already have called to her.

She stood (sand raining down in a distressingly familiar patter) and turned. Except for the thin stone wall in which the locked door stood (she refused to think it was mocking her — she refused to give it that much power), there was only sand visible in that direction as well. There was sand and there was sun and there was Marguerite.

And there was a bag, she remembered. The one Mama Bella had given her. She was still angry with Mama Bella, but her so-sensible body was telling her that there were likely things she needed in that bag. She knelt and opened it. There was a hat on top, a beige-ish color, of woven bamboo. She put it on her head; it fit, of course, perfectly. She resented it for that. She would have preferred it be too small so she would be justified in putting her foot through it. She had just enough self-preservation instincts to wear it if it fit.

Below the hat was a bundle of cloth, beige as well, probably the sensible outfit that Mama Bella had wanted her to wear instead of the big black skirt. She tossed it impatiently aside. Below, several little packages of dried bread and — she forgot, for a moment, to be furious — a waterskin. She put it to her lips immediately and drank deeply. It was too fresh, too clear, too sweet, and already too warm, but it was water. She drank it all, lowering the skin only when even sucking drew nothing more.

She opened her mouth, ignoring the way the wind picked up, the way it seared her cheeks. She breathed once, shallowly, and it didn't sting. She breathed again, preparation for the kind of song that could drown a kingdom.

The wind blew a chunk of her hair into her mouth. Strands were not an improvement on sands. She sputtered, pawing at her mouth rather like a small cat. It made little appreciable difference; she dislodged just enough hair to sweep up and cover her eyes. She raised her arms, rubbing her wrists and forearms across her face, an old gesture half remembered from childhood before the wind became her plaything. The movement pushed the hair away but dislodged her hat. It struck the ground behind her. She felt the wrench and the sudden heat on the top of her head. She spun, for a moment moving with the wind. Her skirts billowed; had she been in a temper to notice it, she would have been charmed at her brief resemblance to a ship in full sail. She did not notice, mostly because she had suddenly realized that her hat was made of very light bamboo and that it was no longer behind her.

She had had far too many defeats in the last few minutes to let a hat add another to the pile. She hiked up her skirts and gave chase. This was a mistake. Marguerite had walked on ice before. She understood how to move when the ground was your enemy. But she did not know how to move on ground that played tricks. She took three steps, hard running steps, the steps of a woman who had never had to be less than herself. The ground shifted as she reached the first dip in the sand, and she pitched forward.

She hit the sand hard and rolled, spraying sand up around herself rather like a wave striking the beach. And like a striking wave, she tumbled for some time, a confusing mess of flailing limbs and fluttering cloth and tangled hair. She landed, finally (it had only been a few heartbeats) on her stomach. The sand cradled her — tricky ground was often tender with those it managed to fool. She pushed herself up, shaking her head, sand raining down around her, in time to watch her hat crest the next hill.

Bemused, she watched it roll for some time, disappearing occasionally into some dip in the landscape and then appearing unexpectedly on a distant hill, until the brown of the sand and the brown of the bamboo blended together. Only then did she put her hand to her cheek and realize it was burning and that if she did not cover up soon, she would have a great deal more to worry about than a bruised knee.

She had read literature with brave young heroines at Mama Bella's and so she knew what was expected of her. She shifted carefully in the small depression her fall had made so she could spread her skirt out in front of her. She seized the hem in both hands and twisted it skilfully, rather like wringing a goose's neck. It occurred to her, after several moments of fruitless yanking, that she had always favored the gothics, with girls dressed eternally and impractically in chiffon and lace, and that her skirt was very sensibly made of cotton. She didn't carry a knife in her boot, which was another thing that brave young heroines sometimes did. She thought of the bundle of beige cloth and her mouth twisted. She decided to be the kind of bird that would dash itself to death against the bars of its cage rather than accept its confinement.

She stood, giving her skirts a flick (it was possible that women were born knowing how to flick their skirts in just such a way). She would go back to the door, and she would claw at it until the tips of her fingers were jagged and white, and she would try to sing until her throat was so raw that every note was a splatter of blood. She would replace every spot of white in her face with red, even her teeth and her eyes. She would let the sun bleach her silver hair to dun and her black skirts to grey. She would not change her dress, would make sure that Mama Bella understood that Marguerite had dressed for her own funeral. The thought of her poor, battered corpse and her mentor's regret made her smile a little.

She wedged a toe in the sand before her and put her full weight upon it. The sand gave way, of course, and again Marguerite collapsed. She didn't roll this time — small mercies — but merely slid backward, landing in a heap even farther from the door than she'd started. The world continued to tilt and dance long after she stopped moving.

She rolled onto her back so that her hair cushioned her head. She didn't understand why the sand had to follow her every movement. Seawater got everywhere. It would encrust you, your clothing and your tongue and your eyes and your lungs until you imagined that your bones had turned to coral and that you breathed in plumes of it like a whale, but it was polite about it. It followed you daintily, dogged you, and plucked at you like a good maidservant. It didn't announce its presence every time you moved. It didn't, at the slightest shift, abandon you. Seawater understood about loyalty, about what it owed a person who belonged to the sea.

There was something cruel about the desert. There was something cruel about the sand's impermanence. There was something cruel about the sky, about the way it didn't seem to have secrets, about the way it didn't cloak itself decently in clouds and mists, the way it didn't shy from blazing its colors. Nothing so red and so sharp should be so proud. The ocean knew how to behave, how to keep secrets, how to keep part of itself back just enough that you knew there was more to be found. The desert was not a lady.

She was tired of heat-too-hot and colors-too-bright. She gathered the ends of her hair and drew them across her eyes until she was cloaked in silver and could pretend that all she was seeing was water shimmer. She closed her eyes.

Sleep — if such an utter surrender to the world around her could be called something as simple as sleep — came quickly. She had hoped it would bring with it a measure of peace.

Instead, Marguerite dreamed. She dreamed first that she sat in a little boat cresting high up in the sky. She did not let it fool her. There were no sails, and the planks were made of something hard and white that gaped strangely beneath her feet, and there was no roar of water, only a continuous shrieking. She stood carefully because mischief was woven into the soul of a boat, even if this wasn't a real boat. She knew boat songs.

The air forced itself down her throat, filling her lungs with a hot, fetid weight. She choked and dropped to her knees.

The sun pressed down on her. She had heard the sun often described as an eye, but this, no, this was a mouth, a great gaping expanse breathing stinking hot air down on her. She gagged and tried to struggle away. The world vanished beneath its desperate, all-consuming hunger.

She discovered that she wanted to live after all.

Her eyes should have flown open: that's what the books told her happened when a person was jolted from an unpleasant dream. But hers did not, chiefly because they were crusted over. She rolled to her side, groaned, and discovered that she was cold. She sat up and rubbed her eyes roughly, smearing grit across her cheek. She blinked a couple of times. Her eyes were sore and perhaps a little swollen, but slowly the world came into focus.

It was not the world she had fallen asleep in. The dunes were still there, and there was still sand beneath her and still probably caked in her hair (she refused to pay the sand the compliment of worrying about it — Marguerite had come to hair combing late and with great reluctance). But the world was dark, the brown and yellow of the sand turned to white and grey and the red of the sky to black. It was a sharper darkness than she had ever known and the stars — ah! They shone like knives. She understood now why some legends painted them as wounds in the sky's skin — but the colors at least were not so hot. If she squinted, she could almost pretend that she was on the shore of a particularly foreign ocean.

She did not squint. Instead, she stood and wrapped her arms around herself, an awkward half-hug from a woman who had received none of them. The night air was chill on her skin;

her skirts were suddenly, if not appropriate, at least not quite so obviously foolish. She turned slowly, careful finally with her steps. But perhaps night sand was kinder than day sand; she did not slip. She smiled a little. Like anger, cold had ever been her ally.

The smile hurt her mouth and something tickled her chin. She put her hand up and took it away bloody. She touched her bottom lip and recognized the cracks she felt across it, though not their cause. Since she apparently did not want to leave a desiccated corpse for Mama Bella after all, she needed to take care of herself. She had best climb her hill and try to work out how she would survive the next year-minus-a-day.

She lifted her foot to take a step, debating whether she should trust the sand so far. She decided it had done little to earn such trust. She lowered herself to her knees and plunged her hands beneath the surface. It was finer and smoother than she would have expected. It reminded her, in the starlight, almost of sugar. She took a handful and let it trickle down to rejoin its compatriots. When it wasn't in her eyes, it was almost — not pleasant, tolerable. Almost tolerable.

She turned her eyes to the top of the dune and began to scramble up. It took more than a few tries to work out the correct way to move, how to brace herself so that her hands didn't slip every time she slid her knees forward, and how deeply she had to plunge her fingers into the sand before it didn't collapse beneath her. She was panting when she at last crested the hill.

Her bundle still lay beside the door, which looked no less mocking at night than it had during the day. She took a step toward it, tentative as the first step onto a sheet of ice. There was a shift of light beside it, the patch resolving into silvery fur and inky darkness opening to reveal gems sparking red even under starlight. She made out an arched back, a paintbrush tail, and ears that were tall and pointed like sails. The ears swiveled toward her.

It wasn't a wolf, although it looked a little like one. Like a child's model of a wolf that had been tugged and twisted so the ears were too long and the snout too narrow and the whole thing small and distorted. She wondered what it was about the desert that made everything sharper. It lifted its head and looked at her. It did not bare its teeth, for which she was grateful. It was a small thing, but she was tired and she knew — none better — how dangerous small, angry things may choose to be. She didn't hold her hand out to it, would never have even thought of doing so. She didn't stand, either, not because she was trying to appear unthreatening, but because she didn't think she would be able to.

They stayed there, for a moment, looking at each other, a pretty tableau of maiden and beast in the starlight. Then it took a step forward and met her eyes squarely. Its eyes were not as red as she'd first thought, more garnets than rubies, with a ring of amber around the pupil. Her left hand contracted slightly and she decided that she would throw sand in those eyes if it approached any closer. Sand had to be good for something.

It watched her for a moment and then turned and trotted away, skirting the ruins and the door and slipping off to her right. It occurred to her that she was very, very thirsty and more than a little sick with it, and that, though not every creature ached for it in their soul the way she did, every living thing needed water. There was no one to see her so humbled and so, as quickly as she could force herself, Marguerite crawled after the sharp little wolf.

It couldn't help noticing that she was following, great clumsy mass that she was, as ungainly on land as any other creature born to the sea, but it didn't seem to care. She didn't know if it was brave or uninterested or simply aware that she posed no threat. She wasn't sure she liked that idea. She had never, since her first song, not posed a threat.

It stopped, the small body arching suddenly like the swell of a wave. It began to dig, the tiny paws beating franticly into the ground, little spurts of sand tossing up into the air around it. Bemused, she watched its movements. It stopped and put its head down, the small body shuddering ever so slightly. Then it lifted its head and turned to look at her again, pupils dilating so the gold seemed to fill its eyes, before it flicked the plume of its tail and was gone into the swells and dips of the sand.

She pushed herself forward, exhaustion having long ago burned off her anger so only curiosity was left. She wanted to know what it had been so desperate to find. The hole in the sand looked very little different than the sand around her, perhaps just a shade or two darker. She extended a single finger and touched it gingerly.

It was wet. For a moment, she thought she had sunk into another dream. But her dreams had never been so mundane. Frantically, she began to claw at the sand, and when that didn't work, she formed her fingers and palms into scoops and threw great handfuls of moist sand up and around her. She paused and watched as the pit filled with water, dull and thick, with none of the clarity and brightness of the water at home. But it was water nonetheless. She plunged her face into the hole and drank.

It tasted like the sea.

Chapter Two

The difference between land and water was this: Water had a memory and land didn't need to remember. Land put down layers of rock, like pages in a book, and waited for someone to come along and read it its history. Water did not share its secrets so easily, or record them for anyone to find. There were no chapters in water. The greatest scholar could not read a river and know what it once was; only the riverbank knew where its ancestors might have run. No one would ever remind a water droplet that it once nourished a tyrant and drowned a queen. So water remembered for itself.

The water in Marguerite's puddle remembered. It remembered the deep quiet of lakes and the bubbling excitement of rapids and the fury of storms and the soft patter of rain. It remembered updrafts and air currents and the brush of bird wings through clouds. It remembered window panes and clay mugs and the hardness of teeth and the gurgle of stomachs. It remembered the exaltation of being hot and the serenity of being cold. It remembered blood and it remembered urine and it remembered tears. And it remembered the ocean.

It was the memory of being seawater that Marguerite tasted. There were other memories, and if she'd wanted them, she could have had them. There were no secrets between lovers, and, though many in this place had needed water, had desired it, Marguerite knew she was the only one with the trick of loving water so it knew and loved you back.

But Marguerite did not want to taste glaciers or cooking vapors or the intestines of another person. She found the ocean memory and she drank deeply until her hole was empty, and then she dug it again and again and again. She drank until her stomach protested, and then she continued to drink until it rebelled and she vomited onto the sand. And only then did she understand that the memory of an ocean in a drink of water could never satisfy the hunger for it she felt.

She cried, just a little bit. Just a breath or two. Just enough to swell her throat and tighten her chest. Just enough to hurt.

Not, this time, a rebellion. Not angry tears refusing to obediently play the hand she had been dealt. It was a quiet acceptance that she was here and that all she could do, all she must do to survive, was learn to bear the unbearable.

She stood eventually. It was easier with water inside her, even if it was the wrong water. The desert was very big and someday she would need to learn to master it. But she would start small. She made her way back to the door, slowly, testing each step before she put her full weight on it, moving like a very old woman or like someone who had been very, very badly hurt.

Her bundle was pulled apart and the pieces scattered, the fault, no doubt, of the sharp little wolf-creature. She let herself down again, carefully, and began to pick through the wreckage. The beige clothing was still there, though a bit tangled. She undid the buttons of her bodice and pulled her dress over her head. Her skin prickled in the night air, but it was a comfortable prickling, a reminder that her blood still pumped, that there was still a little bit of sea inside her. She gave the tangle of cloth a flick and it resolved into three pieces: brown pants, a cream-colored tunic, and a long piece of bone-under-sun-colored cloth that she didn't understand the purpose of. She slipped the pants on. They sat perfectly on her waist and hung loosely around her ankles. She supposed they were meant to. The tunic next, sitting easily on her light frame, the top resting gracefully just over her collar bones. It was the long cloth that gave her the most trouble. It reminded her of a scarf, but she could not see Mama Bella giving her a scarf just because the nights were a little chilly.

The wind gusted up again, dancing under the loose flaps of clothing and flicking her hair into her eyes. She pushed it away impatiently, wishing she had some method of tying the tangled mass back.

The idea dawned quickly but the technique eluded her. She pulled her hair back and tied the scarf around it, but the cloth was far too long: she could see little advantage to holding back hair when the fabric swung just as freely behind her. In frustration, she raked her hands through her hair to undo her efforts and yelped. Her scalp hurt.

She knew very little about the sun, but she was learning quickly and it occurred to her that maybe sun and skin did not get along. Or that maybe they got along too well and if she left her skin exposed for too long, the sun would slip inside and take up residence and continue to burn. She didn't like the feeling of the sun outside and the thought of it inside her, the heat licking her insides, evaporating her blood until only salt was left, horrified her.

It took some time to figure out how to loop the cloth around her head. She experimented with wearing it as a headband before finally twisting it and her hair together into a lump of cloth covering her scalp and neck.

It occurred to her that she probably looked quite a sight. It did not concern her. Marguerite had never learned the knack of being beautiful, which was mostly posture and cosmetics and a little bit of looking like you didn't care while caring very much and having a friendly, or not so friendly, poet around who wanted to *make* you beautiful. She had never had a looking glass, either, or picked up the habit of checking to make sure the right person was gazing back. When Marguerite had wanted to know herself she had looked out into the ocean and found everything she needed.

The bundle of cloth dispensed with, she turned to what else had been in the package. It was mostly, she discovered, a kind of flat dried cake wrapped in oilcloth, and a small leather bag of dried apricots. The cakes were scattered but unharmed; the sharp wolf, she supposed, having been interrupted by her arrival before it could force its way in. It had chewed on the apricot bag as well; there were tooth marks in the leather, though no tears, and tooth impressions in some of the fruit that had spilled out of the bag. Marguerite ate them anyway because she had grown up watching beasts scavenging other beasts' meals and it didn't occur to her that it was unsanitary. She wanted apricots and therefore she ate them, as had always been her way.

She wasn't exactly satisfied, but her basic needs had been met and what emptiness inside that could be filled with food and water and comfortable clothes had been filled. She had a vague sense that a person needed more than that (besides the ocean — always, she would need the ocean) and searched a part of her memory that she usually kept tucked neatly away, the memory of when she'd first come to her place by the sea. A memory of the time before she'd learned to fill herself with salt and spray and ocean music. *They* had given her food and clothing and … shelter, she thought. They had given her a house: a little thatched cottage that let in the wind and the cold and had never felt much like a home, even years later. She didn't have a cottage here or any materials to build one, even if she'd had the slightest clue how. She had a wall that didn't support anything, a door that didn't open to anywhere, and a dress she could no longer wear. If they couldn't do what they were made for, perhaps she could turn them to a new purpose.

Had she any idea of how to actually build a structure, she probably wouldn't have been able to do it, wouldn't have even attempted it. But she didn't understand about things like pegs and struts and dove-tail-joints so she tied her bodice to the door handle and buried the skirt in the sand and, looking at the thing she had made which could generously be called a tent, thought herself very clever.

She took a deep breath, which turned into a tortured yawn. She had not been awake very long but having your entire world upended was tiring. And anyhow, having fulfilled all of her immediate needs, and with no goal in sight, she was already feeling the first nudges of boredom. She dropped to her hands and knees and crawled into her shelter. She curled up into a ball and hummed a lullaby, the first song she had ever sung for herself.

It was a lullaby from her village, although she could not have identified it as such. There were other verses, about chickens and dogs and cherry trees, but she sang only the one about the shorebirds, over and over and over again until the beating of her own heart became the beating of the waves. Her voice under the shorebirds was impossibly light and strong for being so drenched in seawater, lifting them up higher and higher into a sky that was soft and wet and perfectly grey.

Her mouth tasted of salt when she woke. She supposed she had been crying in her sleep.

She sat up and her tent promptly collapsed around her. She flailed helplessly before she managed to clear the cloth enough to poke her head out. She breathed in, one single careful breath. It was dark out, but the air was warm. Not the agonizing heat that blistered her insides. She let herself breathe normally. It didn't hurt.

Her stomach growled, and for a moment, she thought she was back in her dream as the world pitched around her like a storm around a ship. She braced her hands and put her head down, and it subsided. She was hungry perhaps or (she ran her tongue around her mouth) thirsty. Life here seemed to be a constant struggle for dominance between hunger, thirst, and exhaustion.

She stood and stumbled past the ruins to the place where she'd found water before. Her well, if it could be called that, had been filled in at some point during the preceding day, by animals or wind or erosion or all three working together. But the water returned when she dug it out and she was relieved by that. She knelt and cupped her hands and drank. The water didn't taste of anything. She didn't allow it to taste of anything.

She ate a bit of the flat cake. It was bland but not as dry as she'd worried it would be. She sat back and looked out across the desert. She was, she supposed, physically satisfied. She could sleep again but she didn't care to. Her world, so recently so very large, seemed to have shrunk to the door and the well and the hill she had fallen down. She didn't like it. There was something out there, and perhaps it was time to find it. Besides, maybe if she grew as a person or something, Mama Bella would let her come back early.

She repacked her satchel and, in the process, discovered the empty waterskin. It took some time to fill it. Her well was too small and muddy to be dipped into, and the cup she made with her hands was too broad to get much liquid into the container. Eventually, she worked out that she could take a mouthful and spit it in. It was inelegant, and a bit slow, but effective. She was beginning to value inelegant but effective.

She stood and looked out across the desert. She had, if her assumptions about desert weather patterns were correct and it was only evening, hours to walk before it got hot. She had no idea in which direction something worth finding lay, and in some ways that was rather freeing. She closed her eyes, twirled, and pointed. When she opened her eyes, she followed the line of her finger and began to walk.

She was, she thought, beginning on what she suspected might turn out to be an adventure. She couldn't imagine anything worse.

Chapter Three

Marguerite had read adventure stories before. She had even enjoyed them. But she had never particularly been sold on the concept of adventures. They seemed messy and uncomfortable and besides, Marguerite had never believed the motivation behind most of them, even the ones that were about saving the world. Especially the ones that were about saving the world. Marguerite had always suspected that she would do quite well in the aftermath of an apocalypse, thank you very much.

So far, her own adventure was matching up quite closely with what she had come to expect from the stories. She was tired and her feet hurt and her bag weighed far too heavily on her shoulder. But there was one final problem, one that the stories had not prepared her for. She was rather bored by the whole thing.

The first few steps had been interesting, she supposed. She had struck out without much enthusiasm, but with a dull hope that she might find something that was better than her hill and her door and her well. She was still angry (when she remembered to be), and, in some ways, it seemed rather attractive to have something she could take her anger out on in a thoroughly righteous fashion. (A deserving target, in Marguerite's definition, was anything that was in her way. Marguerite had never heard the saying "Might makes right" but, like most people who were usually in the position of might, she lived her life largely by its tenets.)

The sand under the moon and starlight was hard and cold and had a white tinge that was pleasant to the eye. But it still had a tendency to shift unexpectedly, like an undertow, and twist her down on top of it. She was learning how to fall in a manner that didn't hurt and was thoroughly resenting that she was getting enough practice to do so.

She fell again as she was thinking this and instinctively relaxed her muscles. She hit the sand on her side and it puffed up around her, a little cloud almost like spray hitting rock but far too thick and heavy. She let her breath out in a short huff. Not a loud one — she had never learned to ask for help without asking (Mama Bella would say she had never learned to ask for help at all). She did briefly consider just staying there, but she suspected it might be a death sentence once the sun rose, and if she was going to let herself die (and she was not), she wasn't going to do it where she couldn't be found and properly mourned.

She rolled so she could put her knee in the sand and lever herself up. Her knee sunk slightly as she put her weight onto it and she bit back a shriek. There was something sharp beneath the sand. She jerked back. Marguerite knew about rocks that lurked in what looked like deep ocean, waiting to rip a ship up its belly and spill sailors into the water like intestines. She had not expected to find a similar phenomenon in the desert.

Curiosity bubbled up within her. The desert's harshness, the sharpness and depth of its colors, and the unrelenting grip of its sand had tricked her into thinking that it kept no secrets. There were fine things beneath the surface of the ocean: jewels and gold, strange creatures and plants that didn't behave like plants, and secret histories of lands long since drowned and forgotten. She couldn't help but wonder what the desert was concealing.

She dug carefully. Unlike her desperate scrambling for water, there was no need to hurry beyond the threat of the sun's eventual rise, and there was something almost pleasant about not immediately knowing what she would find.

Her fingers brushed over something rough and rigid. She buried her fingers deeper into the sand, following the sides of it down. It was large, whatever it was, and not quite as jagged as she'd first assumed. She cupped her hands away from each other and separated them, pulling the sand apart like wrenching open a carcass. What she revealed was a hard shaft longer than both her hands held together with a pitted surface the color of paper splashed with tea. Had she had expectations for what she would find, it wouldn't have matched them.

She ran the tip of one finger along the ridge. It snagged gently against her skin, not enough to hold her, just enough to disrupt the motion. She followed it beneath the sand until her arm was buried to the elbow. The sand was a heavy weight that reminded her of the press of water on the ocean floor. It occurred to her that not all sharp things that lurked in the ocean were inanimate. Some sharp things meant harm to those on the surface and were very good at seeking them out. The sand's weight became suddenly oppressive, a reminder not of home but of how very trapped she was. She yanked her arm back, watching the sand cave in behind it. Part of what she had been holding came with her. The weight of the sand had, at least for the moment, killed her interest in desert secrets. She tucked the hard, porous thing in her bag, more because it had been an effort to get than for any real interest, and walked on.

She noticed, eventually, that the air was beginning to get hazy, that the stars were vanishing and that flame colors were beginning to bleed into the coal of the horizon in front of her. Morning, she thought with a twinge of dread. Morning. She still hadn't mastered the desert and she had walked away from the one part of it she had begun to understand. She needed shelter, somewhere to hide from the sun's constant, vicious hunger.

She turned in a slow circle. Sand. In every direction, sand and sky and nothing else. She had always guided herself by the sound of water and the smell of salt in the air. She didn't know how to turn the sun and stars into her allies. Didn't even really know if she could.

She walked (because there was nothing else she could do). She walked toward the tallest drift of sand because she needed to aim for somewhere, and a crest of sand could, if she squinted hard enough (and she would be squinting badly soon), look like the crest of a wave. She had time. Sunrise was always slow, the sun creeping gently up the horizon like a spider up a web.

Sunrise was slow over the ocean. It was not slow in the desert. It exploded over the horizon, so quick and bright that she thought for a moment that someone had dropped a torch to some faraway pan of oil. She held her hand to her forehead and tried to quicken her pace.

It took far too long to reach the hill, the arbitrary marker she had set for herself. She didn't sit at its base so much as she collapsed into a graceless heap. She wanted to sleep, to try to escape from the agonizing heat in the only way she could. But if she didn't create some kind of shelter, her escape might well be a permanent one.

She pulled out her poor, abused dress. Yesterday, she had hooked it over the door, but the door was gone and she needed a new way to support it. She shook the cloth and the thing she had collected — stolen, no, acquired — unraveled out of it. She picked it up thoughtfully. It was not tall, but it was perhaps tall enough to dwarf a relatively small woman lying down. She jammed it into the sand, twisting it back and forth until it seemed at least somewhat stable. She spent some moments attempting to impale her skirt on the jagged end and knocking the makeshift peg over before she tied it on instead. Then she crawled beneath and lay with her face toward the tiny gap. It was a dark, claustrophobic space and she suspected that if the wind picked up, it would either blow away or smother her. But it was shelter and it was all she could do. She closed her eyes and willed herself to sleep.

It was dark and it was cold. Both sensations pressed down on her in a way that should have been terrifying, but dark, cold pressure was an ocean feeling so she reveled in it. Shadows passed above and through her, so big they would have blotted out the sky had there been any sky in this deep, hidden place. There was familiar music in her ears, the half moan, half mournful keen of whales calling out to one another across the fathoms. She sang along, their music as much a part of her as the lullabies she had been sung so briefly in her cradle. It should have been a thinner, weaker song but there were storms in Marguerite's voice and a knowledge that she could, if she chose to, sing them to their death. She did not choose to. She sang a love song, the song of calf to mother and mate to mate.

Her face was wet when she awoke, the cheek resting against the sand irritated and sore. She blinked and raised a hand to scrub the moisture and grit away. As the world came into focus, she became aware of many things. The first was that the air was hot. Outside the darkness of her shelter, it was blazing bright, not cold and safe like it should be. The second was the agonizing pain in her stomach. Initially, she thought it was despair, the pain of having everything she loved presented to her and then yanked away as soon as she opened her eyes. But then her stomach made a watery noise that she hadn't heard since she was little and she hadn't understood that flour must be mixed with other things to be edible. She was hungry and she was thirsty.

The third thing she became aware of was that something was rooting in her bag. It lifted its head and she looked into enormous red eyes, the pupils so small as to be almost invisible, giving the effect of two great gaping wounds in the sharp little face. She didn't cry out — one lost the knack of crying out at night when there was no one to respond — but she did jerk back enough to upset her precarious shelter, which promptly collapsed around her. For a moment, she was wrapped in thickness and black, a less welcome pressure than her earlier dreams. She flailed before she managed to free an arm and then her head. The sharp little creature was gone and her bag was scattered. It was a familiar scene. Despite her long (had it been long?) walk, she had apparently not managed to break free of the cycle her life had fallen into.

She looked out across the daylit desert. The dunes swelled and fell in a different pattern than the last time she had looked out across the expanse under the sun's light, but otherwise, she might as well not have moved at all. Her mouth, so lately tasting of salt and therefore of goodness, now tasted bitter and like she had been eating the cliff plants she had quickly learned to avoid as a small girl. She drank to chase the taste away and ate more of the dry bread. She was getting heartily sick of bread and water.

She looked up into the sky, mostly to distract herself from the sand, and saw dark shapes circling. They were too large and didn't ride the winds properly but she thought they were birds. She had never been overfond of bird meat, but it might at least make a pleasant change. She wondered how you brought birds down when you couldn't sing up a maelstrom that would dash them onto the rocks in front of you.

She half-hummed a lilting scale that matched the cries of a gull, hoping to entice them closer with some vague hope that she could twist their necks like a chicken's. The birds continued to swoop and circle, paying her as much mind as they would to someone who had no storms in their voice at all. The wind sprang up, catching her scarf and sweeping it half off her head. She put her hands up and caught it, pleased and a little smug that she had not repeated her misadventure with the hat.

She should sleep and try to wake at a time when the desert was kinder, or at least cruel in a way that she could better cope with. She didn't want to sleep but the world lately seemed to care very little what Marguerite wanted, a change from when it had danced to her tune and her tune alone. She sighed and rebuilt her shelter and curled up in a ball beneath it and did not dream of anything worth dreaming.

The world was dark and cold when she opened her eyes, safer. She rose and ate and drank a little and continued to walk. She had precious little but she had this: the slow setting of one foot in front of the other. She walked and she dreamed a little and she walked. She was so intent on simply staying upright and moving forward that she crested a hill without realizing it until she was stepping out into air instead of grit. She fell, hard, and rolled, tumbling over and over and over, like a rock caught in the grip of a tide going out. She tried to breathe and could not, overwhelmed by the flurry of movement and sand. She thought, for a moment, that she would die.

Then she struck water. Her first thought was that she had died and her soul had returned to the place where it knew it belonged. A distinctly pathetic death for someone who deserved a legend. She was covered in water and facedown. She was not dead. She knew this, not because she hurt all over, although that was the cliché, but because she had inhaled some of the water in which she now lay. Although she was disoriented and still had her eyes closed from the fall, she gasped and choked and sat up.

She rubbed her eyes and opened them cautiously. She seemed to be in a different world, a world of gently lapping water edged by trees standing tall and black against the night. But no, this was still the desert. Beyond the trees was the same expanse of sand she had so quickly learned to despise. She was in some hidden gorge carved out of the heat and the misery. She smiled. She was pleased that she had tamed the desert enough for it to open and offer her this, a sad substitute for a seashore but, she supposed, the best that such an ugly place could do. She wondered if another song would expand it, if she could carve out more of the desert to serve her.

She hummed a few notes she had once used to raise the tides. The lapping of the water did not noticeably increase, although the wind caught her bangs and knocked her scarf back into the water. She sighed, more on the principle of the matter than in exasperation or despair. The wind had miscalculated. Cloth on land was subject to the whims of the air but cloth in water answered only to the water itself. She would teach the wind to submit to water, as she would teach the land.

She stretched up into the sky and let herself flop backward with a splash. Perhaps this was what she had been sent to this desert for, to turn it into a real place, a place of water and salt. To make it *good*. She could do that.

But before she took care of this horrible, hot world, she ought to take care of herself. She stood and stripped in an even, efficient movement. She let her clothes fall to drift freely, wrapping around her like seaweed. She waded deeper into the water and let herself slip beneath it. It was all wrong. Like the rest of the desert, this water revealed too much, kept too few secrets, did not act like it was part of a greater, more fearsome whole. That was fine, for now. It would learn. She surfaced, realizing by its sudden absence how utterly coated in sand she had been. It was still — she reached up — hiding in her hair. She spent some time using her fingers to tease it out, more abruptly and more harshly than Mama Bella ever had when teaching her the intricacies of a comb. Her scalp hurt even more when she finished, but she felt lighter and easier and calmer. She tried another string of notes that had always produced ripples. The water did not change beyond the disturbance of her movement, but the wind blew against her neck. She smirked. With her hair soaking and clinging to her body, there was nothing it could do to disturb her.

She drank, careful this time not to sicken herself. The water tasted of sand and heat and, though it seemed a contradiction, dryness. She made a face and spit it out, then took another mouthful and spit again, delighting suddenly in having enough water to do so. It was a game she had never played before, although, she had watched the porpoises do it occasionally when they went past on some long migration. Marguerite had never much cared for porpoises — altogether too landlike — but perhaps they had had a point with their little games. Remembering another trick, she ducked down and blew bubbles, giggling as they fizzled from her lips.

The giggle snapped her out of her playful mood. She wasn't here to giggle. She had better dress and eat and sleep and work out how to turn this place into what it should be, to work out a song that would cover the entire world in sea. She looked around for her clothes and located them some distance away, past her, out near the center of the pond. She hummed to the water to bring them to her.

Nothing happened. She hummed again and if possible, they drifted farther away. She flushed, lip twisting. She began to stomp toward her clothes or at least as much of a stomp as she could muster. The water deepened. Marguerite yelped as it reached her neck. Her clothes were still out of reach and she didn't think she could walk any further. *How do you go to the water,* she wondered, *if the water doesn't come to you?*

One swam, she supposed. She knew all about swimming, from fish and snakes and seals and whales. She knew the way the water felt when something cut through it, the way it could both raise a body and part before it. There was a trick to moving smoothly through water. She had never learned it, had never needed to part water with her hands when her voice worked so much better. She tried one more song. The only response was a breeze across her forehead. She would have to swim for it.

She conjured up what she remembered of other swimming things. She couldn't swim like a snake or like a fish. Her body didn't bend in the right way. But a whale — whales had always had more than a bit of the land in them, a memory of walking lurking in their bones. She knew she was shaped like a land creature. Perhaps she should take her cue from the whale.

She let her body tilt forward until she was lying face down in the water. She spread her arms out to form angles with her sides. And she moved her legs, a hard up and down motion. She should have propelled herself through the water in a single slick, graceful movement. Instead, her head was forced down, plunging harder and deeper into the water than she had meant to. Her hands came up to grip something that wasn't there and she went deeper. She opened her mouth to sing a song of ice, to give herself an edge to grip. Water flooded in and she gagged and choked and breathed and gagged again. She had often thought of water in her lungs, the salt encrusting the edges, filling each breath with a hint of seawater, but now the heavy burning of it entering her chest didn't feel like home. She tried to reach for the surface, but the water seemed suddenly far too deep. She understood, for the first time, how water could drag a body down as well as buoy it up. She understood, for the first time, what drowning meant.

Not this, she thought. Any death but this. *Please.*

There are some instincts that lie buried deep in the human mind, deeper even than the knowledge of how to sing up a storm. There was some knowledge that even a seawitch's blood knew was important to hold onto. Marguerite's ancestors rose inside of her and screamed at her to kick, to paw, to open her eyes and aim for the light. She did, without understanding why, and broke free of the water's grip. She opened her mouth and sucked in air, gasping a single deep, wet, salty breath. Then her head slipped below the surface again into a world suddenly dangerous and alien. She tried to sob but some instinct forced her mouth shut and only a small stream of bubbles shot out. She kicked and flailed and broke free a second time, riding a little less high in the water. She was afraid there would not be a third.

Get on your back, whispered a small voice that she had never heard before. *Get on your back and you'll float as you were meant to.*

She threw herself backward, kicking her legs until she lay flat on the surface. And suddenly she was fine, a piece of driftwood bobbing on a gentle series of waves. She could breathe. Her chest rose and fell, first quick and erratic, then gradually slow and regular. Her eyes hurt and her abdomen burned. She drifted, moving only enough to keep herself afloat until her head touched something solid. She stilled and her body collapsed into the shallows. She rolled over and, shaking, pulled herself free, letting herself fall to the ground as soon as she knew no part of the water could touch her. The sand clung to her as if staking its claim.

She put her head down and let herself cry.

——— «◊» ———

Her tears dried up quickly, not because the grief was eased, but because moisture in the desert was still precious and had become more so now that she knew that not even water was her ally in this harsh place. She forced herself to take a deep breath, taking the air in slowly and letting it out in a hard whoosh. She sat up and promptly wretched, thin liquid splashing down to be absorbed immediately into the sand. She put a hand up to cover her mouth, a silent refusal to surrender to what was happening to her. Her entire body was gritty, skin almost completely concealed by the grains. She raised her other hand and brushed at her elbow. The sand came free easily, a tiny, tinkling shower hitting the ground. Another sign of sand's disloyalty. Water held on to what it claimed. Even after you thought it had dried away, you would find it clinging in half-unknown crevices, hiding in the tangles of your hair.

She forced another deep breath, brushed the sand from her hands, and then rubbed her eyes. Perhaps she should rest, curl up under her old skirt, and dream of water that recognized its master. She looked around for her bag and didn't see it. Her chest tightened. She tried to retrace her steps, to remember where she had it last. She must have dropped it when she fell down the hill and into this treacherously pretty place. She stood, carefully, on shaky legs and looked around. Her bag ought to be obvious, a spot of dusty brown amid the white, green, and black. She saw nothing but trees and shadows and — she turned back to the water. If she had landed in the water, her bag likely had as well.

She took a step closer, careful not to let even the slightest edge of the lapping water touch her toes. The water was dark, the stars' reflections bleeding into bright splotches of color, flashing like the glowing shrimp she used to watch from her cliff. She didn't see her bag. She stepped back, knelt, and extended her hand. She took a deep breath and felt the ache in her lungs. She lowered her arm until one finger brushed the water's surface.

She pulled it back, drawing it tight against her chest, and sobbed, just once.

She forced her eyes open and looked straight ahead. Her clothing bobbed mockingly, a plain spot right in the center of the dully gleaming expanse. She would never reach it from shore. No food, no clothing, no shelter. She had nothing, which she had dealt with before. But the water had disobeyed her. The water had treated her like she *was* nothing.

The ice inside her flared.

She had been born in a storm and ever since then she had been the storm's master. She had fought armies and won, without even realizing she was at war with them. She had set her voice against an entire frenzy of sirens and outsung them all, forcing them back from the shorelines they coveted and into the cold depths of the ocean where they could torment her no further. She had been exiled to a life alone among the rocks and the spray, and she had survived. She had *thrived.* Marguerite didn't know anything about the world she now inhabited. She didn't know the desert, couldn't read its moods, couldn't uncover its secrets. She didn't know what the funny sharp wolf was called or why the water in this place was wrong. But she knew one thing and she knew it well: she was *not nothing.*

She screamed, an animal shriek of fury and resentment with an odd musical quality from living a life preferring song to speech. She screamed her defiance and threw herself forward into the water, hitting it with a hard splash that threw droplets into the air and sent it pattering around her like the rains she used to call. She struck out toward her clothing with a movement that was half instinctual paddle and half frenzied striking at that which dared to defy her. It had a great deal more anger than skill to it, but anger was a form of power, and a seawitch, even one far from her sea, knew how to bend power to her will.

The water was cold and stung against her skin, sensitized from rolling nude in the sand. She embraced it, let the discomfort fuel her, let frustration with unfair pain block out the fear. One thrashing hand reached out and hit something coarser and softer than the water. She closed her hand around her clothing and continued to force her way through. She half swam, half stumbled onto the sand on the other side, pushing herself high above the tide line. She stopped. She looked down at the sodden bundle clenched tightly in one fist. She looked out across the water.

Marguerite threw her head back and laughed.

Chapter Four

No one had taught Marguerite to sing. No one had heard a core of sweetness in her infant wails and promised to nurture it. No hard-faced teacher had taken her hand and explained the theory behind crescendo and falsetto. She would not have been able to read a sheet of music if it was waved under her nose. Marguerite may have heard others sing, but no one sang to her. And no one expected her to sing back.

And yet, she did. Something in her rose and poured out and called things that had no business dancing to a child's tune. Perhaps it was the sea itself that taught her, playing music that only she knew how to first hear and then make. The ocean had a rhythm, a push and pull as steady as a heartbeat. The wind whistled. Even fish had scales.

When you had been taught to sing by forces so much larger than yourself, it was hard to learn another beat. There was a song that would tame this strange green place, she thought, sitting on the shore in her half-dried clothing, hair tied up in a sodden scarf to delay the inevitable caking of sand. There was a song that would remind it of what it should be, of the way water was meant to behave. The sun and the sand and the heat had clearly confused the water. It didn't know who it was. There would be punishment, of course. Marguerite would not allow her will to be challenged. It was water's duty to bow to her every whim, no matter how shallow or ill-conceived (although, Marguerite knew that no whim of hers was truly foolish; her desires were always perfectly correct). It had always been that way. To be mastered instead of master was for lesser mortals, without magic in their voices. But after punishment would come forgiveness and love (there was love in punishment, too — the love of a parent disciplining a wayward child; a teacher, a disobedient pupil). She touched her sleeve and smiled a little. She had won once. She would continue to do so.

The stars were starting to fade, and there was a faint hint of warmth in the cool air, like a faint stench of rot, more a memory of heat than true heat. The desert was recalling that it would soon be set ablaze. She supposed the sun would reach even here, in this hidden place. The sun here had very few manners and did not seem to care that it was continually penetrating where it was unwanted. She should find shelter and try to sleep. But she was hungry. She had eaten very little these past few days and triumph had made her hungry (it was triumph and not distress that had woken her appetite, she was sure). Her bag was somewhere on the other side, but where, she still wasn't sure. She looked out across the water. She could — no. Not tonight. Not again. Not — not now.

She stood and looked around. There were trees all around the water, funny kinds of trees like none she had ever seen before. Mind, she had never paid much attention to plants, having killed most of them at her cottage with her freezing mists (seaweed delivered by the ocean and dried on the rocks had provided any greenery she needed). Mama Bella had plants but Marguerite, so uninterested in their mincing neediness, had never learned to tell dependant from invader and had rarely been recruited to help care for them. She knew that they were trees because they were tall and thick around, although perhaps they were diseased. Certainly, their trunks didn't have the dainty smoothness of Mama Bella's apples and cherries. Instead, they stuck out in all directions, like someone had grabbed a sea urchin and yanked it into a cylinder. The branches didn't stand tall and proud but hung down as if trying to shield the diseased trunks from view.

But then, perhaps it was not a disease. Perhaps the desert had ruined the trees as it had ruined the water, and they didn't know how a tree was meant to grow. Perhaps that was the true danger of the desert, that its seeming openness and sharpness confused those that dwelled within, made them twist themselves into unnatural configurations because they no longer remembered how they were meant to behave. Well, the trees were on their own in that regard. Marguerite didn't know how trees should behave and wasn't about to go out of her way to find out. She would save the water because she loved it, but she was not a hero and the rest of the desert's residents could find their own way.

She began to walk, carefully circumnavigating the water. She had to pick her way through the trees, careful not to touch them in case what had twisted them up so badly was a disease after all, and a catching one at that. Occasionally she didn't dodge well enough and one of their fronds brushed the top of her head. They were thicker and stiffer than the leaves she was used to. She had a vague sense of where she was going — there was a dark impression near the water's edge that she thought marked where she had fallen. The rest of her passage seemed to have been brushed away by the wind. Had she a little more grace, the concealment of evidence of her discomfiture might have thawed Marguerite's feelings toward the desert wind. But grace was not much needed alone on a cliff, and she was, if anything, more smug at the proof of water's memory and sand's forgetfulness.

By the time she reached the site of her fall, the comfortable deep black of night had been replaced with the yellow-brown sharpness of daylight. The trees under the new sun were so vibrantly green that they hurt her eyes. The water itself was now still as a looking glass, reflecting sky and trees and sand. Marguerite turned away, feeling unexpectedly disturbed by the mirrored world. Water concealed but it didn't lie and she didn't think she cared to be reminded that this water had allied itself to what it reflected and not to her. She would change that, of course, but the reality of it now was — she needed to eat. Food would make things better.

The water was thick and opaque, and she couldn't see into its depths even in the shallows. Too much sand, she thought, sand that crept up from below and blew in from above until the water thought it, too, was a desert. She took a deep breath and forced herself to extend an arm into the water. Her hand stiffened and wouldn't obey her properly as soon as it touched the water, which was colder than she expected. She was glad she was touching the part of the water that reflected leaves and not the part that reflected sand. She did not want to put her hand into an image of the desert. She forced the thought down and concentrated on making slow, circular sweeps with her arm. She felt sand — mud — but she didn't feel her satchel. She sighed. It could, she supposed, have gone anywhere.

She didn't have her rations. The practical things to do were curl up and sleep, hope that the sun never reached her in this hidden place, and try to find her bag on a cloudy night when the water's reflection wasn't so harsh. She rejected this idea immediately. She was hungry *now*. And anyhow, she was surrounded by trees and she knew that trees made food. Mama Bella's trees had had large round red fruit, gleaming in her hand like freshly butchered organs. She hadn't seen anything that looked like meat in the trees here. She checked the nearest one just to be sure. Nothing red, just green fronds and some round purple things that looked like rocks. Marguerite didn't question why a tree might be filled with rocks. Rocks turned up in unexpected places. Tidal pools. Bird's stomachs. The purple things, though, now that she looked at them, might be seeds. Seeds came in all sorts of funny shapes and sizes and she was pretty sure they were usually edible (Marguerite understood about seeds because sometimes they relied on the ocean to bear them to new lands).

She reached up and caught the end of a frond that dangled at the edge of her reach. She pulled it down and stretched with her other hand to grab the purple things only to bat empty air. Her brow furrowed and she tried again, adding a jump. Her fingers still swished past without purchase. She needed something to stand on. She'd stood on rocks before, many times, and on stools. She didn't have any rocks. She supposed one could make a stool out of wood and wood came from trees and she had trees. But she had never understood the alchemy that turned a living thing into a tool or a decoration. She scooped up a handful of sand and let it trickle through her fingers, gazing at it ruefully. Water she could have frozen into a platform, had she been around more cooperative water. But water won't stay in the heat. And sand refused to stay at all. The only time she'd seen it remain in one position for any length of time was —

She glanced back at the depression that still marked where she had fallen, a dark pit among the beige. Water made sand stay. Somehow, water taught sand to be loyal. She stood, went to the water's edge, and brought up another cupped handful. She splashed it at the base of the tree. It made a tiny dark patch that she could nudge into an off-kilter rectangle shape. This might just work if she could make it larger. She went back to the water for another double handful, but when she returned her shape was already crumbling.

She allowed herself to kick it over with a great deal more force than necessary.

When you couldn't sing the water where you wanted it to go, you carried it. But in order to do that, she needed a container and she was fairly certain she had none. She remembered the mud she had pawed through when attempting to find her bag. She rolled up her sleeves and plunged her arms in up to the elbow. It occurred to her a heartbeat too late that she would have to brace her arms to carry the mud any distance and the only bracing she had was her chest. She looked down at the dirty smear across her chest with distaste. She let the mud drop, cleaned her arms, and stripped to the waist, letting the tunic fall onto the drier sand above. Then she gathered another armful and went to work.

It took some time and more trial and error than she would ever admit to discover how moist sand needed to be to sculpt. Still, eventually, Marguerite built a rather respectable platform, which she then stepped on in what she allowed herself to believe was a graceful manner but was really more of a mincing shuffle so she didn't collapse it. She reached up and took hold of one of the funny purple things that might be fruit and might be rocks. It was too soft to be a rock and so she assumed it must be edible. She tugged on it, carefully at first and then harder when it refused to give. It fell heavily into her palm.

She knew enough about fruit to suspect that one wouldn't satisfy her. She tossed the first onto her tunic and followed it with a short rain of others. Then she half stepped, half slid off her platform and knelt by the pile. She pulled her tunic back on before the sun could get beneath her skin again, and then she picked up one of the fruits and held it, inspecting it critically. It was a comfortable weight in her palm, but now that she had it, she wasn't sure she wished to eat it. It would be poetic to say that Marguerite had read books about strange lands where nothing behaved as it should and where eating a single bite of food would doom the plucky young heroine to be trapped there forever and that she feared that desert food would have the same effect. She had, in fact, read those books but it was not that fear which arrested her meal. It was another instinct rising inside her that she hadn't realized she had, this one whispering that she had no idea if what she held was edible. Fruit she had encountered before was round and firm and colored as bright as — jewels was the cliché. The thing she held now was soft and giving in her hand and dull-colored, a deep, dusty purple, like mold. The closest comparison she could think of was the liver from a rabbit she'd once found two days after its death. She had eaten it, because she was hungry, and the days that had come after were such that even the memory made her nauseous.

She sighed and looked down at her harvested pile. After all the effort to get them, throwing them away seemed a last-second defeat snatched from the jaws of a victory she rather felt she needed. On the other hand, she was starting to realize that a prudent defeat might do her more good than a stubborn victory. She chewed her lip but stopped when she felt it tear. She sighed and looked around. There was a slender figure a few lengths away, lapping at the water. Another of the sharp wolves or perhaps the same one, Marguerite had never worked out how to tell furred things apart when they were colored from the same palette. Perhaps it sensed her gaze; perhaps she wasn't as still as she had thought. It jerked up and looked at her squarely.

She didn't know what wolves-that-weren't-proper-wolves ate, but she remembered being small and realizing that bushes birds ate from usually didn't make her ill. Moving slowly, she leaned forward and gently tossed the purple blob in its direction. The creature skittered away a few steps and then, eying her, sidestepped closer. The funny pointed muzzle came down and the purple blob disappeared. The sharp wolf chewed and swallowed and did not immediately keel over and die. That was something.

It watched her, the line of its back arched and tense. When she didn't move, it abruptly dropped to the ground. She thought at first she had killed it after all, but no, it seemed to be resting. It lowered its head to its paws and watched her. She didn't know how long poisoning took but she assumed that if it was willing to eat it at all, it was probably safe. She picked up one of the fruits and bit into it.

It wasn't bitter or sour and it didn't burn her mouth. It didn't taste of anything at all, really, just a subtle sweetness like diluted sugar water. She decided that that was a positive thing; she had a hazy sense that her body would know if something tasted like death and this just tasted like vague disappointment. She chewed, swallowed, and bit into it again. She made her way methodically through the pile of fruit. On her sixth, she discovered that the sharp wolf was still looking at her, with a steadiness that suggested the weight of expectation. She thought seriously about ignoring it, but she had just risked its life to ensure her own and she supposed she might owe it at least a little kindness for that. She tossed it another fruit. It jumped to its feet and snapped the fruit up. It didn't lie back down. Perhaps it was full, or perhaps it realized that she wasn't generous by nature. Its red eyes met hers for a moment and then, with a flick of its tail, it disappeared into the surrounding foliage. Marguerite shrugged and finished the rest of her fruit. She wasn't exactly satisfied, but she wasn't hungry, either, and she intended to count that as another victory. The day was becoming hot and she was beginning to feel sticky. She had lost her tent, but surrounded by trees, she didn't really need it. She curled up under the prickles and closed her eyes.

She dreamed of the ocean, she knew that. She dreamed of water cradling her, of swells carrying her to the air instead of dragging her down. She dreamed that her chest was wide and open and that it didn't cramp and burn when she tried to breathe. She probably dreamed other things, but when she woke she determinedly didn't remember them. She was tired of waking with her face wet and her throat swollen.

On the second day, Marguerite found her bag by crawling carefully through the shallows of the pool and telling herself that she was doing so because that was where her bag would have dropped. Her dress was waterlogged, but unharmed. She had always favored fabrics that didn't mind a good soaking. The breads were soaked and crumbling, but she opened each packet and spread the leather on the sand and they soon dried into something almost edible. She sang to the water and felt no response but the wind, dragging her hair into her eyes and mouth. She ate and drank and slept off and on.

On the third day, Marguerite tried to learn to swim or at least negotiate water that wasn't her ally. She floated in the shallows, on her back, and learned that if she kicked with her legs and paddled with her hands, she could point herself roughly in the direction she wanted to go and move more swiftly than a gentle current alone could propel her. She did not allow herself to drift out deeper than her feet could touch if she stood. She counted this a victory, although her eyes were sore and blurry when she left the water. She walked around the entire place and painstakingly gathered more fruit. She sang while she did it and felt the faint stirrings of something too pleasant to be called misery, too resigned and sad to be happiness. She thought it might be contentment.

On the fourth day, Marguerite had an epiphany (which was a pretty way of saying that she realized she was wrong). She had thought this place belonged to her, that, through sheer force of will, she had cracked the desert open and flooded the gaping wound with water. But this water didn't belong to her. It didn't obey her. It didn't seem to love her. It didn't even seem to remember that it had once been part of the ocean. She had sung to it and all she had ended up with was a sore throat. And these trees that surrounded her, she hadn't chosen them. She hadn't summoned them. She didn't even particularly like the way they looked or the taste of the fruit they bore. This place didn't please her and, therefore, it couldn't have been made for her. It was just a strange little sanctuary in the middle of a harsh and dry expanse.

Marguerite didn't know much about deserts. But she knew about small wet places where a frightened sea creature could dwell and be safe, at least for a time. At home, they were called tidal pools. A long expanse of dry, dead rock, and in its heart, a sanctuary, a little puddle of water, teeming with life. She had never cared for tidal pools. She had rather pitied their inhabitants, whose entire world was a few drops of water, when with a little courage they could free themselves and strike out for the ocean. And she knew what happened to those who dwelt in tidal pools. Their stories always ended the same way. The pool would dry and they would suffocate. Or, every once in a while, a clever predator would fly or sneak across the rocks and tear them from their home. Tidal pools seemed like a place of safety, but they were really more like a trap. One way or another, their inhabitants were almost always damned.

This was a big pool. There was a chance it would last a year, that she could stay the entire time, with just enough to eat and just enough to drink. The idea was suffocating. She was out of her depth and she was — fine, she would admit it — afraid, but she wasn't a barnacle. She didn't think there was an ocean beyond this place, but she didn't know. There might be something out there. There might be anything out there. She wouldn't be the kind of person to hide in a tidal pool. She would be like the crabs she had watched running over the rocks. She would risk the deadly expanse, on the chance that there might be something worth finding on the other side.

She waited for night, of course, the closest thing to any ally she had. In the meantime, she filled her waterskin, wrapped as many of the purple fruits as she could fit in one of her spare leather wrappers, and repacked her satchel. When the world darkened, she hefted it over her shoulder with a grunt and began to climb the dune. She didn't look back. This was partially because she was afraid to leave, but also partially because the climb was difficult and she didn't want to fall. She kept her eyes on the ground, picking each handhold carefully in the hopes that she would, for once, navigate successfully over the sand. The moon had ripened, at least, and the stars were bright, so she could see where she placed her hands. She didn't look up at all, which was why it came as a surprise when she breached the hill and found someone waiting for her.

Chapter Five

She didn't realize at first what she had encountered. She was climbing on hands and knees when she put her palm on something hard and warm: a creature's leg, she discovered when she looked at it properly, so incredibly slender that she could see the tendons stand out on it even under the covering of fine, black hair. Her eyes trailed up the leg across a thick barrel chest and a slender, arching neck until she met nostrils flaring deep and red, and above them, eyes the same gentle blue as the ocean on the sunniest days of summer bordered above with a shock of deep black hair and a fringe of soft red tassels. The eyes disposed her kindly toward the creature, although it stood in her way. She knew what it was or at least could guess. She had seen several ponies in her time and knew that if you took a pony and made it taller and gentler, you had a horse. So that was what this creature was.

It occurred to her a second too late to do her any good that, although horses were found running free in many places, they didn't typically come pre-equipped with soft red tassels. There was a thud from beside her and a heavy hand came down on her shoulder. No one had ever grabbed Marguerite or at least, no one had grabbed her since the before time, the time when she didn't know what she was capable of. In the days after she had learned, she would have frozen the hand and shattered it or summoned a wave to sweep its owner away or a wind to smear his skull matter across the rocks. She couldn't do that now. So she fought with what she had. She twisted and reared back, left hand tightening into the sand and then coming up to fling it in her attacker's eyes. It was a good defensive tactic, although it would have been a better one had she had better aim. The sand splashed harmlessly across the man's chest.

He stumbled back at the same time as Marguerite clamored awkwardly to her feet and half stepped, half fell backward.

"Don't touch me," she snarled.

The man put his hands up, a gesture half conciliatory and half mocking.

"Whoa, there, lady," he said. "I meant you no harm." His hands lowered, dropping to waist height. He was tall, taller than she was, his features broad and smooth. He was wound almost completely in deep indigo cloth, in the same style as her own but much more carefully arranged. There was a sword at his waist, a wicked curved blade where his hand now hovered. He looked as though he understood the desert and would defend it if he felt he needed to. Despite his words, he did not look harmless.

She was a woman alone in a place that was no friend to her and faced with a strange man who probably knew its tricks and secrets. It was a frightening position to be in. But Marguerite had once been worshipped as a goddess. She had never heard the prayers or realized that the gifts people brought were offerings. But a goddess she had been all the same. And when a woman knew she had been a goddess, she would never quite see herself as a mortal woman again. Marguerite did not cower. She drew herself up and looked the man straight in the eye.

"Then you shouldn't have grabbed me," she said. "Never touch me again without my permission."

"I was afraid you would run," he said. He said it confidently, but there was an uncertainty in his eyes, as though he hadn't expected her defiance.

She lifted her chin in challenge. "So you laid hands on me without my permission?" She didn't mention how foolish it was to think that she could have run away at all in this sand. She did have *some* sense of self-preservation, although her instinct was admittedly weak and apt to be easily buried by anger and hubris.

His eyes dropped. She had watched the wolves around her cottage often enough to know that this was a sign of submission and that she had won. She didn't point this out, which counted, for her, as grace in victory.

"I didn't mean any harm," he mumbled again. It wasn't an apology, but Marguerite did not apologize herself and therefore wasn't conditioned to expect it from others.

"Who are you?" she demanded, happy to push her advantage while she had it. (People forgot a goddess's power so quickly, didn't they? Especially when she had no force to back up her anger.) "What are you doing here?"

"My name is Malik. This is Catseye." He gestured to the horse. It bobbed its head in what might have been interpreted by a romantic as a greeting.

She remained uncharmed.

"This oasis is one of the hearts of the desert. I thought it might be a good place to begin my search for you. And it was."

Children learned to feel and shape their feelings on their faces by watching first their parents and then their friends. Marguerite had spent her childhood alone. What feelings she had learned to express, she had learned from the sea. In that moment, she was glad of it. The sea had taught her to rage, but an ocean couldn't feel fear or concern and so she had never learned to mirror it. Though she felt her heart begin to pound, her face remained blank.

"And why are you searching for me?" was all she said.

He looked disappointed. He had meant, perhaps, to throw her off balance. She felt a small thrill at having outmaneuvered him mixed in with the fear.

"There's been a strange song on the wind," he said. "And the foxes are whispering about a pale woman who should be dead and isn't. My grandmother sent me to discover what it meant."

"So you weren't simply afraid I'd run," she said, "you intended to drag me back." She smiled, a stiff, tooth-filled smile she had learned from an eel and perfected with Mama Bella. She didn't like people, but she had learned enough about them to know that they gathered in places where there was food and shelter and where interesting things happened. This man might be dangerous — definitely was — but she had cowed him for the moment and that meant she wasn't in such a bad position as she'd thought. Besides, she wanted to know more about his grandmother, a woman who dispatched children in a manner that reminded Marguerite of Mama Bella dispatching apprentices. "Well, I won't be dragged anywhere but I'm willing to be..." She thought of what they had called it when she left her village. "*Escorted.*"

His eyes flicked across her face. They were clearly brown even by the light of the stars with an edging of gold around the iris rather like a seashell. Had she been interested in eyes, she would have thought them rather pretty.

"Very well," he said. "You'll have to ride with me on Catseye or we won't make it in time to avoid the heat of the day."

He had phrased it like this was a sensible suggestion, but Marguerite could always tell when she wasn't being given a choice. She wasn't being given a choice now. She reminded herself not to be bothered, that she wanted to go with him and therefore he was doing what she wanted. She nodded. He took her bag first, looping it through a strap hanging from the saddle. Then he took hold of the horse's saddle and swung onto its back in one fluid motion. He brought the horse up beside her. She thought she was being offered his hand and so she allowed it. Instead, his arm went around her. She tried to protest. She didn't have a chance. His arm tightened and she was lifted through the air, landing stomach down and draped across the horse's back like a wet sack. She gave a shriek of indignation half muffled by the animal's broad shoulder and the man's hand on her back pushing her down. The horse smelled of sweat and heat and manure. So did the man. His thigh sat right at mouth level. Marguerite opened her jaw as wide as possible, twisted around, and bit him as hard as she could.

As hard as she could was remarkably hard. The man made a sharp, angry noise that might have been a swear, and the hand on her back lifted. He'd left her hands free. She slammed them into the horse's shoulder and slid down as it started away. She stood and faced the man.

"You're a pig," she spat, trembling with what she chose to believe was fury.

He lowered his head as though he would meet her eyes but at the last second, his own slid away.

"What would you have me do?" he said, a breathy tone, half a snap and half a whine. "I had to throw you across my saddle. You might have stolen my horse or my weapon. You're very strange."

"What would I want with your horse?" she asked with genuine curiosity. "It's too big to eat much before it rots, and it smells bad."

He made a soft, snorting noise, half cut off. This time he did meet her eyes. His pupils were slightly dilated and his cheek was twitching. She didn't know if it was amusement or anger and wasn't sure which would have annoyed her more.

"Fair enough," he said eventually, in a tone that even she could recognize was being tightly controlled. "But I do need to bring you back. Will you consent to ride behind me?"

She brushed a speck of sand from the front of her tunic. "Since you finally ask, yes, I will."

He looked away again. She thought she might have shamed him. Good.

He held his arm out stiffly. She took a deep breath, let it out slowly, took another, and finally grasped his arm. Again she moved through the air, but this time, she landed upright on the horse's back, not exactly comfortably perched but at least a little more in control of her position. She let herself breathe again. She didn't know what to do with her hands — she certainly didn't want to put them on the man — so she let them rest on her thighs. He was uncomfortably close, his back so near her face she could have rested her cheek on it. He smelled of sweat, an unpleasant, acrid odor tickling her nose. She pulled back slightly.

"Are you ready?" he asked.

She shrugged, wondering what ready even meant in a situation like this. He must have felt the movement, (or perhaps it had just been a rhetorical question) because his muscles rippled and the horse leaped forward. Her hands tightened into the fabric across her thighs, which did exactly nothing. The horse leaped forward, but Marguerite did not. Marguerite stayed where she was. She hit the sand hard, although at least she pitched off to the side and so landed on her shoulder and hip rather than her head. Her chest burned and for a moment, she couldn't breathe. The world continued to spin long after it should have stopped. The man appeared in the corner of her vision, a blurry figure. His hand came out but stopped just shy of touching her shoulder.

"Breathe," he said. "You've just been knocked around. You're all right."

"I'm not," she gasped out. She pushed herself up slowly into a sitting position, air coming in and out in tight little puffs. She raised one hand to her chest and felt its jerky movements. Some of the tension eased and she could breathe, if not freely, at least enough that she knew she wasn't dying.

The man turned his hand so his palm faced upward. She recognized an offering when she saw one and a moment later, realized what it was he was giving her. She put her hand carefully in his and let him pull her up.

"You're all right," he repeated. "No broken bones. I'm sorry, I didn't realize you were so off balance. I should have been more careful."

It was the first time he had actually apologized to her. Marguerite was too sore to be gracious.

Once she knew her voice would handle it without breaking and shaming her, she said, "Yes, you should have."

He didn't exactly look chagrined, but he didn't defend himself either. She realized that he was still holding her hand. She waited until they made eye contact and then pointedly tore it away. His cheek twitched again.

"You could ride in front of me," he said. His gentle tone was probably meant to be ingratiating. "I'll put my arms around your waist and keep you steady."

"I think not," she said. She chewed her lip. She didn't have to go with him. She could run. No, she couldn't run, not in this sand, he'd catch her, especially with the advantage of Catseye. She could fight him, kick and bite and struggle until it was more trouble than it was worth to drag her back. But — he was stronger than she was and he wanted to bring her with him. She was beginning to realize that there was a possibility she could lose. She didn't think she could handle the risk of turning it into a certainty.

And anyway, she reminded herself, she *wanted* to go where he was taking her. She did.

"I'll ride behind," she said. "I'll" — she steeled herself — "put my arms around *your* waist."

His eyes flicked across her face. She wasn't sure if he was looking for something or trying to intimidate her. Then he nodded, turned away, and mounted Catseye, who had been standing nearby and mouthing at the sand, seemingly unbothered by the darkness. She let him swing her up behind him again.

It was just a torso, she reminded herself, a lump of flesh wrapped in cloth, even if it was attached to someone she didn't much like. Slowly, she brought her arms up and wound them loosely around his waist, trying to keep as much of her chest from touching him as she could.

"Okay," she said in a tiny voice. "Let's go."

His hips shifted beneath her hands and Catseye started forward, at a slower pace than last time. It was still too fast and her arms tightened of their own accord, bringing her cheek to rest against his back. He was very warm, his body heat oppressive even through the cloth, and his mass had a great deal less give than she had expected. She took a shuddering breath. The man still smelled unpleasantly of sweat, but this close, she could also detect some light scent that might have come from a plant, although she didn't know which one. He didn't say anything, barely acknowledged she was there, and she was thankful for that.

Catseye sped up, hooves striking a muffled beat on the sand like the pounding of the surf heard from a distance. The ground slipped away beneath them. Marguerite began to feel ill. She had mounted with a vague feeling that she ought to pay attention to where they were going, in case she needed to get back, but that was probably a fool's dream. The desert all looked the same to her. She closed her eyes and swallowed, tasting bile.

Keeping her eyes closed helped a little. She could almost pretend that the hard, rocking motion of the horse's movement was a boat and not a flesh and blood animal. She thought of peaks and troughs instead of hills and valleys, of the majestic passage of wood through water, of the taste of salt in her mouth, and a friendly wind in her hair. She imagined that what she gripped to steady herself was a mast or a chunk of driftwood and not a man. As Catseye moved still faster, she told herself that they had caught a tailwind and that the stinging of her cheeks was the strike of sea spray and not wind and sand. It was merely a fantasy, but Marguerite was learning for the first time how much such fantasies could help.

She didn't know how long she sat there, clinging equally to the man and to the images in her mind, before the horse came to an abrupt stop. She felt herself thrust forward, pressing briefly against the man's back before she pushed herself back sharply.

"Don't sing," the man said, his face half turned toward her.

"Please," he added a moment later. "Your songs are strange."

She hadn't realized she'd been singing. That disturbed her. She had already lost her mastery of the wind and the water in this place. She didn't want to believe that she could lose her mastery of her voice as well, the one weapon she had left. She gave herself a mental shake, reminding herself that she had been thinking of the ocean and that she often sang to the ocean and it didn't mean anything. Then what he had asked — no, demanded — of her registered. She leaned back so she could meet his one visible eye.

Then she opened her mouth and shrieked a drowning song as loudly as she could.

He jerked around in the saddle and his arm swung back, a hard, sharp motion like a snake rearing to strike. She thought he might want to hit her. She'd never been hit before. It would be a novelty and confirmation that he was a man to be distrusted and hated. His body was solid and his arm was strong. She had a vivid mental image of her cheekbone shattering under his fist. She didn't consciously choose to be quiet; it was more like her voice was snuffed out as soon as her mental image made contact. His arm had already begun to lower when she stopped. She didn't notice.

Marguerite had read books that talked about a single moment seeming to last forever. She had thought it rather a silly metaphor. Time, in her experience, was a fairly stable entity, apt to slip away on a current if you weren't paying attention, but otherwise a steady presence. But sitting there on the horse, watching the arm half raised to attack her and knowing that she had miscalculated, had made a dangerous mistake, she didn't have a clue how to move forward. The whole world seemed frozen. She held her breath, struck with the absurd thought that if she didn't move, didn't do any more to draw attention to herself, then things would stay still and silent, too, and the man wouldn't hurt her. Finally, she exhaled, a quick puff that felt like a lightning strike in the midst of their strange tableau.

His hand lowered back to his thigh.

"You don't know what you do," he said.

She realized that she was shaking and then, that he was as well. She assumed first that it was anger. But it could have been fear. That gave her a little of her strength back.

"I know what you were going to do," she said in a small voice, the only time she could ever remember that she had not let her voice project across the world. She heard his sharp intake of breath and watched the hand on his leg clench. Her next action wasn't a conscious decision: she didn't weigh her options and decide that he was more dangerous than the desert, she just threw herself backward and to the side, half sliding off the horse and half falling. She landed heavily on the sand and for a moment, was grateful that she'd had so much experience doing so lately that she could shake it off quickly. She pushed herself to her feet and began to run, flailing and stumbling, her inertia the only thing keeping her upright. She heard him give a startled exclamation but didn't know if it was directed at her or his own incompetence. For a moment, it seemed he might let her go. Then she heard the hoofbeats behind her.

She fell again and watched the dark streak flash by her. She rolled and clamored to her feet, trying to make herself go, trying to make herself *move*, to find somewhere, in the little time she had before he was on her, where she would be safe from him.

Sand spattered her side. She lumbered forward and smashed into a heaving black body. He had brought Catseye around and blocked her path. She tried to step back, to dodge, and succeeded only in remaining upright. She faced him, trembling. He didn't touch her. If he'd touched her, she would have killed him. She knew that. She didn't know how. She didn't know what weapon she could possibly conjure here in this place that hated her. But she knew that if he tried, she would find a way or force him to kill her instead in the attempt.

"I'm sorry," he said. The words echoed oddly, the wind catching and playing along their edges. His last apology had had an edge of resentment to it. This one was gentle. "I shouldn't have raised my hand to you."

Her head was heavy, as though something momentous rested on her scalp and shoulders. She lifted it anyway and met his seashell eyes.

"No, you shouldn't have," she said.

Silence followed her words. He seemed to be expecting more from her, or maybe he just didn't know how to respond; if it was the former, he would never speak again because she had *nothing* to say to him. She continued to look into his eyes, although all the protective instincts that she was just discovering she had screamed for her to look away, to stop challenging him, to submit. She forced them into silence and continued to look at him steadily.

His eyes slid slowly down from hers like ice sloughing off a glacier. She knew this was a victory and didn't understand why all her victories lately seemed to bring her so little joy. She continued to watch him.

"I'm sorry," he said again. "I shouldn't have raised my hand. I was wrong. But please don't sing again."

"No," said Marguerite, the words flat and unemotional. It wasn't defiance (or at least, it was only a little bit of defiance). It was simply a statement of fact. She had learned new things about herself these past few days, about what she could do and what she was willing to do. But it was a process of discovery, not change. The one thing she was still very sure of was that she was Marguerite. And Marguerite sang. Marguerite would always sing.

The color rose in his cheeks, but he didn't move. His hands didn't even clench, although Catseye pranced a little at what must have been his stiffening body. He let his breath out slowly, a perfect count of ten, although she didn't count along.

"Will you consent to stop singing until we get to my grandmother?" he said, the words clipped, with hard edges.

She tipped her head to the side and considered the proposition, still refusing to look away from him.

"I'll sing every song I know if you're cruel to me again," she said eventually. "And I know a lot of songs."

He jerked at that. Anger, she thought, her own flaring up. Anger that she was still defying him. Anger that she was threatening him. His next words startled her.

"I haven't been cruel to you."

The anger boiled over before she could think to control it, although she wouldn't have even if she could. There was a great, hard blackness in her soul. She hadn't felt like this since her village had first abandoned her, before she had understood that she was better than they. She had not had a name for it at the time, but she thought it might have been hatred. She was filled with hatred for this man and it was clean and pure and *powerful.*

She had stopped defaulting to song to strike down an enemy and he was lucky for that. Even here, in this foreign, unfriendly place, she might have killed him. But she didn't try. Since she couldn't hurt him with a song, she used her voice to lash at him in other ways.

"You hurt me," she hissed, in a voice that had sung to the ocean and knew how to project. "You chased me down. You treated me like baggage. You tried to strike me. *You have been nothing but cruel.*"

She stopped, the last of her words echoing strangely. Her throat hurt, and her eyes burned. She could feel the wetness at their edges, waiting to flow over. She took a deep breath and forced the moisture back. She would be angry in front of this man, and she'd had no choice but to be afraid in front of him, but she wouldn't cry. He wouldn't see that. He never would, she promised herself. She would always be too strong to cry in front of people she hated. She swallowed again and felt the stillness after the storm flow through her.

He was silent, his shoulders raised, his entire body tense. Catseye pranced nervously and tossed his head, the dark hair at his neck rippling across his shoulders. The man shifted suddenly and dropped heavily from the horse's back.

"I'm sorry," he said, a soft, choked noise. He wouldn't meet her eyes.

Coward, thought Marguerite. *I met yours.*

"You're—" He breathed for a moment. "I didn't mean to be cruel. I didn't want to be cruel. But you frighten me."

There was an expectant silence. She wondered if he expected her to be shocked by his fear. She wasn't. She was used to fear. There had been precious few people in her life who hadn't feared her. She took it as expected. It was even, occasionally, pleasant, and certainly it was useful. But he didn't know that. He couldn't know what she'd been. She shifted her weight onto one hip and waited. It seemed her silence got to him because he swallowed and spoke again, all in a rush like water spewing from a former blockage.

"You're so strange," he said. "And the things you do — you don't understand this place. You don't understand what it can do to you. I don't know how you've survived this long, with your white skin and your badly arranged clothes and your stupid bravado. But you have. You should be crawling and beaten, you should be *dying.* But you're fine. You even found an oasis that hides itself more often than it lets itself be found." He took another shuddering breath. "I'd think you were a djinn, but you feel like a human and I've never known a spirit to act the way you do. I don't want to touch you or to have you on my horse. But my grandmother sent me to fetch you. And I wish to do my duty." A final sharp exhale. He finally met her eyes. He seemed to be looking for something —

understanding, perhaps. Remorse. Forgiveness. She knew he wouldn't find it.

She licked her cracked lips and said nothing.

He looked at her for a moment longer and then seemed to come to a decision. He extended the hand holding the leather straps he steered Catseye with. "You're obviously far from home," he said. "You clearly want nothing to do with me. I don't blame you. But my grandmother wants you. Take Catseye. He can probably take you to our camp and I'll draw you a map. You don't have to touch me anymore."

Someone else had once reached their hand out to her like this, on a rocky cliff after she'd drowned the little brown and white floating things. Someone had recognized the frightened girl inside the raging monster and tried to help her. It had been a kind gesture. That meant *this* was meant as a kind gesture. He had listened to her and he was trying to make her feel safe. He was offering her something that would hurt him in order to make up for being cruel. He was trying to prove that she could trust him. The angry flame inside her cooled and then froze and sloughed off into the depths of her soul. He was being kind.

"Okay," she said and swiped the straps from his hand, careful not to touch his skin with hers.

Chapter Six

Catseye tossed his head, but when she pulled on the leather he walked willingly forward, away from the man. The man blinked and his jaw dropped.

"You took my horse," he said. Marguerite gave him a blank look as she continued to back away and Catseye continued to follow.

"You offered him to me."

She tightened her hand on the strap. It was slick and slimy and uncomfortably hot to the touch. Catseye pranced a little, bumping the man with his hindquarters. The man stumbled, looking distinctly put out.

"To be honest, I didn't think you'd agree," he said. "Do you even know how to ride?"

"No," said Marguerite, quickening her pace. She was pleased that the man didn't follow her, although there was a tension in his frame that seemed to hint that he wanted to. "But up until a few days ago, I didn't know how to swim or find an oasis or survive in the desert either and I seem to be managing all of that quite well."

"Don't follow me," she added.

He watched her silently. His cheek was twitching again, bobbing rather alarmingly against the sharp bones of his face.

"I wouldn't dream of it," he said eventually in a strangled little voice.

She wasn't sure she wanted to put her back to him. After a few false starts, she managed to swivel Catseye so the horse was between them and she was watching the man over his back. Then she grasped both sides of the saddle and attempted to pull herself onto the horse's back. She lifted herself perhaps an inch off the ground and then fell back. She peeped at the man again. He hadn't moved, although he was watching her intently. She gave a small jump and tried to use the extra height to lever herself up. It didn't work. She slid to the ground again, almost twisting an ankle and toppling over. She clung to the saddle to keep herself upright and almost fell again when it moved beneath her as Catseye backed up a few steps.

"Do you need help?" asked the man.

Marguerite directed a glare at him. "Not from you."

There was a long silence, broken only by the scuffle as she attempted and failed again to pull herself up.

"Put your left foot in the stirrup and use that to boost yourself up," the man called across the saddle to her.

She couldn't manage a proper freezing glare on her tiptoes and so she bent to scowl at him from beneath Catseye's belly. "What's a stirrup?"

Really, he ought to get his cheek checked (she wasn't really clear on who should check it, but she knew theoretically that Getting Things Checked was the done thing when a person's body was behaving strangely).

"It's the leather loop hanging down his side," he said. "Just put your foot in."

Marguerite gave him another glare on principle before straightening back up and inspecting the saddle. There was a braided leather band hanging down, and it did look about foot size. There was only one problem. It was hanging at stomach height. She looked at it, looked down at her left foot, and grimaced. Slowly, she attempted to raise her leg to stirrup height. She managed about knee height before she tipped over and had to cling to Catseye to keep from falling. The horse swiveled his head to look at her out of one bright blue eye and pawed the ground. She had the disconcerting sense that she was disappointing him. She swallowed and glared back.

"At least I don't smell as bad as you," she said to the horse.

"Do you want me to lift you into the saddle?" the man called.

"No!" she snapped. "I had enough of that the first time." She grabbed the top of the saddle with both hands and tried to lift her foot again. With the added support, she didn't overbalance, but otherwise, it led to a similar result.

"Hold the stirrup leather with your left hand," said the man. "And the cantle with your right. It'll be easier."

"I don't know what half those words mean," she ground out, raising her foot again and giving an experiment hop to see if that would solve the problem.

"The strap the stirrup attaches to is the stirrup leather," he said, sounding pointedly patient. "The cantle is the back of the saddle."

"You can do it," he added, not sounding like he particularly believed it.

She would show him. She grasped the leather strap, just above the ring, and put her other hand up to the saddle. She could put her weight on the strap, she discovered, and lean back to get her leg up. She raised her foot higher and higher and managed to nudge the tip of her toe into the leather ring. Her lips pulled back in a triumphant grin.

Then Catseye began to walk forward. She hopped a few steps before her foot was pulled out of the stirrup and she almost fell again, saving herself only by grabbing the horse's head straps.

"Hold the reins in your right hand," the man advised. "Pull on them if he tries to do that again. And try to get on quickly so he doesn't have time to feel your weight shift and walk away." He paused for a moment. "The reins are what you're holding right now."

Marguerite didn't dignify his advice with an acknowledgment, but she twisted her hand in the reins and brought it up to the cantle, grabbing the stirrup leather with her other hand. She took a deep breath and raised her leg again, sticking her toe into the ring. She tried to push herself up with her left leg and then, remembering her earlier attempt, bounced on her right. She launched herself into the air. For a moment, she was suspended above the horse, all her weight resting on her left foot as she stood tall. She met the man's eyes and forced a smirk. Then Catseye began to walk forward again.

Her first impulse, as she felt her seemingly steady platform begin to move beneath her, was to get down, to retreat to the sand, to try again when Catseye was calm. She watched the man raise one eyebrow and flushed.

I'm riding *this horse,* she thought, and swung her leg over the cantle, accidentally (mostly) kicking Catseye in the hindquarters on the way over. And then she was on him, sitting tall and featherlight on the broad back. She turned her head to smirk at the man. This was a mistake. Catseye began to walk forward more briskly. Suddenly she wasn't master of the beasts, she was a frightened sailor on a swaying boat that was quickly moving out of her control.

"Stop," she commanded and kicked him in the sides in an attempt to get him to listen to her. It had the opposite effect. Catseye sped up, beginning to move in a strange rocking manner that bounced her out of the saddle. Marguerite yelped and leaned forward to grab a fistful of the horse's mane. It was easy with her right hand but her left was still entangled with the reins. The horse jerked his head forward and her fingers were wrenched. She let out a strangled gasp of pain.

"Stop!" she repeated, higher and louder this time. If anything, it seemed to spur Catseye to go even faster.

"Sit up!" She heard the man yell behind her. "Or you'll fall! Whoa, Catseye!" His voice didn't sound any farther away so he must be chasing them.

"I can't!" she wailed. The man's commands seemed to have little effect on Catseye. Perhaps the horse didn't respect him, either. She would have liked Catseye for it if the stupid animal wasn't in the process of running away with her.

"Whoa!" the man yelled again. "Catseye, whoa! Pull back on the reins, that will stop him!"

For a moment, her determination to ignore everything the man said warred with her desperation to stop this horrible runaway animal. Desperation won as she felt herself begin to slip sideways. She tightened her hand and jerked her elbow back as far as she could. Catseye startled, tossing his head and making a strangled whinny, but he stopped.

She leaned over the horse's neck, trying to take deep steady breaths. Behind her, she heard a hurried shuffling. Then a warm palm pressed to her shoulder, shoving her. She made a strangled noise of protest. But as she was pushed back over the horse's center, she realized how far she had listed. Another moment or two and she probably would have been underneath the horse. She spared a glance down at Catseye's hooves. They looked sharp and she knew they were hard. Marguerite suppressed a shudder.

"Are you all right?" the man asked. His hand grasped Catseye's reins, near his muzzle.

She gulped and nodded. His gaze dropped to her hand tangled in the reins.

"I'm fi—"

She'd meant to follow up this reassurance with a comment about how an unpleasant man would naturally have an unpleasant horse, but she never got the chance.

"Never do that!" he snapped. "Never wrap them around your fingers like that." He reached toward her left wrist but stopped before he touched her so she didn't have to claw his eyes out with her other hand. "*Please* drop the reins," he said. "Do you want your fingers to be yanked off if you fall?"

She looked down at her hand. Her fingers were white where the reins covered them, almost gleaming in the semi-darkness, and red on the tips. She consciously unclenched and slowly used her right hand to unwind the strap. Her fingers were numb as though she had a block of ice at the end of her wrist instead of flesh and bone. She gave her left hand a sharp flick downward in an attempt to shake it off. It didn't work. Grimacing, she massaged her fingers until they began to prickle and then burn. Under the circumstances, she decided that burning was the better sensation.

"See?" the man said.

Marguerite wondered if it was quite right to glare at a man when he had helped her out and was in truth correct. She concluded that given all that had transpired up to this point, it was. Besides, it was eminently satisfying to glare down from so high a perch. It was almost like being back on her cliff.

The man seemed irritated by her response, or at least his shoulders were stiffer than they had been a second ago and his eyebrows sloped down at a slightly sharper angle.

"Why don't I give you a hand?" he offered, instead of chastising her.

She felt her eyes narrow and her mouth twist.

"I can do it," she snarled. She turned her attention to Catseye or at least, what she could see of Catseye, a broad black neck cresting like a wave and the pricked ears framing the desert. She leaned forward a little. "Go home," she said, enunciating carefully. "Take me to your wisewoman."

Catseye stretched his neck in what must be preparation to move. Then his head began to shake wildly. The shaking traveled down his entire body until it reached the point of his back on which Marguerite perched. She yelped on finding herself tossed like a leaf in a storm and would have toppled off had the man not put up a steadying hand.

"He tried to throw me!" she cried indignantly when the shuddering finally stopped and she had pulled herself back more or less upright (without help from the man, although he had seemed like he was offering).

"He's just bored," the man said in a tone that was obviously meant to come across as *extremely patient* but had a certain nasal whine to it. "Are you sure you don't need help?"

"*Yes*," she said and then added, "I'm sure." (Just in case the man was beginning to think that she was softening toward him. Softening was for springtime and Marguerite liked to think that her heart had never left the dead of winter she had been born into.)

She took a deep breath and reminded herself of wind beating and waves smashing.

"Take me where I want to go," she commanded in what she hoped was an approximation of the voice that had conjured and then controlled that fury.

Catseye snorted and his front hoof thumped once, twice, three times down on the sand, a dull and dispiriting thud. She threw the reins down across the horse's neck in a fury. She didn't strike him, though it wasn't compassion or prudence that stayed her hand, it was simply that she had never needed to use her fists to do another harm. Had she had an iceberg available, her story and that of Catseye and the man would have taken a very different turn. Since bringing all the rage of the sea down on the horse's head was not currently an option, she settled for turning her anger on the man.

"Why won't he listen to me?" she demanded. "What have you done?"

The man had caught Catseye's reins when she'd thrown them down and now held the twin straps in a loose grip.

"I've done nothing," he snapped. "What exactly do you think riding *is*?"

Her lip curled. "You tell the horse what to do and he does it."

The man heaved an extremely heavy sigh which she considered rather overplayed. "That's the gist of it," he said. "But you're telling him what to do in human language. You need to tell him in horse language for him to understand."

If she could make an ocean understand what she wanted, she ought to be perfectly capable of communicating with a horse, which after all was bred to do what people wanted. Still, this was the desert, and if there was one thing she'd learned about the desert, it was that everything was harder here. She chose to keep her silence.

The man looked up into her face, waiting to make sure that she would keep his gaze even when she wasn't pointedly defying him.

"Look," he said. "Riding is extremely complicated. It takes years to master. It's no wonder you're having trouble if you've never been on a horse before. Why don't I—"

He didn't get to finish his sentence. He didn't get to finish his sentence because Marguerite, instead of listening to him, had been slowly going over what had happened when they rode together and when Catseye had moved forward as she sat alone on him, and she had come to a conclusion. So she sat back and she kicked the horse in the stomach on both sides as hard as she could.

Catseye shot forward like steam through a shaft. Marguerite shrieked and attempted to throw her arms around him, succeeding largely only in bashing her nose on the swelling arc of his neck. She wasn't sure where the man had gone. He had disappeared under the black onrush, sand spraying up from the horse's passage, but also, perhaps, from his tumble, if he had indeed merely fallen and not been beaten under the horse's hooves. She thought he was fine because vaguely, around the wind and the thudding and her own shrieks, she was sure she could hear blistering swearing.

"Stop!" she howled.

Catseye did not. He continued to run, bearing her easily up the swell and crest of sand that rose before them. In that she was lucky. If he'd run on flat ground, she would have fallen under his hooves and her head would have shattered like ice. But the force of his movement and the rising of his body pushed her back in the saddle. She didn't sit with the kind of height that a horse needed to feel commanded, but she didn't slump so low that the ground began to anticipate her landing.

She did fall, of course. They reached the peak of the sand and began to gallop down into the trough and she slipped free as easily as a water droplet separates from a puddle on a high surface. She hit the ground first with the flat of her left shoulder and then with the point of her hip. She didn't tumble end over end as she had last time she had fallen down a hill. Instead, she slid a short distance, her shoulder grinding into the sand until she hit what might have been the bottom or might merely have been the point at which she'd gathered enough sand in front of her to act as a stopper. Her left side hurt far too much to move. She squirmed and arched her right shoulder far enough to propel herself onto her back. The sand was still cold under the night sky and it soothed her a little. She was so very, very tired of falling.

She didn't move at the sound of footsteps, not the dull thud of Catseye's hooves but a light, shuffling, uneven step that she supposed must be the man's. She didn't move even when he appeared as a dark shape in her peripheral vision and then blocked her view of the stars as he leaned over her.

"Are you dead?" he asked.

She didn't answer, mostly because it occurred to her that perhaps she was and she was trying to process how she felt about that. But she blinked and licked her lips, which must have given him his answer.

"*You*," he said, "are dangerous."

"Yes," she agreed, wondering why his eyes darkened like she wasn't supposed to take the compliment as it was offered.

"You're not riding my horse," he said.

Her eyes narrowed (both to express her confusion and because it eased the strange metallic aura she was seeing around the man's outline). She idly wondered if he'd struck his head. It was, after all, quite obvious that she wasn't riding his horse since she was lying on the ground, and she wasn't sure why he thought she should be informed of the situation. But then, perhaps he was fine. Most of his actions up to this point hadn't made much sense to her. Or perhaps he was fine and she was the one who had hit her head and that was why things didn't make sense.

Marguerite put that thought away neatly in a dark corner of her mind with most of the things she had been thinking since she entered the desert (and every thought she'd had between the ages of five and six) and went back to ignoring the corner's existence.

"I mean it. You aren't riding my horse," he repeated.

She contemplated his words. Apparently he wasn't going to let up until she responded. She was fairly certain that on a normal day, she'd have waited him out. But her side hurt and she was beginning to feel a harsh pounding at her temples. If she acknowledged him, he might let her alone. (Little chance of that, based on previous behavior. But any port in a storm.)

She prefaced her words with a deep and pointed sigh, an action which made her head throb but hopefully made it clear even to him that she was speaking under duress. "No," she said.

One dark eyebrow lifted. It gave his face an elegant tilt. She resented him for that, a sharp spike in the background resentment she had felt for him since they met.

"You're being very agreeable," he said and bent a little nearer, his eyes holding hers more intently, as though looking for something.

She turned her head away, not enough to break eye contact, just enough to let him know that his attentions were unwelcome.

"Of course I'm not riding your horse," she said, rather pleased that clearly it was him having the comprehension problem and not her. "I'm on the ground."

He made a strangled noise, half angry (she had learned his angry noises by now) and half a sound that she thought might be laughter, although it didn't sound much like Mama Bella's or her own (not that she had much experience with her own laughter).

"No," he said. "I mean you're not riding my horse to my grandmother. You'll kill yourself. And you'll kill him. And you'll probably kill me."

"I'm all right with two of those," she mumbled before his words registered. She attempted to sit up sharply, although the movement with her bruised limbs was more the flop of a freshly caught fish. She caught herself on her elbows, just high enough off the sand to make the rigid lines of her body clear.

"You told me I could!"

"That was before I realized how little you can ride," he shot back. "I won't subject Catseye to your attempts anymore."

"I won't ride with you," she said, and gave herself the gift of looking away. "You said I didn't have to."

"You are a liar," she added, enunciating clearly. The wind picked up again, pulling at her hair and the man's clothes.

He was silent for a moment, the soft rattle of the sand the only noise. Then he sighed heavily and put a hand to his forehead.

"You're right," he said. He didn't say anything else. Perhaps he simply didn't know how to solve this riddle, how to put an angry woman and a disobedient horse together into a solution. Perhaps he was hoping if he waited long enough, she'd give in. He'd be dead before that happened, Marguerite promised herself. So would she, probably, but if that was pride's price, she'd pay it. And pay it more easily than he would. There was no one waiting for *her* return.

He began to chew his lip, looking like he was thinking deeply. When his teeth disappeared back into his mouth, it seemed that he had found one.

"You won't ride with me," he said slowly.

She nodded, although he didn't seem to be questioning her, merely clarifying the situation in his own mind.

"And I won't let you ride alone."

She nodded again, interested in spite of herself.

"If you rode," he said, even more slowly, rolling the words around his mouth as though he was tasting them, as though the sharps and flats of them would tell him the idea's quality. "And if I led him, we'd both get what we want. And we'd still move faster than walking alone."

She considered. She wanted to go quickly and his solution would be slow, despite his claim to the contrary (although she supposed almost anything was quicker than her stumbling shuffle). On the other hand, if he kept his hands on Catseye's reins, he wouldn't touch her. It wasn't ideal, but she supposed it would suit her. She would, just this once, accede. She wondered if this was what was called a compromise. She wasn't sure she cared for the concept. She liked it much better when everything went her way.

"That would be acceptable," she said.

The man's shoulders slumped and he almost smiled. His mouth at least lost its hard lines.

"Good," he said. "So get up and I'll catch Catseye." He extended his hand to her.

She turned her head away and concentrated on rising without him. It was a more complicated process than it had been before. There was precious little strength in her left side. She experimented with pushing herself straight up, but when that failed, she painstakingly listed to the side until she could get her good arm underneath and push herself until she was sitting upright. Her legs shook a little. Her arm wouldn't push her to a standing position. She slowly slid her left leg forward and up until it was bent and she was half kneeling. Like rising after a fall on ice, she used it as a platform to get to her feet. The man didn't help her, to his credit. But he didn't look away, either, so she felt quite justified in continuing to despise him.

When she finally stood before him (tall and stiff-backed, although it ached to hold herself so), he stepped back a little He formed a crescent with the thumb and forefinger of his left hand and raised it to his mouth. A sharp, shrieking whistle broke the relative quiet of the desert night. Marguerite started, shoulders jerking up and nearly knocking the last wrapped edges of her scarf loose. She peeked at the man out of the corner of her eye. He didn't seem to have noticed. She chose to accept his ignorance at face value and concentrated on fiddling with her head wrapping. When he whistled again, her hands jerked only a little, the cloth tightening momentarily around her throat and then loosening as she forced her muscles to unclench.

There was a soft, rhythmic thumping. Catseye came trotting up, reins hanging from one side of his neck and tail swishing through the air violently. The edge of his tail caught Marguerite's shoulder as he came toward the man. It was a harder strike than she had anticipated, her arm stung as though she'd been whipped. She couldn't read the body language of a horse, but she didn't think he looked as contrite as he should. The horse trotted neatly up to the man and bumped his nose against his shoulder. The man smiled and put a hand up to stroke his cheek. Then he grabbed the straps and looked at her.

"I don't suppose you'd let me lift you into the saddle?" he asked.

She attempted to raise an eyebrow but raised both instead. She was pretty sure it still got the point across.

"Not a chance," she said. "Anyway, I can do it on my own. You saw me do it."

"I saw you do *something* but I'm not sure it was mounting," he mumbled. But he turned Catseye and led the horse toward her, stopping when her eyes were level with the saddle. With the hand not holding the reins, he made an elegant swooping gesture that she supposed was meant to be encouragement.

She huffed and tried to remember how she'd done it before. She had grabbed the strap, she remembered, and sort of half-bounced, half-hauled herself into the saddle. She imitated the movement she thought she'd made. For a moment, she hung suspended from her arm and the toe of her boot in the stirrup. She felt Catseye shift forward but the man's hand steadied him and he didn't run. Her side throbbed, her heartbeat swelling in her ears. For a single sharp huffing breath, she wanted to let herself slide back to the ground. If the man hadn't been standing so near, she might have. But he was and so she tightened her jaw and forced herself the rest of the way up. She sat heavily in the saddle, feeling a sting in the warm part of her body where thigh met thigh and a dull ache farther back. She looked down at the man, enjoying that he had to tilt his head up to meet her eyes. It was pleasant being the one who was looming, rather than the one being loomed over. She grinned down at him in triumph, the kind of grin she'd learned from the wolves, which showed all her teeth and had no warmth.

"Let's go," she said. "Bring me to your grandmother."

He had one advantage over Catseye. He obeyed her command.

Chapter Seven

The man walked forward briskly, his steps far swifter and steadier on the moonlit sand than hers had ever been. A small, sneaking part of her (not the part that had taught her to swim — what a lot of new and largely unwelcome parts she was discovering in herself!) wanted to ask him how he did it. She stifled it immediately. And then she forgot the man's movements because Catseye walked forward, too, his steps matching the man's in speed and confidence. Instinctively, she hunched over the horse's neck, clutching his mane to keep herself in place. Now that she didn't have to concentrate on making the horse obey, she realized how very big his movements were. She felt rather like a sailor on a boat being tossed by a bad-tempered sea. She hunched lower, although the movement strained her bruises and shortened her breath. She tried to force herself to exhale in a normal rhythm.

Her eyes dropped to the man's head. *He* wasn't bent over. He was striding forward, confident in his role as the leader of their little trio. Confident in his place as the alpha. That made her the weak one, bent over as if she were submitting to him. As if she ever would. She straightened her arms, pushing her torso backward, ignoring the fire that raced up her side, and forced herself to sit upright. She might be so far out of her depth she was being crushed but she'd be damned if she'd acknowledge it to *him*. When he glanced back at her, she was sitting as tall and rigid as if she was on a throne and not a horse. His eyes flickered and his mouth pulled up strangely on one side. She didn't recognize the expression and reminded herself again that it didn't matter because she didn't care what he thought.

"You can relax," he said.

She glared at him. "So nice to have your permission," she said drily and smirked when his eyes narrowed.

"I *meant*," he paused, seeming to weigh his words and piece his sentence together cautiously. "That Catseye won't take off on you again and it'll be easier on you and on him if you're less tense."

"Usually I sing when I'm relaxed," she said, keeping her tone carefully neutral, trying to tell him that this was, for once, not defiance, that she was merely giving him a fact and letting him choose what to do with it. She didn't know if he understood, but at least he didn't raise his hand to her again. The wind gusted gently against her. Her scarf was half pulled loose, one end trailing over the pommel of the saddle (and she was holding too tightly to the saddle to fix it).

"I like this part of the desert," he said.

Marguerite blinked rapidly several times.

"Why?" she said. It was meant to be part of a longer sentence, a demand to know why he was telling her this. Why on earth he thought she would care about his opinions on any part of the desert (especially this part, which was clearly unpleasant and unfriendly and unmannerly and, well, perhaps she could understand the appeal to this man). Besides, it had nothing to do with their previous words. She was unaccustomed to social niceties, but it occurred to her that this was perhaps the point.

He didn't seem to understand what she had meant by the question. Instead, he glanced back at her briefly and almost smiled a little. It looked different than the other smiles he had given her. Less stiff and his teeth weren't as visible. Then he shrugged and turned away again.

"It's peaceful," he said. "Catseye and I can gallop for hours without seeing another soul. There aren't really any bandits. And it reminds me of the stories my grandmother told me."

There was a follow-up question there. Marguerite didn't ask it. It was not a conscious choice. She simply didn't realize that it was lurking behind his answer. Instead, she let herself look around (she had survived the horse practically galloping before — surely a mere turn of the head wouldn't knock her completely from her perch). Peaceful was not a word she would have used for a place where everything was hard and sharp, where the sun was an enemy and not merely a way to mark time, where water hid itself in sand and valleys instead of gushing forth cleanly as it should. She supposed there weren't many people about (all to the good, since the one she had met she liked so little). She hadn't particularly considered this remarkable. She wondered what shape his life had taken, that a place with few people was a novelty and a pleasure.

She didn't say anything. His head kept flicking back toward her, like a bird moving from tree to ground and back again. Whatever he wanted from her, he seemed eventually to give up on it and faced forward again. Her side continued to throb, ebbing and flowing with every step the horse took. When she was sure the man was no longer checking on her every second moment, she let herself slump, just a little. Once the novelty of their relatively swift progress wore off, it was dull being led through the desert. She hadn't liked traversing it on foot, but the constant threat of being lost and drying out or starving or being torn apart by wild animals at least made the process *interesting*. She assumed there was no such threat now. Certainly the man seemed to know his way, judging by the sureness of his steps, although she didn't know how he was managing to navigate. The desert rose and fell around her but there was no pattern that she could discern. He could have been using the stars, she supposed, like sailors did. (Marguerite had never learned the knack, of course. Why consult the sky when the sea itself would tell you where you were? The sky had no power to send you on your way with the right aria.)

She leaned forward a little more, letting her left arm, which was resting on the pommel, take most of her weight. It eased some of the soreness in her back. She watched the stars, mostly because watching the sand running past underneath her made her feel ill. She didn't recognize their forms. She'd read that other people saw shapes, saw *legends* in the stars. She squinted, trying to pick out the things that she knew. One cluster of stars might be a school of fish, if the viewer was feeling generous (she wasn't sure if she was), and she could almost see the arch of a boat's prow in the line of another. The world around her felt soft and misty as she gazed up, falling into something that was half a trance and half a doze.

She was beginning to notice that the stars were getting harder to see when Catseye stopped abruptly, throwing her forward and sending a sharp spike of pain shooting up her side like being struck by a harpoon.

"The sun is rising," the man said, turning to face her. "We need to make camp. It's dangerous to travel in full sun."

She blinked, raising one hand to rub her eyes in an attempt to make sense of a world that was suddenly hard and sharp again.

"You said we'd make it back to your grandmother before the sun rose," she mumbled. Not an accusation. Merely confusion.

Perhaps he'd become so accustomed to her anger that he saw every statement through that lens. Perhaps he was merely embarrassed. In any case, his tone was defensive. "That was riding together at full gallop, not walking you like an invalid." He shook his head, shaking off his annoyance like water droplets after a bath. "Anyway, I need to set up the tent. Do you need help getting down?"

Yes, said the part of Marguerite that housed her survival instincts, vocal despite how often she slapped it down. No, said the louder part of her, a jumble of emotions she was so far refusing to untangle and investigate.

"I can do it," she said. She'd had enough practice coming off this stupid animal over the past night, doing it by choice ought to be a simple enough matter. It wasn't. Marguerite gazed at the ground for a moment, knowing that she wanted to be there and wishing it had the sense to rise up to meet her. She tried to mentally reconstruct all the times she had left the horse's back before. She was more tired than she realized or she might not have reached the conclusion she did. She drew herself up in the saddle and tipped to the side.

The man squawked a distressed, wordless cry and raced forward, grabbing her shoulders when she was nearly parallel to the ground. Her head fell to rest against him.

"What are you doing!" he shouted. The noise made his chest vibrate strangely under the ear that she had unwittingly pressed to it. She could hear her heart pounding, a staccato rhythm to a racing tempo. But no. Her own heart was calm, she could feel it in her breathing and in the looseness of her chest. Anyway, her heart pounded in her throat. This beat came from her ear. She was listening to *his* heart. Her one good hand clenched over his shoulder.

"Let me go," she said, pleased that her voice remained steady.

"You could have killed yourself," he said, slowly walking backward until she was pulled free of the horse. Then he set her on her feet and stepped away. Despite the way the air was beginning to warm, the side that had been pressed against him felt suddenly cold.

"But I didn't," said Marguerite.

The man's face twisted in that look that was becoming quite familiar, although she still didn't quite understand what it meant. Then he smiled at her, just a quirk of the lips without meeting her eyes.

"You didn't," he agreed, somehow managing to sound like he wasn't agreeing to anything. He walked past her (she stepped a little to the side so he wouldn't brush against her) and put his hand up to the back of Catseye's saddle. He undid a strap and tugged. Part of the saddle came loose into his hand. It was a cloth of some kind, canvas perhaps, rolled up into a tight cylinder. She'd thought it was meant as some form of backrest, but apparently it had its own function and was just being carried on the saddle. He undid the strings holding it together and with a flick of his wrists, it flared out into a sail.

She gasped, just a little. A mere intake of breath, soft as a sigh. She was glad that he hadn't seemed to hear her because, as she watched him fuss with it, she saw that she had misjudged the situation. It was not a sail. Instead, the man transformed the canvas into a cloth building, a protective vanguard against the ravages of the sun.

"There," the man said, standing back and putting his hands on his hips. "That'll do, I think."

It would do. It would be a better shelter than she had had for quite some time. The man slapped his hands together as though he was cleaning them and walked toward Catseye again. He pulled a few small bags loose and let them drop onto the sand. None looked like the roll he had pulled out before.

"Where's yours?" she asked.

He turned to look at her.

"Where's my what?"

"Where's your shelter?"

He turned back toward the horse, dismissal in every line of his body.

"It's right there. You saw me set it up."

"Then where's mine?" she demanded.

He turned to look at her again, brow furrowed. "I've only the one. We'll have to share." He smiled again. He had a lot of smiles. This one looked like he was hoping if he smiled widely enough she'd smile too. "Don't worry, I don't snore."

"No," said Marguerite.

His smile dropped off. His whole face slumped, like a cliff finally eroding into the sea.

"I know it isn't ideal, but it's the only one I have so we'll both have to make the best of it. It's certainly big enough. It has to fit Catseye too."

"No," said Marguerite again.

The man sucked in a breath and let it out in a hard whistle like escaping steam.

"Yes. We have to share a tent. We only have one."

"I have a shelter," she said.

He raised an eyebrow at her (it gave his face a deeply judgmental slant). Marguerite resolved to learn how to do the same. And do it *better* than he did.

"You don't have a shelter."

"I have a shelter," she insisted.

She walked past him, head held high, and began to yank on her bag. Catseye tossed his head and sidestepped. The man reached past her to unhook the strap. She pulled her bag free and ducked under his arm. She opened it and dumped the cloth and the white rod on the sand.

"I have a shelter," she repeated.

The man looked down at the dingy little pile, the black cloth already bleaching to grey, the rod showing yellowed cracks.

"That's not a shelter," he said.

She attempted to raise a single eyebrow but couldn't manage the refinement and ended up with an expression closer to a surprised owl.

"Neither was yours when you first took it off Catseye," she said. She tried to turn her back to him so she could set it up. It was harder than she'd thought it would be. She took a deep breath and forced herself to turn and kneel.

It was strange, how quickly she had forgotten the trick of making it stand, considering the hours it had stood as the only barrier between her and an all-powerful, unforgiving enemy. (How quickly one could forget something once it ceased to be needed. Marguerite was not alone in remembering that which made her happy and not that which kept her alive.) She started with what she remembered. The rod had to be thrust deeply into the sand, she knew that. And she remembered tying the cloth around the top because that had been difficult and difficult things always make a deeper mark than easy things. The rest she could intuit; there wasn't really any skill to it. Most of her effort went into ignoring the man's gaze on her and hiding the vague stirrings of an uncomfortable new feeling that twisted her stomach and warmed her cheeks. Finally, she stood, dusting her hands together in unconscious imitation.

"I have a shelter," she said for the fourth time, giving him a triumphant glare (it wasn't nearly as satisfying to do when she had to tilt her head up to meet his eyes rather than gaze down at him from horseback).

His eyes traced her shelter's sagging lines. Her own flicked to his tent. It was tall and sleek and proud, snapping slightly in the wind like a ship in full sail. Her shelter was a sad, slumped little dinghy. But a dinghy, she reminded herself, would often take you where a galleon couldn't sail. And it was *hers* and therefore known and, as much as anything in the desert could be, trustworthy.

"I guess you do," he said eventually, grudgingly, the words drawn out of him as if by force.

Her smile grew wider, lips unconsciously falling to hide her teeth so it communicated pleasure instead of challenge.

"We should eat and drink before we rest," he said. "I suppose you have very specific food preferences too?"

Marguerite stopped and considered the question. Food was a thing she had always conceived of in absolutes. She had it. Or she didn't. She had never given much thought to the specifics of taste and texture.

"I don't like meat that's been out more than two days," she said eventually.

He turned to look at her, his eyes widening in a way she would have found comical if it hadn't felt so judgmental. Hers narrowed in response.

"It hurts my stomach," she added and hated how high-pitched and defensive her voice sounded.

He watched her for a moment longer, as though she had introduced some strange new puzzle he was trying to solve instead of having commented on her tastes. He shook himself.

"You needn't worry," he said and turned again to Catseye's saddle, pulling yet another pack loose. (Was there some strange magic going on, that he seemed to have everything he needed packed into such a small space? Or was this what people did when they couldn't sing up a squall to serve them? Did they make plans and pack things tightly so they'd never be caught alone and vulnerable, as she was?) "I've no meat. I'll shoot it fresh tomorrow if we don't make it back to my family's camp and if we spot something worth the shooting. Only bread and dried fruit tonight."

He had been rooting through his bag as he spoke. He came up with a few waxy pouches, similar to the ones that she carried. He handed one to her; she took it without thinking and unwrapped it, settling herself neatly on the sand where she'd stood. The pouch was, luckily for her bruised and battered self-respect, easy enough to undo. The wrappings fell away to reveal a flat type of bread much like the ones she'd been carrying around with her, although darker and softer, filled with a dark, wrinkled mass that she didn't recognize. She bit into it. The bread had a sharp savory taste — some herb she didn't recognize — and the dried fruit tasted a little like the swollen purple things she had eaten in what the man called an oasis, though the flavor was deeper and richer. It didn't occur to her to check for poison, and if it had, she would have quite sensibly reasoned that he wouldn't kill her now, after having spent what he'd made very clear was a frustrating night looking after her. Dimly, she was aware that he had dropped another package on the sand in front of him and tossed a larger package to Catseye. When he sat down, close enough to count as sitting next to her, and opened his own packet, she didn't move away, although she started a little when he suddenly extended his arm. He didn't reach for her. Instead, he grabbed a leather bag sitting on the sand between them. He undid the top, drank deeply, and then held his arm out straight, silently offering it to her. Marguerite turned her head away and reached for the water in her own satchel. His eyebrows drew down over his forehead as he watched her drink, but he didn't comment.

He finished his meal and then stood, giving his clothing a light shake to free any crumbs. She rose with him, reluctant to let him loom over her any more than was inevitable with their differing heights. His hand shifted against his side — perhaps he'd meant to offer it to her — but she was up and facing him before he had a chance.

"We should sleep," he said. "The heat of the day will be upon us soon."

She shrugged, the closest she would give him to agreement, and moved toward her shelter, tugging cautiously at the edges as she tried to remember how to enter without bringing the whole thing down in a tangled jumble. If she'd had any exposure to gentlemen, she would have expected him to insist on taking her poor little shelter and offer her the tent. But she had not and so he didn't disappoint her when he turned away and left her there to crawl beneath her shabby cotton ceiling.

She lay on her stomach, pillowing her head on her hands so she could keep her mouth high above the sand, and closed her eyes. Despite her misgivings about the man resting far too close to her, it had been a physically and emotionally taxing night and sleep came easily. Marguerite sank swiftly and willingly into the wreck of a great sailing ship, its timbers encrusted with barnacles in every shade of sea foam and all its sails replaced with anemones, waving in a hundred currents at once instead of a single wind. She slipped below the deck, hearing the hold groaning under the weight of the fathoms of water above it and watching the darting of tiny silver fish who felt no pressure at all but would have flown apart if ever they were taken into a softer sea. The groaning grew louder, no longer a pleasant reminder of oceanic strength but a ringing in her ears. She surged up through the water and as her head broke the surface, she woke.

"*Lady*," the man said, in a scratchy, exasperated tone that suggested this was not the first time he had said it. "Lady, we must be off."

She opened her eyes. Part of her made ready to jerk away in case he was too close, maybe even about to *touch* her. Another part noted that he was not. That he was standing apart from her, one hand at his side, the other holding Catseye's reins, stars ringing them both. She didn't know what to do with this information and so she responded to both parts at once, half pulling away so that her elbow caught the cloth and jerked the supporting rod to the side. She waited, breathless, to see if it would collapse around her. It did not and slowly, she crawled out. Her injured side seemed to have shrunk in her sleep, the skin tightening like leather after it had dried, and now movement was difficult. She stood carefully, trying to hide the slight tremble in her limbs. She turned away from him — even harder to do — and rolled the cloth around the rod. She stashed the bundle in her satchel and took a sip of water. The bag was getting disturbingly light and it no longer sloshed when she raised it. She allowed herself to hope that they would find another water source soon. The alternatives, whether it was dehydration or sharing with the man, were deeply unpleasant to contemplate. Finally, when she could put it off no longer, she turned to face him.

"Good morning," he said.

It wasn't morning, of course. It was the first blush of evening. She did not correct him. It didn't occur to her that she could have. Marguerite had spent most of her life setting her own hours and the shift in thinking to a near fully nocturnal life was not difficult. She had often stayed up all night dancing when the rhythm of the waves was just right or avoided sleep for days to watch a particularly good storm play out.

"Hello," she said. She didn't say anything else.

"We should get going," the man said. "If we make good time, we can be back at my camp before sunrise. I've already packed my tent. Give me your bag, I'll hook it back on the saddle. Can you eat and ride at the same time?"

Marguerite shrugged, wondering how he expected her to know that. She could eat, certainly. She'd had plenty of practice at that. And she could ride, she supposed, if riding meant sitting like a lump on a leather pad and not making any decisions about where horse and rider would end up. He didn't seem to get her unspoken message. His eyes rolled, just a little, and he took the bag that she slowly held out, arm straight to put him in as little contact with her as possible. He took it with the tips of his fingers, although his arm dropped a little, as though he had underestimated the bag's weight.

It was the work of a moment to attach it to the saddle. Then he turned back to her.

"Get on," he said. "Eating on horseback isn't hard if you don't have to steer." He made a quick encouraging gesture, close to his side, with the hand that wasn't holding Catseye steady.

Marguerite raised her hand and strode toward the horse. He was standing farther back than he had yesterday. She appreciated it, although she assumed it was a fluke. She put her hand up to the strap, the movement already starting to feel familiar. She supposed the one benefit of falling off so often was that she had had plenty of practice getting back on. Her hand tightened and she tried to lift her leg. It wouldn't rise, the skin that yesterday had been sore but supple now rigid and unyielding. She put the leg down, gave it a shake, and tried again. Again, she felt the pull but as much as she strained, there was no give in her body.

"Hurry up," said the man, in a voice just to the side of angry. "We have to go."

Marguerite let herself down slowly and swiveled so she could glare at him.

"I can't," she snapped.

His eyes narrowed.

"What do you mean you can't?"

"I mean I *can't*. My limbs don't work the way they did yesterday," she said, making sure to say it in a tone that implied it was his fault, although she hadn't quite worked out how yet (beyond that he made her very unhappy and when she was unhappy things didn't go right for anyone).

His gaze ran down her body. Perhaps he finally noted the stiffness in the way she stood because the corners of his eyes crinkled a little.

"I'll lift you up," he said, and though he'd made no move toward her yet, she stepped back sharply.

"No."

He didn't sigh, although he inhaled deeply as though he wanted to. Instead, he bit his lip, before exhaling in such a slow, deliberate manner that he must have been trying to sound calm and casual.

"I could give you a leg, I guess," he said.

Marguerite was about to retort that she didn't see how that would help, since she already had the normal allocation of two, and anyway, he couldn't possibly have a spare just sitting around. But then she remembered that he seemed to be able to pull just about anything from those few bags and rolls on Catseye's back and she was worried that he would prove her wrong. So she held her tongue. The man shifted and then, to her utter astonishment, knelt in front of her, one knee pressed to the sand, the other calf still vertical, as though he might get up at any moment. He smiled at her and patted the raised knee.

"Well, go on."

She blinked down at him. It wasn't that men had never gone on their knees for her before — she assumed they had, anyway — but they'd never done it in *front* of her. Some of her discomfiture must have shown on her face because he laughed a little, a softer noise than the defiant one she had forced out in the oasis.

"Don't you know how a step works? Just put your right foot on my thigh and then your left in the stirrup."

She looked down at him (she really did prefer it when he was lower than she was), swallowed, and slowly lifted her foot to place on his leg. It didn't make a good platform — it was round and bony and much of the bulk of it turned out to be the pants he wore, rather than his flesh and bone — but it worked. She didn't have to lift her foot nearly as high to get it into the stirrup and as she moved to swing up, he rose, the extra boost in height tossing her over the saddle. Again she perched on the horse, one hand already twisting into Catseye's mane to keep herself stable. The man smiled up at her, looking almost happy. She didn't smile back, but when he held another package of bread and fruit up to her, she wasn't quite so careful to avoid letting his skin brush hers.

He caught Catseye's reins and they began to walk again. A splinter of ice so cold that it burned ran down through her buttocks and down her thighs. Marguerite bit back a cry of pain. She was suddenly hyper-aware of the bones in her seat, feeling as though all the flesh had been stripped away and the only thing left was the hard line of her pelvis jabbing into her skin. She shifted, trying to find a position that eased the discomfort. Catseye trotted a little in response and the man, after running forward a few steps to slow him, looked back at her.

"All well?"

There wasn't an answer that wouldn't draw attention to parts of her anatomy that she didn't particularly want him contemplating. She glared down at him and nodded aggressively until he shrugged and turned away. She kept her movements smaller and subtler, eventually deciding that leaning slightly forward, though it strained her arms, at least kept the actively aching parts of her from direct contact with the saddle. The package she still clutched in one hand, but it would require both to unwrap it and so Marguerite let it be. She wasn't really terribly hungry at the moment anyway.

She could wait at least a while. Perhaps even long enough for them to make it to the man's camp.

If the man's estimation was accurate, she would be meeting his grandmother tonight. His grandmother who knew things, who sent her children's children without complaint to collect mysterious strangers that she shouldn't have known even existed. Marguerite had never met a grandmother before; her own had died long before she was born or perhaps had lived nearby but was such a nonentity that even her existence had made no impression on her granddaughter. She wasn't sure, then, what to expect. This grandmother knew things. She made commands. She understood how to hear when the desert spoke, a trick Marguerite herself would like to learn (knowing what a thing tells itself was often the first step to knowing how to speak to it in a manner that would make it listen). *And,* Marguerite thought, remembering one of the very few things the man had said that hadn't seemed like some form of attack, *she told stories.* That confused her. Storytelling was for books. What was the point of doing it with your voice, an instrument that could be turned to much greater work?

"Why did your grandmother tell you stories?" she asked.

The man's shoulders jerked and he stumbled a little. Catseye halted (reacting to his master's surprise or pulled to a stop, she didn't know which) and the man turned to watch her face. Again. (She didn't know what he kept thinking he would find there.)

"Because she wanted me to know them, I think," he said eventually. "To teach me about the world we live in. And to entertain me, I suppose. I was a … demanding child." He grinned back at her.

She didn't recognize the invitation to laugh and so didn't. After a moment, he sighed and turned away. It was quiet again, save for the thudding of footsteps as steady as a tide and the occasional flash of wind ruffling clothes and hair and making the sand dance across the desert's surface.

"I could tell you one?" he said in a small and strangely tentative voice.

It was her turn for her shoulders to jerk, and her eyes widened as she looked down at him. She didn't remember anyone ever telling her a story before. Well, it would perhaps answer the question of why a story should be spoken instead of read. She nodded and then realized he couldn't see her.

"Yes," she said. If she had ever learned to say please, she would have said that too. The man didn't seem to expect it of her.

She watched his shoulders rise as he inhaled deeply. And then he began to speak.

Chapter Eight

"A long time ago," the man said. "Before my people came to the desert, it was not like the desert we walk in today. It was not like a desert at all. It was very cold, not just at night but during the day as well. So cold that the cold would creep inside you and make all your bones as brittle as glass, so that if you moved too quickly you risked fracturing them from your body. I spoke of night and day, but the truth is, there was no night or day. There was only blackness, so deep and complete that it was never pierced by even the tiniest prick of light. And because it was so cold and so dark, the dark and cold would press down so hard that it was impossible to breathe. And in this cold and dark roamed monsters, so large they would have blotted out the sun, if the sun had been visible, and so bizarre and unearthly that, if you had been there, you would have been glad it was too dark to see them, for to look upon them would drive you mad."

He paused. The pause stretched on and on and on.

"And?" Marguerite prompted when the silence stopped being atmospheric and started being dull.

"And that's it," said the man.

Marguerite made another valiant attempt at raising an eyebrow. He wasn't looking at her so it worked near perfectly, of course.

"That's it? The desert used to be slightly less terrible? That's the story?" She pursed her lips. "Do you understand what a narrative structure is?"

He still wasn't looking at her but now it seemed a tense, uncomfortable kind of not looking.

"It's better when my grandmother tells it," he mumbled.

She had trouble believing that — she was pretty sure a story without a plot was a story without a plot in even the most deft hands — but then, she knew very little about grandmothers. Perhaps in a grandmother's voice, a story felt like a story even when it wasn't a story at all.

"Wait," the man said, though he didn't stop the horse (she took this as an interjection, rather than an order, and so refrained from pointing out that while he went forward, she could not, in fact, wait). "Did you say you thought the desert in my story was *better* than the one we're in now?"

"Yes." She began what would have been a careless shrug, felt the pull of taut muscles, and slowly lowered her shoulders. He wasn't looking at her anyway.

"You'd prefer to never see again?"

"I'm not afraid of the dark. And the light here hurts my eyes."

"You'd prefer cold so deep it could shatter your bones?"

"As opposed to heat so searing it lives inside you long after the sun is gone? Yes."

"You'd prefer," he paused, swallowed. "You'd prefer a life surrounded by monsters lurking in the black?"

She let the question lie long enough that he would begin to suspect she wasn't planning to answer. Then she spoke. "I used to be the monster lurking in the black," she said. "So I'd be in good company."

It was a conversation-ending statement, as she had meant it to be. He was already turned away from her, but by the twitch in his shoulders he'd have liked to twist on his heel rather than face her, would have liked to rub her face in his deliberate rejection (or maybe she was just projecting).

She sat back, winced, and leaned forward again. She was becoming accustomed, at least a little bit, to Catseye's movements, and her stomach was starting to feel rather like a cavern at low tide. She continued to hold on with one hand and used the other and her teeth to rip open the package that she still held. It was another bundle of bread and dried fruit. She bit into it and watched half the fruit dribble from the sides and roll down the horse's shoulders. The tiny morsels were lost in the sand before she even had time to look down (not that she would have; Marguerite had learned quickly that looking straight down the side of a moving horse matched — well, she had never experienced seasickness herself, of course, but she knew of it). She made an unhappy noise, consisting largely of a snort like a whale's blow but with a hint of huff and a hint of growl mixed in. The man's head shifted slightly but she didn't catch the whites of his eyes so her frustration must not have attracted too much of his interest. She contemplated her meal or at least what was left of it. Putting her other hand to it might help steady it but she dismissed the possibility immediately. Falling had hurt enough when she was able-bodied. She didn't want to do it when she was already damaged.

She took another bite and watched another cascade of fruit disappear into the desert. There was only a small morsel left in her hand. She sighed and slammed her palm into her mouth, getting most of it inside and leaving her with the empty package and a few crumbs. She contemplated the scrap of leather as she chewed. She was finished with it and so she supposed she could just let it go, let it drop into the desert as she had dropped the bits of the package that she actually wanted. She was still hungry and therefore out of temper, but she didn't intend to ask the man for more. Let him think she could survive on dust and moonbeams. It would serve him right if she just dropped the leather. She was sure it was rare; she'd seen very few animals since she'd arrived here, certainly fewer than she'd seen up on an isolated cliff. On the other hand, if it was rare, it was valuable and perhaps she should keep it. It might be useful. She didn't care to hold it balled up in her hand the entire time so she tucked it carefully in the space between saddle and blanket on Catseye's back and made a mental note to remember that it was there.

Meal finished, she looked around and took careful stock of her surroundings. The desert looked the same as it had every other night. Perhaps the peaks of the sand were a little higher. Perhaps the moon was a little brighter, although she hadn't paid much attention to its shape (when it wasn't pushing and pulling the tides, she had very little interest in the moon). She saw no sign of life besides herself and the horse and the man. The sea had sometimes seemed this lonely, to the unknowing eye. A single boat adrift on a dark expanse. But there was life beneath the surface, in greater and more varied numbers than there ever was on land. Marguerite didn't think that there was life beneath the desert. She certainly hoped that there wasn't. Life under the ocean hadn't always been … merciful. She hadn't needed mercy from the ocean, would have been offended had it been offered. It would offend her now, in the desert, but that was pride rather than practicality speaking. Wolves in the desert were small and sharp. She didn't want to see the desert's equivalent of a shark.

It was dull, though, the desert, now that she was fed and watered and moving toward a goal. She had spent most of the previous night watching the stars and contemplating her life and her bruises. She didn't think she could handle another night spent the same way. She looked at the man, his steps as steady and even as they had been the last time she'd looked. She could have used his walk to keep time, if she'd meant to sing.

"Do you know any other stories?" she asked, because, as she told herself, it was the only thing she *could* ask without potentially diving into something more personal than she cared to.

He didn't startle this time. Apparently he was getting used to her ways.

"You didn't like the last story I told you."

"That wasn't a story. That was a description. A story has structure. It has a beginning and an end and a plucky young heroine to get you from one to the other."

The man snorted. It didn't sound like a contemptuous snort so she wasn't sure why.

"A heroine? I know one about a woman who becomes the queen of the bandits. Will that do?"

Marguerite nodded, remembered that the man was looking ahead, and spoke. "Yes."

It was a better story than the one he'd told before, at least in the sense that it had a plot. He kept mentioning things that she didn't understand — foxes and sandstorms and buzzards and cacti — so she had trouble following it, but the heroine was appropriately brave and the ending, wherein she became absolute ruler of all the bandits of the desert, spoke to her. (She wasn't sure what bandits were, either, but context suggested they were the desert equivalent of pirates.)

"Better?" the man asked once he had finished describing the Bandit Queen's wedding (because most stories ended with a wedding it seemed, even in the desert).

"I guess," she said. She wondered if she could wring a third story from him. She wasn't sure she particularly liked his stories (the desert took far too much of a starring role), but judging by the position of the moon, they at least served to pass the time.

"Your turn then," he said.

She blinked. He'd better not have meant her turn to lead the horse. That would end with the three of them very, very lost. She was quite committed to that. Even if he gave her directions.

"My turn to do what?" she asked.

"To tell me a story, of course."

"I don't know any stories."

"You know an awful lot about 'proper story structure' for someone who doesn't know any stories."

She didn't shrug, but she tossed her head slightly. "I read books. But I don't know any *stories*."

"Didn't your mother ever tell you any stories? Your father? Your grandparents?"

She could have shocked him into silence, then. He probably wouldn't have known how to respond if she'd told him about her parents. But she did not wield that weapon. She would have if she'd known how powerful it might have been, but she, who had never known a grandmother, didn't realize what a loss he would have seen it as. Either way, she had just enough emotional intelligence to know that staying silent would have prompted questions and not peace. So she asked a question instead.

"How far is your home?"

"You're looking at it," he said.

She squinted, trying to find buildings camouflaged in the sand. But the soft crests and dips all refused to resolve into sharp corners and solid walls. She returned to glaring at him, refusing to feel embarrassed at not being able to pierce the illusion. Perhaps he sensed her anger because he snorted again.

"All the desert is my home," he said.

Marguerite's eyes narrowed. She was, for the moment, disappointed that he wasn't looking at her so she couldn't impress upon him the full weight of how little his answer pleased her. She considered throwing something at him but the only thing she had to hand was the scrap of leather she had crammed under Catseye's saddle and she didn't think it would fly properly. If she threw something at him, she wanted it to connect, not flutter pathetically down to the sand.

"I wander free. All my people do. But if you're asking how much longer until we reach my grandmother," he continued, an amused lilt to his voice. "I'd say it will be less than an hour now, an hour more at most. Just enough time for that story."

She would have liked to fold her arms and rest her chin on them. She made do by folding her wrists. "Go on, then. I'm listening."

He did glance back at her then, a quick flick of his head like a bird striking a seed.

"You're really committed to the idea that you can't tell a story, huh?" His head stayed pointing forward. "Not much storytelling in your family, I guess."

It would be the height of pointless drama to declare that she didn't know the meaning of family, and inaccurate besides. She had books. She could *read*. And she did remember her parents, or at least she remembered that she had had parents. She'd had people who gave birth to her, anyway, and someone must have cared for her before she'd sung her first storm. She prided herself on her cleverness and independence but even she would grudgingly admit that a baby couldn't feed and shelter itself.

But that wouldn't be the kind of family the man had, she thought suddenly. He still talked to his family. Presumably he remembered their faces. He probably even knew their *names*. (Like every small child, Marguerite had never even conceived of the idea that her parents had a signifier beyond what she called them. And by the time she'd understood that they had names, she'd been in no place to ask what they were. Or, indeed, had any interest in knowing even if it were possible to find out.) What did a life lived in the embrace of family look like? She tried to picture it and failed.

"I'll be seeing your family soon," she said, voice rising just enough at the end of the sentence that it might be mistaken for a question.

"Some of them," the man said. "Not all."

"Why not all?" she asked. Who was it that left? She did not ask. He would know the second half of the question.

"Because not all were needed," he said, sounding irritated.

Good. He'd been on far too even a keel lately. She liked him unsteady.

"The only person who wants to speak to you is my grandmother. So she is who I'm taking you to."

"Just your grandmother?" No mother, then, or father. Not a surprise. And the fewer people, the better. If she had to run or worse, to fight, her chances would improve if her only opponents were an old woman, however wise and commanding, and one man, however threatening and disconcerting.

"And my sister," he said. "My grandmother is teaching her."

Sister. She had forgotten that some people had siblings, that some parents didn't give up when their first child was not what they had imagined. She wondered if parents were kinder with two children because they could spread their disappointment around or even more uncaring because there was always a spare. She wondered if the man was the spare. She wondered if being the spare made you bold or if it simply made you sad. She didn't think the man was sad, but then, she didn't actually particularly care to look for the signs, either. (Were there signs of sadness that didn't involve weeping down a hurricane? She didn't know but assumed there must be.)

"Teaching her what?" she asked.

The man shrugged, a loose, easy movement that she, still stiff and aching, resented him for.

"Things," he said.

"What things?" she demanded, too used to getting whatever information she pleased to recognize a brush-off when she heard one.

"Desert things," he said.

She contemplated the back of his head. (She was getting uncomfortably familiar with the back of the man's head and the arch of the horse's neck.) Desert things. Part of her wanted to learn desert things, to master this place before it destroyed her. Part of her worried that mastering it would be her destruction, that since the desert distorted wolves and ground and trees and light and even water, if she allowed herself too much intimacy with it, she would be distorted as well. She didn't want the shadows that played across her form or the hidden hollows of the notes that she sang to turn into something sharp and stark.

"Looks like there's an owl flying overhead," the man said abruptly, voice pitched high to be sure he caught her attention. "Do you know what owls are?"

"Yes," she said. She had known owls on her cliff, although she hadn't much cared for them. She didn't trust birds that spent most of their time over land, instead of over sea, nor any creature that moved so silently. She liked birds that called, even if you had to struggle to hear the melody in it. Anyway, the few owls she'd eaten had been stringy and the meat had tasted rancid.

"But you've never seen a desert owl?"

Marguerite did not dignify that with what she believed was an obvious answer.

"Are they bigger, where you're from?"

She couldn't shrug exactly, but she tilted her shoulders forward in a way that she hoped got the message across that she did not spend her time *measuring birds,* here or anywhere else.

"Ours fly rather funny," he said. "You might be able to see it if this one moves past the moon."

She didn't care about owl flight any more than she did about owl size, but she supposed if she had nothing better to do…. She leaned back as far as she could go without hurting herself or feeling that she was about to pitch off Catseye.

She grunted, wondering how the man expected her to see a single silhouette across an entire expanse of darkness. The owl could fly across the moon, as the man had said, but it was not a full moon nor even the crescent of romantic art, merely a wedge like the rim of a seashell stuck upright in some glittering black rock. He was muttering something, but she didn't particularly care to hear him speak when he was trying to make himself heard so she wasn't going to go out of her way to hear him when he couldn't be bothered to raise his voice.

The wind struck her cheek suddenly, whipping around her hair and tugging at the ends of her scarf. She raised her hands to keep the scarf in place, tearing her eyes from the sky. Her gaze fell forward, following the silvery strands of hair that the wind managed to snatch. Suddenly the owl and the wind were no longer of interest.

The desert was dancing. She had no other word for the way the sand rose in front of her, twisting higher and tighter into a soaring, spiraling crescendo. She had seen water turn like this, when the currents were right, but it had never risen so high nor moved so lightly. There had been power, always, behind the water, a sense of primal forces being compelled grudgingly into the movement. There was no hesitation in what she saw before her. The sand flew delicately around a central core, swelling and falling and swirling, always swirling.

And then it died. The sand dropped back to the desert floor, a delicate sprinkle so much gentler than the pounding of even the lightest of falling rain. But the air did not clear to show more of the endless pale expanse. Something did arch out of the sand, but it wasn't sand itself, or at least it had not been sand in a long, long time. A great shelf of rock jutted out, curving like the back of a wave. And below it, a tent, the same style as the man's but vastly bigger and painted with red designs that she couldn't relate to any seascape or sea creature. She felt the muscles of her jaw go slack. She made a mental note to close her mouth as soon as she could spare the mind power to do it. She had not known that the desert could do this. That someone could *make* the desert do this.

"You weren't supposed to see that," the man said, sounding distinctly put out.

She didn't spare him a glance. The tableau in front of her was moving. Two hooded figures emerged from the tent and began to walk toward them. One was tall or tallish at least — bigger than she herself, perhaps, but not bigger than the man. The other was small, hunched, scuttling along like a crab. That didn't comfort her. Crabs were small, but they could crush a bone in their claws.

The figures reached them. The man shuffled and made an awkward movement that she thought might have been a kind of bow, although she had never seen one done so high or with so little grace.

"Grandmother," he said. "I've found her. I brought her to you."

"And no doubt scared her half to death to do it," said the small figure in a dry, creaking voice, wind through reeds or scales over stone. No voice so weak should contain so much power. She pushed her hood back and looked up at Marguerite. "Well, get down from there and let me have a look at you."

Chapter Nine

"No," said Marguerite.

The man made a noise. It might have been a quickly swallowed curse; it definitely had notes of both exasperation and anger in it. She ignored him. She didn't think he would hit her in front of his family. And, much as she had done with him, she would be damned before she established a precedent for *anyone* in this desert to order her around. She had not been (very) afraid of Mama Bella and she was not going to be afraid of this wisewoman.

She was a strange-looking creature. Small and shrunken, like a clump of seaweed left out in the sun too long. She had not thought of the sun's ability to make things smaller, but perhaps, in this world where it reigned uncontested, she should have been more concerned with it. The woman's face was craggy beneath her headscarf, incised with such deep lines that Marguerite was reminded of cliffs that had taken the pummeling of the waves for hundreds of years. She wondered idly what had pummeled this woman. It would have been poetic, in this shrunken, dried-up face, for the woman to have had eyes that blazed out like stars. Marguerite was pleased to see that she did not. They sank into her face beneath the crevices of her skin, a filmy brown like water doused in dirty oil. They sank even deeper, suddenly, as the woman's mouth cracked open and curved upward.

"*Will* you come down and let me have a look at you then?" she asked, voice pitching higher and breathier.

Marguerite debated. She'd have to get off the horse eventually — presumably the man would want Catseye back at some point, for reasons that still rather escaped her — and the woman had asked this time, rather than commanded. She should probably reward that. On the other hand, there was power in being so much higher than everyone else. Power in being able to turn and gallop away if she was threatened, even if she was unlikely to get far before she fell and was caught. There was power in defiance, however ill-conceived. And she had never managed to descend from Catseye gracefully. She supposed the man would tell his grandmother that, even if she achieved grace now. She glanced at him out of the corner of her eye. He stood at Catseye's head, his body stiff, his back so straight she could picture a rod jammed up his robe behind him. If she tried to remain on the horse, he would probably lift her off.

That decided her. She kicked off the stirrups and leaned forward carefully, ignoring the way her taut muscles pulled and protested. She swung a leg over and tried to let herself down slowly. Her arm gave out instead and she fell heavily to the sand, remaining on her feet only because she still held Catseye's straps. The taller of the two figures, still hooded, started forward. Marguerite arrested the movement with a glare, allowing her lip to curl when the person stuttered to a halt. The shadows of the cloth and of the night itself still fell across their face — her face. The man had mentioned a sister. The sister did not try to move again and Marguerite turned her attention back to the old woman.

Now that they stood together, she was taller than Marguerite had thought, almost her own height. Had she been able to stand up straight, she might even have towered over her, as the man kept doing. She was unashamedly glad that the woman could not. Her dark eyes explored the curves of Marguerite's face. Marguerite had already inspected her from the saddle, but she stared back anyway. She didn't think she had ever met a woman so obviously old. She herself was, according to the storybooks, at least, a maiden. Mama Bella had been flushed with the grace of middle age, old enough to be confident, young enough that her body had not begun to degrade and betray her. This woman was a hag or perhaps a crone (this would have been an insult coming from anyone else, but in the books Marguerite read, crones lived alone and knew secrets and occasionally cursed people horrifically, and therefore, becoming one had always been somewhat of a life goal for her).

The crone reached up, fingers grasping for the single lock of silver that had come untangled from Marguerite's scarf. Marguerite leaned back, not far but pointedly. The hand withdrew and the crone smiled again, a disconcertingly earthy look, as though she had confirmed some hidden expectation.

"Well met," said the crone. "I trust your journey was not too difficult."

"I was stuck with a stinking beast," said Marguerite. "And the horse smelled bad, too."

A soft snort came from beneath the sister's hood. She couldn't see the man's expression from where she stood, but the abrupt movement of the side of his head suggested he wanted to glare. It interested her that he apparently couldn't choose which woman to glare at, as his head twitched between Marguerite and his sister. She wasn't sure how to feel about that. It was *her* insult, after all, and she considered it a pretty clever one, especially since she'd had very little practice insulting people to their faces. She didn't appreciate the sister getting just as much credit merely for finding it amusing. On the other hand, it had been a bit of a low blow and perhaps it was safer if he portioned out his anger between the two of them.

The crone didn't laugh but she didn't *not* laugh, if that could be said to be a reaction. Her smile didn't suddenly seem fixed, the crinkle in her eyes didn't smooth. Marguerite couldn't tell if she was amused, but she showed no signs of anger either. Marguerite chose to take that as a good sign, although she wasn't truly sure that it was.

"I'm sorry that you've been unhappy with Malik," was all she said in acknowledgment. "But please, come with me. We'll drink tea. And then we'll *talk.*"

She had *talked* with Mama Bella. Such talks could rarely be said to be pleasant. But they were ... illuminating. And, though she now found herself in a place where the sun seemed to be the sole arbiter of life and death, Marguerite thought that she was rather in need of illumination. She nodded, short and sharp, and when the crone turned away, she followed. The sister trailed behind her. Out of the corner of her eye, she watched the man turn Catseye and lead him away. She had seen only the one tent, but she suspected that there was more to this camp than what they were choosing to show her. The desert hid more secrets than she'd originally believed. The revelation pleased her a fraction more than it frightened her.

The crone pushed aside a flap and led them both into the tent. It was rude to stop in the entryway, but Marguerite did so anyway, feeling the sister's garments brush her back. Only the garments. There was no sudden shock of warmth as skin met skin even through cloth. The sister had anticipated Marguerite's halt or perhaps merely had fast reflexes. Both options made her a threat. Marguerite resolved to pay more attention to her before she took a slow look around the tent.

The man had said that his people wandered and so she shouldn't have been surprised that the space she found herself in was so sparse. She still was though. Her own cottage had been relatively empty — a bed, a table, and a small stove had been the only things to fill the stone walls — but she hadn't chosen her cottage. She hadn't furnished it, and she hadn't, really, spent very much time in it. And she had walked away at the first chance she was given when Mama Bella arrived. Mama Bella's home had been just full enough to feel loved and not cluttered enough to be suffocating. Marguerite had thought that people who chose their spaces liked to keep them filled. But the tent felt as empty and vast as the desert itself. It was about the size of her cottage, she estimated, although it seemed so much larger. The walls weren't like her own damp and molding stone but starkly white and airy, vibrating slightly in the wind that had still been pulling at her hair when she walked in. The floor was not a floor at all, she discovered, giving it a light tap with the tip of one foot, but a woven mat of what seemed to be reeds. The furniture was likewise light. In the center of the room stood a sleek low wooden table, the legs carved into some sinuous shape that might have been the coil of a snake or the curl of a horse's neck or some desert creature that she hadn't yet encountered. It was bare but for a lamp in the center, an odd-looking thing, the flame encased in a glass orb, wound around with copper flowers, which arched up and over it to form a platform. There were woven jars in one corner and in another, a carved chest of drawers, too small for clothing. Around the edges of the tent were piled rolls of leather or cloth, similar to the ones that the man had carried on his saddle, but much larger.

The crone gestured to the table, an apparently universal movement that indicated that Marguerite was to sit.

Her eyes narrowed. She would actually have liked to obey. Her side still hurt and a chair that didn't *move* sounded thoroughly appealing. But there was no chair, only more rolls. Perhaps these people could balance neatly on such a thing, but Marguerite could not and she didn't intend to try, especially with her thighs already aching and beginning to feel chafed.

The crone smiled again and then slowly lowered herself down on one side of the table, sitting directly on the ground and putting her back against the roll. It didn't look comfortable, but Marguerite followed her lead, allowing herself to slump down in what she convinced herself was a graceful settling like a blossom landing on water. She tucked her feet along her calves and waited.

The sister did not immediately sit. Instead, she walked over to the chest of drawers and bent, retrieving a small metal container that rested beside it. It was elongated and the handle curled out and around itself before meeting the side again. The slosh of water and the spout, however stretched, told Marguerite that what she held was a kettle. She placed it on the lamp's platform and returned to the chest, this time opening one of the drawers to retrieve three tiny round cups, metal and, as Marguerite saw when one was placed in front of her, delicately incised with images of flowers that Marguerite had never seen, but were surely too large and flamboyant for the desert. Finally, the sister sat beside her grandmother (in the same kind of movement that Marguerite herself had attempted but with markedly more success — although she presumably hadn't been stuck on a horse for two days so that was only to be *expected*) and pushed back her hood. And everything changed.

Everything changed. How poetic; how utterly meaningless. Every movement, every choice, every second lived changed the world. Everything was always different. Every now was always brand new. The sister took off her hood and things were different afterward. But things had also changed when Marguerite met the man and when she first rode a horse and in all those hours she spent by the oasis convincing herself that she was still powerful. They changed the first time she bit into a desert fruit and the last time and all of the times in between. Marguerite changed the world with every breath she took in and every breath she let out again. So did the man. So did the sister and the crone and the horse and the sharp wolf that might have been many sharp wolves. So did every lap of water in the oasis. So did every glint of every star on every grain of sand. The world was constantly being reinvented by everything that inhabited it.

So things changed when the sister took off her hood and shook back long thick hair, rich brown and gleaming red with each flare of the lamp. And when she met Marguerite's eyes with her own, brown rimmed with gold just like the man's and yet ever so much brighter, the world changed. The wind gusted and the lamplight flickered and the crone took in another breath and Marguerite went from living in a World Without Her to living in a World With Her.

I didn't know there were people like her, thought Marguerite. *People like me.*

And then, *I hate her.*

Some storms on the ocean screamed their rage for everyone to hear, destroying everything in their wake and strewing the wreckage across a thousand leagues. Some storms swirled and bubbled below the surface, their fury boiling fathoms and yet going unnoticed by those resting just above them.

"Now then," the crone said. "We are settled and the tea will soon be ready. Perhaps we should start with our names."

Marguerite met her eyes with icy composure. "Perhaps we should," she said. She held her silence and the crone's gaze, resisting the urge to glance at the sister.

The crone laughed, a harsh little noise rather like the shriek of a hawk just before it struck prey.

"You may call me Saqr," she said. "My granddaughter and apprentice is Än."

Än lowered her head slightly in acknowledgment. Her seashell eyes glittered as though the sunlight had caught them just so. Marguerite wrenched her attention back to the crone.

She had read that there was power in names and she supposed she believed it, in the sense that names were spoken aloud and there was power in a voice. But she had never believed in a name's power to command if its owner didn't choose to follow. Even Mama Bella had not been able to compel her purely through that single word, unless it was spoken in anger. There were many things that only had power in anger.

"My name is Marguerite," she said.

"Well, then," said the crone — Saqr. She folded her hands. "Now that we've been introduced, tell me, girl, who do you love and who loves you?"

Marguerite blinked. "What kind of question is that?" she said. "And also," she added, beginning to get angry. "Why did I bother introducing myself if you're just going to call me 'girl'?"

"It was two questions, actually," Saqr said, her face cracking open again, so wide it seemed her lips would tear. "The only questions that matter. I've always found that the answers to those two questions tell you everything you need to know about a person." The smile slumped just a little, worn and yellowing teeth disappearing again behind ravaged lips. "And you're right. So, *Marguerite*, I ask you again: who do you love and who loves you?"

The ocean, thought Marguerite, immediately. She wasn't sure if that immediate response was an answer to the first or the second question. It didn't matter. The ocean, the ocean, the ocean. Its waves still washed through her veins with every heartbeat. When she bit her lip, she still tasted its salt on her tongue. When it was dark and there were no words and no wind, the silence she heard was shaped by its murmurings. The ocean, the ocean, the ocean, always and only.

"I love not getting asked personal questions by strangers," she said.

The sister — Än, she must remember that — looked away suddenly, her teeth (not white as pearls, that was poetry again, but certainly whiter and fuller than Saqr's) coming down over her bottom lip. Saqr sat back, her lips twisting together much like her grandson's often had during their time together. Then she threw her head back and laughed, long and heartily.

"Well parried," she said after she had finally finished, her breath still coming out in throaty gasps.

Marguerite allowed herself a tight smile, just enough to let the woman know that she was aware of her victory, not enough that she would think it came as a surprise to her.

"The tea is ready," the crone continued and gestured.

Än rose to her knees, an easy graceful motion, and poured a stream of amber liquid into first Marguerite's cup and then her grandmother's. Marguerite supposed that the same logic she'd earlier used to assume that the man wouldn't poison her would apply here. She waited until Saqr drank anyway. Better safe than screaming with a belly full of fire. She blew at her cup gently, watching the steam waft. She could feel the tea's warmth in her hand, although it quickly cooled. Even in a tent, the heat of the desert during the day was not preserved. Like she watched Saqr, she noticed Än watching her. When she finally drank, the girl smiled.

Marguerite had never been much interested in fire, except as a tool. You could tame water, but she had always considered fire truly domesticated. It ran wild occasionally, of course, and people were injured or killed, but it spent most of its life confined and used for its gifts. It demanded respect, but it also demanded fuel, and if you didn't feed it or if you fed it wrong, it would die. The sea was not so weak. You could get rid of every tree, every bit of paper or straw, every charred brick, let it never see another human again, and it would still be as vast and as deep.

But she had used fire, because she was still human and meat still needed to be cooked and winters could be cold even if you were the one encouraging the frost, and she had not always been as careful as perhaps she should have been. And her mouth had occasionally been filled with smoke. The tea she delicately sipped tasted like those mouthfuls of smoke, although it didn't make her cough and choke. And there was an aftertaste, she discovered when she swallowed, something that burned even without heat. She put her cup down, fairly certain that she didn't care for it.

The crone raised an eyebrow at her (or, at least, Marguerite thought that was what the sudden rearrangement of the crags in her face meant).

"Are you enjoying it?"

"No," said Marguerite.

The crone didn't laugh although she looked rather like she wanted to. Än ducked her head again. Carefully, Saqr lowered her cup to the table. It rattled against the wood as it made contact. Marguerite lowered her own cup, meaning to let it clink softly against the surface. Instead, it struck the table hard and tipped to the side, splashing red liquid across the surface. It was, in fact, amazing that the liquid didn't drop to the floor, as the room seemed to suddenly be tilting wildly. She put out an arm and grasped the edge of the table, afraid that if she didn't hold on, she would slide across the floor and perhaps out of the tent completely. Slowly, the world righted itself and when she realized that her fingers burned, she slowly unlaced them from the table and sat up. The two women were looking at her. Än's eyes were wide and soft. She couldn't read the crone's face.

"You're tired," Saqr said. "Perhaps you should rest before we speak longer. Do you wish to bathe before you sleep? It will likely do you good."

Marguerite was already nodding before she had time to fully register the question. Yes, her skin felt dry and sore, and more importantly, she had, however briefly, pressed against the man when they had ridden together. She wanted to remove any trace of his scent (however much ... not-completely-unpleasant it had been) before it had a chance to sink even further inside her.

"Än will show you where you can wash, then," Saqr said, gesturing to her granddaughter. "Then you can rest. And then, when I have spoken to my grandson, we will speak again."

Marguerite thought of warning her that whatever nasty things he said about her probably weren't true, but on further consideration, she held her tongue. To call him a liar to his grandmother's face would not likely engender any sympathy toward her. Instead, she merely nodded.

Än rose, the same smooth movement of a snake pulling itself up to scent the wind. Marguerite tried to follow suit. Immediately, the muscles in her thighs and in her back made it known that they were moving only under protest. She rose an inch, froze, wavered, and managed to get one knee up to catch herself. She put a hand to it and pushed herself to her feet, keeping her eyes to the ground (only for guidance, of course). The room swayed and warped as she rose, but it settled once she reached her full height. Only when she stood, trembling slightly, did she face them again.

The crone had remained seated (Marguerite took solace in the knowledge that her rising would likely be even more ungainly). Än stood impassively, one hand resting palm down against her pants. (She wore the same style of clothing as her brother, although the cloth was a deep reddish brown, rather than the dark indigo of his. It was a more flattering shade against the bronze of all of their skins.) Her other hand was slightly raised and extended, as though she had been about to offer it and then changed her mind. Marguerite wondered if she had changed her mind because she didn't want to show compassion or if she didn't want to show pity. Neither alternative pleased Marguerite; she wasn't sure which was worse.

"I'm ready," she said, swallowing (her mouth felt thick and the liquid she swallowed tasted more like bile than saliva).

Än turned and led her slowly out of the tent. Marguerite didn't look back. To do so would have indicated that she cared about Saqr in some fashion, even if only as a possible threat. And she didn't.

"Were you really out there alone for days?" The voice had a smoky quality to it, a burning sting that lingered after the sentence had already finished.

Marguerite's first, irrational thought was that the tea had spoken to her. But no. It was Än, paused just a few steps beyond the tent and looking back at her, eyes fixed on her face, lips slightly parted. So she could speak after all; Marguerite had begun to wonder if she was mute (a mute companion might have been pleasant, actually, except that Marguerite would probably have been expected to understand what she wanted anyway).

"Yes," she said, flatly.

Än's eyes widened, the gold in them becoming even more prominent. It was not a pretty effect; it gave her the appearance of something predatory. A hawk or a large cat. Or perhaps it wasn't the gold at all but something deeper, some hunger inside her that leaked out as she tried to feign polite interest.

"And you survived?"

No, thought Marguerite. *I'm a ghost.* She didn't say it. Her reticence had nothing to do with manners (Än's presence so far was less irritating than her brother's, but her mere existence still chafed at Marguerite, much like the sand they were surrounded by). It was just that — it was just that acknowledging her death, even in joking form, would birth the thought into this world that the desert could kill her. That she'd had a narrow escape. That the desert would get another chance to strike at her when these people got what they wanted from her or realized that she couldn't (or wouldn't) give them what they sought and threw her back out under the sun.

Apparently her silence said more than she had meant it to (consciously, anyway). Än bit her lip and looked away.

"I suppose that was a silly question," she said.

"Yes," said Marguerite and then wondered why her companion's eyes dropped even lower.

"There's a crevice where water collects," Än said, after a moment of watching the ground while Marguerite watched her and tried to work out whether she ought to say something else and if so, what. "I'll take you to it."

Marguerite nodded, a brief jerk of the head that set the world swinging again. Än looked like she might be willing to wait for her, but Marguerite kept her head up and walked forward, spurring the other girl on with the threat that she would pass her and wander freely through the camp. They circled the tent, coming face to face with the great red rock that supported and sheltered it. It was not particularly imposing when Marguerite stood directly beneath it. It was lower than it had seemed on her approach with the man. Perhaps it had seemed to dominate the landscape merely because it was the only thing she had yet seen that dared jut out from the sand instead of tuck inside it. But it wasn't truly large; she could see the sand dunes rising above them on every side. She reached out to touch the rock. It was smoother than the rock of her cliff and not as uniform a red as it had originally seemed. Instead, it appeared to be made of layers of different shades, all pulled from the same palette: some of the lines in the rock were rose red, others had hints of brown or gold or dun. One line near the bottom was the same red-brown as Än's hair. She smiled, without really knowing why. There was simply something *friendly* about the rock she touched.

She turned at the sound of a pointed choking noise. Än was leaning against the rock face directly behind the tent at the midpoint, her fist near her mouth. Not a cough, then, but some passive way of drawing her attention. When their eyes met, Än gestured to a shadow on the cliff beside her. Which was odd, actually, because the moon and stars provided a decent light and there was no reason for a shadow to be that black in that particular spot, especially given the angle of the moon and — oh. Not a shadow, then, she thought, as Än slipped through it, turning sideways in order to fit. Marguerite walked to the entrance and put a hand to it. She would fit, of course. It was tough to tell through the bulk of her clothing, but she was fairly certain that Än was larger than she was and she had seemed to have no issue, beyond, perhaps, a need to exhale when passing through. So Marguerite would fit. Rock had no give. It didn't part for you the way water did. The way even sand did (though she hated to credit sand with anything). It would wear away, but that took time and a power that she didn't currently possess. She looked at the crack again. She couldn't see much through it, beyond a vague impression of light. Marguerite would fit, of course.

She stretched her arm inside and didn't meet resistance. She turned slowly and began to step through. At the last moment, she closed her eyes.

She pushed herself through harder than she should have. The crack widened immediately and Marguerite stumbled into a tiny cave, bumping hard against Än. Än stumbled, her arms going out to support the lamp she had apparently been lighting and placing. For a moment, shadows danced across the walls, taking shapes that seemed almost familiar, before Än steadied herself and they became mere outlines of the cave walls. It *was* a cave they were in, a small chamber just barely too big for Marguerite to stretch her fingers from wall to wall. She attempted to do so anyway, pawing delicately and ineffectually at the air around her. Though the space was narrow, it didn't feel particularly suffocating, probably because it rose high above her head, ending eventually in a circular opening which let a weak shaft of moon- and starlight in. The walls were smooth and, until they curved to converge on the chimney hole, remarkably straight. The only blemishes she could see were a gash in the wall, so rough and raw that it must have been carved out for a shelf, on which Än placed the lamp, and a pedestal of rock that swelled out at waist-height from the floor and the wall beyond it. She approached the pedestal, brushing past Än to do so (a faint scent of something sweet and spicy wafted up). The rim, smoothed and indented, just reached her chest (Än and the man would have been able to easily bend over it). She leaned over and peeked inside.

Time and pressure had eroded what was presumably once a flat surface into a small basin in which a pool of water now lay, glinting dully in the combined light of the lantern and the sky. She cupped her hand and dipped it into the water. Her arm sank lower than she expected, almost up to the elbow. The water was warm and lapped gently against her tired flesh. She lifted her hand and put it to her mouth. There was no memory of the ocean in the water, but it tasted kind, like time and patience and the way water could support the world if it was hammered into the right shape first. She swallowed and licked the last remains from her lips, surprised to find that they already felt less cracked and painful.

Something soft nudged her elbow. She half turned to see Än holding out a soft length of cloth.

"To bathe with," she said. "I'll leave you be so you can strip and bathe in peac— *oh*! You're already—"

Indeed, even while Än was speaking, Marguerite had already unwound the scarf from her head, swept off her tunic, and was wrestling with the tie around her pants. The knot had become stiffened by the sand and her own sweat. She grunted as she scrabbled at it, finally getting the edge of a nail underneath and swiftly pulling herself free. She kicked off the trousers and bent over the basin, soaking the offered cloth and using it to rub the grime from her skin.

She had been dustier than she'd realized; now scrubbed, her pale skin showed up like a second shaft of moonlight in the cavern's gloom. She put a hand up, wondering if she dared risk attempting to detangle her hair and decided that the night had been long already and that at this point sleeping on it again would do no further harm. She straightened and stretched, feeling the tight muscles in her back loosen. Should she dress again? Her lip curled at the sight of the trousers on the ground. She had often dealt with cloth so impregnated with salt that it might as well have been carved of stone, but salt did not chafe as sand did. She bent and, slowly, pulled only the tunic over her head.

Marguerite turned and looked for Än. Despite her statement, the other girl hadn't left. She was standing stiffly at the entrance to the cavern, back turned. It was a strong back. Solid like a — a tree maybe but not like any tree that Än would have ever seen, judging by the ones Marguerite had encountered in the oasis.

Marguerite had never had to attract a person's attention before, and she found that she wasn't quite clear on how to do it (her instinct, a frigid gust of wind, would be impossible here and probably unwelcome besides). Should she make a noise? What kind of noise attracted attention? A scream, obviously, but the man would probably hear and roll his eyes at her, and besides, after a few days of more talking than she had ever done in her life, her throat was rather sore.

She settled on words.

"I'm done." It was, at least, to the point.

Än turned. Marguerite watched her eyes widen and followed their path as they trickled down her body.

"Are you sure?"

She also looked down at her legs. They appeared even paler in contrast to Än's clothes and skin. She shrugged and nodded.

"The trousers are dirty. And it's not like I need pants to sleep."

Än's eyes had risen again and were fixed firmly, almost manically, on her face. She swallowed and gave herself a little shake. It reminded Marguerite of a wolf shaking off water; she wondered what Än was attempting to shake away.

"Very well." Än turned and led her out of the cave.

They didn't go back into the large tent in which they'd had that strange fiery tea. Instead, they walked past it. There was, Marguerite realized, another tent tucked in against the big one's side. It was much smaller — only up to her own head — and Än would have to duck to enter. It was a plain little thing, without the intricate designs of the other. Än held the flap open and, after a moment's consideration, Marguerite slipped through the entrance. She was in a narrow, dim space, not as bright or as airy as the last tent that she had shared with the girl next to her. The only furnishing appeared to be a flat rectangle on the floor which filled most of the available space. She knelt and prodded it. It was soft, likely some form of bedding. She squinted at it. She thought it would fit one with room to spare, two if they slept close together. Remembering her night with the man, she turned to face Än.

"Are you expecting to share with me?" she asked.

Än started a little.

"Did you want me to?" she asked, voice pitching high.

Marguerite narrowed her eyes.

"*No.*"

"Good, because I didn't intend to," Än said. There was a strange edge to her voice. "You may sleep here for now. *Alone.*" Her hands rose to her chest, fingers churning against each other repeatedly. Marguerite watched in silence.

"Dream of water," Än said eventually and turned to go.

Marguerite gasped and threw herself forward, clutching the first part of Än that came to her hand. "*What did you say?*"

Chapter Ten

Än gazed down at Marguerite's white-knuckled hand tangled in the leg of her pants. Her mouth was a flat line, but there was a slight wrinkle in the corners of her eyes.

"I wished for you to dream of water," she said slowly. "It's what we say, here, to wish a person a good rest." Her hand reached down, grasped the cloth of her trousers, and twitched it from Marguerite's grasp. "I apologize if I distressed you. It was not my intent."

Marguerite unclenched her hand and withdrew it, balling it up instead against her chest.

"It's fine," she said, between clenched teeth. "You're free to go. I can fall asleep on my own."

But Än lingered, her brows knitting together.

"If you have some other way to say good night," she said after a moment. "I'm willing to use it."

Marguerite turned her head away. "I don't."

"How do you normally wish someone well before they rest then?"

Marguerite scooted backward and flopped down pointedly, curling on her side.

"*I don't.*"

She didn't look back, but she heard the rustle of cloth, and the tent was plunged suddenly into deeper darkness as Än let the tent flap fall. She inhaled and let it out slowly. Her bedding smelled faintly of horse — she thought the smell was horse. It smelled like Catseye had smelled, anyway. It was less acrid than human sweat, she supposed, but she still didn't care for it. She shifted into a more comfortable position, taking the weight from her damaged side. This bed was far softer than any she'd had since coming to the desert, and she was looking forward to not having to shake the sand free of her hair and clothing when she woke.

She didn't like the man and she didn't like Saqr and *she didn't like* Än, but she supposed that things could be worse. They'd been rude, and Saqr in particular had been impertinent, but they had not, except for when the man had initially wrenched her arm in grabbing her, hurt her. And they had food and clothing and water that didn't fight back, and they knew the desert. She could leave perhaps. But what would be the point? It was wiser, at least for now, to stay. She closed her eyes.

Dream of water, Än had said. She might as well have told her to breathe.

The water she dreamed of that night was warm and gentle, lapping shallowly against the shoreline, the sun's sparkle catching on the delicate ripples. But, Marguerite knew, as she would always know when it came to the ocean, that the smooth-pebbled beach had once been a mountain, beaten by the waves over lifetimes until all that was left were a few round stones.

She dreamed, too, of the wind, pulling at her hair and then at her clothes. She dreamed that she opened her eyes and that there were voices in the tent with her, riding the wind like tiny boats on a current.

"What's your impression of her?" That was Saqr's hard croak.

A pause. An intake of breath, too smooth to be the crone's.

"She might be a monster that kills us all." The man's voice was smooth and deep. It might have been pleasant if he wasn't always using it to be unkind. "She might just be an overdramatic brat who knows a few tricks." Another intake of breath. "She might be both."

Some part of her wanted to sit up and start shouting. But then the waves bore her gently away again, and she watched them reduce another cliff face to a handful of grit and pebbles.

《》

She woke up angry. It was not an unusual feeling. She often felt the dull ache of a world that didn't please her and rarely bothered even to try. But this anger was sharper, focused, even targeted. A pity that she didn't know what the target was.

She sat up slowly, letting the blanket that had been haphazardly draped over her fall across her lap. The inside of the tent was dim and the air was comfortably chilled. Night, she concluded, and well-advanced, since she felt none of the day's lingering warmth. She yawned and put a hand up to her head. Her injured side didn't pull at her anymore, for which she was passingly grateful. Her hair was still a tangled mess. She would have to unravel it at some point or, as Mama Bella had threatened more than once, it would soon need to be shorn from her head.

She leaned forward, letting her weight fall on her hands, and crawled to the entrance of her tent, pulling the flap free.

"Good night," she heard the man drawl. "Finally decided to grace us with your presence, have you?"

She started and pushed herself forward, trying to find where he had concealed himself. He was to her left, she discovered, leaning casually against the rock face and gazing down at her with a small, easy grin on his face. She freed herself from the tent and scrambled to her feet, brushing her hand angrily down her tunic to shake loose the sand that even that simple movement had picked up.

"The night isn't that far gone," she snapped (wilfully ignoring her previous conclusions). "You can't have been up that much longer than I have."

"It's well gone," he said cheerfully, his eyes remaining fixed on hers as he pushed himself away from the wall. She instinctively stepped back just a touch. "And even if it weren't, there's work to be done during the sunlit hours."

She caught the evasion in his words. "But were you the one doing it?" she asked, keeping the triumph out of her voice since she hadn't truthfully won yet.

He started and then his eyes crinkled. "You caught me," he said. "I was up before you but only when the light turned. I had a lie-in, since I was tired from fetching mysterious, disagreeable strangers."

There was probably meant to be an insult in there, but she couldn't find it. She was a stranger to him, she was willing to admit that she could seem like a bit of a mystery to those who didn't *understand* (which was most people) and she saw no shame in not agreeing to go along with someone who refused to stop taking objectionable actions. She huffed, half acknowledgment that he had spoken and half just to remind him that she didn't like him.

"Anyhow, it doesn't matter," he said. "You were obviously tired and you're much less trouble when you sleep. Come and have a wash and something to eat. Maybe Än will even lend you a pair of pants." He paused and raised an elegant eyebrow. "I hope you weren't expecting one of us to wash yours."

"No," said Marguerite, surprised. "Why would you?"

Apparently that wasn't the answer he was looking for, or at least not the one he was expecting. He looked fully into her face for the first time, his mouth arching up on one side.

"Why indeed?" was all he said, after a pause while his eyes raked her face. He turned and began to walk away, in slow measured steps that were clearly inviting her to follow. She debated walking the other way on principle, but her mouth was dry, and — she prodded her feelings — a meal would definitely not go amiss. She followed him at a firm distance, ready to bolt if he reached for her. He didn't. Instead, he led her to the same cavern she'd washed in before. He stood outside the crack, his hand moving out in a graceful invitation to enter the crevice. She was half expecting him to follow, perhaps offer to light the lamp as a flimsy excuse to bother her. But a few minutes' wait showed that he was either kinder or lazier than she had thought.

Without the lamp, the cavern was dim, the deep shadows making it seem smaller than it had when she had occupied it with Än. She still remembered its layout, moving briskly forward until her outstretched arms met the rock pedestal. Along the way, her feet struck something soft and she nearly tripped. She knelt and picked up her pants. They were still gritty, but they were less stiff than they had seemed last night. Shrugging, she pulled them on. Then she stepped up to the basin. She bent, taking a sip and splashing some of the water on her face. She tried to smooth her hair back and grimaced. She wondered if Än had a comb she'd be willing to lend. (A strong one. She'd shattered the only ivory comb she'd ever used and broken half the teeth from the wooden one that had replaced it.) Or perhaps Mama Bella had packed her a brush and it was somewhere hidden in the folds of her bag. Her bag — it had been attached to Catseye the last time she had seen it. Presumably it had made it to the camp. She would have to locate it; she had liked no portion of it except for the rapidly bleaching dress, but it had been useful. She wondered where Catseye was. She hadn't seen or even heard the horse since the man had led him away. There must be more to the rock they sheltered under than her tired mind had comprehended. She scooped up another handful of water and used it to push some of the flyaway ends of her hair from her face. That would do for now. It was probably best not to keep the man waiting in case he barged in after all.

She stepped back into the night air and paused outside the gap to let her eyes adjust. The moon was bigger tonight. That had meant something to the ocean. She doubted it had any significance at all in the desert.

The man had been leaning against the wall again. His chin was tilted down so the shadows fell across his face in a way that hid his eyes from her. She found that she didn't care for that. She liked being able to see where he was looking, and she liked being able to at least guess at what he was thinking.

He stirred and faced her. She was learning to read him a little, at least when he was in an extreme of emotion. He wasn't right now, although he was probably annoyed. He always seemed annoyed. She assumed he must simply be a naturally cranky person because, after all, there was nothing *she* had done to annoy him. She hadn't asked him to come find her and drag her back to deal with a pushy old woman and a disconcerting young one. *She* was the victim.

"You're done?" he asked, voice level and uninflected.

There was a sarcastic answer there that rose unbidden to her tongue. She remembered that he had access to food and water and allies, so she swallowed it.

"Yes," she said.

He half turned and beckoned to her to walk with him. (All of his motions were slow and smooth and elegant. She had moved like that, she was pretty sure, before she'd come here and lost all her grace.)

"Good," he said. "Come and eat something." His face half swiveled again so he could watch her from the corner of his eye, a movement that brought an odd, lurching memory of the way he had spoken to her when he led her through the desert. "I promise the meat is younger than two days old."

She started. She had forgotten she had told him that. And, though his voice had pitched higher in a way that she suspected was meant to mock her, he had remembered. She wasn't quite sure how she felt about that, and so she stayed silent. He turned his head back and led her around the large tent and in through the opening. It was arranged much as it had been before, although Saqr and Än now sat at opposite sides of the central table. They both turned as the two of them entered. Saqr merely nodded, her face wrinkling up. Än half rose, an ungainly rearrangement of limbs like a newborn animal learning to walk for the first time. What she meant to do remained a mystery; when she seemed to realize that she wouldn't be able to rise properly, she flushed and subsided, limbs folding down again like reeds breaking or a long-legged seabird nesting.

"Well met to you both," Saqr said, her croak shattering the silence.

Marguerite looked at her. She appeared much the same as she had the night before, the face as creviced, the eyes cloudy but somehow still piercing. A few white hairs escaped from the scarf she wore and dangled beside her face.

Än had her hair braided back; the few wisps that escaped framed her face rather than making her look unkempt.

"Sit," said Saqr. "Eat. Drink. And then we will speak."

You will speak, thought Marguerite. *You can't compel me to.*

Malik moved forward suddenly, skirting Saqr and sinking down beside her. If she chose to follow their arrangement, she would sit in the free space beside Än and across from Saqr. She was not sure that she cared to and wondered idly if there was another place to sit. Än did not beckon but her face turned up toward her. Her eyes were golden again in the lamplight.

Marguerite sat.

The same teapot — probably the same teapot. She hadn't paid that much attention, but presumably a person only needed one fancy teapot — sat on the same brazier in the center of the table. But there were other dishes, too, arranged to each side of it. They were too thick to be metal. They might be some form of ceramic, glazed and burnished to a deep, gleaming red like blood in the very deepest meat of a fresh kill. There was meat on one, lozenges of some grey-brown, scaly meat. There was an uncomfortable jerk in her stomach before she realized that it was almost definitely snake and not fish. Next to it sat a dish piled with the same flatbreads that she had found in her bag and that the man had given her while they traveled together. These ones must be fresh; steam rose in tiny spirals from the plate. There were more of the things she had eaten in the oasis, the fruits that looked like organs, and another, unfamiliar kind of fruit, red and prickly. The final plate held mounds of leathery-looking strips.

The man leaned forward and picked up a piece of flatbread in the palm of his hand. He then used it to grab a palmful of fruit and meat. He sat back, caught her eye, and raised the meal to her in a salute that might have been meant as mockery or might have been a demonstration. She snorted. Part of her was tempted to shove her bare hand into the food, just to defy them. But she still didn't understand what they wanted from her and the price for disrespecting food in this strange family might be the loss of access to it. She sighed and reached for the flatbread, at the same time as Än did. Their fingers bumped and then bumped again as both reached forward a second time, having clearly expected the other to withdraw. For a moment, they paused to glare at each other. Then, quick as a snake strike, Än's hand darted under Marguerite's and came back with the prize. Marguerite snorted and retrieved her own bread.

The meat was flaky, with a texture much like fish. Its flavor was mild and, to Marguerite's mouth, slightly rancid, although she didn't believe it was actually rotting. The organ fruits were sweet, as they had always been. The red fruits were sweet, too, although she found them slightly unpleasant. They had a fruity richness to them that the organ fruits lacked, but there was a perfumy quality that stuck to the roof of her mouth. The leathery strips turned out to also be meat, heavily spiced with something similar in taste to the smoky tea. She had read that one could dry meat to preserve it, although it had always been too wet and too foggy at her cottage to try it.

She ate sparingly, just enough that her stomach no longer felt pinched and tight, and then leaned back on her palms to watch her companions. The man ate heavily, the two other women lightly (proving her accusation that he had risen just before her). Eventually, the plates were emptied. She didn't see Saqr give any signal. She didn't even seem to glance at her grandchildren. But, as one, the man and Än rose, gathered the plates in their arms and, before she could protest, left the tent, abandoning her to the old woman.

They faced each other across the table. Saqr's face was calm. Marguerite was fairly sure hers was as well. She could leave, she supposed — the old woman couldn't stop her — but unless she abandoned the camp completely, this confrontation would come at some point. Best to get it over with so at least she knew where she stood.

"Have some tea," said Saqr. As opening volleys went, it wasn't a particularly threatening one.

"I don't like your tea," said Marguerite.

One side of Saqr's mouth twitched up.

"I suppose it would taste strange to you," she said. "But it's good for you. If you intend to be here long, I suggest you develop a taste for it."

Any answer to that would reveal more than Marguerite cared to. She folded her hands in her lap and waited.

"Will you give me your hand?" Saqr asked after a moment, extending her own appendage.

She didn't want to. Only one person who'd taken her hand had ever even seemed to mean her well. But life in this vicious place seemed to mostly involve doing things you'd rather not. She held out her hand. The sudden tightening of Saqr's fingers around hers felt like the grasp of a striking bird of prey.

"Do you remember what I asked you yesterday?" Saqr asked, bringing her other hand up to press her palm to the back of Marguerite's hand.

Marguerite flinched but didn't pull away.

"You asked me several questions," she said flatly, although she suspected she knew what questions in particular Saqr was referring to.

The old woman smiled again.

"I asked you what you loved and what loved you," she said. "You refused to answer."

Her fingers tightened around Marguerite's hand. "How a person answers those two questions tells you everything you need to know about them." She smiled again. "You revealed more than you think."

Marguerite did wrench her hand away then, pulling it back to cup it hard against her chest, to rest against her suddenly pounding heart.

"You know nothing about me," she said. "Nothing."

"I know your hands are always cold, even in the desert."

It should have sounded like a conversational tangent. She knew it wasn't. The old woman's eyes held hers. Though they were cloudy, she could see the similarity to her grandchildren's eyes. The flecks of gold had tarnished, but they were still there.

"I wondered," she said. "How someone like you, so pale, so lost, could survive so long in the desert without burning to ashes. So did Malik. So did Än. I understand now. There's ice in your soul, girl. There's a frost in you so deep that it can't be melted even with all the sun's power bent against you."

For a moment, the tent was silent but for the wind, which slipped in under the tent's flaps seemingly solely so it could catch Saqr's words.

Marguerite broke the spell, her laughter ringing lightly and easily. "Tell me something I don't know," she said.

Saqr had obviously been expecting a different reaction. She drew back, her brow wrinkling, forming even deeper crags and crevices. She didn't, to her credit, immediately speak, demanding answers to questions she couldn't form. She sat, and clearly, she thought, long and deep. Marguerite didn't interrupt, although she badly wanted to. She sensed that a decision was being made. She would let it happen, so she knew whether she would soon be running or fighting. Saqr sighed, a gust as sharp as the wind still playing along the room's boundaries.

"I don't know who you are," she said. "I don't even know what you are. I don't know why the wind seems to love you so. The only thing I am sure of is that you don't belong here, lady of the pale skin and silver hair and ice in your soul. But," she paused. "I think I will feel safer if you're somewhere I can keep an eye on you. So, with harm to none, you will stay here, with me and the young ones, at least for now."

She held a hand up to forestall Marguerite's protests. Marguerite, undeterred by a simple appendage, protested anyway.

"So I'm to be a prisoner?"

Saqr smiled. "Is that what you heard? No, strange one, you may leave if you wish. But I don't think you're as big a fool as that. There's food here and water and shelter. My grandson said you wanted to learn about the desert and I will teach you, at least a little." Her smile widened, a great gaping cavern. "You may think of yourself as a prisoner if it soothes your ego. But we will think of you as a guest."

A guest or a prisoner. Her pride said prisoner, that although it was phrased in pretty language, she didn't truly have a choice. That she would probably die if she struck out on her own and that Saqr knew that. She had spent most of her life being forced into places she didn't terribly want to be. This was the first time the people forcing her had stuck around. She didn't know if that was a good thing. But it was novel.

Prisoners were ill-treated. But guests were looked after.

"I will be your guest," she said, and then, because she was Marguerite, added, "For as long as I care to."

Saqr nodded. "Very well then. My grandchildren will show you around the camp and then you can help prepare the next meal."

"If I'm a guest," she said slowly, drawing on the descriptions in books she had read. "Doesn't that mean I don't have to help out with chores?"

There was a long silence, although it was far less charged than the last time neither of them had spoken. Then Saqr began to laugh, a harsh sound like a bird's shriek.

"You might be strange and dangerous, girl," she said. "But Malik was right. You have an interesting way of seeing the world."

Birds and fish puff up when angered. Marguerite's movements were similar.

"I do *not*," she snapped.

She wasn't actually sure what Saqr and, by extension, the man had meant by that, but she knew that she didn't like him, and she was pretty sure he didn't like her and therefore it was probably an insult. Her furious denial didn't seem to have much effect on Saqr, who continued to chuckle.

"I have nothing more to ask you," she said instead. "And you've made it clear that you have little you wish to say to me. My grandchildren are waiting for you."

Even Marguerite could recognize the dismissal. She wanted to find some pretext to stay purely to prove that she wouldn't be commanded. But there was none, or at least none that her pride would let her use, and she had spent enough time with only herself for company to know that more time with Saqr would only make her unhappier. She wasn't quite sure whether they were at war with one another, but she knew if they were, it was on a battlefield that she had never seen before and didn't understand. So she rose and she nodded, just a little (an acknowledgment, not a bow, never a bow), and she walked to the tent entrance in slow, measured paces. She pushed aside the folds of cloth and slipped out.

Two figures rose from the shadow of the cliff and moved to face her. Än was smiling; the sharpness of it and the way her eyes flashed gold made her look more wolf than woman. The man's face was that special kind of blank that even Marguerite could recognize meant that he was concealing deep feelings. She was fairly certain that they had been standing too far away to hear the conversation she had just had. She wondered idly if they had sprung away to that position when they realized that the meat of it was over or if they truly respected Saqr enough to restrain themselves from eavesdropping. She didn't ask, not wanting confirmation that they knew her secrets or that Saqr had that kind of command.

"You're to show me around the camp," she said, before either could speak.

Än's eyebrows rose. The man's face didn't change, except perhaps, for the slight upturn of one side of his mouth.

"So we are," he said and turned, leading her away from Saqr's tent.

Än fell into step beside her. It felt more like a guarded escort than it did gentle camaraderie. They circled the rock, remaining in the shadow of its crest despite the fact that there was no sun to dodge. Marguerite let her eyes trail over the undulations of the rock, mostly so she wouldn't watch her companions. There were symbols carved on the rock, high up and (her eyes flicked downward) low to the ground, nowhere that was easy to access. Some had sweeping lines like wings, others evoked memories of the way Catseye had run so swiftly over the sand. Some had the heat of the sun in them and some the gentler light of the moon. Some were unrecognizable. She didn't know if this was a language, new or ancient, or simply an idle doodle from a bored inhabitant. Or magic, she supposed. There was magic in the voice and the voice could be captured, weak as the capturing was, in symbols. Perhaps magic could be captured too.

They rounded the edge of the cliff and suddenly there was a white mass in front of her, and something hard and warm caught her elbow and pulled her, stumbling, in a new direction. The white mass was a tent, she realized, as plain as the one she had slept in last night but larger. And the warmth around her elbow was Än's hand, fingers curling against skin and bone to create pressure but not pain. Marguerite pulled her arm free anyway and did not have to fake the narrowing of her eyes or the flush of rose across her cheeks.

"Don't touch me," she hissed.

Än raised her hands to her chest and stepped backward, eyes wide, some of the wolf going out of her smile. The man had turned to face them. She recognized the edge of anger in his face and didn't understand why he was facing his sister and not her.

"I wasn't trying to hurt you," Än said, voice low and calm, a slight sharpness under the smoke. "I only wanted to prevent you from walking into Malik's tent. He pitches it too close to the peak."

"The horses need space," the man said. The anger in his voice was bleached like it was the color from a shell left too long on the beach. He sounded, instead, an equal mix of amused and some tired emotion that echoed of frustration — boredom, perhaps. Evidently the siblings had discussed this before.

"Horses?" said Marguerite, latching onto the one part of the conversation that seemed to be of relevance to her.

The man faced her fully, smiling a little.

"I supposed you've wondered how Catseye is," he said. "Come and see him and the others."

She hadn't, in fact, given much thought to Catseye, although she supposed she wished the horse well enough. She shrugged and followed him. They rounded the tent, to see — not a tent. A canopy might be the best term, a huge square of cloth or leather, stretching out from the cliff and anchored with two yellowing rods. Beneath it stood three horses, clustered around a heap of some grass-like substance like crabs around a dead fish. The black shape lifted its head to face her and whinnied. She was caught again by Catseye's blue eyes. She found that she had, after all, hoped that he was healthy after the journey. In response to his movement or perhaps merely in response to their presence, the other two horses also raised their heads. One horse, smaller and rounder than Catseye but taller than its unknown companion, , was dark beneath the moonlight, although she thought in the light that its coat would warm to a rich red-brown. The delicately pointed ears pricked toward her. The eyes were not blue, but neither were they particularly dark. In a brighter light, they might have been amber. Its mane lay along its neck in braided scallops, although its tail swished free. The third horse, facing her across the hay, was the slowest to greet them. It was the shortest, the thinnest, and the palest. Its coat was grey, not a single solid hue like Catseye and the brown horse, but spotting darker and lighter across its body, as though dozens of rocks had been dropped into the pond of its skin and ripples had just begun to spread. Its short mane was a dark line across its neck, a branch lying across the pond's surface.

Beside her, the man whistled, the sharp noise piercing what had been a remarkably peaceful scene. Catseye immediately turned and trotted toward them, stopping in front of the man and dropping his head into his raised palm. The man ran a gentle hand along the broad cheek and smiled, the kind of easy smile that Marguerite had never seen directed at her. His head turned, some of that comfortable warmth lingering.

"Well, give him a stroke," he said. "He's been looking after you the past few days and I think he's wondered where you were."

She reached up, the movement stilted, and gingerly uncurled her fingers. She had never petted an animal before and she wasn't really sure of the protocols involved. Catseye had been a nice animal, but he had run away with her and after her, and she was well aware that he was big enough and powerful enough to shatter her bones. She laid a hand on the horse's cheek in imitation of the man and gave it a few gentle pats, more like beating down bread than rewarding a living being. If she wasn't doing it right, she at least wasn't doing it so wrong that Catseye felt the need to move away, as the one visible blue eye remained fixed on her. She smiled: a mere crescent rather than a waxing moon.

Her arm jerked suddenly, as a sleek neck was thrust underneath it. Catseye's ears pinned back against his skull, and he sidled away as the rippled horse pushed between them and thrust its nose into Marguerite's chest. Startled, she recoiled.

"Enough, Eyas," the man growled.

Beyond him, Än echoed a similar sentiment, her arms sliding from the brown horse's neck as Catseye's retreat forced it to the side as well. Neither reprimand seemed to bother the horse, as it continued to move forward, forcing Marguerite backward until the sand shifted beneath her and she sat down heavily. It was not a safe position to be in when an animal so much larger than she was wanted something from her. But the hooves didn't strike her. Instead, the horse bent its head and caught a few strands of her hair between its teeth, giving them a tug as gentle as a lover's (as if Marguerite had ever had one or, indeed, even bothered to imagine what such a touch would be like). Grimacing, she raised a hand and laid it against the warm muzzle. She had meant to push the horse's nose, but the breath against her palm was gentle and the fur beneath her hand surprisingly soft.

"*Enough,*" the man said again and the nose vanished as he pushed the grey — Eyas, he had called it — away.

He held a hand out to her, although far enough back that she could rise without touching him if she chose to. She did choose to and pushed herself up stiffly, only then meeting his eyes. His look was half smile and half grimace, a look not focused on her, judging by the angle of his eyes, but remarkably similar to the ones that he kept giving her.

"My grandmother says she likes a horse with spirit," he said, shifting his position to stabilize it as the grey rubbed its cheek against his shoulder. He sighed and pushed its cheek away again. "I wouldn't, personally, recommend so young a filly to so old a woman." He grinned a little, wryly. "But Grandmother is also old enough to do as she pleases. Hence Eyas, who needs no introduction, as she introduces herself."

He pushed the horse's head away again.

"And this is Nahr," Än said from behind them, hand resting on the thick, gleaming brown neck. Apparently the single touch was all she needed to lead the brown horse toward them. Its ears swiveled back briefly to press against its head when it looked at Eyas and then thrust forward toward her.

"Give her your palm," Än instructed, demonstrating with the hand not pressed to the horse. "Unlike Eyas, Nahr is a lady and must be greeted politely."

Some wild and slightly hysterical part of Marguerite wanted to inquire what made a horse a lady, what the horse system of monarchical hierarchy actually was, and if she would soon be meeting the horse queen. But she did know what Än meant. So slowly, she extended her clenched hand, fingers unfurling like an anemone to rest under the horse's nose. Briefly, Nahr dropped her head, the whuff of her breath across Marguerite's palm as hot as the rest of the desert air, but blessedly moist. There was another smile lurking behind her teeth and she barely bit it back.

"Tomorrow," said the man, his voice firm and deep. "We'll teach you to ride."

Chapter Eleven

The man was as good as his word (he mostly did speak true, it seemed, or at least he spoke the truth as he saw it, however misguided his perception of the situation happened to be). He and Än pulled her from her rest the next day well before the sun had gone back into hiding. She went without protest only because, muddle-headed, she was too tired to marshal her arguments into any kind of formation. The previous night had been, after the horses' introduction, uneventful (besides the brief thrill of being trusted with a knife to help prepare the night's final meal and the subsequent discovery that organ fruit — which they called dates — required only an extremely blunt blade). The others had retreated to bed well before sunrise and she had done the same. It had been, perhaps, a mistake. With the night's air still cold and beckoning on her skin, she had had trouble falling asleep, and when dreams had finally taken her, there had been no crashing waves or beating rain, but only the slow retreat of puddle into air.

After a splash of water to her face, a quick meal, and a cup of tea — the flavor still confused her — had restored her, she bitterly protested being dragged back under the sun. Perhaps it was not their enemy, although given their nocturnal behavior so far, she'd assumed it was, but surely they could see that hard work was impossible in the heat. Än laughed.

"Hard work is also impossible in the dark," she said. "This place is shaded and the moon only occasionally penetrates. Horses do better when they can see. I'm sure you do too."

It was a very nice laugh, truthfully speaking (bell-like, in fact, although the description in Marguerite's mind didn't match what most people's conception of a bell-like laugh was, Marguerite having only heard distant church bells calling the hour). Emotionally, it was not so nice. Even Marguerite could hear its mocking edge. She grappled for a response and found none. Her only comfort was that they had fed her beneath the shelter of the cliff, with Saqr absent and thus unable to bear witness to her discomfort. She growled and threw back the rest of the tea, ignoring the way it scalded the back of her throat. Her singing voice was useless here anyway, and so the damage hardly mattered.

The man didn't laugh, although he turned his head away in a movement that might have been hiding one. If he was laughing, it was too subtle to hear, and so Marguerite didn't add it to the mental list she'd been keeping of injuries he'd done to her (she had such a list for all of them, although she had to keep crossing through some of Än's entries, in grudging admission that things like 'eyes too gold' were not exactly a deliberate insult). He waited and then he half-offered her his hand, as though afraid she wouldn't take it.

"Shall we go?" he asked.

She didn't take his hand, but she nodded, shifting her weight to sit over both legs, instead of resting on one hip, and looking inquiringly at Än. The other girl shook her head.

"I have work to be done," she said. "I'm not Malik. I haven't time to babysit little lost souls."

Her eyes were crinkled and her mouth quirked up. Perhaps the gentle expression was meant to make up for the insult. It did not. Marguerite closed her lips against a song for a storm that would never come and substituted an uncaring toss of the head, sending silver tendrils whipping through the air (Än had indeed had a comb she was willing to share the night before and so for the first time in a week, Marguerite's hair was free to move like a wave instead of a mat of seaweed). Beside her, the man's bronze cheeks reddened to copper. He did not otherwise acknowledge his sister's statement.

It was Marguerite who began the walk toward the horses, brushing deliberately past Än. It was meant as an act of dominance, stepping into her path to force her backward. But Än — too clever or perhaps simply too domineering herself — remained in place, so that for a moment their flesh pressed closely enough for Marguerite to feel her heat. (Was Än also warmed? There was ice inside her, of course, but Marguerite had never before wondered how it chose to manifest itself on the outside.) The man followed, tossing a grin that appeared loaded with meaning that she couldn't decipher over his shoulder.

"You're lucky," he said, catching up to her and matching his strides to her. "Än is allowing you to borrow Nahr. She'll be slightly less wild as a mount than Catseye."

"I'm riding Catseye," said Marguerite, not bothering to acknowledge either of their statements with eye contact.

The man made one of those noises he made around her sometimes that didn't seem to mean anything.

"You are, are you?" He did like to repeat things for no particular reason.

She had yet to understand it.

"I am," she said.

"Don't you think you should ask if it's okay to ride Catseye?"

"Why shouldn't it be?" she said, tilting her head enough so that she could catch his eye. "Is he sick?"

"Well, no, but he is my horse."

Marguerite stopped and looked the man full in the face, waiting patiently until he made eye contact with her.

"Doesn't he own himself?" she asked, voice inflecting to show him that she was truly waiting for the answer.

The question, though phrased aggressively, was genuine. Marguerite had been raised with wolves and snakes and seabirds, with the wild beasts of the seashore. She had killed them, mostly for food, sometimes in self-defense. She had owned some of them, she supposed, in the sense that she had made use of their corpses — drawing another few days of life from something's meat was perhaps the deepest form of ownership. But she had never thought of them as hers or at least, no more than she had thought of everything the sea touched as hers. She had never considered herself in control of their movements (not when she wasn't killing them, anyway).

The man did that thing he had done so often before, his eyes scanning her face, trying to find something he seemed to think was hidden there, curling in the edge of her mouth or twining through her eyelashes.

"I suppose you're right," he said, words drawing themselves out of him slowly and carefully. "I suppose he does own himself." He paused, biting his bottom lip. "I love him. He loves me. In that sense, he's mine. You always belong a little to the ones you love." He paused.

What a weak sort of love he practiced, Marguerite thought, to give himself to it only partly.

He smiled suddenly. "But I own the riding of him, at least. And I'll lend it to you, since you're willing to brave his back again." The smile widened. "You needn't thank me. I'm half doing it because I know you'll regret it."

"I wasn't going to thank you," Marguerite said, turning away and beginning to walk again toward the horses.

They were clustered around the crack in the rock face, the bigger crevice that would fit a horse's head and which also led to a small pool. Catseye greeted her — the man, actually, probably — immediately, with a shrill, high-pitched whinny. Eyas trotted over and was prevented from headbutting her only by the quick movement of the man's arm, which shot in front of her to block the narrow grey head. Marguerite stepped back and narrowed her eyes, reminding herself that she wasn't grateful for being saved from something that experience told her would be uncomfortable but ultimately harmless.

"I suppose you aren't going to thank me for that, either," he said.

It was a comment disturbingly close to her own thoughts, so she glared and remained silent. He grabbed a fistful of Catseye's mane and led the horse away from the other two.

"The first step to riding," he said. "Is preparing the horse. You'll need to brush him and pick his hooves."

Marguerite's eyes dropped to the horned crescents on the end of Catseye's legs.

"Doesn't he already have hooves?" she asked in honest surprise. "Why do I have to pick them for him?"

The man laughed, the kind of warm, comfortable laugh she had only heard around the horses.

"Picking means cleaning," he said. "I'll show you how."

Preparing a horse was a more complicated process than Marguerite, having only seen them fully tacked, was expecting. Brushing the sleek black body was a simple, rhythmic task that would have almost been pleasant if the man hadn't been standing over her correcting her stroke length and arm movements. But picking hooves meant letting the horse rest its weight on her knee as she did so, an easy enough task for a man used to it but a tricky prospect for her ("My grandmother can do it," the man had pointed out unsympathetically when she tried to plead physical weakness in an attempt to weasel out of the work). The saddle was heavy and apparently it absolutely *had* to be straight, and the strap around the horse's belly had to be tight (the man had to grudgingly help her with that step). The bridle was comparatively easy, once the man taught her to loop it around Catseye's neck to prevent him from tossing his head out of reach. (Before he taught her, the task was ... less easy. She suspected her shoulder would be sore the next day.) Finally, the horse stood before her, fully prepared for riding. The man walked around the sleek black body thoughtfully, pausing to adjust a strap here and there.

"Not bad," he said. "For a first time anyway. You'll do it alone tomorrow." He turned to look at her and arched an eyebrow (she would really need to find a looking glass so she could practice the trick herself). "Well, get on."

"Just levitate up there, shall I?" she asked and was gratified to see the split-second widening of his eyes as he considered if she was serious, before recognizing the sarcasm.

"You know how to get up," he said. "Kind of."

She did know how to get up, theoretically, the same way she knew how to bake bread or weave lace. The actual prospect seemed far more complicated. Logically, she knew Catseye hadn't actually grown, that he had always been a big horse, and it was only familiarity that had made his bulk seem manageable before. Logic was rarely a help in these circumstances. She grasped the strap and tried to lift a foot to place it in the stirrup. She slipped, coming down hard, and knew through the shift of his body that the only reason Catseye hadn't run was that the man was at his head, holding it, and soothing him. To her credit, she tried again. And again. And again. When she landed heavily on her hip for the third time, she sent the man a look that might have been an appeal if it hadn't been couched in the body language of command.

"I can't get up," she said.

"I can see that," he replied. "You're not very good at asking for help, are you?"

She let her eyes slant slightly to the side as she faced him, the only acceptable substitute for the looking away she badly wanted to do. "It hasn't come up very often."

There was a long pause. "You have a strange way of making my feeble jokes not funny at all," the man said. "I'm not giving you my knee again, but I'll make my fingers into a stirrup, if that will do."

"It will have to," Marguerite said flatly, turning away to grasp the saddle (and for absolutely no other reason and definitely not so she wouldn't be tempted to ask what he had meant). She had been worried that his hand wouldn't support her, but his linked palms were solid and strong. The horse's back was strangely familiar, considering how little riding she'd actually done. It was not a comfortable familiarity — everything below her waist already twinged, and even when they weren't out in the middle of the desert the horse stank. She sighed and leaned forward.

"Sit up straight," the man snapped. "Gather the reins in your hands properly. Now, nudge him forward with your legs. *Gently!*"

The clarification came too late.

"I hate this!" Marguerite shouted over her shoulder as Catseye took off from the camp into the dunes, the other horses tossing their heads and rearing in response.

It didn't end in disaster (Catseye stopped a few steps out), but the rest of the lesson continued roughly in that vein, and when the shadows had disappeared into night and Marguerite was finally allowed to slip from the saddle, she was grumbling and sore, a state that wasn't improved when the man also made her remove the tack and brush the horse out again.

"You don't have to do this," she said.

"I don't mind," the man replied, apparently under the impression that she was worried about him and not her own bones and flesh. "I teach all my little cousins to ride. You're just a bigger, crankier, somehow even less cooperative version."

"You just get children dumped on you?" Marguerite asked, in some surprise (and consciously choosing not to be insulted by a description that was clearly meant to be unflattering but was also not untrue). Would that have been her fate, had her parents had any siblings? She added a silent sigh of relief that they had not.

"Just temporarily," he said. "I'm a *very* good rider." He paused. "Don't you spend time with your family?"

"Don't have any. Probably wouldn't even if I did. I'm sure I wouldn't like them."

There was something sharper in his gaze now and the easy smile had disappeared.

"No family? What about your parents?" His voice was clipped and hard.

Än's voice had had a similar hungry quality when she had asked how Marguerite survived the desert. The hunger had been almost appealing in that smoky voice. In the man's, it was merely disconcerting.

"I said I don't have any."

"You mean you don't have parents? Are they dead? Who birthed you?" His voice had risen and quickened, not resembling his sister's now so much as her own when she'd first demanded his identity.

"My parents, of course," she said, forehead wrinkling and eyes narrowing. "Who else would have?" She shrugged, a deliberately casual movement, putting as much dismissal as she could into her movements and tone. "They might be dead now. They might not be. They're gone, anyway. Why does it matter? They're not here."

"I suppose it doesn't matter," the man agreed, the hunger vanishing from his voice and his breath evening out. "You must be hungry. We'll take a meal with Grandmother and Än. Then I'll teach you how to repair equipment."

"I can hardly wait," Marguerite said dryly.

Än met them as they turned the corner and gestured them into the tent. Her eyes were bright and wide, while Saqr, already seated, had a calmly pleased air that Marguerite found suspicious. She refused to be drawn into conversation, devouring meat and bread and fruit and tea with forced single-mindedness. The man, perhaps taking his cues from her, perhaps merely hungry himself, also finished quickly and set her to sewing together straps. She took an amount of pleasure that even she would admit was slightly obscene in demonstrating that not only was she adept at threading a needle, thank you very much, but that her eyesight for such detail work was better than his. Her skill seemed to surprise him, as it did whenever she demonstrated some practical ability. She refrained from pointing out that she had spent years creating and repairing her own clothing, mostly because she didn't want to let any of them that deeply into her life.

The thin leather horse blanket she held in her lap while she patched it smelled of horse and sweat. So did she and so did he. The smell didn't bother her nearly as much as it used to.

He settled down across from her, a heavy leather strap in his hand, and began to close a gaping wound in one section. She turned her eyes back to her own sewing. She didn't notice Än's approach until the rug beside her shifted, and suddenly her peripheral vision filled with red. She turned. Än smiled at her, a vast expanse of red leather, far thinner than the strap or even the blanket, held in her lap, and then her eyes turned downward. It wasn't repair work she was doing but stitching delicate black designs into the material she held, designs that Marguerite thought she recognized from the cliff. Apparently neither of the siblings was interested in speaking, and after a moment, she let her attention stray back to her own stitch work. She had never engaged in a task with others before, unless she was doing it while Mama Bella critiqued. The sound of other needles wasn't as distracting as she had expected. In fact, the sound of breath in chorus and the pull of thread and the feeling of concentration was ... warm. Not warmth as she had so often been subjected to lately, sweating and stifling and suffocating. Warm in a way that sunshine breaking through storm clouds had once been.

———— «» ————

He dragged her out of bed far too early again the next day, stiff and complaining and too tired to have dreamed of seawater, and thrust a bundle of clothes into her arms. The clothes turned out to belong to Än, the man having noticed that hers were becoming unbearably soiled. It took some time to get into them. The layers took skill to arrange, skill she didn't have, and the spicy scent was distracting. Än, despite the deftness of her fingers across Marguerite's waist when she came to her aid, was no help.

Marguerite bathed and grumbled, ate and grumbled, prepared Catseye and grumbled, and was finally thrust onto the horse's back, grumbling. Her mood was not improved when Än wandered up to watch and spent the entire time giggling. She ate, avoided speaking to Saqr, washed her clothes, sewed, ate, and slept again.

The third day proceeded much the same, except that she was back in her own fabrics. Än was the one to wake her up this time, the man apparently preparing the early meal. Catseye's back seemed to get harder and more jagged by the day, although his straps were easier to tighten, and he didn't run away with her quite so often. After her lesson, she didn't sew but was given a mortar and pestle and forced to grind leaves until her shoulders protested too bitterly and she stomped off to her tent (her shoulders, admittedly, had a low threshold for repetitive movements and she spent a great deal of time lying awake in her nest of blankets, knowing that it was far too early to sleep but too late to return to the tent).

She dreamed that night, the only kind of dream that mattered. She dreamed of boats, veering into each other's paths and smashing, splinters of wood scattering across the ocean's vast expanse. She might have interpreted it as metaphorical, if she believed in poetry.

The man shook her awake far too early, even earlier than she had been woken the previous three days. Rubbing crusted salt from her eyes, she glared at him.

"Must you torment me so early?" she asked, a wave of anger, as always, concealing a core of true inquiry. "I don't want to ride, anyway. I hurt."

"Then fortune smiles on you," the man said, grinning widely. "No riding today. Catseye needs to rest. And anyway, we have need of you, unskilled as you are." He paused to acknowledge her frozen glare with another grin. "The rain comes tonight."

She sat up as swiftly as someone whose muscles must have shrunk in the night, they were so stiff, could do.

"There's rain in the desert?" she asked. The man laughed, and then abruptly cut himself off, brow wrinkling as he watched her with sudden interest.

"Of course there's rain. Where do you think the water comes from?"

True water comes from the ocean, Marguerite thought. *But yours doesn't behave. It might come from anywhere.* She didn't answer, of course, because she never did answer his questions. He seemed to expect it because he was already moving away from her tent.

"We'll break our fast and then show you what to do," he called over his shoulder.

She crawled from the tent and bathed slowly, giving herself time to think before she would have to confront them again. What she could see of the sky through the shaft in the cave ceiling was still the same harsh, unflinching blue it had always been, so bright and unchanging it seemed that someone had laid a ceramic bowl over the desert. She knew the color of a sky before rain. A sky before rain was grey. Grey — storm clouds and mud and seals — was a water color. The blue of the desert sky was not. The world didn't taste of rain, either, and that was a taste she had carried in her mouth for years. She felt no water on her tongue and no anticipation in the air. There was power in the sky, but it was the same steady power of an unrelenting sun. A rainstorm — that was the power of change. The scent of upheaval in the air. She could use a little upheaving. She sang, a single note chiming out into the cavern and spiraling up to the opening above her. She had not sung in too long and it came out harshly, without the strength to lift waves, if waves there had been to lift. It certainly didn't lift the oppressive blue of the sky. The rain didn't suddenly fill her mouth. The only response the desert gave was a gust of wind, whipping down the chamber and pushing the loose tendrils of her hair away from her face. She sighed and went to face this new cruelty.

The first meal of the day went as it usually did, at least for Marguerite, who ate and said nothing and watched them all. Saqr did most of the speaking, which was unusual on its own, and the words she said weren't cheery conversation-making but orders, thinly disguised as information sharing (Marguerite was not fooled, and she had just barely enough respect for the siblings to admit that they were probably not fooled either). Saqr dismissed them early, and Ma — the man disappeared immediately to see to the horses. Än didn't follow. Instead, she knelt in the corner of the tent and began to fiddle with the chest of drawers. Marguerite knelt next to her.

"What are you doing?" she asked, voice pitched softly enough that Saqr hopefully wouldn't overhear, recognizing even as she did that this might be an invitation to assign her a task. Somehow, in all the chatter, Saqr seemed to have missed her and she'd been given no direct instructions. That was fine. She was bored of sewing and a little tired of horses.

"Preparing," Än said shortly.

"For what?" she asked.

"For the rain."

She swallowed. The air was still dry. It did not taste of excitement or the heavy slumber that precedes a nightmare.

"When will you call the rain?"

That did win Än's eyes. She jerked up so they were face to face and then began to laugh, a strange sound that was half filled with the amusement that Marguerite was used to from her and half filled with something that sounded almost like pain.

"You can't call rain," she said. "You can call horses and you can call foxes and you can call the wind, if you're very clever and if it likes you. But rain comes only to please itself."

This was wrong, of course, but everything in the desert was ugly and harsh and wrong so Marguerite accepted her words without bothering to explain. It was only the illogical part of the statement that chafed her.

"How do you know it's coming, then?" she demanded. "It isn't the air or the colors of the sky."

"I can't call it," Än said. Her voice was low and carefully spaced as if she was measuring each word with a little cup that said 'enough for our strange guest to know.' "But I can — we can, it's one of the things I was sent here to learn — tell when it's coming. Sometimes."

"Show her," came Saqr's voice, stronger than she had ever heard it before. Her cup clinked as she placed it back on the table.

"But Grandmother!" It was the first time Än's voice had held overt notes of anything other than curiosity or amusement.

"Malik will handle most of what needs doing," Saqr said. "And I'm not so old that I can't do the rest. Show her. Help her understand the desert. Malik is giving her a piece of his heart every time he puts her on a horse. Just this once, give her a piece of yours."

"It isn't the *giving* I'm afraid of," Än mumbled (Marguerite barely caught it, engrossed as she was in being offended at the idea of Malik giving her *anything*), but she complied, her movements becoming less erratic and more targeted. She pulled a glistening metal bowl from the lowest and largest of the drawers.

"Come with me."

Marguerite had been half-hoping that she would take her somewhere new, that she would reveal some magic place in the desert where one could sing in full voice. But no. Än led her to the bathing cavern and dipped the bowl into the basin, filling it almost to the brim.

"Don't jostle me," she said. "Even a single spilled drop will turn it against me."

It? Marguerite thought but didn't say. Did Än's words refer to the drop itself? A single drop was no danger, but water called to water and an ocean could be a vicious thing. Respect for water seemed to be one of the few things she had in common with the people of the desert. Än led her back to the now empty tent (Saqr had disappeared she didn't know where, although a process of elimination suggested she must be with the man and the horses), slipping inside with a single, smooth movement that Marguerite envied but couldn't imitate. She laid the bowl in the center of the cloth room, twisting it back and forth to make a hollow in the sand below the carpet before she took her hands from it. She stood and walked to the back of the tent.

"Is that it?" Marguerite asked, following her. Än gave her a narrow-eyed look that had more than a hint of disgust in it.

"Of course not," she said. "I need the other half of the spell."

She knelt before the chest, pulling drawers open briskly and systematically, her left hand diving in and dropping the contents in her cupped right. First a few twisted petals, of a color that might once have been pink and releasing a faint scent of dust and roses, a lover's bouquet entombed for a thousand years. Then a pinch of something green and pointed and glinting dully. Then a dried fruit, not one that she had eaten before but something large, something that would have been round and bursting before the desert had stripped the life from it. A small strip of bark, which Marguerite thought had come from the same trees she had seen at what the man called an oasis. A few black seeds, shining like jewels or eyes against Än's dark skin. And finally, she dipped her fingers into one drawer and came away with them coated red. Not blood, too bright for dried blood. A hint of the smell wafted over. It was the same spicy, smoky scent as the tea she was almost starting to get used to. Än closed her fingers over the small mound in her palm and walked to the bowl. She opened her hand and let the contents fall into the bowl, giving it a quick brush with her hand to free the last sticking remnants.

It was time to sing. Surely whatever strange spell Än was weaving was completed now and needed only a chime to set it off. Marguerite waited but no voice rang out. The other girl didn't even tap her fingers. Instead, she merely watched the bowl's surface. Marguerite sighed and turned her attention away from Än's profile.

For a moment, nothing happened. Then the water shuddered and began to ripple, thousands of circles beginning and radiating out across the surface, until the sad pile of dried plants disappeared completely beneath the onslaught.

And then it was over, and the water smoothed out again, no more disturbed than a perfectly poured glass plane. But things had changed in its depths. The fruit was swollen and golden, and the pink petals had unrolled and bloomed into a single, perfectly formed bud.

She raised her eyes to meet Än's. The gold was dominating again, almost sparkling despite the lack of direct light, and a smile danced across Än's mouth the way the ripples had just danced across the water's surface.

"Well?" she asked, the smoke in her voice almost roiling out of her mouth.

"Is that it?" asked Marguerite.

Än jerked back, wide eyes suddenly distressed instead of pleased. Her mouth slumped. It occurred to Marguerite for the first time that perhaps she should try moderating the tone of her voice, since it seemed people were constantly getting offended by what was meant as an innocent question. Än had not sung, had not even whistled or hummed. Her mouth had stayed firmly closed. How, then, could her spell be over?

She didn't know how to ask so she fell back on her old strategy of staring the other person down. It had always worked on the man. Eventually, he would shrug and turn away. Än did not turn away and, though the gold had dimmed almost to bronze, there was still a sparkle in her eye that refused to be ignored. There were words that could fix this. She knew there were words that made hurting another person a little bit better because people were cruel and yet people stayed together. But if you had never spoken an apology, how did you conjure one up? She wet her always dry mouth and offered the only gift she could. She tried to explain.

"How can you be done?" she asked. "Where is the magic?"

It wasn't a very good peace offering, but perhaps the fact that she was making one at all swayed Än a little. Some of the hardness in her face softened.

"It's in the plants, of course."

"There's no magic in plants."

Än sighed. She looked suddenly very much like her brother, or at least how her brother always looked at Marguerite.

"You just saw it."

She sighed again, raising a hand to her forehead when it became clear that Marguerite would not respond. Her shoulders slumped and then squared, and she raised her eyes again. "I know you don't like it here. You think it's too bright and too hot and too dry. And you're right, I suppose. It is bright and hot and dry. But" — her smile wasn't friendly, but it was still the curve of lips — "don't you think there's something a little bit magical in being able to blossom in such a place?"

No, she did not. Magic didn't lurk in the curl of a leaf or the arch of a petal or the steady lines of a trunk. Magic danced in every note of a song and every drop that hurled from a wave. Magic was in water and in music and in what happened when they came together.

But it hadn't worked here. She had sung until her throat hurt and nothing had happened. Nothing had changed. No power had swelled in her throat and been matched by the swelling of the desert. The only power she had seen had come from Än, carefully mixing a handful of crushed and dried greenery. Än hadn't sung. Saqr had never sung. Malik had told her a story once but even he had never given her a song.

There didn't seem to be any music in the desert.

Her shoulders slumped and she let her gaze drop to the bowl. Plants don't mock, of course. They grow and they spread and they die. But it felt like the petals slowly drifting in the depths of the bowl were laughing at her.

"All right," she said, to the plants or to Än. It was the closest she had ever come to a surrender.

Maybe Än sensed that. Or maybe she was simply willing to take anything that wasn't a vicious denial.

"All right," she echoed. Her hand came into Marguerite's view. A large hand, with well-shaped fingers. A strong hand, the calluses showing how hard she worked and how much she did. She paused.

Marguerite heard a sharp intake of breath. And then Än's fingers covered hers.

It should have been electric. It should have been like the striking of a storm. There should be a reason she felt like she was boiling over, like every drop of water in her body was rising and dancing. There was only a steady warmth, the slow steeping of tea, or the feeling of Catseye's back moving under her thighs, and yet her heart was a percussion in her ears and throat and chest.

If Än had said anything, Marguerite would have reared back. She would have pushed her away. She would have stomped out, and she would have walked into the desert, and she wouldn't have stopped until the last drop of spit evaporated from her mouth and she collapsed into the sand. But she didn't. They sat together and ignored the few drops of water that darkened the legs of Marguerite's pants. When the spots began to dry, Än squeezed her fingers, just once, and then rose.

"I'm sorry," she said. "But I'm glad too. Grandmother was right. I'm glad you saw this." She turned away and walked to the tent opening. "I'm sure there's still work to be done," she said over her shoulder.

Marguerite watched her back — strong just like her hands, she thought — and hummed a little in response. Än's instincts were good. A little time with Catseye would at least be a distraction.

A last ripple crossed the bowl's surface as Än turned away, the water slopping so high that a single drop crested the bowl's rim and spilled onto the table's surface. One last remnant of the spell.

Marguerite shrugged and followed Än from the tent.

It hadn't felt like Än's magic had taken long at all, but Saqr and Malik had apparently had more than enough time to completely alter the camp (admittedly, Marguerite had never seen a clock or kept to a schedule so her ability to estimate time was near nonexistent). The awning that sheltered the horses had been dropped, and the sheet lay flat against the cliff side. The horses themselves stood anchored along the wall, Nahr's back already heavy with bundles. The extra tent — it probably wasn't extra, actually, it probably belonged to the man, which had never occurred to her before — had disappeared.

"Are you moving?" she demanded, addressing the question to him rather than one of the women, not out of respect or fondness but because he mostly did answer her fairly.

"Yes," he said, without turning from the bundle he was rolling. His voice was even and so she assumed that he looked away because he was busy and not because he was annoyed at her again for some reason. "But not far. Only to the top of the dune."

"Why?"

It was Än who answered, brushing past her to kneel and tie the bundle as the man held it in place.

"You must have noticed we're in a valley," she said. The packing movement must have been familiar, as she was able to face Marguerite while she did so.

Their eyes met squarely; Än's looked unusually soft and velvety. Marguerite turned away. Of course she knew they were in the lowlands, although she had been calling it a trough rather than a valley. She didn't see the relevance.

"There's a risk of flooding," Malik clarified. He still hadn't looked up, his lean hands weaving a leather thong around the bundle until he pulled away and left a perfect knot. "So we're retreating temporarily. We'll return as soon as the rain ends."

"It won't be a bad one this time," Än added. "I know." This more softly.

Marguerite shrugged and wondered idly if these people in their sun-drenched and sun-dominated land knew how heavy a rainstorm could truly be or if they would consider an hour's patter a downpour.

The man stood, wielding the bundle easily.

"Why don't you make yourself useful and take down your own tent? Can you manage it?" He grinned. "It's not hard, but I've seen what you think erecting a tent looks like."

"Mine worked!"

The corners of his mouth twitched, but he didn't respond. Huffing to herself, she turned away and proceeded back along the path she had just traversed. It was a small tent, at least compared to the large one that Än and Saqr seemed to occupy, and was presumably simple for a single person, even of no particular size or strength, to handle. She knelt and contemplated it, chewing her lip slowly and carefully. She'd never retrieved her personal possessions from the man (she'd have to do that someday, even if most of it was useless and her dress was ruined) so the only thing in the tent was the pile of blankets she had been sleeping in. She wondered if she should retrieve them before she took the tent down. They were cloth and the tent — well, she wasn't sure if the tent was cloth or fine leather. There was probably a way to tell if you cared — but anyway, they had the same consistency. It would be an excellent time saver to drop the tent on top of the blankets and roll them up together.

There were no pegs. The tent's arch was created from sticks thrust into the sand at fore and aft, and it was held in place by large stones placed in each corner. She removed the stones first. They were almost perfectly rounded, but the surfaces were rougher than they would have been had they come from the sea. It was to be expected. Sand didn't smooth. It only irritated. The poles were trickier to take down. They were longer than she had been expecting, certainly longer than her own sad little rod, and buried far more deeply than she'd ever managed. They were slender and not heavy, even for her strength, but they were unwieldy with the weight of the tent hanging over them. She struggled for some time, cursing under her breath (a mixture of the ones she had made up herself and the curses that had been carried over the wind to her — having lived near the sea all her life, she knew some good ones). She didn't so much pull the sticks free as her efforts eventually threw her weight hard enough against them that the whole contraption collapsed beneath her. With a tense grumble, she proceeded to try to roll everything together as she had seen the man do. It didn't work well. The bundle of cloth was thick and didn't take direction easily.

By the time she had forced it into a more or less even cylinder, the gleaming blue of the sky had darkened to a matte grey and the wind that batted the sweat from her cheek smelled, not exactly of water, but of anticipation. She tilted her head up, tasting it, and felt some of the tightness in her chest ease.

Red flashed in her peripheral vision and she started as Än knelt next to her, slender hands coming to rest beside hers.

"Malik is going to laugh when he sees this," she said. "You really have no idea about tents, do you?"

Marguerite pulled away, eyes narrowing into the familiar resentful glare.

"You wanted it down, it's down," she said, not bothering to help as Än wrapped a few cords around the bundle, even as she struggled to knot them.

"This is the last of it," Än said, when she had finished. "And just in time. You take one end and I'll take the other."

Marguerite straightened and looked around. While she had struggled with her own tent, the larger one had been taken down and the space under the rock formation was as empty and barren as the rest of the desert she had wandered through. Without quite knowing why, she suppressed a shudder and was suddenly glad that Än had come to find her. She crouched and caught the other end of her disemboweled tent, rising quickly enough that it strained her arm. She nodded in Än's general direction and began to stride forward without waiting to see if she would take the cue. This was a mistake, she realized quickly, as she was unsure where she was meant to go. The siblings had merely told her that they were going.

Än was grinning a little when she turned questioningly to her, apparently aware of her dilemma. The other girl tossed her head a little, a deliberate gesture designed to show off her own comfort with the situation (as well, perhaps, as the red gleam of her hair which hadn't dulled even with the loss of sun and fire). Or maybe she was merely pointing the way, as she began to walk in the direction her chin had indicated, letting Marguerite either maintain the pace she set or drop their parcel. The climb up the side of the valley was not as tricky as she had feared. Instead of hiking straight up the sides, they followed a furrow between two dunes and emerged on higher ground, without even Marguerite panting, to see the large tent standing as though it had merely been swept there by wind or wave. Malik puttered around doing nothing in particular that she could see. He didn't, in fact, laugh but his face went through some rather extraordinary contortions when he saw what they held, and he made a noise rather like steam escaping from a pot as he took it from them and stored it with the other campsite flotsam in the tent.

"No sense in putting all the tents up for such a short stay," he said, without prompting from her. "We can share for a night."

"You finished just in time," Saqr called from the more or less clear place in the center of the tent. "Come in before the storm starts."

Än slipped inside immediately, but Marguerite reeled back. "In?"

"Yes, in," said Än. "Where else?"

"If you're worried about the horses, don't be," Malik added. "They're hobbled around the back. They won't come to harm."

"I'm not worried about the horses," Marguerite said with a little less indignation in her voice than there would have been a week ago. "But why would I shelter from *rain*?"

The three inside the tent exchanged a look, then Saqr turned away and the man flopped down beside her, pulling another strip of broken leather from his apparently inexhaustible repair pile. Än paused halfway between her brother and Marguerite, biting her lip. Then she stepped forward and dropped into a graceful crouch right at the tent entrance. Marguerite looked at the rest of them and then, sighing, sunk to the ground, carefully outside the tent's coverage.

The air was starting to feel not just anticipatory but charged. Her blood responded, rising and dancing in her body. Rain. She hadn't realized the desert could produce something as simple and as good as rain.

And then the warmth in her blood stopped. She had met water once before in this place. She had avoided thinking of the oasis, telling herself it was because she was busy and for no other reason. She thought of it now. That water had not been her ally. It had not even been a well-meaning stranger. Perhaps all of the water in this cursed place was twisted and wrong. Perhaps that was why the people who knew this place hid from it.

A water droplet struck her in the nose. Another hit her in the cheek. In the space between one breath and another, she was soaked, water pouring down around her. She closed her eyes and listened to the rhythm of it. It wasn't the drumbeat of waves on rock or water striking water. But water has a rhythm, whatever form it takes and whatever instrument it uses. The sand could dull its percussion but not hide it completely. She opened her mouth. It tasted of dust and heat and death, but it also tasted of life and cold, and it spread across her tongue the way water should and the way the dry desert wind never had.

"I love this," said a voice beside her. "I always have."

She started and turned.

Än had moved from the shelter of the tent and knelt beside her, her face also upturned to catch the rain. It ran down her face, catching the gold of her eyes, her eyelashes flashing like they'd been coated in facets of amber. Her hair streamed, lying dark against her back, and her clothes pressed against her, the water turned their clasp into a caress. Marguerite turned away. The wind swept around her, catching her hair and pulling it into a silvery curtain until her face cooled. Än said nothing more and they bathed in the world together, until Marguerite's eyes began to flutter shut, the almost familiar beat lulling her into a sleep that was nearly peaceful.

She dreamed of flooding, of rain that never stopped until it filled the desert, until sand disappeared beneath wave and everything she had hated was swept away.

She woke to a world transformed.

Chapter Twelve

Once, in her youth, before she had decided that she preferred a cloudy day, there had been an unusually hot summer, the sun bright and relentless (back when she thought she had known what a relentless sun was). She had looked down into the ocean and seen not the gentle blues and greys she had already grown to love but green. Green, stretching toward the horizon, eddying and dancing on the waves, a green so rich it had seemed possible to live on just the color of it.

The desert reminded her of that long-ago day. The searing yellow and beige had disappeared completely under a coating of green, lush and brilliant and gentle on her so very tired eyes. She had never noticed it before, but there was a kindness to the color green, a softness even when it was saturated with itself and should have burned her.

She sat up, slowly, and blinked, rubbing one hand across her face and not, for a wonder, feeling the rub of grit on her palm. When she looked again, the green was still there. She reached a hand out tentatively to touch it and noticed for the first time that she was no longer lying in the desert. Someone had pulled her just inside the entrance of the tent, so she was sheltered as she slept. It was a gross violation, to touch her when she was so helpless, but she supposed it had been kindly meant and so she probably shouldn't kick the man awake in order to yell at him. She rose, wobbling slightly, and stepped outside.

She had half expected the verdant world in front of her to disappear as soon as she breached the tent's entrance. But it remained. Her foot came down, not on the smooth, treacherous surface she had grown used to, but on a rough, mottled surface covered in plant life. She knelt and pressed her palm down. The green she had known on the ocean had been slimy and warm and unpleasant to the touch. The leaves quivering against her skin now were soft and dry and weak and gave easily even to such a delicate touch. But they were undeniably real.

"It's beautiful, isn't it?" Än said behind her.

Marguerite rose and shifted so the other girl could stand beside her.

"Why are you always sneaking up on me?" she griped.

She saw Än's grin in her mind before it sliced across her face.

"Because you don't pay attention to what's going on around you when something interests you," she said. "I assume that *this* interests you?"

"Why?" Marguerite asked. And then, "Where are we?"

There was a pause. Peeking sideways under her eyelashes, she noted that Än seemed unsure of how to arrange her face.

"We're here," she said finally. "Where we've always been. This is what the desert is after rain."

"And a thorough pain it is, too," Malik said behind them.

Marguerite rolled her eyes and let Än make room for him.

"Good for the horses, though," he added. "If you'll excuse me, I need to make sure they haven't been washed away." He swept past them, crushing a path through the little plants. Marguerite dropped to the ground again and pulled a few leaves free. They were velvety and cool. The pressure of her fingers damaged them a little and clear, green-tinged sap oozed out.

"It won't last," Än said. "Not long at all, not up here."

"How far does it go?" Marguerite asked. She could see no end to it, the green lasting until it turned abruptly to the deep blue of the horizon.

"Why don't you come with me and see?" the man's voice sounded behind them. He came around the end of the tent. "I have a few things to check on and I wouldn't mind the company."

He paused and sighed, a low, gusty noise she had also heard come from his horse.

"I assume you still refuse to ride with me?"

"Yes," Marguerite said flatly.

"She can ride Nahr," Än broke in quickly. "She's easy to handle."

"Why can't I ride Catseye?" Marguerite demanded.

Malik favored her with one of his more unfriendly looks.

"Because *I* am riding Catseye."

She considered reopening her argument with him. Catseye was, after all, the best horse, and therefore the horse she should be riding. But she supposed that he had been riding Catseye long before she ever came to the desert and perhaps that did entitle him to certain privileges. Anyway, it might be fun to ride the horse belonging to Än. Perhaps she'd learn something worth knowing.

"Okay," she said.

The man started a little, and his head tipped as he looked at her. He opened his mouth, then closed it abruptly, as if rethinking whatever he had been about to say.

"Good," he said finally. "I'll get the equipment and you can help me tack up."

"Good," she echoed him.

He disappeared into the tent. Left without orders, she shrugged and made her way slowly around the tent to where she assumed the horses were. Indeed, they were arrayed just behind the tent, gleaming heads bent as they cropped eagerly at the newly awakened greenery. None of them acknowledged her approach, even when she attempted a whistle.

"Catseye, Nahr!" Malik called behind her.

The heads lifted in unison, swiveled, and both animals walked briskly past her to meet the man, his arms loaded with leather and padding. He grinned at her expression.

"You do Nahr," he said, shifting the bundle he held. "On top there. I've the brushes in my hands underneath, so if you'll just—"

She did, lifting the saddle with one arm supporting each side, as he had shown her. The strip of leather she held was much smaller than the saddle she was used to. Before she could stop herself, she looked at him quizzically.

"For speed," he said. "Usually I use a saddle that can carry a bit of weight but we won't be gone long."

He shifted his arms and held a brush out. She took it.

It would be a delightful act of defiance to brush Catseye instead of Nahr, but she should probably start getting to know the horse before she expected it to carry her on its back. She ran the brush down the warm side, enjoying the way it pulled on the brown to reveal gleams of gold. Some of the scalloped braids were coming loose; she hoped she wasn't going to be expected to fix them since she didn't have the first clue how. But no, when she turned to face Malik with Nahr saddled and bridled, he said nothing about the horse's mane, just smiled a little. He was already prepared, of course, and sitting easily on Catseye's back. He tossed her a waterskin (she just barely caught it on the tips of her fingers) and spread one hand in a gesture encouraging her to mount.

Nahr was a little easier than Catseye, being shorter, but it was still a struggle to pull herself all the way onto the horse's back, especially without the support of a larger saddle. She found herself caught halfway up, left foot in the stirrup but body hanging free, having not quite given herself enough momentum to throw a leg over. She shifted her grip slightly, preparing to lower herself down and try again, when a gust of wind ran up her back. Startled, she jerked up and then over. She faced Malik with a triumphant, if flurried, grin. His mouth smiled back at her but his face looked troubled.

"Shall we go?" was all he said.

She nodded. He turned Catseye and began to ride away from the camp, a faint scent of life and salt and growth following him as the horse crushed the plants beneath his hooves. She touched her heels to Nahr's sides. The horse began to move immediately. Despite her apparent willingness to obey, the horse was hard to ride, her gaits choppier and her broader sides straining Marguerite's legs in a way that Catseye's had mostly stopped doing. She took a deep breath and forced herself to sit straight.

Än and Saqr were standing outside the tent, seeming to be in consultation about something. Malik lifted a hand and waved it languidly in farewell. Marguerite briefly raised her own before returning it to the saddle.

"We'll be back before full heat of the day!" Malik called.

"See that you do," Saqr responded, her voice unexpectedly harsh.

Än just waved back. Then they were past them, nothing ahead of them but the vast green expanse. She was a rider now, if not a particularly good one. She shouldn't be following him around like a lady in waiting. She dug her heels into Nahr's sides. The horse shot forward for a few steps but then returned to her slow, stately walk. She watched his arms flex and then Catseye slowed so they were walking side by side.

She had been afraid that he would try to speak to her. The last time they had journeyed together, words had flowed from his mouth almost constantly. Not all of them had been unpleasant, exactly, even if he had sometimes been needlessly confrontational, but having to keep up with his babbling in case she missed something important had been exhausting. Today, however, he didn't seem to be feeling talkative. He barely looked at her, his eyes fixed on the horizon and his lips curled into a faint, comfortable smile. His only words were the occasional direction or encouragement to one of the horses (usually Nahr, who was apparently a great deal lazier than Catseye). Marguerite smiled and relaxed, leaning back in the saddle as he was always telling her to do, and let herself glance around a little.

It was a softer desert she looked across, the green so much less harsh than the yellow. No puffs of dust raised beneath the horse's hooves. The air smelled clean and bright. It would hurt again, probably, when the sun rose higher. Though few parts of the desert were kind, the sun was the greatest monster. But the heat of the day was some amount of time off so the plants would live and spread and cushion the desert a little while longer. It was peaceful, this slow procession, knowing that she had water and food beside her and a means to get ... well, not home but at least somewhere with reliable shelter. She had never had anywhere to come back to before. Her cottage, she supposed, had been hers and only hers, but she had never felt the slightest urge to leave it until the day she walked away with Mama Bella forever.

She didn't know how long they walked, over and around leaf-coated dunes, before the man pulled them both to a stop. They were in a trough between four sand peaks, to her untrained eye equal in height, but she could see nothing else special about the place. Malik dismounted, swinging easily to the ground. He knelt, ran his hand over the leaves, and plucked a few, tucking them into the bag at his belt. Then he nodded solemnly and swung back up. He didn't tell her what he was looking for and, resenting his expectation that she would question it, she didn't ask.

They rode again, mostly walking, occasionally engaging in a bouncy movement called a trot (Malik kept having to rein back suddenly in order to catch her as she toppled sideways). They stopped again, in a place identical to the first (perhaps it was the first again; she had no sense of space in the desert). The third place at least was distinct. It was arranged the same as the first two (first one?), but the peaks were higher and the trough lower, so it felt like they had ridden into a hole instead of merely an undulation of sand.

The man dismounted and knelt, doing whatever it was that he did. Marguerite sighed and put a hand on the back of the saddle so she could lean back and stretch. Nahr's ears pricked. Malik had told her that meant she was hearing something. Marguerite tilted her head, wondering if she could pick it up as well. She could detect nothing, until the wind rose and brought her the sounds. It was a low rumble, a muted sound that reminded her of the sound of raindrops hitting sand but magnified a great deal.

"What is that?" she asked without preamble.

"What's what?" He didn't look up.

"That sort of thumping, rumbling noise. In the distance."

He turned his head to look at her. He didn't look terribly impressed, but he rose and made his way slowly to the top of the dune, looking around him. In a snap decision, she slid from Nahr's back and followed, watching him. His body stiffened and he came down a great deal more quickly than he'd gone up, a swift, stumbling gait she associated more with herself than she did with him. His face was pale, as though someone had drained the rich hues of his skin from it. She opened her mouth, but he cut her off immediately.

"Can you shoot?" he asked, voice clipped.

"Shoot what?"

"And that answers that question. I don't suppose you know how to use a sword?"

She felt her face scrunch up. "I know which way to point it so it doesn't go into me."

"Oh well, no worries, then. You can save us both." A smile rippled briefly across his face before it was replaced by something tight and serious.

Abruptly, he surged forward, his hands seizing her waist. She howled and kicked as she was lifted into the air and he attempted to propel her toward the horses.

"Put me down!"

"Would you please for once in your life cooperate?"

Instead of yelling again, Marguerite twisted in his arms enough so she could get a fist to his shoulder (she'd been aiming for his face but at least the point of his shoulder was bony enough to produce what felt like a hard strike). He said a word she didn't understand but by its timbre was probably a swear and continued to push her at Nahr. Marguerite kicked out in front of her. The chestnut startled and moved away.

"What are you doing?" she demanded.

He swore again and dropped her to the sand, letting her propel herself away, although he kept hold of her arm so she was whirled to face him.

"Bandits," he said shortly. "You need to get on Nahr and get out of here. Gallop away, fast as you can, doesn't matter what direction. When you can't see any other figures even after a five-minute wait, give her her head and she'll take you home. She knows the way. Don't worry about me, I can handle myself."

"I *know* you weren't planning on worrying about me," he added before she could speak. "I can't help saying it. Now go. *Please.*"

He reached for her again, and she pulled away, watching his face. She couldn't remember him ever saying please to her before. She wasn't sure anyone ever had. It was rather a nice feeling.

He saw her hesitation, although of course he didn't understand.

"If you hated meeting me," he said. "You'll hate them more. They're … very rude."

He had censored himself. She was just savvy enough to know, although she didn't know what he was censoring. He had never prettied up his language for her before. She nodded, once, but continued to pull away.

"I can get on myself."

"Fine." He seemed relieved, and she supposed he had been expecting her to protest more.

She turned away, and when she was on Nahr, she discovered that he had mounted too. He leaned over, grabbed Nahr's bridle and they both began to walk up the dune.

Despite her agreement, she paused on the rise. She had never seen a bandit before. She saw nothing now, except a great cloud in the distance. It was darker than sand should have been at the bottom so she supposed the shadow must be their figures. It was impossible for her untrained eye to pick out how many there were. More than two, she could say that confidently.

"Yah, Nahr!"

She heard a meaty slap behind her and suddenly the horse was moving, sand churning beneath them as the chestnut legs pumped. She threw herself forward before she could be thrown back. She yanked her concentration from the horizon and focused on staying aboard. She didn't know how long Nahr galloped, but judging by the lack of stinging in her legs, the horse slowed to a trot and then to a walk quickly. She pulled the reins back until she stopped entirely and turned to look behind them.

The dust cloud had disappeared. But there were three figures framed against the horizon.

She knew that the smart thing to do was turn around, kick Nahr as hard as she could, and hope they didn't catch her. Instead, she tightened her grip on the reins and squinted, trying to pick out their features. They were mounted, she could tell that much from the flashes of light at ground level as the horses moved. They were large or at least their clothing was bulky. She could pick out no other features. It seemed they were moving toward her, although she knew well enough that the desert could be tricky.

The black blobs became bigger and bigger. There were three, riding on darkish-colored horses. She thought they might be galloping.

It occurred to her for the first time that if they were silhouetted against the horizon, so was she.

The small part of her that understood the definition of self-preservation grabbed the reins, both physically and metaphorically. She whirled in the saddle and drove her heels into Nahr's sides.

The horse's head flew up and she shot forward. The first spurt, however, did not move into the smoothness of a gallop. Nahr slowed and her head dropped so she could crop at the plants. Marguerite kicked her again. Again the horse started and moved forward another few feet before she again slowed and eventually stopped. Marguerite risked a look behind them. The three figures were much, much closer. She could hear them behind her, laughing and whooping. There was joy in the sound, but it was an ugly, mocking kind of happiness. Rude, Malik had said. She understood a little about what rude could mean in a cruel man. She swore, bent low, and kicked Nahr even harder. They were galloping now, a proper gallop, but it was a slow, sludgy movement, with none of the whipping grace she had felt on Catseye. It was not the kind of gallop that offered any chance of escape.

They crested another dune. The trough below it was deep and there was another rock formation in the center. It was a little like the one their camp had been sheltered against but paler and crisscrossed with dark lines. Crevices, she realized. Perhaps even paths. If she rode through them, she could lose the bandits. Maybe. It was a chance, however slim, and she seized it with her customary hunger. Again, she urged Nahr forward. The horse tossed her head and wobbled down the sand, not so much galloping as stumbling down the steep incline. She pointed the horse's head toward the nearest dark line and kicked her, once, twice, three times, four.

Apparently even a horse had a limit. On the fourth kick, the horse's neck suddenly disappeared from in front of her and her back rose as swiftly as a whip crack. Marguerite catapulted, flailing as she tried to catch herself. She got one hand wrapped through and braced on Nahr's mane. Then the horse abruptly went sideways, a movement so smooth that Marguerite barely detected it until the horse was no longer beneath her. She hit the sand hard. More of it showered over her as Nahr's hooves dug in. When the world stabilized, the first thing Marguerite saw was the horse's back disappearing over the ridge. She cried out and tried to stand to give chase, but her shaking body wouldn't hold her. Painstakingly, she pulled herself into the rock's shadow.

They would catch her. Undamaged, she couldn't outrun a mounted rider who knew the desert. Malik had taught her that. Injured, she had less than no chance. She didn't know what they would do to her, but she remembered the look in Malik's eyes, his tense grip on her waist. She didn't know what they would do, but she could guess that it would hurt. Perhaps it would do worse than hurt. She closed her eyes and began to quietly lay out her options, less with a hope of salvation than so she would know that she hadn't gone down quietly. She couldn't run. She could hide, but presumably they were smart enough to work out where she had gone and find her. She couldn't hope for rescue in time. Malik wasn't here. For all she knew, he had been captured or killed. She doubted the women knew anything was wrong. They weren't expected back yet, and so no one would search for them until it was far too late. The only person who could rescue her was herself.

She allowed herself a single moment of remembering a time when bandits would have found her the hunter and not the prey, when she would and could have summoned rain to beat them into the ground and ice to grow beneath their skin. She couldn't do it here. Hadn't Än already told her that? She heard the girl's soft, smoky voice in her mind.

"You can't call rain. You can call horses and you can call foxes and you can call the wind, if you're very clever."

She remembered the wind, the way it was constantly playing around her, the way it had pressed against her as she mounted Nahr, the way words she couldn't quite hear were suddenly swirling around her.

"You can call the wind, if you're very clever."

I'm clever, Marguerite thought. And I'm desperate.

She tried to think of the wind, tried to remember the feel of it on her skin and tugging her hair, the rustle of it against her clothes, the way it smelled.

"Come," she said.

But the desert remained still and silent save for the whooping of the bandits. They were closer now. She could begin to make out their voices. The things they were shouting raised bile in her throat. She was almost out of time. Anger filled her. When the wind had irritated her, it had seemed to be a constant presence. But now that she truly needed it, it had chosen to shy away.

When had the wind first come? She tried to remember. It seemed that it had always been there, pulling at her, stealing her things, reaching down her throat to grasp at her voice — she had been singing. She had felt it first in that angry moment when she thought she could sing the desert to her will.

She opened her mouth. It should have been hard. She hadn't sung in what felt like a lifetime. But the music came to her easily, the song to call a storm or a single rogue wave. She closed her eyes and sang a song of need, a song that called for aid, a song of pleading and of begging and with just a hint of command beneath it. The wind picked up, slowly at first, caressing each note that came from her mouth and spiraling delicately around her body, then building with every crescendo she reached until it howled around her, its whistling a countermelody to her own.

She could ask for a windstorm. That would deal with the immediate problem of the bandits. But she didn't truly need revenge or even defense. What she needed, what she really *needed* was a ride. What she needed was one of the few things in the desert that she could almost trust and, she thought in despair, one of the few things that the wind might not be able to bring her.

She took a deep breath and began to sing a new song. She sang of gentle, widely set eyes and softly flaring nostrils and a long, elegant face dipping slightly in the middle like a platter. She sang of a powerful chest and a back so broad she could lay across it. She sang of hooves harder than ice that never melts. She sang of long limbs, almost too delicate for the body they carried but kicking up so highly in the air that they seemed almost ready to spring into flight. She sang of a mane spilling across an elegantly cresting neck and a tail lashing everything around it like a storm. She sang of breath huffing out in a warm, wet gust, and felt it pressing into her palm.

She opened her eyes.

It was beautiful. That was her first thought. There was wonder at what had happened, as well, but what first took her breath away was how lovely the horse that stood in front of her was. It was tall, taller than Nahr, taller than Catseye, its shoulder rising above her head even as it dipped its nose into her hands. She had never seen anything so white. Even first snow seemed dingy in comparison to the brightness of its coat. The horse raised its head and shook it. Its mane, which had formerly flowed over its neck and shoulders in a smooth curtain, rose as delicately as flying sea foam. It lifted a single hoof, clear and faceted and sparkling like ice under sun, and pawed the sand, sending it puffing up far higher than a single strike should have done. Its eyes turned back toward her, the soft pale grey darkening to something deep and wild.

She walked quickly around the horse, letting her hand run over the sleek, sinuous body, feeling its muscles ripple. Despite its size and clear strength, the overall impression was of slender grace. She ducked her head slightly. The beast was male. No gender to the wind, but perhaps it had modeled itself after Catseye when it took form. She heard yelling and remembered that she had summoned the horse for a reason. The narrow, perfectly formed head swiveled and the thick neck arched as the horse turned to her. The sight of it blurred a little but she smiled.

"I didn't know what I was asking for," she said. "I'm glad it was you."

The head nodded, the eyes darkening to black. She raised a hand to its shoulder and froze.

She had missed something in her first awe. The horse was beautiful, but it wore no saddle and no bridle. She wasn't sure even Malik could have pulled himself onto such a large animal without either pommel or stirrups. She couldn't escape from the rapidly rising voices on a horse she couldn't even ride. But surely, surely it wouldn't have come to her merely to mock her. Surely there was a way to mount.

The yelling was so loud. They must be so close. She touched her forehead briefly to the center of the horse's and sang a song of calming, a song to soothe a wave before it broke on the shore. The horse shuddered. The great back heaved. And then the horse knelt in the sand.

It was still large, but she was able to throw a leg over the broad back and pull herself onto it. The horse rose in a swift, easy motion like a wave breaking. She was held, suddenly, far above the sand. The back she straddled was hot, without burning, and the horse's coat so smooth it felt like her legs were gripping ice rather than flesh. She was not afraid. She had not believed in anything but herself for a long, long, long time. But she believed, with everything she was, that he would not let her fall.

The hooked ears had turned back toward her. She leaned forward.

"Let's show them who rules this desert," she whispered.

The shift from standing still into full gallop was so smooth that she didn't realize they were moving until the dune began to grow toward her. No need to kick this horse. It would run itself to death for the sheer joy of movement, if such an animal could even die. She grinned and tightened the grip of her calves, feeling her hair blown back from her face.

They crested the dune and cascaded down into the midst of the bandits. Their mocking cries of joy turned into cries of alarm as suddenly the great white beast was among them. One of the horses screamed, throwing itself and its rider into the air. Another dropped low and spun, its rider hitting the ground with a jarring thump. The third man yanked at his horse's mouth, sawing the reins to keep it from bolting. The wind horse danced to the side, the tone of his gleeful whinnying exactly mirroring that of Marguerite's laughter. It was too much for the rearing horse, which threw itself down again and ran, its rider barely clinging to its neck.

The third man fumbled at his waist, his eyes large and terrified as he pulled his sword, pointing it, shaking, at them. Marguerite laughed again and moved with the horse as they rose into the air, one glittering hoof raising and coming down to shatter the man's arm. He swore and dropped his sword, bringing the injured arm up to cradle against his chest. There was no blood in his face, his skin so pale and his eyes so desperate he looked like a corpse. Something in him seemed to break. With his one good hand, he grabbed his horse's reins and drove his heels into its sides. It snorted and ran.

She felt the wind horse's hunger rippling through it. It wanted to run, to continue to play, to chase, if not the third bandit, then the second, the one who had fallen and crawled away, or the first already long gone. She felt the temptation, too, to follow, to continue to fight. But there was another feeling, bubbling above the bloodlust. She was safe. And she had never truly watched a man be hurt before.

She had no reins to command the horse, so instead she put her arms around its neck and squeezed. Something in the horse subsided and it stilled, becoming suddenly a becalmed ship instead of a tempest.

Marguerite burst into tears.

Chapter Thirteen

The sun was fully up, and her eyes had dried crusty and sore. Scrubbing at them as her new horse carried her at a smooth gallop, she considered. He needed a name. The other horses had names. Her horse, which was the finest horse, must therefore have a name. She didn't know what people called their animals, if there was some common theme that she had never learned. Zephyr was a little too apt. Ice or Snow suited its coat but how could she give a winter name to a desert beast? Ocean — merely thinking the word hurt. She couldn't name her horse after it without breaking her own heart every time she called him.

She watched his neck rise and fall as he moved and remembered the way that first gallop had reminded her of a wave breaking over a bow. He carried her, and he carried her burdens, and in a way, his movement, too, was decided by the wind.

"You bear me over the desert like a boat over sea," she said aloud. "So you will be Caravel."

Caravel whinnied, lighter and with a softer, whistling lilt to it than the other horses' heavy, wet noises. It was an acknowledgment of her voice, if not her words. She didn't know how much he understood. He knew what she needed of him. He did as she wished him to. But everything he had given her so far had come from feeling and not from speech. Her emotions had guided the wind horse. He had offered himself for her fear, not because she had begged, and his galloping had come from joy, not encouragement. She didn't know if he even knew what words were, beyond something he could toss around or offer her like a child with a trinket. It mattered little, she supposed. If song was all he understood, well — she had always known what to sing. It might be nice to be around someone she didn't have to speak to. Words, she had discovered, were slippery things, apt to twist themselves into meanings she had never asked for.

They were going back to the camp, or at least she was pretty sure that was where Caravel was taking her. She had considered going back to where she had left Malik. She certainly no longer feared the bandits. But he'd seemed like he knew what he was doing, she was forced to acknowledge, albeit unwillingly. He had been afraid. She knew he had been afraid. But his fear had been focused on her. He hadn't run. He had grabbed her. He had sent her away. He had tried, in some limited way, to protect her. Surely, if he didn't think he could handle himself, he would have run and left her to her own devices. Anyway, she didn't know how far she'd gone or in what direction, and she didn't know how to steer Caravel to a place she couldn't find herself.

She couldn't find the camp, either, of course, but it was a wet place and a place with people and the wind had played with her there so she was fairly certain that Caravel knew where they were meant to be going. He was moving confidently, anyway, his long, slender legs bearing him and her swiftly across the desert. Despite the rising heat of the day, his body grew no warmer. The peaks and troughs of sand and tangled vegetation, already dulling and shriveling under the sun, slid easily past her. From her perch on his broad, rocking back, the desert seemed almost — well, not pleasant, but not the implacable enemy it had been for so long. She smirked a little, looking forward to rubbing her self-rescue in Malik's face.

She hoped he was okay.

Only so she could really make him boil, of course.

She was fairly certain that they had ridden together for only a few hours, and she couldn't have gone much farther on Nahr, considering how slow and uncooperative the mare had been. On the much swifter and more agreeable Caravel, she should be almost back by now.

It occurred to her for the first time that they had not simply come upon the rock that first time. Malik had done something to conjure it. He had said words. She didn't know what the words were and knew she couldn't intuit them. She knew no desert magic. Even summoning a desert wind into the form of a horse had been seawitchery transposed.

Perhaps in response to her thoughts, perhaps for reasons of his own, Caravel slid suddenly to a stop, the great white neck surging up to catch her as she pitched forward. She looked around. She could see nothing that would make him halt — no hazards in the sand before them, no bandits, not even a hawk above them in the sky. She laid a single hand on the side of his neck, a silent question. The horse flicked an ear back but didn't otherwise respond. They stood together. With the wind below instead of around her, the desert was frighteningly still.

Two shapes exploded from the sand in front of her. Caravel half rose on his hind legs and danced, a graceful, pattering movement. The grey and black blur wheeled and resolved itself into Malik and Eyas. The black and amber became Än and Catseye.

They looked a great deal less composed than they had when last she'd seen them. Half the hair had slipped from Än's braid, billowing around her face and sticking to her cheeks, half covering her widened eyes. Malik's clothes were dusty and torn, and his right arm hung from his shoulder in a sling. Even Catseye looked the worse for wear, his chest wet and gleaming, his mouth flecked with foam. Only Eyas seemed bright-eyed and eager, and much the horse she'd been that morning.

Än and Malik spoke at once, babbling out words in a syncopated rhythm that she couldn't make out, but seemed to be in the key of questioning. She waited for them to finish, mulling over in her mind how to start the story she had to tell.

The flow of words eased to a trickle and then stopped. Marguerite met Malik's eyes calmly.

"My horse is better than yours," she said.

She had never heard anyone make quite that noise before. It certainly refused to resolve itself into mere words.

"What happened to you?" she added and gestured to his arm.

Malik continued to make the noise.

"We were about to ask you the same question," Än said sharply.

Catseye moved forward until he and Caravel were almost parallel. Catseye's nostrils flared red, his snorting providing a counterpoint to Malik's distress. Caravel stood still and silent, his only movement the whipping of his tail, which never seemed to cease.

"When Nahr came back empty-saddled and in a panic, we feared the worst." Än's eyes traveled over Caravel, sliding down the arch of his neck and caressing the curves of his body. "Where did you get *that horse*?"

"I was very clever," Marguerite said, waiting for the delicate flash of gold.

It didn't come. Än's face remained blank and confused and a little frightened, as though their previous conversation had meant nothing to her. Marguerite sighed.

"I'll tell you the story when you let me back into your camp. I don't care to repeat it twice."

Än's eyes were still cool and murky, but she nodded a little and something in her face softened. She turned and murmured to the expanse before them. It was a less impressive rush of sand than her brother had conjured, although perhaps it was merely weighed down by leaf and root, but when the soft puffs cleared, Marguerite was looking down again on the familiar red rock, its surface half covered in withered leaf matter. Caravel whinnied, a sweet little chime, and bounded down the slope in a series of movements that was more hop than gallop. Marguerite bounced along easily, clouds of silver rising above her shoulders, as she listened to Än and Malik scrambling after her.

Saqr was waiting just on the lee side of the mass, her hands raised to Nahr's soaked sides. She turned. Her eyes widened. Caravel approached her at a smooth gallop, stopping abruptly in front of her a mere breath away. He whinnied, just a little, and dropped his nose so it just touched her chest. She raised a crooked, shaking hand and laid it on his forehead. Finally, finally, she raised her eyes to Marguerite's.

"What have you *done*?" she whispered.

Marguerite looked down at her coolly and didn't answer.

"I'd like to know the same thing," Malik said, coming up from behind her.

Eyas sidled along beside him at a strange angle that seemed meant to keep her as far from Caravel as possible.

"Something amazing," said Än, her movement a wide swath around Caravel to give both herself and Catseye space. "She keeps surviving things she shouldn't. She went out alone into the desert and she found a horse. A *beautiful* horse." There was the gold, just a tiny glitter of it.

"She's found nothing," Saqr said. Her voice had always been harsh, but it had deepened now and sharpened. There was something jagged in its tone. "She's stolen it. She's stolen the wind."

"I didn't steal anything!" Marguerite snapped, offense prompting speech where manners never could. "I called. He answered." She crossed her arms pointedly over her chest. "He *likes* me."

Caravel raised his head, shaking it high in the air and letting out a soft whuff of breath. He danced for a moment, his icy hooves flashing in the sunlight. Saqr stepped back, her brows knitted.

"It's wrong," she said. Though the words were quiet, they hung heavy in the still air.

Än turned her head away. Malik was still.

"Why are you so angry at me?" she asked, not bothering to force her voice into evenness. "Än is the one who gave me the idea." The younger woman started as Marguerite rounded on her,

her head shaking jerkily. "You *said* I could summon the wind if I was clever." Her eyes dropped. "Well, I am clever."

"*Clever*," the word came out in a hiss, as tight and scathing as escaping steam. "You think you've been *clever*?"

"I think it's clever," Än said before Marguerite had formulated a suitable reply. Though her shoulders hunched and she seemed unable to meet Saqr's eyes, the gold gleamed from under her eyelids. "I think it's incredible. And she saved herself. You can't deny that." Her cheeks darkened. "Maybe it was a little my fault, anyway. If Nahr hadn't run—"

Her voice dwindled and died. Grandmother and granddaughter faced each other silently. Though Marguerite had never known how family spoke to one another across generations, some instinct told her silence was a wise choice. At least, it seemed always safer not to draw Saqr's attention.

Malik stepped forward, hands held up with his palms out. His eyes flicked briefly toward her, but he turned them away before resting his hands on Caravel.

"What's done is done," he said, addressing his family. "It's no use being angry at her, she doesn't listen."

"I listen, I just don't—"

He continued to speak over her. "She probably shouldn't have done what she did. She definitely shouldn't have." This correction came after a look from Saqr. "I don't even understand how she did it, although I'm getting used to that from her. But what's done is done. We can't change it. She can let the wind go, and I don't suppose having it tamed for half a day will do the desert much real harm. And," — he took a deep breath — "Än is right. She would have been killed otherwise. That fault lies with us as much as it lies with her."

Än said nothing but her hand reached out and took her brother's. Saqr hunched in a little, her body softening as she gave up the struggle to remain upright and commanding.

"I'm not giving up my horse," said Marguerite.

She noted for the first time that all three pairs of eyes were really quite similar, as they all turned to her in varying attitudes of disbelief (Än's wide, Saqr's narrowed, Malik's tired-looking).

"He's my horse," she repeated. "Malik has a horse. Än has a horse. Even Saqr has a horse, even though I've never seen her ride. Why should I have to give my horse up, just because he's *better* than the rest?"

"He is not!" Malik snapped, over the protests of the two women.

They quelled him with a look, although he subsided into offended mumbling rather than silence.

"You've no right to it," Saqr said, each word carefully enunciated, beady eyes fixed on Marguerite's with a fierceness that demanded she hold the contact.

She would have done so, anyway. Maintaining eye contact was a challenge and this was a contest she had a true investment in winning.

"He chose me," she said, a lilting sing-song tone making its way into her voice (every bit of power helped).

Caravel's ears immediately swiveled backward to listen.

"If you want him gone," she added. "Dissolve him back into wind yourself." She accessorized her wolf challenge with a wolf smile: all teeth and no humor.

Saqr held her eyes, hard and furious. But just for a moment, her gaze wavered, dropping to the side before she brought it back up. It was the hesitation that told Marguerite that it was the young challenger who took the prize.

"You're not welcome here," the old woman finally said into the tense silence. "Not while you have that horse. You're right, I can't compel you to let it go. But I'll be damned if I share our shelter with you while you hold it." The eyes that finally held hers blazed again.

She reminded herself that she had already found one oasis when she was alone and scared and that now she was very, very far from alone.

She shrugged, the movement slow and deliberate. "All right," she said. "But I want my things back. You still have them." She turned her eyes from Saqr and focused them on Än. "You'll bring them to me?" She tried to lilt her voice upward, to make it not a command but a question (if not a question with an assumed answer).

Än nodded, looking no more unhappy than she had before Marguerite had spoken, so Marguerite assumed she had succeeded.

Marguerite nodded and turned Caravel's head away. He bounded up the slope in three enormous leaps. When she turned to look behind her, there was only desert, stretching out into the horizon.

She dismounted, finally, but kept a steadying hand on Caravel's shoulder, half afraid that, after her show of defiance, he would disappear as soon as she left his back. But he didn't seem interested in running, nor did he shrug her hand off. Instead, his head lowered and he began to lip at the sad remains of the plants growing in the sand. She leaned her head against his shoulder and exhaled, letting her eyes slide closed. It had been a long day. He wasn't as warm as Catseye, but the feeling of life and solidity was still a comfort.

She opened her eyes only when she heard the soft shuffling of footsteps through the sand. Malik reached the dune's peak, a thick pack slung across his back.

"Hi," he said.

Marguerite peeked up at him from the shelter of Caravel's neck.

"I thought Än would bring it," she mumbled.

"Än is trying to convince Grandmother that you're more stubborn than she thinks," Malik said, lips twisting slightly. "I made the same argument, of course." His eyes turned, so sharply that he seemed compelled, to Caravel. He held a hand palm out, letting the horse come to him slowly. Caravel extended his neck, nostrils flared, stepping forward only when Marguerite grudgingly stepped aside.

"So, this is the form the wind takes when it wants to be loved," Malik murmured.

Marguerite shrugged, nodded.

"I don't know much magic," he said, in a soft, gentle tone that might have been for her or might have been for Caravel or might have just been him putting his own thoughts in order. "Oh, I can activate a spell that's already been set up. I can open up the way, if someone shows me the path. But magic has always been Än's gift, not mine. Considering even the family wisewoman isn't quite sure how you've done this, I know I don't have a chance of understanding the spellwork. But," he paused. His hand ran down Caravel's neck. "I know horses. He's got good conformation and he stands square."

She was, in spite of herself, interested.

"Square is good?"

"Square is good." He walked slowly around Caravel, the hand on his neck running over his shoulder and down his leg, until Malik grasped the horse's ankle and lifted his hoof.

"Weird hoof," he said. "Never seen anything like it. Looks more a jewel than a nail. But it's got a nice shape to it and the consistency of the frog is good." He dropped the hoof, continuing his slow stroking and circling. "Nice muscle distribution. Good weight. He carries his tail high when he moves, which I always like to see." He stopped finally and turned to face her. "I'm still not sure how you did it, but you've acquired yourself a fine figure of a horse." He grinned a little. "You can take that as a recommendation. I'm generally held to be the best in the family at horses."

She snorted. "Big deal. Your family is three people and Än's horse is bad."

He turned his head to look at her blankly. "You realize I have more family than just a grandmother and sister, right? I'm pretty sure I've talked about them before with you."

She covered her sudden confusion with an irritated huff. "Why would I remember that? I've never met them."

"No, you're being kept contained in one safe place because you're clearly dangerous. But my family lives all across the desert."

"Really? How many?" It was hard to imagine that there could be more people out in the world like Än and, though Malik might not actually be the worst person in existence (definitely wasn't — she was fair enough to admit that the bandits were probably worse), she still didn't like the idea of more men like him running around.

"Lots," he said. She thought he was brushing her off, but he patted Caravel and continued. "My parents, of course. Two older brothers and their wives. Plus a whole mess of aunts and uncles and great aunts and uncles and nieces and nephews and varying degrees of cousins."

There was a gap there. She filled it. "No wife for you?"

"No wife for me. Too young and too much of a wanderer."

"And," she paused, licked her lips, sought composure. "No wife for Än?"

"Husbands usually for women. And no." He grinned. "Not even any flirtations. Än always says she has too much else to do to bother." There was a great deal of meaning in his shrug, although she couldn't read the implications that were clearly meant to be there.

She wondered if he would ask about her marriage and if so, how she would explain the complicated bond between her and the sea. He didn't. He smiled again, smaller than when he was talking about horses or his family, warmer than when he had first greeted her, and shrugged the pack off onto the sand.

"I'll leave you to get set up," he said.

"Who says I'm staying?" she asked, as if she'd had plans other than hanging out at the rim of their shelter and pointedly sulking.

He never took her bait anymore. "The fact that Än is arguing for you and will probably be up later to tell you the results," he said cheerfully. He walked away with a casual wave and disappeared halfway down the dune in a puff of sand.

She sighed and knelt to inspect the pack, pushing away Caravel's questing nose as she did so. It was, now that she looked at it, a great deal thicker than she remembered, so swollen it was straining the seams. She pushed the flap back. A waterskin sat on top, so filled with water it didn't even slosh when she raised it. She thought it was her own, although she had mostly forgotten its appearance. But there was another waterskin below, similarly filled, and she knew she had never had an extra. And below that, she found a great pile of tiny, leather-wrapped pouches, a small sewing kit, and a bundle of cloth which, when shaken out, turned into the same loose kind of riding outfit that Malik favored. A second, thicker bundle, with something rigid through the center, transformed into a small leather tent cover, wrapped around a great many rods of plant matter that fitted together in what would probably be a frame.

Marguerite contemplated the pile in front of her with dismay. Malik had given her the *wrong bundle*. This one must have belonged to him; he had no doubt prepped it for another journey like the one they had taken this morning. He was probably going to be furious when he discovered he had accidentally given it to her. Well, she wasn't giving it back, she thought with the self-righteous fury that could only be conjured by someone who had just won an argument in their own head. It was his mistake, even if he did try to blame her for it (which — well, he *might* not). But — her expression narrowed — she had asked for her bundle and hadn't received it. Where were *her* things? They might have been sort of useless and probably ridiculous to drag around with her, even now that she had Caravel to do her carrying for her, but she would be damned before she gave up anything that belonged to her.

Caravel snorted, plunging his nose into the pack and inhaling. Marguerite pushed him away again, with a single stroke to his broad cheek to reassure him that she was exasperated but not angry with him. She looked into the pack again and noticed for the first time that the darkness at the bottom was irregular. She reached a hand in and touched cloth that didn't match the rest of the pack. She reached in and pulled out her own black dress, torn and faded to a smoky grey, but as intact as she had left it, and the white rod she had been using as a tent support.

It was her own bag then.

It was her own bag, filled with a great many things that she had never placed inside.

She had a shelter now. She had water. She had food. She had clothing.

She remembered the last time she had sung a song of power and then been given shelter and resources.

She knew how to handle it now. That was something. She rooted around inside herself until she found the kind of anger that causes productivity, rather than the kind that hurts and burns and accomplishes nothing. The burning kind of anger would have insisted that she leave the bag behind. But clever anger knew that surviving from spite was far more powerful than dying for pride. So she calmly repacked the bag. She calmly threw it over her shoulders and mounted Caravel. And very, very calmly, she kicked him into a flying gallop.

'Away' was not a cardinal direction, but it was the only heading she gave him. Someday soon she would need to find an oasis. But she had, for the moment, water. She had food. They could run and run, until either the desert ended or they did. She gripped his mane and urged him to go faster.

It was well into the night before she could no longer hold herself upright, and the only thing halfway keeping her on Caravel's back was her fingers twined in his mane. He must have felt her weight shift and stopped, kneeling so that she could topple to the ground without tearing her fingers. She spent some time lying across his side, untwisting each numb and whitened digit and trying to massage the life back into her hands. Caravel blew into her hair but did not otherwise shift.

She knew she should set her tent up. But she had no strength to stand and Caravel's sleek body made a kind of bed. He wouldn't move while she lay against him. She was almost certain of that. She laid her head across his powerful shoulder and closed her eyes, letting out a choppy exhalation.

She didn't cry, of course. Why should she?

Chapter Fourteen

She dreamed of flooding again that night. She saw a desert covered not with a sea of green but with a true sea, a sea of blue and white and every shade of grey. She dreamed that the undulations of the dunes were replaced with flat, glassy water. She dreamed of a sun draped always in mist and spray. She dreamed that the only proof that the desert had ever existed was the bloated corpses of its inhabitants floating on the tides.

She woke soaked in sweat. She had slept well into the heat of day, she thought, pushing her dripping bangs from her forehead and squinting across the flaring gold sand (ignoring the soreness of her eyes, which were absolutely not red and sore and salt-encrusted). She was still leaning against Caravel, although he had shifted at some point in her dreaming. His legs were folded neatly beneath him, but his head was pointed out across the desert and his nostrils were wide.

She pushed herself up. The minute her hands dropped away from Caravel, he stood, a single, fluid heave. Her own rise was weak and stuttering and filled with false starts. She reached for him and he shied away, consenting to be touched only after she dried herself on the outside of her pack.

She stroked his neck for some time as she took stock of her situation. She wasn't badly off (she *wasn't*). Even if her chest did hurt a little and the world kept blurring unexpectedly (she was fine). She had water and food and shelter and the best horse in the world. She was still stuck somewhere she was rapidly beginning to believe was not an actual place but a personalized version of hell (that Marguerite was important enough to deserve a personalized version of hell she never questioned, of course). But she was pretty sure she was now adequately supplied to survive the whole thing, rather than relying on her own stubbornness to overcome all challenges, so that was a step forward.

She should probably pick a goal. Something to work toward. It had been nice, this last little while, having reasons to do things.

Having a feeling of accomplishment when she did something she set out to do. It didn't match the pleasure of conjuring up a tidal wave or a whirlpool or a battering storm, but in the absence of the ocean — well, victories had to be taken where they could be found, that was all.

Resources were not an immediate issue. She would have to track down an oasis at some point, but with Caravel, that was hardly a concern. She could, she supposed, simply find somewhere to settle down. Pick a crevice somewhere with water and fruit nearby and live out the rest of her sentence in relative comfort. The idea was not appealing. She'd spent most of her life staying in one place. With the sea nearby, it had been a good place. But lacking a sea, small dwelling places in the middle of nowhere had little to recommend them.

She didn't have to stay anywhere, she thought suddenly. Her shelter was portable; her horse was swift. Neither dehydration nor predation was much of a threat. And she knew already that the desert hid strange places in its dunes. Saqr had not taught her any of the desert's secrets, as she'd hoped. But she didn't need her. (Never had. Never would.) She could explore the desert on her own. If it wouldn't tell her its secrets, she would tear them out.

And if she met any more bandits, some particularly jagged little part of her whispered, she was more than ready to tear them apart too.

There was a certain satisfaction in coming to a decision, even if, as she quickly discovered, she would have to delay implementing it. She did mount Caravel and attempt to begin her noble exploration of the desert, but the sun was high and hard and the air close and sticky and she was soon forced to admit defeat. Her tent, once erected, was too small to fit Caravel, but she reasoned that, since he wasn't a true horse, and he was already so much warmer to the touch than Catseye or Nahr or Eyas had ever been, he was probably perfectly tolerant of high temperatures. She let him drink a little from her cupped hand and then crawled into the tent, curling up on her spare pile of clothing.

Sleep came, as always, quickly and easily. Her dreams were wet and glistening, and she woke with the taste of tears in her mouth and Caravel's nose nudging her cheek. Salt and sorrow were becoming a familiar morning reveille, and the movement of hand to lips to wipe it away was so natural the only thought it required was the diversion to stroke her horse's nose.

There was still a touch of red on the horizon but night had fallen enough that traveling would be bearable. Breaking camp was easy when it was just her. (Much easier. Much more pleasant, too, when she didn't also have a rotten old woman and two self-satisfied idiots to cater to.) She ate and drank and, after a moment's thought, stripped so she could slip into the clothing Mal— the man had left for her. It fitted a little more tightly than her own loose tunic and trousers, the pants billowing around her thighs but coming in sharply at the knee. There was a spare scarf that she eventually conjectured must be a sash and indeed, it wrapped neatly around her waist. Despite the tighter fit, it was neither uncomfortable nor stifling. She admitted grudgingly to herself that people of the desert probably did know a thing or two about designing clothes for their environment.

She ate a few dried fruits and, at the insistent nudging at her elbow, fed a few to Caravel. He knelt for her, an easy, graceful movement and she mounted more or less smoothly. Her thighs burned, and it took her a moment to realize that it was not the heat of her horse but her own body, and that, even if you had started to become used to riding, a broader back was still a strain. She shrugged it off. She had learned from Catseye that the pain would disappear if you waited long enough, and that eventually it would stop returning. Still, she braced herself when her horse stood, and her first breath ended sharply.

There were ways to navigate without tools. There were stars that didn't move and stars that moved in just the right way. There were bodies of water that flowed only to other bodies of water. There were, even in the horror of a desert, places that didn't look like other places and could be used as landmarks. But she didn't need to navigate beyond not returning to where she had been. She was free to pick a direction and strike out as she pleased.

It was an exhilarating and definitely not overwhelming freedom of choice.

In the end, she chose to move in the opposite direction to the last spot of red she had seen on the horizon. Even she had watched the sun enough to know that it moved across the sky. Therefore, she would go toward its rise. The sun had been her tormenter often enough. Today it could serve as a signpost. When she saw it, she would know to make camp.

Riding through the desert alone turned out to be scarcely more interesting than walking through it alone (and, she admitted after several hours with a grimace, scarcely less painful). They walked through dunes and over dunes and sometimes around dunes, the only change in the landscape being how tall the dunes were and how desiccated the waning vegetation became. Sometimes they trotted. Occasionally, when she thought her hips would stand it, they galloped.

The horizon began to redden earlier than she had been expecting. She supposed she had been dreaming a little, the monotony of the desert lulling her into something that was almost, but not quite, sleep. What she had been dreaming of — well, it hardly mattered. She dismounted, made camp, and curled up in her tent. Caravel circled once or twice and then settled beside her, poking his nose through the flap so they could rest together.

She woke drenched in sweat again. She dried herself and they continued. The second night passed much like the first. The only point of interest came halfway through when the expanse of sand was interrupted by a single anomalous shape, perhaps a little longer than the length from her elbow to the tips of her fingers. She had wanted to discover interesting things, and, though she had been hoping for something a little more impressive, she dismounted and approached. The lump resolved itself into a bird, plastered against the sand.

It was an ugly creature, the feathers of its head burned away to reveal reddened skin, patched in places with white and blue. Its feathers were blackish-blue, the same dark indigo shade as the man's clothing. Its beak turned so far down it resembled a fishing hook more than it resembled a mouth. The bird watched her approach silently, its green eyes large and bright, its wings half lifting as she showed no sign of stopping. The wings moved freely, the feathers lying smoothly along the bone. Except for its heaving chest, the bird showed no signs of injury. When she reached a hand out to touch it, the wicked beak struck downward, narrowly missing the delicate connection between thumb and forefinger as she jerked away. But, though her attentions were clearly unwelcome, it did not fly away.

She took a half step back and watched the bird thoughtfully. Easy enough to kill, if she wanted a meal. She had had fresh meat only once or twice since coming to the desert. But she wasn't particularly hungry, and she knew enough of wild birds to know that a beak so sharp meant a predator and a predator was rarely good eating. Besides — she took a hard sniff — despite the gloss in the feathers, the bird smelled a little rancid and she was leery of spoiled meat.

Caravel came up behind her and then pushed past her, catching her hair briefly in his teeth as he did so. He stepped up to the bird, which watched him without apparent fear, and thrust his nose beneath its chest, attempting to raise the bird into the air. It cooperated a little, spreading its wings to balance on the arch where forehead became snout. But the bird did not fly, and with a snort, Caravel lowered his head again to the ground. He turned and gave her a look loaded with meaning. Unlike when Malik gave her such looks, she thought she understood. She didn't think it was usual for horses to want to help birds, but then, Caravel was not a usual horse.

She circled the bird (it swiveled its head to watch her warily), unknotting the scarf from her hair as she did so. Abruptly she pounced, throwing the scarf over the bird's head and then scooping it up into a tight embrace, pinning its wings to its sides. It was bigger than any bird she had caught on her cliff, but the principle proved to be the same. Eyes covered and movement restrained, the bird settled immediately. She tucked it under one arm and gestured to Caravel to kneel. He did so immediately, his eyes soft and trusting. Getting on one-handed was harder, but Caravel helped and soon she was remounted. Well, she had a bird now.

As Caravel began walking again, she cautiously unbound the bird's eyes, making sure its body was still held close to her own. But even sighted, the bird was calm, resting against her without protest. When her arm tired, she moved it to her lap and then, slowly, pulled her hand away. It shifted just enough that it was facing forward, perching just above Caravel's shoulder, wings half spread. It held itself rigid, only its head darting around to investigate its surroundings. Its belly was pale. Against Caravel's back, it had a yellowish tinge, but in the sky, the bird probably looked white. Its head — she pressed it gently — was not burned after all. The ridges and mottling were natural, although what purpose they served she couldn't tell.

Even up close, she could see no damage beyond the bird's apparent exhaustion. She wasn't sure what she could do with it, beyond giving it a place to perch while it rested, but it was a quiet companion and, except for shifting her slightly out of position on her horse's back, not troublesome, so she resolved to let it stay as long as it pleased.

They found the second bird an hour or so later, a tiny falcon smaller than the length of her hand. It was a pretty little thing, its back a soft shade of russet, and its head capped with a patch of grey that reminded her of a storm's height. Like the bald bird, it showed no damage and, on being brought aboard, perched happily between Caravel's ears.

The third bird was a hawk, an enormous, vicious-looking creature, its beak glinting gold even under moonlight, its feathers a deep red like Än's — like heavily steeped tea. It perched, without trouble, on the arch of Caravel's tail, the stallion carrying high it as the crest of a wave about to break.

She didn't find the fourth, fifth, and sixth birds but was instead found by them. Three little finches exploded from the sand ahead of her and, tiny wings beating a rhythm that was steady but far too swift to dance to, fell upon Caravel's hindquarters. He was a broad horse and their miniature feet were as stable on the broad expanse of him as they were on the ground. She had hoped they would sing but, though their orange breasts provided a pleasing splash of color on Caravel's searing white, it was only her eyes and not her ears that they charmed.

"I'm out of room," she told the seventh bird, a small black owl with a sweet face like fruit sliced lengthwise. It watched her with solemn red eyes before hopping to her shoulder. It was a surprisingly heavy beast, and the extra weight unbalanced her. She took a deep breath and readjusted herself. Her hair piled on top of her head and bound tightly with her scarf created an acceptably stable perch and, if the owl was still heavy, it was at least an even heaviness.

The sun began to rise, and still none of the birds stirred from their perches, even when she called Caravel to a halt and dismounted. Even the owl remained, an unwieldy headdress as she shrugged her bag off and put up her tent. Caravel lowered himself carefully to the sand, the birds' wings opening as one to steady themselves but not otherwise acknowledging the movement. She drank, poured a little bit of water into her palm for Caravel, and then, with a sigh, a little for each bird. She would need to find an oasis sooner than she'd expected. She had more mouths to fill now, and she was drinking more than she had the last time she'd wandered alone (alone-ish). Most of the birds also took a strip of jerky. The little finches did not, but when she placed a dried fruit on her palm and laid it on Caravel's hindquarters, they consented to surround her and pick out the seeds.

The owl didn't move from her head until she had crawled into the tent and laid herself down, and then it only relocated to her shoulder, crouching low in the tight space. The finches settled by her cheek, the tiny falcon anchoring itself in her hair, where it was so light as to be undetectable beyond the pinpricks in her scalp. The hawk and the ugly bald bird remained in the entrance of the tent, sheltered half under its roof and half under the arch of Caravel's head. She had slept more comfortably, but she had also slept more uncomfortably. If they wanted to stay, that was their business, and lucky for them she never shifted much in her sleep.

She had expected to dream of seabirds, but instead, her dreams were full of ships wrecked upon rocks. She woke less wet than she had been, though still damp, to a soft cooing. The owl was pulling at the hair on the nape of her neck, a soft but insistent tugging. She nudged it away, gently, and remembered to pat the finches out of the way before pulling herself forward on her stomach. Only when she was free of the tent did she stand, slowly, letting the falcon hop from head to shoulder and then to hand and then to the ground before she rose fully. The owl clung to her back, its spread wings as heavy a weight as if they were her own.

Caravel was waiting for her and the hawk beside him. It had, sometime during the day, been hunting, and the bloodied corpse of the longest-eared rabbit she had ever seen lay under its talons. It met her eyes with an expression disturbingly like Saqr's before pointedly hopping backward. She knelt and inspected the rabbit. It appeared fresh, the fat and muscles still glistening. She didn't much care for raw meat, but she had no fire or means to make one, and at least fresh meat was rarely dangerous. She had apparently interpreted the hawk's actions correctly because it did not protest when she lifted the rabbit and bit into it. After so much dried meat, the taste of iron in her mouth was almost unbearably powerful, but it imparted a strength to her limbs that she hadn't felt for some time. She bit off a smaller chunk and fed it to the owl, and then gave a smaller still bite to the falcon. The ugly bird refused the offer, but its beak was newly reddened and so she assumed that it must have fed itself recently.

Meal finished, she pulled at Caravel's mane until he knelt. It was getting easier to vault onto his back and easier to sit there, despite his breadth. The birds joined her, taking the same positions as they had the night before, before Caravel rose. So they would be joining her again, at least for a little while. Their company had been charming, if odd, before. But it had been a full sweep of moon to sky and sun from horizon to horizon and still, they showed no interest in flying away on their own. It was ... concerning.

She was still thirsty, she reminded herself, and still needed an oasis. She would find one and she would leave the birds there. There would be water and fruit and probably the kinds of little chittering things that hunting birds ate. They could rest and recover from whatever ailed them in relative safety. She was no healer. She could do no more for them than that. She leaned forward, one arm steadying the bald hawk, so she could sing in Caravel's ear, a soft little song of lapping water and of nourishment in a place that normally killed such things. He whinnied, a delicate fluting that punctuated her notes more than a horse's cry, and began to walk, steps firm and confident.

She didn't know how long they rode. Long enough for her seat to begin to get sore again, long enough for each bird to briefly drop down to the sand and then rejoin them. There were probably things you were supposed to do when you traveled with such a large party. Jokes to tell. Ribald songs to sing. (She wasn't sure she knew any ribald songs. She had caught occasional snatches from sailors on the wind, but most of their songs had been vastly less interesting than the duets she sang with the ocean and so she had never learned them.) Long enough for boredom and then dreaming to set in.

The sky began, eventually, to lighten. Time to make camp, she thought, wakening from her half trance and turning to the sun. She froze. There was red and orange and the crests of dunes in front of her, but there were also black shapes.

Figures, silhouetted suddenly against the horizon.

Chapter Fifteen

Not (she sternly told her suddenly swift heart) anyone she knew. Too many and they didn't ride like Än or Malik. The red of the dawn would have set off an answering gleam in Än's hair, and Malik would never have allowed his horse to carry its head so high or tense. He had told her, more than once, that a horse should arch underneath her, not sink away. Anyway, even so far away, there was a suggestion of fear in the way the riders held themselves. Än and Malik were sensible, even when things were bad. They would not hold themselves so rigid.

She could have turned Caravel away. He could outrun anything and do it so smoothly that none of their odd passengers would be jostled. But she was disinclined to disrupt her mission, now that she had one, and they would have to go far indeed before she felt safe making camp. Besides, she was not afraid. Her horse was worth all twelve of theirs and more besides, and she had seven birds, while they clearly did not (she wasn't actually sure of the advantage of having seven birds, but seven was more than zero and therefore there had to be one). She took a few deep breaths, slow in, slower out, and nudged Caravel in the direction of the figures. His ears pricked forward, his steps becoming bouncier. The figures disappeared and reappeared as they wove through the sand. They were growing larger much more quickly than she had expected. They must be coming for her, as she was coming for them.

Though they drew closer and closer, she could pick out few details. The horses were shadowy, brown shading lighter and darker across their bodies. The riders were dressed in tan-colored clothing, almost a match with the warming desert around them. Their faces were covered, their eyes the only thing she could see. The horses were moving faster than she was, at first galloping, then, as they drew closer, trotting, and finally slowing to a walk. They had been in a line when first she saw them, but every time they disappeared into the sand, they came out bunched closer together. She could have hurried to meet them but why jostle her birds without reason? The meeting would come soon enough. She was not afraid to face them, but she refused to make them think she was eager, in case they construed it as a compliment.

Almost as one, they came to an abrupt halt at the peak of the dune nearest to the one that she and Caravel were mounting. She stopped as well at the summit. She could go no further without running straight into them or stopping in a position that would require tilting her head up to speak with them. A single drop of sweat trickled down her neck as she watched them silently. They shifted, the horses spurred into restlessness by the tension in their riders' bodies, but did not speak. She stroked the bald hawk's back and waited. She had, admittedly, met very few people. But she had yet to meet anyone who could hold a silence longer than she could.

It appeared they would not be the ones to beat her. The whole bunch of them rippled and then one broke or perhaps was thrust free.

"Well met, lady," he said.

Even if she hadn't made it a personal policy to dislike all strangers upon first meeting, she wouldn't have liked him. He was a large man, the rolls of fat obvious even under the looseness of his clothing, and it seemed to her a little obscene to be so large in a place where there was so little to eat and drink. His tone was polite, almost over-polite, but there was something in his manner that reminded her of Malik as she had first met him, the Malik she still disliked.

She didn't respond right away. Instead, she let her gaze run over each of them. The bald bird half-lifted its wings as her hand on its back suddenly spasmed and grasped a few feathers. The man on the end ducked behind all the others and cradled his arm against the pommel of his saddle. She was almost certain it was the one whose arm Caravel had broken.

Bandits, then. Bandits that she had tangled with before and who would have no fondness for her. The revelation was more a relief than anything. She would have felt a little (only a very little) guilty about being rude to family of Än and Malik. But bandits had chased her (and injured Malik, although it probably served him right and was definitely not a concern of hers even if it hadn't) and she was quite content to give back twice whatever they threw at her.

"I disagree," she said. Perhaps it was a gesture of support, perhaps it was merely an unconscious shifting of her head in dismissal, but the owl punctuated her words with a soft hoot.

A wave of exclamations broke over the assembled riders. She couldn't hear what they said, but she could hear the babble of their words as they murmured together well enough to know that they were not admiring.

The man in front, leader or merely elected spokesperson she didn't know, spread his hands, splaying his fingers out on either side of his horse. It was probably intended to make him look open and friendly, but there was something subtly menacing about the gesture. Though his hands were open, they looked like they were grasping.

"So harsh," he commented, in the same coaxing tone that Malik had used on Eyas. No, not quite the same tone. There had always been warmth in Malik's voice, especially when he spoke with the horses. There was no warmth in the man in front of her. "We've done nothing to harm you. We only want to speak with you."

"The only reason you haven't harmed me is because I'm very clever," she said flatly, not insult or boast, just plain statement of fact. "Do you think I don't recognize the man behind you?"

The fat man's shoulders rose and then dropped abruptly. His eyes crinkled. There might have been a smile beneath his wrappings. Or there might not.

"If you know who we are, then there's no need for the two of us to dance around one another," he said.

She had thrown the contents of a stew pot from her cliff once. There was something of the oily glimmer of fat on waves in his voice. She must be careful not to let him coat her as he coated his words.

"I wouldn't dance with you," she said. "And you'd best not to try to attack me again. My horse hasn't gotten any slower. And now I have these birds, too." She gave a subtle jab to the bald bird so it lifted its wings in protest and was rewarded with another wave of murmurs.

The man laughed. She hadn't liked it when Malik laughed at her, and she had hated it when Än did so (even if Än's laugh was rather a nice sound). She would, she decided immediately, rather have heard either (or even both) laugh a thousand times than be the victim of this man's mockery. Perhaps it was time to end this entire charade and gallop away. Caravel was swift. They would have to ride through the day, but they could leave the bandits in their literal dust.

He must have seen a shift in her face or posture. Abruptly, the laughter cut off and he raised a hand.

"Forgive me, lady," he said. "I didn't mean for you to feel mocked. I couldn't help laughing at how badly you have misinterpreted us. You see, we mean you no harm."

Raising an eyebrow wasn't a very effective gesture from so far away, with a scarf and an owl covering her. Besides, she wasn't sure she was doing it properly anyway. But it felt satisfying and she hoped it at least got the point across.

"Truly," the man said. "You thought we were hunting you out of anger?"

She shrugged.

"No, my lady. I'm sorry that my men frightened you. It was not their intent."

An eyebrow was not sufficient. But a snort in chorus with Caravel seemed to communicate their feelings well enough. The man's eyes crinkled again.

"No, my lady—"

"Not *your* lady," Marguerite interrupted.

The man bowed a little, a strange, awkward movement. She hoped he would fall from his horse, but he remained stable.

"Not yet," he said. "Which brings me to my offer. My men told me that there rides a pale lady who can conjure magnificent horses from thin air. Although they did not tell me how beautiful you were."

He bowed again. Marguerite, unfamiliar with the ways in which men tried to flatter women, was unmoved by the compliment. There were things in the world that she cared about less than whether a bandit found her attractive — but not many. She certainly, upon being asked to describe herself, would not have used the word beautiful. Would not have seen any reason to desire beauty. (She wasn't, in point of fact, beautiful. She should have been. A laundry list of her features would have made a poet salivate, and the description of her said poet wrote would render her a veritable Venus. Her hair was silver, sea foam and moonlight, her skin a milky shade of cream. It should have been magnificent, but the effect was rather more that of a smooth-faced grandmother than a nymph. Her body knew it was meant to be picked out in shades of brown and black, and her extraordinary coloration sat uneasily on her features, a bad paint job on a portrait of someone the restorer had never seen.)

So she stared at him, and as she waited for him to get to what he truly wanted to say, she watched the crinkle gradually disappear from his eyes. It took him a moment to rebalance, a moment to recover after having clearly budgeted time for 'maidenly simpering'. He cleared his throat.

"My proposal is this, lady. To ride alone in the desert is a dangerous prospect. You have need of companions. And we could use someone with your skills. Join us. Take my hand and I will make you our queen."

He spread his arms again in the palms up gesture, as though he was offering her something. She was aware of the men around him shifting slightly, but she kept her eyes on his. She wanted to laugh derisively at him. But something about this situation wasn't funny at all.

"I reject your offer," she said flatly. "Leave me alone."

He laughed again. It was an even uglier sound this time, the thin veneer of courtesy gone.

"You misunderstand me, lady," he said. "To be queen of the bandits was an offer. But joining us was not. In some form or other, you will be ours. Now, perhaps you would like to rethink our proposition."

Marguerite looked at him. She looked at the men and perhaps women arranged behind him. They were suddenly tense, leaning forward. Some had their hands on their waists. She knew what lived there. She returned her gaze to the leader.

"I really wouldn't," said Marguerite.

The bandits were moving suddenly, as though her words were some kind of signal she hadn't intended. They galloped toward her, their hands moving to their hips. The leader, in one smooth motion, reached downward and then extended his arm. Something large and black reeled out, settling around Caravel's neck, a jarring black line like a wound against the white. The falcon started, lifting itself partly into the air. Another line went across her horse's neck and then across her own torso. Her arms were suddenly bound to her sides, the owl half-spreading its wings and shrieking above her. She turned to face the throwers, and two more lines wrapped around Caravel from the other side. She turned just in time for one to be thrown over her head and another to be knocked away by the owl. The bald bird rose without a sound, and the hawk behind her screamed. Caravel lifted himself, suddenly, into the air, the shriek of wind through ruin suddenly filling the air. The bandits flinched, but their hands were firm, and Caravel was yanked back to earth.

The leader was too close. He was grinning at her, the sweat pouring down his neck. She could smell him from here, the odor of his natural body overpowered by the rank smell of some perfume. She said a silent apology to Catseye for ever complaining about the clean scent of horse sweat. His covering had fallen from his face. She had learned to smile from wolves and only later learned what the gesture meant from humans. The smile on his face had something very lupine in it.

"You should have said yes, lady," he said.

Caravel was quiet under her, contained and huffing. She could feel his fury or perhaps she could merely feel her own, reflected and amplified by his presence. They shouldn't have been cruel. They shouldn't have made her angry. Anger was a weapon in her hand, not theirs.

She didn't sing a storm. Not for their sake. For her birds, because she liked their company and she knew what a storm did to birds caught in its grasp. For Caravel, because she liked his form now. Instead, she sang of foggy mornings, of mist sliding into keyholes and creeping through cracks. She sang of wind whistling through the smallest openings and destroying the peace within. As she sang, she felt Caravel's body dissolve for a moment underneath her. The ropes dropped to the sand. She heard the bandits exclaim, and felt the slackening of her own bonds. One movement pulled them free. And then Caravel surged up beneath her, her horse once again. He screamed one last storm's cry and then he jumped, straight into the air and over the bandit's head.

They hit the sand at a full gallop, implacable and unstoppable as a flood. Caravel's powerful legs churned the sand, throwing it up behind him and coating the bandits. She heard cries, human and equine, but no answering hooves. They were free and no horse in the world could catch them now. Never could, really.

They had been mean and they had been dishonest, or at least deceitful. So she let herself have one indulgence. She stopped on the dune where they had first met her and swung Caravel around to face them. None were moving toward her. Most of them were still trying to bring their horses under control. The leader had fallen or been bucked and was struggling to rise, shouting orders or merely swearing at the other men. He turned to face her, his attention drawn by the movements of the birds back onto their perches. Marguerite grinned.

"I decline your proposition," she called. "I've already been a goddess, you see, so *queen* seems a bit of a step down."

His mouth opened, but she didn't wait for his words. She touched her heel to Caravel's side. Caravel wheeled and they, horse, rider, and birds were gone.

There was something pure and clean about a desperate run for freedom, especially when the runner thought she would make it. Something about her hair being pushed back from where it had clung stubbornly to her face. Something about the birds, their wings fully extended, even the finches managing to survive and stick. They galloped and they galloped. They galloped long after all fear of pursuit had vanished. They galloped until Marguerite's clothing began to darken. They galloped until the sun was well risen and the day was far advanced. She pulled Caravel to a halt only when the sun in her eyes grew too bright.

"Nothing in this desert can stop me," she told Caravel.

And then she quietly toppled to the sand.

Chapter Sixteen

There had always been water in Marguerite's mind, in her heart, in her blood and bone and sinew. But she tasted it now in her mouth, felt it slide over her tongue and down her throat. There was a strange taste to it; though it was as light as water, it felt like drinking mud. She swallowed and tried to open her eyes. They disobeyed her command, though she felt her skin straining. Her eyes felt gritty and sore. When she lifted a hand to them, she felt only sand, hardened over and sealing her face closed. She scrubbed, desperately, at it. Something hard batted her hand away and then water poured, not inside her, but over her, washing the sand away. She choked a little, but when she tried again, her eyes opened, little good though it did her. The world no longer had shapes in it, only blurred blotches of light, although there was a great red shape like a spout of flame in front of her. She blinked and slowly, slowly, as though she was surfacing through layers of water to finally see the sun, it came into focus.

"Hi," said Än.

Marguerite tried to sit up, but her limbs were no more cooperative than her eyes, and there was a tiny, delicate tremble through her body that she had never felt before. She swallowed again — her throat burned — and contented herself with looking up.

There was a subtle wrongness to Än's appearance that she credited first to her weakened eyesight, but as she continued to blink and the world continued to sharpen, she realized she was seeing true. The red cast to the hair was still there, but it was dulled, the normally neat braid straggled, hairs working themselves out to paste against Än's neck and forehead. Her bones pulled sharply on her skin, which held an underlying greyness, and the hollows under her eyes were bruised, a purple overlaying them like overripe fruit. The eyes themselves were the same, though, the gold still faintly glittering. It was that which convinced Marguerite that it was truly Än she was seeing and not some trick.

"Hi," said Marguerite. "What are you doing here?"

Än laughed. It was a strained sound, her voice struggling like she had earlier been shouting or perhaps crying, but the echo of bells was still in it. It chased some, though not all, of the tightness from her face.

"Saving your life, apparently," she said. "How are you feeling?"

"Bad," said Marguerite, requiring little assessment of her own body and position to answer. "But you didn't save my life. I escaped the bandit king on my own."

She was gratified to see that the raised eyebrow was hard for Än, too, judging by how both had just shot up.

"Bandit king?" Än asked, the bells chiming again just under her words. "I'm looking forward to hearing that story. But *I'm* talking about your collapse from the heat. We only just found you in time."

Marguerite liked to think that she was the only one with water in her voice, but somehow, it lurked there in Än's, too, and she didn't quite understand why.

She broke eye contact and looked around. She was lying in one of the tents (not her own, which was smaller and wouldn't have accommodated Än sitting comfortably ramrod straight). Beneath her was something soft and smelling of horse (horse-horse, salt and effort and a bit of dirt, not Caravel-horse, which smelled mostly of dust and heat). It was dark-ish in the tent, and a glance beyond Än to the entrance told her that twilight was just now coming on.

She pointed to it. "I can't have been that hurt. I've only been unconscious for a few hours."

"You've been out for two days," said Än.

It didn't register at first. Two days? Impossible. She had never — not even when she had been young with aching joints, a burning forehead, and an insistent pounding at her temples.

"Where's Caravel?" she gasped. "What have you done with him? And my birds?"

Än held up a hand, the way Malik sometimes did with the horses. It didn't have the same effect.

"Caravel is fine," she said. "We haven't done anything with him, except feed and water him." Her brows drew together. "I'm not sure we could do anything else, even if we wanted to."

As if to prove her honesty, an enormous white head was suddenly thrust through the tent flap. Caravel saw her eyes on him and made a soft noise, half whistle, half nicker, all welcoming. She pushed herself up a little and put a hand out to him, glad for the tent's height so he could thrust his neck far enough inside for her to stroke his nose. She did so and exhaled slowly, some of the tension sliding out of her chest.

"And my birds?" she asked, eyes still on her horse.

"There were seven birds arrayed on Caravel when we found you," Än said. "Is that what you're talking about?"

Marguerite nodded.

"They're around the oasis somewhere. We brought you to the nearest one. It seemed the safest place to treat you."

The pronoun finally registered. She turned her head to Än. "We?"

There was a noise outside the tent and Caravel withdrew his head abruptly, his white form in the opening replaced by a dark and slender one.

"All's quiet, I think," Malik said. His eyes turned downward and met hers. They widened slightly. "You're awake!"

She nodded again.

His expression twisted, the way it often had when they first traveled together. "What were you thinking? I told you to wait for us! Why did you run off like that? You could have died! It's a miracle we found you in time!"

Marguerite looked up at him and then turned away, annoyed at having to explain something so obvious.

"You sent me away from your home and gave me the resources I needed to survive. I know what that means," she said, in the kind of voice she would have used to speak to a child if she had ever met one.

There was no comprehension in Än's eyes.

Marguerite huffed. "You don't want me. So I left."

There was a long silence, not a comfortable one like most of the evenings she had spent in a tent with the two of them, but tense, the air as charged as though a storm were coming. It was broken by Malik clearing his throat.

"That explains so much about who you are as a person," he said. Though the words were harsh, his tone had softened, more like the way he spoke to the horses or occasionally his sister than the way he usually spoke to her.

Än shifted, opened her mouth, closed it, opened it again.

"That's not — I want — I mean, *we* want," she stopped. Her eyes dropped to her lap. She reached out and rearranged one corner of the bedding Marguerite lay on. She inhaled, deeply. "You should have waited for me. We would never just abandon you to the desert. I came out for you after I spoke to Saqr and you were gone. You were just gone," she repeated in a smaller voice, more to herself than anyone else in the tent.

It was that, more than anything, that suggested to Marguerite that perhaps, just perhaps, she had been a little bit wrong about what they thought of her.

"What did Saqr say?" she asked because Malik had said Än was talking to Saqr and suddenly it was vitally important to know Saqr's answer, as it hadn't been before.

Än's eyes, which had risen to meet hers, dropped again, and when she looked at Malik, his face was turned away.

"She said, as long as you have Caravel, you aren't welcome in our sanctuary," Än whispered.

Marguerite swallowed, the movement suddenly strained and difficult.

"Then why did you bother coming after me?"

Neither of the siblings spoke.

She let her breath out in a hard snort. "If you followed me just to tell me to get rid of Caravel, you can forget it."

Another silence, then broken by Malik's loud exhalation.

"We followed you because *someone's* got to look after you," he said. "You've got no idea how things work in the desert."

Än nodded, escaping wisps of hair flying around her head in her enthusiasm. There was a faint redness on her cheeks.

Marguerite looked at them. She had ridden a long way, she knew that much, and on a quicker horse than either of them had. They must have pushed themselves hard to find her. No wonder Än and, now that she looked, Malik, looked so tired. They had worn themselves out to find her. Because they thought she needed them.

Marguerite turned her face away from them, covered her head with an arm, and burst into tears.

It hurt to cry, her body already wrung out and desiccated, every hitch of her shoulders pulling on strained muscles. She was faintly aware of noise around her, rising and falling like the tide and then evening out into a low murmur. There was a soft touch on her shoulder, more warmth and pressure on her knee. As her sobs became less a tempest and more a gentle storm, the murmur and warmth resolved into Än and Malik. Än patted her shoulder, a light, tentative motion, her words a rush of, "It's okay, it really is, oh please stop crying, it's okay" in repeating patterns. Malik's hand rested on her leg, rubbing in slow circles, his voice low and soothing and authoritative, telling her again and again that she would be fine. Though she had read of it, she had never in her life heard someone say the words "There, there" as he was saying to her now.

She sobbed once more, hiccupped, and then pulled out from under the hands so she could wipe her eyes.

"Better?" Malik asked. He had moved to sit beside Än so she could face both of them at once.

She nodded and swallowed. Än handed her a waterskin and when she had swallowed a few mouthfuls, she felt strong enough to speak.

"Better," said Marguerite. And then, after a moment's careful consideration, she added, "Thank you."

Malik's eyes widened a little and the gold in Än's glittered. Malik cleared his throat again.

"Yes, well, you're certainly welcome, of course." He paused and seemed to steel himself. "Are you sure you're all right?"

She nodded, wondering why he had asked. Än nudged him, her face turned away.

"She should eat. We should *all* eat."

They both moved, Malik out from the tent and Än to the head of it where a bag rested.

There was fresh meat to eat that night, not rabbit but something smaller and slimmer, and fruit and tea, of course, and, for Marguerite, some form of broth. She ate more ravenously than she had expected to. She had eaten little these last few days, as she had eaten little on her cliff, but perhaps life with the siblings had accustomed her to heartier meals. She lay back finally, replete, and feeling that maybe the world was only terrible and not completely awful after all. She dropped off to sleep before she realized she was tired and dreamed of sunlight gleaming on waves.

She was better the next day, well enough to sit herself up and stumble out to check on Caravel and the birds, who all proved to be fine. The oasis itself was much like the one she had inhabited before, although larger and, after having been home to three horses for days, more trampled. She leaned against Caravel and sighed, feeling something dangerously close to contentment.

She became aware of steps behind her and half-turned her shoulders to face them, keeping her cheek pressed to Caravel's side. Än and Malik watched her, their eyes strangely concerned. Än was biting her lip.

"What?" asked Marguerite, disturbed by their obvious discomfort.

The siblings exchanged a look, and then Än spoke. "It's about Caravel."

Marguerite nodded, wondering why they looked so serious. Perhaps they wanted to try riding him. She would allow it, briefly, if Caravel did.

"We're here," Än said, her words coming slowly, as carefully chosen as someone picking through a tidal pool for dinner. "You — you'll be safe enough with us. You can — you can let the wind go."

Marguerite's eyes narrowed, and the tightness returned to her chest.

"You *said*," she forced out. "That Saqr was wrong. That Caravel was fine."

"We *said* she shouldn't have sent you away!" Än snapped, the composure slipping from her face and voice. Marguerite had never seen her so wild. "We didn't say you should keep him! You can't, you must see that, now that you're safe!"

She shook her head and refused to meet Än's eyes.

"Is it because you want more freedom than we gave you?" Malik asked, in his taming-a-skittish-horse voice.

She changed her mind about preferring it to the bandit king's, who at least could be kicked if he spoke in a way that displeased her.

"You can borrow Catseye, how about that? Not forever but until we get you your own horse. A proper desert horse. A real beauty. Any one you want. If you can ride the wind, you can ride anything."

She shook her head. "I have a horse. The best horse."

The siblings looked at each other again.

"But you're hurting the desert," Än said. "He's — can't you feel it? Can't you feel how smothered it is, how heavy the air lays? We need the wind. All of us. There are *birds* following you because riding Caravel is the closest they can get to a wind current! Didn't you wonder about that?"

Marguerite jerked back. She had not wondered why suddenly birds were following her. She had assumed — because things were going okay and because she liked them, she had let herself believe they just liked her. But they weren't her birds after all. They were Caravel's. She buried her face in Caravel's shoulder and shook her head.

"You're hurting us! You're hurting *me*!" Än said, her voice shattering at the end. There was water in her voice again and salt on the air. "Don't you care about anything here?"

The words hung in the air, a sodden mass, dripping hurt and fury in equal measures into the sand.

"I care about Caravel," Marguerite said, quietly, because thinking about other things was hard but caring about her horse was easy.

There was a rustle of cloth against cloth, and then Malik spoke. "I don't think you're as hard-hearted as you pretend," he said. "Why is this so important to you? Why are you clinging to him so hard?"

She turned to look at him, then, to look at them both. Malik's hand rested on his sister's shoulder, her eyes wet and blazing, the gold in them not just glittering but molten.

No one had ever asked why she did the things she did.

They had followed her, when they didn't need to.

They had saved her life, even though her death might have freed the wind, might have given them what they wanted.

There was a rolling boil of feelings inside. She reached in, felt around, tried to find words amid all the emotions so she could give them that much.

"Because there's no music in the desert," she said finally.

They started, both of them, and Än looked again into her face. The gold cooled a little, not yet set but no longer searing.

"What do you mean?" Än asked.

Marguerite had never before been asked to explain herself, or at least, not by anyone she actually cared to answer. Normally she let herself retreat into silence. She didn't think she would be allowed to this time, nor did she want to. She fumbled, trying to find the words to explain ocean music to people who had never seen the sea. They let her fumble, waited and demanded no more, letting her string words into something resembling coherence.

"I sang," she said eventually. "And it was good. I could make the world be what I wanted. But then I came here and it hurts and there isn't any music. But I forced the music out and then Caravel came." She blinked and the world blurred. "The desert doesn't like my music and it doesn't have any of its own."

There was a long, long silence, broken only by Caravel's soft whinnies as he nuzzled her hair. *I've never been anywhere that someone hasn't brought me*, Marguerite thought. *You are the closest thing I have ever had to freedom.* She touched his nose and rubbed her eyes, finally looking at the siblings again. Their bodies were softer now, and the gold in Än's glittered as it had when they first met, when Marguerite had been a puzzle and not a person. Malik's eyes were dark, his eyebrows drawn together.

"That's it?" he asked. "This whole mess is because you haven't heard any music?"

"You don't understand," Än said, flaring up before Marguerite could. "You're not a magician." She turned back to Marguerite, holding out her hand. "There's music in the desert," she said. She paused, biting her lip again, the gesture this time thoughtful rather than nervous. "I can prove it to you. If you'll let me."

There isn't, Marguerite wanted to say, because if there was music in the desert, she would know it. She didn't speak because some sense told her that it was a wrong thing to call someone who had been good to you a liar. Malik shifted, breaking the tension between them.

"Please don't make me sing her a song," he said. "You know I only sing to my horses."

"Because they're the only ones you can force to listen to you," Än replied, the words coming as soon as his last syllable ended, the response clearly instinctive and oft-repeated. She laughed a little, and he laughed a little. And Marguerite laughed, first a tiny noise and then a great whoosh, swelling as the siblings laughed alongside her. It moved through her, a wave from stomach to mouth, and when it was done, it had taken something dark and hard with it.

When she stopped, when they all stopped, the siblings were looking at her again, Än once again composed, Malik with just a touch of wonder on his face.

"I've never seen you sound so happy," he said.

Marguerite shrugged. If there was a polite answer to that, she didn't know it.

"Okay," she said instead. "Prove it. Show me desert music."

The siblings exchanged another look, Malik's questioning, Än's calm.

"I can sing," Malik said carefully. "If that's what you want. If it will help."

He had told her stories once and, though she had complained, she had liked it. Perhaps she would like his song too. But before she could open her mouth, Än cut her off.

"Very nice of you," she said. "But I'm trying to prove that there *is* music in the desert. I'll take her to Madinat Alghina'. She'll understand there, if she'll understand anywhere."

The name meant nothing to Marguerite, of course. But the name must have meant something to Malik because he nodded.

"Do you need company or shall I return and try to beg for mercy from Grandmother?"

"We'll be fine." Än met Marguerite's eyes, her shoulders rising and tightening. She stepped forward, once, twice, until they were close enough for their breath to stir one another's hair.

Än reached out and took Marguerite's hand in hers. Her thumb ran over her knuckles, leaving little prickles of fire in their wake. Up close, the gold in her eyes was almost painfully bright.

"Will you trust me?" she asked. "Just a little?"

She had forged their hands together, it seemed, since Marguerite couldn't find it in herself to pull away.

"Depends," she said, because she would never lose herself that far. "On what you want."

Än took a deep breath, the swelling of her chest pushing them a little closer together. The heat of her body, even at night, was so intense as to be a little painful.

"The desert is sick," she said. "You know that. You've felt it. You know birds aren't meant to ride with you, not the way yours have been doing." She bit her lip again. "You can see how sickly they look. How sickly *I* look. You've been sick, too." Her eyes wandered to Caravel.

"*No.*"

She was getting tired of the looks that Än and Malik kept exchanging whenever she said anything. She was getting tired of feeling like every human in the world spoke a secret language that she seemed to be missing. Apparently something had been decided. Än's shoulders rose and straightened.

"You don't have to let the wind go now," she said, in the same kinds of coaxing tones that Malik and the bandit king used. "But after we've been to Madinat Alghina' — after I've *proved* to you that there is music in the desert — you'll let it go then. All right?"

She didn't know the secret language. But she knew well enough that words have power, just by speaking them.

"Maybe," said Marguerite.

Än flushed. Her previous blushes had warmed her face like a sunset; this one was splotchy, looking more like a rash than the movement of blood.

Malik put a hand on her shoulder and shook his head.

"Little steps," he said. "Remember?"

Än nodded and her rigid shoulders slumped, more a sudden landslide than any kind of relaxation. She exhaled, loud and slow.

"Okay," she said.

——— «» ———

They packed quickly. Marguerite, who had of course never unpacked, had only to throw her messy bundle over Caravel's back (and ignore Malik's cringe as he looked at it). The siblings took a little longer to clear away their own belongings, although they were ruthlessly efficient. Marguerite had been excused from helping with the justification that she was still recovering, but she suspected that they just thought they would move faster without her in the way. There were familiar flutters of movement in the spiky trees and the occasional rustle of wings. Once she heard an owl — her owl — Caravel's owl — its own owl? — call. Her birds were in a safe place, the kind of safe place she had meant to leave them. Would they stay here or would the wind's presence, however solid its form now, be too much for them to resist?

There was no flurry of movement when she mounted. No winged shadow burst from the shelter of the leaves to perch on her or on her horse. No invisible weight bowed her head or shoulders. The only rustling came from Än's last-minute adjustment of her bundles and from the seamless movement of Malik from ground to saddle. Though he was fully packed and clearly prepared, he seemed reluctant to leave them.

"Mind yourselves," he said, his voice breaking her concentration. "Are you sure you don't want me to go with you?"

"We'll be fine," Än said. Though the words were reassuring, she sounded petulant, even sulky. "I'm a big girl, Malik. And Marguerite has proven that she can take care of herself. Mostly. Besides," her voice smoothed out, became almost smug. "Someone has to speak to Grandmother."

Marguerite hadn't much liked any of her conversations with Saqr, but she hadn't realized that the siblings felt the same way. Judging by the look on Malik's face, which she was learning to read, it was obvious they did. His expression was aggressively patient, which meant that he was feeling put upon. She grinned at him a little, half sympathetic, half mocking. He looked up and wrinkled his nose at her.

"If you're sure," he said, sounding anything but. "I can escort you as far as—"

Än huffed, loudly, and kicked Nahr. The chestnut mare started forward, beginning the climb up the hill. It was not a very impressive movement, less surge and more lurch, but it got the message across. Marguerite gave him another grin, and then Caravel was flying up the slope, cresting the hill long before Nahr reached it. She waited for the other horse, Caravel dancing beneath her, his hooves striking a constant rhythm on the sand. When Nahr finally joined them, he didn't seem to want to walk beside her. He kept prancing forward, tossing his head, at one point even breaking into a gallop in circles around the mare. She had to lean over and hum to him a little before he would settle and walk more or less patiently beside her.

Riding with Än was different than riding with Malik, in ways she had not expected. She had known that Än was smaller, that her horse was slower, and there had been little hints in conversations that Malik had spent more time simply wandering the desert.

She had expected these things. But she had not expected to be so keenly aware of Än, in a way she had never been with Malik, even when she had been afraid of him. Än kept drawing her eye: the rise and fall of her chest, the subtle movements of her hips and thighs as she adjusted to Nahr's steps, the rigid line of her back and shoulders. Malik had only ever been that tense when he was angry with her. She didn't *think* Än was angry at her, or at least not very angry. She had been angry earlier, about Caravel, but Marguerite was pretty sure that their compromise had cooled her temper. But if anger wasn't causing that tension, what other possible explanation could there be? She wondered if she should say something (probably), and what it should be. Än kept glancing at her, subtly, from the corners of her eyes, which seemed to suggest that she was expecting something.

The problem was solved, momentarily at least, by a sudden dark shadow rising up and cannoning into her back. It resolved itself into the owl, which shifted to perch on the crest of Caravel's neck. The horse burst into a trot, and she had to yank on his mane to get him to slow again. Despite the disruption, she was … pleased to see the owl.

"We call that a moon owl," said Än, her speech unexpectedly rushed, spewing out as though the owl's arrival had struck a geyser. "Because normally you can only spot them during a full moon."

"There are lots of animals in the desert," she added. And then she was off, a gushing babble that seemed to have little purpose or direction.

Marguerite learned that the bald bird was called a vulture and that it ate carrion. She learned that the sharp wolves were called foxes and that they were extremely clever and that they had helped Än to find her (she owed them something for that, she supposed; she learned also that they were susceptible to bribery). She learned that Catseye and Eyas were half-siblings, bred from the same stallion, who belonged to Än's mother and was their family's finest stud, which seemed rather irrelevant to their discussion of wildlife, but she filed it away anyway as potentially useful information.

She didn't understand why Än spoke so much. She couldn't remember the other girl ever being so chatty before, and the words spilled out so quickly that she didn't think she was merely getting a lesson (although she was learning and trying to retain the new knowledge). On her cliff, sometimes, in the early days, she had sung merely to fill the silence. Perhaps Än's babble had a similar motive.

The noise bothered her surprisingly little.

"What about you?" Än asked abruptly.

Marguerite, who had been sneaking looks, turned her head to face her fully.

"What about me?"

"You said you were abandoned?"

Marguerite looked at her blankly.

Än's cheeks reddened again, and she turned away. "I'm sorry, I'm probably bringing up bad memories, just forget I said anything, do you want to know all the flowers that grow in the desert?"

"I'll just forget them," Marguerite said frankly. She sucked her cheek. "You aren't bringing up bad memories. I don't remember saying I was abandoned."

"You said you went away because you'd been sent away before. I thought — I mean, I know you can be difficult, but why would anyone simply get *rid* of you?"

A sluice gate opened in Marguerite's mind. "Oh, *that.*" She shrugged, needing no deliberation to make the movement easy and casual. "As a little girl, I showed I was powerful. My village was afraid of me." She shrugged again. "It worked out. I learned more alone than I ever would have from them. Why are you looking at me like that?"

Än's shoulders jerked and she turned away again.

"In my family," she said, voice unnecessarily loud, as though she was trying to wash away the remnants of their conversation that might be lingering in the air. "Children with gifts are celebrated. All gifts. Everyone knows that Malik has a knack with horses and a good sense of direction. But magic especially. We think magic needs to be trained." Her words trailed off, and her head turned away a little. Her cheeks were flushed again. "They caught my gift early. I've been training with Grandmother since I was little. You never had that?"

It was strange, the way Än seemed fixated on that part of her childhood, a part she herself didn't think much on.

"I had Mama Bella later," she said. "But I already knew what I could do by then. I think she taught me other things," she added, somewhat doubtfully. "I wasn't with her for very long."

There was a long silence. It wasn't the comfortable silence of working on chores together or the silence of riding next to Malik while he did whatever it was he did (she should probably find that out at some point). There was something fraught in the air, the charge of a coming storm.

"I wish you'd had a Saqr there for you," said Än eventually. She sounded sad, and Marguerite didn't understand why.

"I don't," she said.

Än started and looked fully at her.

She shrugged again. "If Saqr had taught me, I'd never have tamed the wind."

Caravel pranced a little in acknowledgment beneath her, tossing his head so his mane whipped around them both.

"There is that," said Än. She didn't sound like she thought this was necessarily a good thing, but she didn't sound angry either.

Marguerite decided to take the victory. The conversation seemed to have killed Än's desire to speak. They rode on without saying anything more. She dropped her eyes to Caravel's shoulders. He seemed unsettled tonight. He kept glancing upward, although what he was looking for, she didn't know, and occasionally he would spurt forward, kicking dust and grit at Nahr.

She didn't know how long they rode — she never did know how long things took — before Än suddenly pulled Nahr to a halt in the hollow of a dune.

"We should camp," she said.

Marguerite looked at her questioningly and then at the sky. It was still dark, no hint of sun even on the horizon. In front of her, the owl raised its wings and beat them once, twice, disappearing into the darkness.

"We need time to set up," Än said. "And I want a fire. I want tea and the jerky and bread are better when they've been soaked."

Marguerite nodded, nonplussed, and slid from Caravel's back. She had barely pulled her bag free when he took off, trotting in circles around the dunes, body occasionally rising in a graceful half rear. She watched him fondly for a moment, before pulling her tent free and beginning to shake it out.

"You don't have to do that," Än said, her voice quick and high. "We can share. I mean, I have the big one, big enough for both of us and Nahr."

She couldn't remember a time when she had ever shared a space with anyone. But, after all, she told herself, it would be convenient not to have to set up two tents. Very convenient. Really a very good idea to share a tent with Än.

She caught Än's eye and nodded, unsure why Än's gaze immediately slid away, unsure why her own matched it.

It didn't take long to get the tent up, the only delay coming at the start when Än unwrapped and dropped a bundle at Nahr's feet. She doused it liberally with water from her canteen before letting Nahr dig in. Caravel came up long enough to take a mouthful or two before trotting away. The tent was much taller and longer than

Marguerite's and wider as well, she assumed to accommodate Nahr. Though they would share, she and Än would not be pressing particularly tightly together.

She wasn't in the slightest disappointed about that.

Not in the slightest.

The tent set up, Än began to pull packages from her bag. Some Marguerite recognized as food similar to her own. There was also a canteen, with what she assumed was the tea inside. There were, however, some glaring omissions.

"I guess we're not having a fire after all," she commented.

Än glanced up. "What makes you say that?"

"No flint or tinder," said Marguerite. People in the desert always did seem to miss obvious problems.

Än grinned at her, looking, for the first time since they had met again, totally relaxed.

"Watch," she said. Her hands moved to her waist, where several tiny pouches hung. She opened one and pulled out a handful of some dried plant matter. She had told Marguerite once that desert plants had magic in them.

(If she'd known she would need to carry magic with her, perhaps she would have filled one of her skins with seawater before she left. But probably not. You could remove a plant and it was still a plant, but seawater removed from the ocean became merely water.)

Än dropped the small handful into a hollow in the sand. She covered it with her hand and whispered something, sweet and intimate. Though she leaned in, Marguerite caught none of the words. Än held her hand still a moment longer.

When she lifted it, a tiny fire crackled on the herbs.

Some of her surprise must have shown on her face because Än's smile was both proud and a little impish, the gold in her eyes flickering in time with the flames.

"Maybe Grandmother could have taught you something after all," she said, her smile widening.

Marguerite shrugged. "Perhaps." But she doubted it. What fire would be willing to come to her call, even if she could learn to call with words and plants instead of song? What fire would risk being quenched by responding to someone so filled with the ocean?

Än turned away, placing the canteen in the fire. It overwhelmed the flames, only the occasional tongue flicking up over the side to indicate that it hadn't been completely smothered. They both watched it silently for what felt like a very long time. The sun was finally beginning to burst up from the sand when Än finally raised the canteen, took a drink, and passed it to Marguerite. She had expected it to burn her mouth. Though she could feel the warmth of it, it was nowhere near to boiling. They ate silently. Än was no longer smiling, and her shoulders were tense again. She didn't speak until they had cleaned up and crawled into the tent, lying side by side on their backs, laid out like corpses with their shoulders barely touching.

"It's usually bigger than that," she said.

Marguerite shifted so she could look at her, but Än's gaze continued to rest on the ceiling of the tent.

"The fire, I mean. I'm not as good as Grandmother. She can make fire dance. But I'm usually better at conjuring it than this."

"Okay," said Marguerite, because Än seemed to expect her to say something and she could think of nothing else.

Än didn't speak again, and Marguerite was a little sorry that she had apparently come up with the wrong answer.

She slept fitfully and woke up feeling sweaty and ill. She had dreamed of water, leeching up from the sand and filling the tent, filling the entire desert. And she had dreamed of the bodies of the desert's residents, bobbing on the waves. It took the entirety of their meal and a great deal of staring as they broke camp before she shook away the image of Än's pale, bloated face.

Caravel had been standing high on a dune, looking out across the desert. He didn't respond to having his name called; she had to sing-song the syllables together before he flicked an ear back and trotted down. He didn't rear underneath her when she mounted, but something in the tension of his muscles told her that he wanted to.

They walked and occasionally trotted in silence, Caravel stepping high, his ears constantly swiveling around his head. Though it was night and a dark one at that, the air felt as heavy as if the sun had been soaking it for some time, and Marguerite's hair stuck to her neck. The sand lay flat and smooth. Had it been water instead, she was sure she would have seen her face reflected perfectly. She had never paid any attention to the way the sand used to ripple, and yet she now found she missed it.

"It's usually much better," Än said abruptly, shaking her from her thoughts. "The fire, I mean."

She was looking steadily out across the desert through the window frame of Nahr's ears, refusing to flick her eyes to the side even when Marguerite pointedly looked at her.

"So you said," said Marguerite, which she knew wasn't the right answer. But she couldn't think of another. Why Än was making such a fuss about it was something she still couldn't manage to understand.

"And I'm the best at predicting the rain," Än continued. She sounded a little desperate. "Out of everyone Grandmother has ever met."

"Good?" said Marguerite, when she paused, because she was pretty sure that predicting the rain was considered a good thing here.

"It is good," Än continued. "No one else can do it like I can. Grandmother says it's because I sympathize with the water." She was still looking away but the shadows in her cheeks had darkened substantially.

Sympathize with water? She had never thought of it as sympathy. To know the water, to feel it inside of her, to ride its moods as a blown leaf rode its swells wasn't a conscious choice. On her cliff, water had encompassed her whole world. To live in the world was to live with water. She had never thought you could describe a relationship with the ocean in a single emotion.

"I like water," she said finally because Än seemed to be expecting her to say something again, and she kind of liked the look in her eyes when she met Än's expectations.

She hadn't done it this time or at least she hadn't managed to really impress her because there was a lot of brown in the eyes that looked over at her. But she didn't think she had displeased Än either because she was smiling, one of those smiles that looked like a human smile and not a wolf smile. Än touched her heels to Nahr's sides, the horse springing forward into a trot and then a gallop. Caravel halted, tail swishing. She was about to nudge him forward when a hard shadow hit his neck, and the owl took up its place on his crest. It was panting, its chest heaving with exertion, and most of its feathers stood out in jagged lines. Caravel must have been waiting for it, because he took off on his own, quickly overtaking Än and Nahr. They spent most of the night like that, Nahr pounding steadily, Caravel spurting forward and then hanging back.

The scent of morning was in the air, heat hanging like perfume, when they halted and camped. Än conjured a fire again, but it was even smaller than last night, more a smolder than a true flame, and Än snuffed it out quickly with a clenched fist. Marguerite dreamed of fire that night, of flames dancing on a beach washed out by a rising tide, and woke feeling hot and uncomfortable. Än's sleep was apparently fitful. She sat up with mussed hair and bleary eyes and didn't speak while they broke camp. It took longer than it should have; Caravel was clearly feeling playful. He kept catching the ropes of the tent in his teeth and yanking them out of their hands.

They were well on their way before Än seemed to come fully awake, but then, perhaps feeling that she had to make up for her earlier lethargy, she babbled most of the night. Marguerite had earlier warned her that she wouldn't remember the names of desert plants, and so she didn't feel guilty when she spent most of her time trying to calm Caravel's steps. By the time they camped, she had only learned that roses grew somewhere in the desert (she had heard of roses but never seen one, so this was not particularly useful information).

Än didn't bother to make a fire and seemed out of sorts when they crawled into the tent together, although perhaps she was merely tired. In the light of dawn, Marguerite could see the bruising under her eyes, as though the ride had not just exhausted her but pummeled her as well.

She dreamed again of waves lapping at a shore, not extinguishing this time but playing with the soaked remains of previous fires. She woke up once, as she never had before, gasping for breath. Though nothing rested across her face, she felt like she was being smothered. She fell back asleep or perhaps passed out and would have put it down as a dream if she hadn't woken at nightfall with her chest strained and hurting.

"If we ride hard and into the day a little, we can be there today," Än said as they broke camp, her voice strained, the gold in her eyes tarnished.

That was right. They were actually going somewhere. Marguerite had forgotten that she was once again being *brought* somewhere. But Än had said it would please her. That was enough of a novelty for the situation to be acceptable, she supposed. She nodded.

They walked only when they had to that night, spending most of it trotting or galloping across the sand. Nahr's slow pace seemed to frustrate Caravel; he kept shooting forward, prancing at the highest point of the dunes until Nahr caught them up again. The owl rode as it had before, on his neck. It, too, seemed dulled, its wings barely rising even when Caravel threw himself into the air.

Day dawned, already hot and heavy, revealing a mass of rock sprawling across the horizon in front of them, a sheer red cliff many times wider and higher than what Än had called the sanctuary. It was apparently their goal, although what there was within or on top of it to impress her, Marguerite couldn't work out. Än led her to a dark line in the cliff, which revealed itself as a massive ravine, more than wide enough for them to ride abreast. Caravel seemed to know this place. His ears flicked forward, and his steps became even more energetic, every single one throwing them both high into the air despite the fact that they had slowed to a walk. They turned in one of the ravine's many twists and came out, finally, from the semi-darkness into light. A jarring, unbearable light, white and gleaming.

Marguerite put up a hand to shade her eyes and gasped.

"Welcome to Madinat Alghina'," Än said beside her.

Chapter Seventeen

It hurt her eyes. The whole desert hurt her eyes, but this was a different kind of hurt, a searing jab not just into her eyes but straight through them so that she felt the light must be bursting from the back of her skull like a prism. She blinked, trying to force herself to adjust, and rubbed at her eyes. The vision in front of her wavered, and finally, finally, she began to make out lines through the blur of light.

She was standing on a ledge or perhaps just an overhang, the ground in front of her sloping down to meet — well, what it was meeting she didn't know. The thing in front of her was rigid and angular. She hadn't realized how soft the desert was, really, without the jagged edges of ice or ripped-apart flotsam or cliffs torn down by the beating of waves. Everything wore down slowly in the desert, all smooth undulations and the occasional sand-rounded stone. Even the sun, sharp though it was, had surrounded her with its heat, not struck her at one particular place.

There was no softness in Madinat Alghina', each flat plane of it was hard and glittering, catching the light and sparking it away in thousands of colors, colors she had seen arcing across the waves or the sides of fish and colors she wasn't sure she had ever known before. Ice was her first thought. Something so hard and so clear and so gleaming could only be ice. But in the desert? Impossible. Impossible because of the heat, because of the sun, and because she would have known it was here if it had existed at all. Ice would have called to her. She would have found this place on her own or at least, when Än said its name, she would have felt a spark of recognition. Looking out across the shining expanse, she felt no surge of welcome. If it had been made of ice, it would have been made for her, and she would have known it.

"What is it?" she asked.

"Glass," Än answered, her voice hushed.

There had been a thousand ways to answer that question. Marguerite wondered if she should be disturbed or flattered that Än had known exactly what information she was seeking.

She squinted at it and the shapes finally resolved themselves into something she could recognize. It was a city, stretching out across the canyon in all directions. The sharp lines, she realized, delineated buildings. Small ones near where they stood, only a room or two, the roofs lying flat and catching the sun. The streets, too, were paved in glass, looking too smooth to have ever been trodden by human feet. Her eyes followed one, letting it lead her deeper into the city's heart, to buildings that flew up multiple stories, ending in roofs that arched into elegant curves or swirled into great squatting bulbs. Everywhere the glass gleamed, catching the light and reflecting its surroundings, until it seemed that she was not looking into one city but a dozen.

"Why?" she asked eventually when the light overwhelmed her again and she had to turn away. And then, "How?"

She heard the rustle of Än's clothing and guessed that she was shrugging.

"I don't know," she said. "No one in my family does. I don't know if anyone in the desert knows anymore. There are stories about what happened, about how it was changed into this." She paused. "I can tell you some, if you want, on the ride back. Malik said that you like stories." There was a hint of laughter in her voice. "Although he said you have strong opinions on how they should be told."

Marguerite turned to her, closing one eye to block out the city's gleam.

"When stories are the only way you learn about the world," she said. "You like them to be told correctly."

It must have come across more harshly than she had intended because Än's eyes pulled down the way they did when she was unhappy.

Marguerite tried to soften her comment. "But I'd like to hear them."

That seemed to help. Än smiled at her, a sort of wry smile that wasn't quite happy but didn't seem particularly sad or angry either.

She turned her gaze back to the city. It really was a lovely thing. Caravel shifted beneath her and tried to spring forward. She twisted her hands in his mane and sat heavily, just as Malik had taught her, silently begging him to hold back. He tossed his head but subsided.

She looked over at Än.

"It's beautiful," she said.

Än's smile widened. It was amazing the way a slight shift in lip position could warm a face so dramatically. Or maybe it was her eyes, widening so that the gold filled and heated them.

"But I don't hear any music," she added because even Än's happiness couldn't distract her from their goal.

She had expected the smile to drop away but it didn't. If anything, it widened, becoming that smug look she had noticed sometimes when she asked a question that Än knew the answer to. Än didn't speak right away. She leaned forward and swung off Nahr, landing easily on the ground.

"Come and explore," she said, raising a hand to Marguerite. "You'll have to dismount. Horses have trouble here."

Not my horse, Marguerite thought, and Caravel tossed his head wildly, as though agreeing with her. But she had promised — more or less, anyway — to give the place Än had brought her to a fair trial. So she, too, swung down, steadying herself on the broad white shoulder as Än hobbled Nahr.

Än turned to her, offering a hand. When Marguerite looked at it instead of taking it, Än flushed and half-pulled it away.

"You don't have to," she mumbled. "But the ground can be hard to walk on if you're not used to it."

She could walk on ice, Marguerite wanted to point out, and glass couldn't look so similar and yet be so terribly different. That was just logic. But she sort of liked it when the siblings were nice to her instead of bossing her around. So her hand darted out and her fingers wrapped firmly around Än's. It was a nice hand, anyway, callused and strong, and Än didn't grip too tightly. Marguerite appreciated knowing that she could pull away freely, if she cared to.

They approached the city together. The transition from sand to glass was smooth, like a wave washing onto a beach but never receding. Än crossed the boundary first, her soft boots making almost no noise on the slick surface. Marguerite stepped after her. The heels on her boots were solid. There was a faint tinkle as she put her foot down. She was suddenly grateful for Än's steadying hand in hers. Ice was slick and treacherous, but its surface moved and danced, and if you were clever, you could step from safe place to safe place. The glass road was a flat plane, no variation in texture or incline for as far as she could see ahead of her. Her hand tightened on Än's as she stepped again, another soft clink filling the air. Än's fingers briefly constricted. She had never asked for comfort in a handhold before. It was ... pleasant to have someone squeeze back.

She walked a little more confidently, the click of her steps settling into a constant beat as she found her rhythm. It was only small houses on the city outskirts, very simple. She peeked in the doorway of one. It was virtually empty but for a brazier in the center, exactly like the one that Än used but all of glass. One handle caught the light and sent it arching into her eyes. She put her free hand on the edge of the doorway to steady herself and skidded slightly, her palms sweaty after only a few minutes of sunshine. As her hand moved along the thick rim, it rang out, a musical whine filling the air. She jumped back, staring at her palm. She looked to Än. The other girl winked, licked her finger, and ran it along a windowsill. The soft ringing filled the air again, like a single bell strike extending on and on and on.

She opened her mouth and then closed it as regular staccato chimes burst out behind her. She turned. Caravel had followed them into the city. The horse moved confidently across the slick surface, each hoof striking brief and hard so that the clinking of his passage filled the air. There was no hesitation in his movements. He explored the city confidently, thrusting his nose against walls and through doorways. But then, he was the wind. He must have been here before.

Though his noisemaking was clearly deliberate, it suddenly dawned on her that he seemed calmer, and his ears were relaxed, swiveling easily instead of laying flat against his head or pricking forward like spears. He almost seemed to be having fun.

It was her horse's joy that spurred her on. She licked her palm and ran it along the doorway, as far as she could reach. A glassy moan rang out, overlaying Caravel's steps into something like a rhythm. Än rang her finger across the windowsill again, a higher-pitched whining joining with the clinking and moaning to form a strange kind of symphony. It was like no music she had ever known before. But it was music.

"This is what you wanted to show me," she said to Än as she lifted her hand from the glass, raising her voice slightly to be heard over Caravel's romping.

Än nodded. The colors of the city reflected in the gold of her eyes so it seemed that her face was encrusted with jewelry.

"Come and explore," she said and pulled at Marguerite's hand, tugging her after her.

They walked through the city together, wandering randomly, as far as Marguerite could tell, their passage turned into a kind of dance by the constant accompanying clicks of Caravel's hooves and her own boots. They found a market, dozens of square buildings bordered with glass boxes, covered with slender glass awnings, glass beads hanging from glass fringes. Clotheslines stretched above their heads, ropes of glass so thin they seemed on the point of shattering and glittering so brightly in the sunshine that they appeared to be made of sunlight. They found a plaza, with a great fountain in the middle, glass spouting up from its center, the edges gleaming as though they were water that was frozen in time and space and ready to burst forth at any moment. They found an aviary, a great dome of interwoven glass bars, slender perches rising from the floor, mirrors hanging from the ceiling. They found a garden, beds of glass dust bordered in panes of glass. Glass orchids rose from the beds, each petal no thicker than a true flower petal. Stamens projected from the flowers, thinner than a blade of grass, the ends glittering like tiny stars. Above them towered glass trees, the leaves reflecting one another into a great bush of foliage, each apple and pomegranate a great, smooth globe. Everywhere, she let her hands run over the glass, and everywhere, it responded, filling the still air with ringing.

They sat, after a time, when they found a bench, a great smooth expanse, its legs shaped like those of some slender, catlike animal, its back a sweeping arc like a seashell. Marguerite closed her eyes, glad of the relative darkness the action provided. The city was beautiful, but there was no break in the clear, gleaming surfaces except the girl beside her.

"You like it?" Än asked beside her.

Although they were no longer exploring (and Marguerite's feet had steadied long before; she had heard of sea legs, and perhaps she had gotten her glass legs), they had not let go of each other's hand. Surrounded by hardness and harsh, unforgiving lines, the touch felt wonderfully warm and alive.

Marguerite nodded. "I do."

There was a pause. While they had explored, it had been an adventure. They had smiled, even laughed a little together. But there was something in the air now, some faint touch of an oncoming storm.

"You know," Än said gently. "It's even better when the wind is running through it."

Marguerite had always been cold inside. It had never hurt before. But now it seemed that the day's warmth had leeched from her bones, leaving something empty and hurting behind. She had forgotten that there was a price to this adventure.

"You want me to let Caravel go."

Än had been angry last time she had asked — demanded — this. She didn't seem angry now. Her eyes were gentle, her mouth soft. It felt like grief. Somehow, that hurt more than anger.

"I think I've proven that there's music in the desert. And..." She paused again, seeming to be selecting her words with care. "Wild things shouldn't be caged. Don't you think?"

Her words fell even heavier in the smothering air, as though there was some added significance that Marguerite was meant to pick up on. She shook her head. Caravel wasn't caged. He was fine. He loved her. He loved her voice. But she remembered his restlessness on the journey to the glass city, his seeming impatience with Nahr's slow pace. The way he had watched the desert. The way he wandered now, a horse where no horse belonged. He had come to her when she needed him. But perhaps, when Än and Malik had found her, he had known that she didn't need him anymore.

She felt warmth over her heart and opened her eyes. He stood in front of her, his nose just brushing her chest, his eyes dark on hers.

You are the only freedom I have ever known, she thought. She remembered a little girl, alone on a cliff. *If I throw you away, how can I say that I care about you?*

But that cliff had been a prison, too. She had known she couldn't leave, or at least, until Mama Bella, she had believed it. She had made happiness because she had to.

Maybe love could be about letting go, as well as holding tight.

"You'll come back?" she asked. "If I need you again, you'll come to me?"

Another nod, harder, a rough nudge to her sternum. Catseye had done the same, once or twice, when he wanted to be petted. She embraced the large head, christening him for the last time with her tears. Then she stepped back.

"Then go," she said.

He raised his head and looked at her. He was beautiful. He had always been so beautiful.

She had heard the laments, sailors lost at sea or merely leaving their sweethearts for warmer ports. Funerals, mournful music playing as bodies were consigned to the water. Her own first songs, alone and afraid. She had always known the music of loss.

She sang it now, a song of parting, a song ripe with goodbye. His nose dropped into her palm, his last touch mirroring his first.

Then he was gone. The wind blew through the city and chiming filled the air, each separate piece of glass striking and whistling, half cacophony, half symphony. The city blurred, shapes disappearing into a multifaceted blur of color and light.

She closed her eyes and dropped Än's hand as she raised her own to her face. Her shoulders heaved once, twice, and then something warm dropped across them. She was pulled forward and encircled until she felt herself pressed against Än. It wasn't particularly comfortable. Her body was twisted around to rest against Än's chest and shoulder, which was surprisingly bony considering how muscular she was, and, though the air had lightened with Caravel's disappearance, the embrace was still stiflingly hot.

It was strange, then, that she felt no urge to pull away.

Instead, her fingers twisted in the fabric draped around Än's waist. Some small part of her let go. She sobbed. She had sobbed often enough in her life. Alone, mostly, with her head in her hands. Since coming to the desert, occasionally against Caravel. Once, with Än and Malik there, concerned spectators to her grief. This was different. It felt as though she was grieving *with* Än, that Än was not just watching but sharing in her sorrow.

There was something in the sharing of sorrow that soothed it a little, in a way that anger or stoicism never had.

Her crying eased. That was something she had always liked about tears — they ended. One could grieve for years. But tears always stopped. Her tears stopped now, and perhaps some of her grief fled with them.

"Thank you," Än said above her.

Marguerite pulled away so she could look into her eyes.

"I know that was hard," Än continued. "But the desert needs the wind. So thank you."

There were things a person said to being thanked. Marguerite didn't know them. She was not often thanked, and to be thanked for fixing a problem that she could admit she herself had caused? There had to be special words for that, and she didn't know them. She wiped her eyes and became aware that the wind was pulling slightly at her hair and brushing against her cheeks.

"Tell me about the glass city," she said.

Än's laughter rang out, the bells in it setting the city chiming again.

Chapter Eighteen

They stayed the day there and the night. The city was different in the dark. Calmer, softer, and perhaps a little more real. It felt more solid, without the sun catching its edges and setting the whole city glittering. She could focus on it without harming her eyes. She could see the lines of each building, complete unto themselves and not endlessly reflecting their neighbors. She could pick out details she had missed before, lines etched into the glass: veins on leaves, embroidery on cloth. Symbols in doorways.

Everywhere they went, the city moaned its strange song around them. The clotheslines rattled, a staccato counter-beat. The apples rocked against one another, striking occasionally just right to cause a great booming bong. Her own footsteps were drowned in the rhythm that the wind coaxed from each building, playing each glass piece like the entire city was one great instrument.

They slept, eventually, exhausted. She had wanted to borrow one of the houses but Än had refused, insisting that, though they could visit, it wasn't their place. They set up a tent, right at the edge, and the sound of the city singing lulled Marguerite to sleep, the whine of wind through glass melting into wind through rigging.

"We should be returning to the sanctuary," Än said when they rose and broke their fast with the evening meal.

"I suppose I'll be allowed in now," Marguerite replied, thinking for the first time of what letting Caravel go meant for her own future. Though they had not left the city, even she could feel that the desert was happier now. The air hung less heavy and the night before she had heard the soft cry of an owl and seen powerful wings arcing above her. She was still sad, but it was a strange sort of sadness, a sadness lapping at the shores of happiness.

"Yes," Än said immediately. "I'm sure you will. We've been working on Grandmother, Malik and I. I'm sure she won't push you away. At least," she said and paused, her brow wrinkling. "I'm pretty sure. Malik will have been home for some time now. I'm sure he's calmed her down." She blushed. "We, uh, didn't have permission to come find you."

And yet they had come anyway. Marguerite was struck, again, with the need to say words that she didn't have. Luckily, this time Än didn't seem to expect anything. They packed the tent, tying Marguerite's pack on with Än's larger one. Then they slowly made their way up the slope and away from the city.

She glanced behind her, one last time. The city spread itself under the night sky, its gleam dulled, winking occasionally as the wind disturbed some slender glass rope. She could still hear it singing. It didn't have the power or the beauty of ocean music. Like everything else familiar in the desert, it was a distorted version of something she loved. But it was music. There was something soothing about knowing that music could be found here.

She turned back as they crested the slope. Än's hand dropped from hers as she stepped forward to stroke Nahr's nose. She swung the bags onto the mare's back and tied them on with practiced efficiency. Then she swung up.

It occurred to Marguerite for the first time that she had no horse and therefore, practically speaking, no way to get anywhere.

Än nudged Nahr over and extended a hand.

"Well?" she said. "I know she's not the wind but—"

"No," Marguerite said flatly.

"I know you didn't have a good experience with Nahr last time," Än said. "But she's really a good girl. Please?"

She had certainly not had a good experience with Nahr last time. Not at all. But it had led to good things and, she thought grudgingly, if Än trusted the horse, she couldn't be all bad (mostly bad, maybe). Anyway, if she really hated riding Nahr, she could always call Caravel again. He had promised to return to her if she needed him.

That should probably be left as a last resort. She had a feeling Än would not continue smiling at her so warmly if she called the wind back at the first inconvenience.

She nodded and let herself be helped up. Än was a smaller mass than Malik, the desert still clearly visible over her shoulder. It felt strange to simply sit behind her, hands balled against her thighs, so slowly and tentatively she put her hands on Än's shoulders. When she wasn't shrugged away, she relaxed, just a little.

They remained still for a moment, Än apparently giving her time to adjust. Then Marguerite felt her shift to touch her heels to Nahr's sides and they were moving, through the ravine and out into the desert's vastness, the city's cries quickly fading into the night.

She looked back for a moment, straining to see any gleaming. Her weight shifted and she tipped backward, but the wind pressing against her back steadied her. She leaned forward again and reminded herself to focus on staying aboard. She tightened her grip slightly and felt muscles shift beneath her hands.

Travel was different with Än than it had been with Malik.

The muscles rippling on Än's shoulders matched his, but she was smaller, the bones Marguerite clung to a little more slender. Her body was cooler, the furnace heat of their confrontation gone, maybe calmed by the wind's return, maybe only ever really present in Marguerite's mind. She smelled like Malik had, fresh sweat and effort, but while he had reeked mostly of horse, her horse smell was undercut by something else, something faintly floral that wafted up from her waist when she shifted, probably from the tiny pouches she wore. It was easier to move with her than it had been with him, although perhaps it was just that Marguerite was less afraid now.

Än clicked suddenly and Marguerite felt muscles shift beneath her. Än clicked again and Nahr began to trot, a slow drawn-out movement, none of the leaping forward of other horses she had ridden, either flesh or wind. Catseye's trot was swifter, but Nahr's smoother (Caravel's, of course, was superior to both). She felt herself tipping slightly sideways and tightened her grip on Än's shoulder. Än cleared her throat.

"You can…" She paused. "You can hold my waist. It's more secure that way." The last sentence came out all in a rush.

Marguerite shrugged and shifted so she could put her arms where she had been told to. Än was right. There was a soft, narrow place between hips and breasts where Marguerite's arms fitted perfectly. She held on loosely at first but when Nahr stumbled a little, her arms tightened. It brought her head to rest strangely close to Än's shoulder so that she was almost leaning on her.

Än's shiver matched her own and she pulled away.

———— ‹›› ————

They rode most of the night like that, Marguerite alternately clinging and pulling away as terrain and discomfort demanded, Än's body stiffer than she could ever remember Malik's being. They made camp before dawn, and Än finally conjured a fire that actually looked a little like a fire, although it was still a restrained thing. They slept side by side, and Marguerite's dreams were full of dark shapes darting through harsh currents. Än seemed quiet the next evening, a little unhappy, and did not speak until Marguerite did, well into the night's ride.

"You're sad," she said, which she knew wasn't a terribly good conversation starter, but at least it was something.

It was strange to speak with Än without watching her face. Marguerite had always gauged her feelings from her eyes, and those, even when she turned back slightly, were hidden, especially in their current position. Bowing to her own lack of balance, Marguerite had twined her arms loosely around Än's waist, pulling her into the longest sustained contact she had ever had with another human being. Perhaps that was what made her extra interested in Än's emotions.

"I'm not sad," Än said. She briefly laid one hand over Marguerite's, perhaps in reassurance. "I'm just … frustrated. I wanted to show you a really big fire last night. But I just can't seem to manage it."

"I don't care," said Marguerite, pleased to be able to speak with complete honesty and yet be fairly sure that it would soothe rather than anger.

There was a pause.

"I do," Än said quietly. "I wanted to show you my mastery of fire. But it seems all I can do is sympathize with water."

Silence fell. Then Än's body expanded as she took in a breath.

"They say you can't depend on water," she said quickly. "They say it's unpredictable, that it's treacherous, that just when you think you have a hold of it, it slips through your fingers. They say it's a pity that we need it because it doesn't need us, not the way fire does, or plants, and so you can't call it or trust it to stay. I was always told, growing up, that you can never trust water."

She looked back, a quick twist like a bird's. Her eyes were downcast.

"But I like it," she said in a near whisper.

There was something there. Marguerite could almost see it, hovering in the smothering air between them, some vague shape that was apparently quite clear to Än. She was meant to understand something. There was an undertow to Än's words, but she had somehow floated right past it instead of being caught in it.

She didn't say anything because she didn't know the words or, indeed, the tone, and besides, they never got very mad at her when she was silent. Än's shoulders slumped with the weight of unsaid words between them, and she suddenly urged Nahr into a canter, as though by running quickly enough they could leave the words behind.

———— «》 ————

Än didn't speak again until they stopped to make camp and then only to tell her that halting was what they were doing. They watered Nahr and set up the tent silently.

"You're mad at me," said Marguerite. There was probably something else she was meant to be saying in this situation, but she had never in her life broached another's feelings. Normally, if she saw them at all, she waited until they had passed. But Än had been happy with her, and she had liked that, and now Än was not happy, and she had a vague feeling that she could fix it if she only understood why.

Än looked at her, eyes very wide, and then away.

"I'm mostly mad at me," she said. "You've been unsympathetic, but you've made your feelings quite clear." One booted toe kicked at the sand, over and over, a dull and unhappy rhythm.

Marguerite looked at her for a moment. And then she reared up and shouted, "No, I *haven't*!" And it felt good. It felt good to get angry, to lash out at Än, to stop trying, however fumblingly, to please her. It felt good to let her frustration bubble over, to let it froth on the sand between them.

"I haven't made any feelings clear because I don't know what my feelings are because *I don't know what you want.* I never know what you want! You and Malik and Saqr push me around and get mad when I say things that are true to me! You all always *want* something from me," she added, quieter and a little breathlessly, hearing the whine in her voice but too frustrated to banish it. "And I don't know what it is. I never know what it is. Why can't any of you be clear?"

An looked at her. Her eyes were very, very golden. She walked forward, slowly, a little like a fawn taking its first steps, a little like a cat stalking prey, until she was standing right in front of Marguerite, so close their bodies almost touched. Marguerite held herself still because even if Än attacked her, the one thing Marguerite would always hold onto was herself and her place in the world.

Än leaned forward and put her mouth gently on Marguerite's.

It was a kiss. She knew that much, had read that much, although she couldn't remember anyone ever having done it to her or having done it to anyone. It wasn't an unpleasant sensation, the pressure not much harder than the wind pressing to her mouth when she sang. If she had ever wondered what Än's mouth would taste like (which she definitely never had at any point in her life ever), she would have guessed fire and ash, that her lungs must be full of flames to produce the smoke of her voice. But Än's voice did not taste of fire or even particularly of tea, which would be a more sensible guess, given how much she drank. It didn't taste like much of anything, really, except maybe a little of sweat and desert and exhaustion.

Än pulled away, her pupils so wide that the seashell brown had disappeared and the gold was only a gilded rim on the blackness.

"Is that clear?" she whispered.

"No," said Marguerite frankly. "Not at all. But I liked it."

Än's face contorted, the way Malik's sometimes did when Marguerite said something he seemed to find particularly bizarre. She didn't think it was an angry contorting. Än's eyes were still wide and her body hadn't stiffened the way Malik's did when Marguerite upset him. Her face contorted further, and then she laughed, just a little, a short, sharp bark like the popping of a cork.

"I'm not good at this," she said, looking calmer, her head tipped to the side, her voice soft, as though confiding a secret she was excited about sharing. "I don't have much practice."

Before Marguerite could point out that she'd had no practice at all, Än continued quietly, "I always loved the water. And you remind me of it — of a rainstorm and an oasis and everything bright and wet. When Malik brought you to the sanctuary — you were the most beautiful thing I had ever seen."

The bandit king (leader — she was pretty sure 'king' was him putting on airs) had called her beautiful as well, as though it was meant to be something that pleased her. It hadn't affected her then. It affected her a little now. It was nice to be complimented by Än. It was nice to know that Än had admired her, that Än had seen the ocean in her blood and bones and seen that it was precious.

She wondered if she should say something in return. She had never considered beauty in the context of a human before. The ocean was beautiful. A storm was beautiful. Caravel was beautiful. Än was just Än, just shaped like a person, not much different than most other people.

But then, if Än was just like any other person, why, from the moment they had met, had Marguerite been unable to stop watching her?

"I like your eyes," she said finally, because it was true and because it was a safe thing to say. There were other things she liked, she was pretty sure, but they were amorphous and hard to describe. If Än wanted to know what Marguerite liked about her eyes, she was pretty sure she could chart it.

Än didn't ask for more. She smiled again and took Marguerite's hand in hers. Marguerite had mostly only held things that were smooth. She decided she didn't mind the calluses that covered the strong fingers.

"Small steps," she said, smiling. "We'll take it slow, for both our sakes." And then she said, "We should eat. And get some rest."

Marguerite wasn't sure she had ever taken anything in her life slow. Things happened all at once for her. Things were the same for years and then suddenly they would change, not a shift in the tides as much as a sudden flood. Taking things slow sounded … nice.

She nodded. They ate and drank and then crawled into the tent. It was harder, somehow, than it had been before. She didn't know how to arrange herself and neither, it seemed, did Än. They shuffled for some time, Än apologizing every time they brushed up against one another and Marguerite pulling away harder in her version of repentance. Eventually, they settled on their backs, lying side by side. Marguerite's hands were folded across her stomach; she wasn't sure where Än had laid hers except that they weren't within casual reach.

Sleep, as always, came easily. Her dreams hurt, in a way they hadn't since she first came to the desert and maybe in a way they never had because it didn't hurt the same way. Dreaming of the ocean before had hurt because it wasn't there. It hurt that night because it was. She felt herself being dragged beneath the waves. Her mouth, when she tried to sing a protest, filled with seawater. She choked and tried to cough it away, but it continued to pour in, filling her throat and then her lungs until she was so weighted with it that she sank beneath the surface.

She woke up gasping, her eyes sticky with salt.

"Are you okay?" Än asked, propped up on one elbow and looking nervous.

Marguerite nodded and pushed herself up.

They broke camp silently and had mounted before Än spoke, breaking their silence. "I'm sorry about yesterday. I thought you — you seemed okay with it at the time."

"The kissing?" Marguerite asked, after more than a moment's review of the previous night.

Än nodded.

"I was — I *am* okay with it."

"You seem upset."

Marguerite shrugged, fiddling with the scarf around her hair, glad that Än couldn't face her so that she wouldn't have to force herself to meet her eyes. "I had strange dreams. It happens. I don't think it had anything to do with you."

"If you're sure," Än didn't sound sure herself.

Marguerite wondered if she should kiss her again, just to reassure her. Wondered if you *could* kiss on horseback without falling off, or if she'd have to dismount, and if that would be awkward.

She didn't get a chance to try. Nahr took off, as much as Nahr ever did take off. It felt strange to put her arms around Än's waist now, although it shouldn't have. She was pretty sure it should feel good to put your arms around someone you cared for. And she supposed she had to care for Än because surely you were only supposed to kiss people you cared about.

She wondered what they were to each other. People in books who kissed and called each other beautiful were usually married or at least about to get married. She was pretty sure she and Än weren't married because marriage involved a ceremony, she knew that much, and she didn't think they were about to get married because she was pretty sure you were supposed to know before it happened. She was also pretty sure that she didn't want to get married, at least not right now. Marriage seemed to involve a lot of complicated emotions, and Marguerite had worked out by now that she wasn't very good with other people's emotions. Wasn't really good with her own, come to think of it, except anger. Anger was always a friend.

Maybe when Än had said they would take it slow, she had meant that they would get married a long, long time from now. That might be all right.

They didn't say much for most of the night, but it was a more comfortable silence than it had been before. She didn't have much to say, and neither, apparently, did Än. She was glad that she could be quiet with Än. She was glad that they could be quiet together and that she could still know Än was there.

They were getting good at making camp together. Än set up the tent, leaving Marguerite to care for Nahr. The horse thrust her nose into her hair, snuffling deeply. Marguerite sighed and stroked her cheek. Nahr had been worse than useless around the bandits, but she'd been helpful during the journey. She was no Caravel. She wasn't even Catseye. But she was really rather a nice horse in the end.

"Can I kiss you?" Än asked, once they had eaten and doused the fire, the sun just brushing the horizon.

"Yes," said Marguerite immediately, who had been wondering if they would kiss again. Who now wondered if they would have to ask permission every time they kissed one another. The idea sounded tedious.

The second kiss was nicer than the first. Än's mouth moved against hers, and, she realized, she could move her own mouth against Än's. She could even part her lips or change the angle of their connection. Än tasted like the meal they had just eaten. It wasn't a particularly nice taste on another's lips, but the warmth of her mouth made up for it.

They held hands when they settled down in bed together. Än half turned to face her, and Marguerite, after a moment's thought, mirrored her. Än's breath ghosted across her face when she closed her eyes. It was a strange touch, almost like wind, but so very much softer and moist in a way even ocean air hadn't been, tempered as it always was with salt. For the first time, she had trouble falling asleep and had to force herself to close her eyes instead of checking that Än was still there.

She dreamed of rain, hard rain, rain that didn't nurture the earth so much as beat it down, rain falling to the rhythm of a military drum. She woke, tense and sore and sweating, and for a moment, doubted that she had woken at all. Her dreams seemed to have followed her waking mind into the desert. She heard the pounding of rain on the tent's roof.

Chapter Nineteen

She had been caught, once or twice in her life, in that place suspended between awake and dreaming, like a beach caught between tide and cliff. And so she didn't move. Some time during the day, she had shifted to lie on her back. She remained there, listening to the beat of the rain, waiting for the sound to shift into the moan of the wind or the pattering of grains of sand or whatever other noise had conjured rain in her mind.

The rain didn't quiet, and she became aware, eventually, that she couldn't be half dreaming. She had never been sticky in dreams or felt the ridges of a tangled blanket digging into her back. She opened her eyes, and they came apart easily or at least willingly, although crusted salt from sleeping tears pulled a little at her eyelashes. It was daytime, the height of daytime it must be, because the interior of the tent was, for a tent, bright. She could see the shadows of something spattering the roof and knew it must be water by the way it slid down. She shook her head slightly and the last dredges of sleep cleared from her mind.

She turned. Än was sitting up beside her, her head tilted to the sky. Even in the shadowy interior of the tent, Marguerite could see the tension in the lines of her body and the way her fists clenched in her bedding. It was a strange position for one who professed to love the water.

"Rain," she said aloud, to let Än know she was awake and to nudge her into speech.

Än glanced down at her. Her eyes were wide and dark, the way Eyas had looked when she started at shadows.

"There shouldn't be," Än whispered. It wasn't an intimate little noise. It sounded more like Än was trying to conceal her speech, not from Marguerite but from something outside.

It felt strange to lie back when Än was so alert. She sat up, folding her arms across her knees.

"Why not?" she asked, not bothering to lower her own voice. In the rain, even in the desert, she was sure she had nothing to fear. "It rains here. You like it."

Än's expression tightened for a moment, and then she seemed to realize that Marguerite was only asking for information, not making an accusation. She chewed her lip and then shrugged a little, a small, helpless gesture.

"It feels wrong," she said. "I don't know if I can explain it more than that to someone who doesn't know the desert. It — it doesn't fall like desert rain. The pattern is wrong."

Rain that fell wrong? Marguerite tossed her head in unconscious rejection. Rain fell in a thousand different ways, to a thousand different beats, fast and slow and soft and hard and sweet and cruel. How could any one of them be judged right or wrong? She shifted, pushing herself forward and nudging Nahr out of the way, so she could look out the tent's opening.

There was nothing wrong with the rain. She had half wondered if Än had seen something that she hadn't, if she would discover the rain falling from the ground to the sky instead of the sky to the ground or some other strangeness. But it was a familiar rain that met her eyes, a rain that she had seen fall hundreds of times from her cliff. She held out a hand. The drops felt like water and tasted — perhaps a little less of dust than most of the water she had sipped in the desert but otherwise, just as water ought to.

She slipped fully back into the tent and shrugged at Än.

"Seems fine to me." The last word ended in a yawn. Surprised, Marguerite only covered the end of it. She was, now that she thought of it, tired. Very tired. It had been a long and difficult few days, and the rhythm of rain on the roof was a comfort. "It's still day," she said. "I'm going back to sleep."

None of the worry left Än's face, but she nodded. Marguerite crawled back to her bedding and curled up, letting the sound of rain carry her away to the seashore. When waking rain became sleeping storm she didn't know.

She woke at the turn of night. The rain still beat at their roof. Än was sitting up again, awake first or never having lain down at all, she didn't know. Her eyes were still afraid.

They ate inside the tent and drank, Än from a waterskin, Marguerite from a palm cupped under the sky.

"We can't travel in this," Än said when they finished. "We'll have to stay under shelter. It's all right. Rain during this season never lasts very long." Her voice shook a little. She didn't sound like she believed her own reassurances.

Marguerite shrugged. She didn't see what was so wrong with traveling through rain, but she supposed Än had her reasons. Perhaps Nahr didn't care for it. The horse certainly seemed distressed, the whites of her eyes clearly visible against her coat now blackened from the rain. Marguerite wondered if she should comfort her and then decided against it. Nahr was Än's. Än would know what she needed.

She missed Caravel.

That wasn't a useful thought. Nothing about this situation was useful. They couldn't travel, she had cared for herself already, and she had no horse to look after. It was too dark to sew, even if she had anything to mend, and she had no tack to clean. With nothing else to do, she lay back down and fell asleep again.

Än shook her awake perhaps midway through the night, the rain still dancing above them. She blinked up at her, or at least the outline of her in the dark of the tent, head still fuzzy after being abruptly pulled from the ocean.

"Are we going after all?" she asked.

Än shook her head. "No. I was worried about you. Are you feeling okay?"

Marguerite squinted her eyes and took a quick mental inventory of herself. The fog of sleep was still there, but it was quickly rolling away. She ached for Caravel, but the weight, though heavy, was not too much to carry. She hadn't moved much and had ridden hard before, so her muscles were a little tight. Her hair was getting twisted enough to be uncomfortable, and at some point, she should probably work out something to do with it besides cramming it under a scarf. But these were all minor problems, not worth being woken over.

"Why shouldn't I be?" she asked.

Än smiled, looking a little embarrassed. Marguerite was glad that she seemed to be learning to recognize when she wasn't trying to be combative.

"You've been sleeping a lot, that's all."

"There's nothing else to do," Marguerite pointed out, trying to keep her voice cool and neutral. "My hair is tangled but otherwise, I'm fine."

Än laughed a bit. The sound was less pleasant than normal, the bells in it corroded and harsh. There was tension, still, in her body.

"Do you want to borrow my comb?" she asked. She paused and lowered her head.

Marguerite thought she recognized the shape of a blush in her hands, although her face wasn't visible in the dark.

"If you want," Än said, "I could braid your hair back for you."

A braid. Än braided her hair back often, so clearly it was a useful style in the desert. It had been some time since anyone had brushed her hair for her. Mama Bella had done it when Marguerite first went to live with her and refused to do it herself. It had not been a pleasant experience, and Marguerite had quickly taken over the task. It hadn't been a pleasant task when she did it herself either, but pain self-inflicted was always more tolerable than pain inflicted by another.

She wondered if it would hurt to have Än brush her hair. Mama Bella hadn't always been gentle, and she hadn't always been patient, but she had known Marguerite's limits better than she herself had. Än, she thought, knew her in ways that Mama Bella had not. But she wasn't sure she knew her in that way. Anyway, it didn't matter. A braid sounded like a nice thing, and her hair had to be less knotted now than it had been back then, without the storm to twine it together and the salt to encrust it.

She nodded and turned, letting Än move behind her and gather a handful of her hair. She ran the comb lightly over it first, barely letting the tines touch it. On the next sweep, she was bolder, burying the comb deep in Marguerite's mane and pulling it through. The sweep lasted only a moment before it snagged and Marguerite yelped.

"Sorry!" Än said behind her.

Marguerite shrugged, philosophical about the pain. She had heard that, with regular brushing, hair never became too knotted. But she had never experienced it, never much bothered to experience it. Tangled hair and the occasional taming of it, when it got too wild, was almost as familiar as the sea.

Despite her calm, her initial reaction seemed to have worried Än. The comb in her hair became gentler, and Än used her fingers to slowly work some of the knots loose before the comb teased them out. It was a long process (she thought, anyway. She was starting to suspect she didn't have the strongest sense of time passing). Though it wasn't particularly comfortable to sit still (mostly still) for so long, she was unbothered. They had nowhere to be, and she had a vague feeling that it was good for Än to have something to concentrate on, rather than worrying about the continued rain.

Eventually, the comb stopped stuttering through her hair and began to cut through it smoothly. Än seemed to judge that to be the finish. The comb was removed, there was a pause, and then Än's hands were dividing her hair into three. She twisted the strands together so quickly that Marguerite couldn't follow the pattern and then tied off the end with something.

"All done," she said, giving the end of the braid a pat, her fingers just brushing Marguerite's waist.

Marguerite reached behind her, running her hand down the braid. It was strange, to have her hair, which usually whipped around as it wished, condensed into one place. She felt rather like a ship that had just been rigged. The tie felt like a small piece of leather, tied tight around the hair. She tossed her head a little, feeling the braid lash behind her.

"Careful!" Än yelped and she felt the other girl fall back.

She swiveled and reached behind her, catching Än's wrist. "Did I hit you?" she asked.

"Yes," said Än. "But I pulled your hair first, so I guess we're even."

"I guess," said Marguerite, mostly because she was pretty sure being even was a good place to be with someone you were kissing and might marry someday.

"Thank you," she added, because now that she was starting to get used to the braid's weight, it was quite comfortable.

"You're welcome," Än said, sounding pleased.

Marguerite was still holding her wrist. She let her hand run down Än's arm until her fingers met Än's. They twisted together, a different kind of braid but, Marguerite hoped, just as sturdy. She lay down and pulled Än to her so they shared a single piece of bedding. Under the beat of the rain, their breaths mingled.

———— «◊» ————

She woke feeling nauseous and sweaty. It was day again and still the rain poured. She wasn't sure how much of the night Än had spent with her. The other girl was now sitting at the entrance to the tent, looking out into the desert.

"We have to go," she said, having apparently heard Marguerite stir. "I — I should be with Grandmother. She'll need my help."

Marguerite sat up and moved to join Än at the entrance, cupping a palm out in the rain and drinking from it.

"Why?" she asked. "Saqr knows what rain is."

Än turned to look at her. Her face was tense again.

"This rain is strange. She'll need my help to understand why. I might be able to help fix things."

"Fix things?" Marguerite asked. "Why?"

It was another of those moments, like when she had told Än about her childhood, that she felt like they were speaking to each other across a chasm. Än's eyes were wide, the gold rims gleaming.

"If you tap into the energies of the world to do magic, you have a duty to steward your home," she said, clearly repeating a lesson. "You have to take care of things, make sure every force stays in balance," she added since Marguerite's confusion must have shown on her face. "You do magic. You must have done the same, where you came from."

Marguerite thought about it, because Än deserved that much. But not for long. The ocean was the ocean, vast and terrible. Even she, whom it loved and obeyed, was a small thing beside it.

She shrugged and shook her head. "Where I come from, things look after themselves."

The answer must have surprised Än, given her widened eyes, but she didn't protest. Instead, she shook herself, as though shaking off the conversation, and dug inside her bag.

"Besides," she said. "We're running out of supplies."

Marguerite didn't point out that as long as the rain fell, they had water. Än had seemed curiously reluctant to even allow the rain to touch her, much less drink it. She forced herself out into it now, the tension in her body so thick it seemed to twang as she slowly pushed herself out of the tent. From one heartbeat to the next, she was drenched, her hair, even braided back, hanging lank across her shoulders, her clothes molding around her body. They were kissing each other now so Marguerite felt she had permission to appreciate the sight while she ate a quick meal and Än prepared Nahr for the journey. The mare was clearly unhappy. She stood, shuddering slightly, her eyes pinned so flatly against her head that it seemed she was trying to drive them into her skull. It seemed that nothing of the desert liked this rain. The tent was soaked, and it took both of them pushing with all their strength to roll it up (Marguerite, at least, pushed with all her strength, and if Än had any in reserve, it wasn't obvious from her heaving shoulders). The mare balked at having the sopping bundle roped to her back, and since it required both of them to heave it up, they had to try to block her in from both sides to get it on. Marguerite was grateful that they had waited so long that it was day again. With the sun blocked by rain, there was little heat, and she couldn't imagine trying to maneuver all of their supplies together in the dark.

Finally, finally, they were ready to move, and Än swung into the saddle, pulling Marguerite up behind her. She had scarcely settled herself before Än drove her heels into Nahr's sides, and they were off. She could feel the tightness of Än's body and knew that she was trying to urge the mare to a quicker pace. It didn't work. The mare seemed to be struggling in the wet sand, sinking in and then stumbling around. It was an uncomfortable ride, even more uncomfortable than her first experience with a horse, which at least had the advantage of being in circumstances that Catseye's equipment was designed for. The saddle was slick and slippery in the rain, and her clothes squelched uncomfortably every time she shifted, which was often as she tried to move in time with the mare's lurching, usually barely managing to keep from falling. It would be faster, she thought with a certain degree of disgust, to walk.

Apparently Än agreed because she pulled Nahr to a stop and jumped off, holding a hand up to Marguerite to indicate that she wanted her to do the same. Marguerite did so, although more slowly, carefully letting herself down the stirrup leathers, rivulets of water trickling down her arms and through her bangs, charting a tiny river map across her skin.

"She's having trouble," Än said, raising her voice a little. "Lightening the load will help. Do you mind walking?"

Marguerite shook her head and meant it. She had not enjoyed the ride, and though it squelched uncomfortably, wet sand was less treacherous than dry. It shifted but only downward or occasionally, when she shifted her weight wrong, to the side. She strode forward easily.

Än seemed to be having more trouble. Her soft boots, though they made her steady-footed on the sand she knew, were not built for the sodden ground. She slipped and stumbled, mirroring the struggles of her horse. The third time she disappeared from Marguerite's peripheral vision, and Marguerite turned to see her flailing around, Marguerite reached out to catch her arm. Their eyes met. Marguerite wondered if she dared and decided that she did. She took Nahr's reins, shifting them to her right hand, and then tucked Än's arm in hers. Än started, and then her hold tightened. They proceeded in that manner, Marguerite dragging both Än and Nahr with her through the muck.

———— «◊» ————

The journey back to what Än called the sanctuary was long and uncomfortable. Both of the desert dwellers continued to struggle, and by the end of the fourth day, even Marguerite was beginning to feel strained. They pushed themselves as hard as they could, even jogging when the footing was steady enough, and slept only when they were too tired to continue, not even bothering to set up the tent. Instead, already soaked as they were, they laid a single cover on the sand so they wouldn't sleep directly in the muck. They kissed only once a day, as they lay down to sleep. There were, Marguerite was discovering, different kinds of kisses. These ones felt like gratitude and like comfort.

On the fifth day, Än pulled on Marguerite's hand. She had been doing that a lot, these past few days, but the tug this time was deliberate, and when Marguerite turned, she was still standing upright.

"I can open up the way from here," she said. "To the sanctuary, I mean. We're almost there."

Marguerite snorted and wondered if the rain had scrambled Än's navigation skills, as it did every so often to birds. She didn't know how far she had actually gone, on her own and then to the glass city, but she knew that a few days walking under difficult conditions did not equal travel on the fastest horse in the desert or even a slow mare like Nahr.

"We haven't gone that far," she said.

"No," Än agreed. "But there are … shortcuts through the desert. Now, stand back."

Marguerite did, moving to stand by Nahr's side and giving the mare's dripping forehead a stroke (Nahr looked so miserable nowadays, soaked and sand-streaked, that Marguerite was feeling positively benign toward her). Än squared her shoulders and began to mutter. She didn't know if they were the same words that Malik had used when he had first brought her to his family, what now seemed so long ago, but the cadence was similar. The effect, though, was decidedly less impressive. The desert had danced for Malik. It did not dance for Än or, at least, the dance it did was mangled and tortured, drawn out and weak. Sand rose shuddering into the air, without spirals or dips, and fell heavily, thudding hard into the ground. Still, it worked. The sanctuary rose before them and already a dark figure hurried to meet them.

It resolved quickly into Malik, storm-drenched, the smile on his face warm but his eyes worried. He and Än met each other, embracing tightly, sinking into one another until their two figures seemed to meld into one. Then he stepped back. His eyes met hers and he extended one arm to her, his palms open, his body wide. An invitation to her as well.

She wouldn't hug him. There were things she still wasn't ready for, maybe would never be ready for. But he had offered, and he had offered as soon as he saw her. His eyes hadn't moved to check for a great white shape behind her. So she gave him her hand and was grateful when he merely squeezed it and didn't pull her in. Then, and only then, did she see him note that they were accompanied by only one horse. He turned his eyes back to her.

"You let him go?"

She nodded. He squeezed her hand again.

"That must have been hard."

She shrugged, unsure what to do with his sympathy, although perhaps she should have expected it. Än knew about magic. But Malik had been the one to give her horses. Perhaps he alone really understood what she had given up. In the end, she squeezed back, just a little, and then let his hand go.

He and Än stepped back as well, giving each other looks that were clearly meaningful.

"Grandmother wants you," Malik said.

"I'd better go to her, then," Än said. She turned, caught Marguerite's hand, and swung it slightly, before making her way to the large tent. Malik turned to Marguerite.

"Want to help with the horses?" he asked. "You can groom Catseye, while I try to get Nahr a little less bedraggled."

"Okay," said Marguerite, after a moment's thought.

Catseye and Eyas, sheltering under the sanctuary's tarp, were clearly restless but were relatively dry. They made a happy noise of greeting as they approached, and while Marguerite knew it was likely for their companion and for their caretaker, she allowed herself to believe that it was for her as well. Malik immediately went to work on Nahr with cloths and brushes, and the mare's ears slowly rose from their position pasted flat to her head. It took her a few minutes before she could work on Catseye. Eyas, clearly bored, kept butting against her and demanding attention until she stepped beside her and scratched her neck so hard that Eyas's head lolled to the side. Catseye greeted her more gently, lightly touching his nose to her shoulder. His black coat was sleek and shining, wet sand not even splattered on his ankles. She ran a brush over his side anyway.

She had never cared for Caravel like this. She had never groomed his blindingly white coat or checked his hard and glittering hooves for rocks. She had fed and watered him only rarely (whether he needed it at all or whether he was just humoring her, she still didn't know). He probably didn't need the care, but she wished suddenly that she had done it anyway. It was nice, to care for an animal you loved. He had carried her on his back wherever she wanted and stayed with her until far past the point when she no longer needed him. She should have been more tender with him.

Thinking of Caravel made her chest ache in a way that previously only memories of the sea had. They were the same, she supposed. Things she had loved, had tamed, and then had lost. She reminded herself that she had given Caravel up willingly, but it had been only half a choice, really. If she could have justified keeping him, she would have.

A blast of warm air to her cheek startled her, and she realized she had stopped brushing some time ago. Catseye's broad nose touched her cheek and he breathed on her again. His breath smelled of small, growing things. Caravel's had smelled only of dust.

She turned and put her arms around the great black neck.

She didn't know how long she stood there, pressing her forehead against the horse, until Malik cleared his throat. She lifted her head slightly and glared at him, glad suddenly that she was soaked and he wouldn't be able to see any extra water on her face.

"It's okay to mourn," he said gently. "He was the wind. But he was also your horse."

"I'm tired of feeling sad," she whispered.

"I know," he said. His arm was really around his horse, not around her, and so she closed her eyes and let it happen.

——— ‹›› ———

She didn't see Saqr or Än at all for the rest of the day, although there was a strange tension in the air like the beginning of a storm that, after some thought, she attributed to them. She and Malik finished with the horses, then Malik pulled food and water from his tent, which he had shifted so that its entrance stood directly beside the lean-to. He offered the tent to her to change into something dry (she shrugged and stripped down where she was, letting him splutter and turn away) and then to sleep in so she could stay more or less beneath shelter. Before she could ask, he assured her that he would sleep out with the horses.

His tent was about the size of the one she had shared with Än, although much more crowded. One corner held a small wooden chest, carved with images of — what else? — horses and, to be fair to him, other animals she recognized as desert creatures. The rest of the tent was filled with bits and pieces of horse equipment, brushes, saddles, and miscellaneous strips of leather whose purpose was unclear. It was, she thought wryly, a very good thing that she had gotten used to the smell of horse because his tent reeked of it.

Perhaps it was grief, perhaps she missed the feeling of Än lying next to her, or perhaps it was merely the smell, but her rest was fitful and disturbed. She dreamed of a storm, as she often did, but this one was raging, not with her but around her, thrusting against her, dragging her ragdoll body until it felt like a chasm was opening beneath her feet that it wanted to thrust her into.

She woke disoriented. There was something very wrong, something missing, an emptiness filling the tent that she couldn't immediately place.

The rain, she realized. Its steady rhythm had stopped.

She didn't understand why that pleased her a little.

Chapter Twenty

Än's face was the first thing she saw when she rolled out of the tent (Än's body, she supposed, to be precise, but her eyes quickly found her face). The smile when their eyes met warmed her in a way she realized the desert air had not. Än extended a hand and helped her to her feet.

"The rain's stopped," she said, because she knew that had mattered to Än. Än smiled again, but it was a tense little smile and her bones stood out in jagged lines from her skin.

"What's wrong?"

"I—" She was learning to recognize the difference between Än prevaricating and Än seeking the words to explain. This was the latter. Instead, Än took her hand and tugged her out from under the shelter and out into the desert.

It was green and lush. She had expected that. It was exactly what had happened last time, and for a moment, she didn't understand Än's concern. The desert dry and dead after the rain, now that would be cause for worry. But the desert blooming? Green stretched as far as she could see across the horizon.

It was, now that she thought about it, a much darker green than she remembered from the last rain, a green so dark that in the shadows cast by the dunes, it appeared black. She knelt and inspected the plants more closely. They looked different too. The leaves were not small and neat but long and sinuous, trailing across the sand and entangling with one another to form not a strange garden but a thick mat. She had seen plants like this before, she was fairly certain, but she couldn't place them.

She wondered idly how bad of an idea it would be to taste one of them.

Pretty bad, she decided. She looked up at Än instead.

"Not proper desert plants?"

Än shook her head. It had been a while since Marguerite had seen her hair dry. She had missed that flash of red every time it moved.

"They're like nothing I've ever seen," Än said. "I thought when the rain ended…"

She trailed off. Marguerite didn't like the tired, tense look on her face. She knew now that people could comfort each other through physical touch. An embrace seemed like a little much. She stood and gave Än a pat on the shoulder. It brought a smile, though strained, to the other girl's face. She caught Marguerite's hand in a tight grip for a moment.

"Grandmother should be awake by now. Come wash and have breakfast with us."

She followed Än back to the sanctuary. She had forgotten, almost, the little crevice that was like an altar to desert water. The pool was as full as ever. She let it splash on her face and took a sip. The taste had improved, or maybe she was just used to the stale water she had carried with her. There was less dust in it. It tasted fresher. It tasted welcoming. She had missed this place, she supposed, and now that she had given up Caravel, she thought she had earned the right to be here.

There was no one waiting to escort her to breakfast when she emerged, but that was all right, she knew the way now. She let herself into the large tent. It looked much the same, even to the people arranged around the table. They all looked up as she entered and she swallowed her surprise. Saqr had always appeared ravaged, her face more like eroded rock than flesh. But it had been a good kind of ravaging, signs of a life lived long and every trial overcome. Her face had resembled a cliff, but one that still stood proud against the elements.

The face turned to Marguerite now was that of an old, old woman. Her skin had seemed strong before, even solid. It was as thin as sea foam now and an ashen color, closer to Marguerite's own tone than that of her grandchildren. Her eyes had always been foggy, but now they seemed damaged, clouds cutting off any warmth in them. She had reminded Marguerite, at first meeting, of a crab. She still did but not, now, a crab scuttling across the ocean floor but one washed up on a beach. But then she smiled and for the first time, Saqr's smile when she looked at her expressed no curiosity or wry humor but merely kindly welcome.

"Hello, lady-who-admits-to-loving-nothing," she said and there was strength still in her voice, though it shook a little. "My grandchildren tell me you did a hard thing and let the wind go."

The response that rose first to Marguerite's mind was to tell Saqr that she had done harder, and anyway, Saqr had better not try to take credit for Marguerite's choice because none of it had been about her, thank you very much. But she suppressed it. She was tired of sparring with everyone she met. Saqr had sent her away, but she had fought bandits and seen a city that sang and gotten kissed and someone had come for her so it had worked out okay, and anyway, if Saqr truly saw herself as a steward of the desert, as Än had said, even Marguerite could grudgingly admit that her actions made sense. Also, if she was maybe going to marry Än someday, then she was pretty sure that meant Saqr would be some sort of relation to her, and she should probably refrain from antagonizing her, where possible.

"Yes," she said. "It was hard." There was more she could have said but she swallowed it.

They all seemed surprised that she had answered more or less honestly and without poison under her tongue. Saqr held her hand out, and, hesitantly, wondering what it was with these people and holding hands, Marguerite laid her fingers across it. It was more like a chunk of coral than the hand she had held before.

"My grandchildren said I was too harsh on you," Saqr said. "I am glad, now, that they came for you. You are welcome in this place."

"Thank you," said Marguerite, after a moment of very deep thought. It was the first time she had ever said the words that she was pretty sure someone wanted to hear. Saqr smiled and Malik smiled and Än, when she sat down, smiled and squeezed her hand under the table.

They ate quickly, the happiness of their (probably momentary) truce overshadowed by the strangeness of the desert's behavior. As soon as they had finished, Saqr and Än rose and slipped out to inspect the thick green plants. Marguerite stayed, with some vague thought that she would help Malik with the horses, but he rose, too, and said that he intended to have a long and proper wash, since he had been busy calming them upon waking. With nothing else to do, she wandered out to find the women.

Though the sun was well up and the day was hot, the plants hadn't wilted at all. They gleamed, a sickly, oily green. Än looked worried again. It was hard to pick out tension in Saqr's posture since movement in general was obviously difficult for her, but she seemed a little more hunched over than normal. They were murmuring together when she joined them.

They both lifted their heads to greet her immediately. She wasn't sure if it was manners or it was just that neither wanted her to hear their conversation. Än's face was starting to resemble Saqr's, drawn and tight and sallow, her cheekbones and the point of her chin standing out sharply on her face. She smiled a little, though, in greeting, and though it distorted her face so she looked more like a leering corpse than a pretty girl, there was happiness in it. Marguerite didn't smile back exactly, but she nodded in greeting to both of them.

"Bad?" she asked. Saqr nodded, and Marguerite fancied she could hear the rasping of old bones together.

"It's like nothing I've ever seen." The old woman shook herself all over, much like a horse did. "Än and I have conjuring to do."

"Can I come?" Marguerite asked. "I'll be quiet."

One filmy old eye rolled up at her, but Saqr was gracious enough to not point out that this was not much of a promise, since Marguerite rarely spoke to her anyway.

"Very well," she said. "If there's harm you can do, I cannot see it. And it might help to have the eyes of someone around whose mind runs through the strange, twisted channels yours does."

That was probably quite an insulting thing to say, but, since Marguerite tended to protest only those things which she saw as untrue, she accepted it as cheerfully as she ever accepted everything.

They walked back to the tent together, Saqr leaning heavily on her granddaughter's arm, Marguerite pointedly looking anywhere else so she could claim she hadn't noticed the need to help. They made their way into the tent, Saqr pointing Marguerite to a quiet corner where presumably she would be out of the way. She flopped down, watching as Saqr let herself down slowly in front of the table they ate from and directed Än as to which plants to pull from the little carved chest. It was a double handful this time, poured into an enormous clay bowl covered with markings that might have matched the ones carved on the cliff or might have just come from the same language. The two women sat across from each other and began to speak softly together. It wasn't a conversation. It was almost like a song — the intonation was right — but there was no music in it, or at least nothing that Marguerite could recognize. It was more like a chant. An invocation: that might be the word.

Saqr said something, sharper than her previous words, and the bowl burst into flames, delicate curls that just brushed past the rim of the bowl but which were hot enough so that Marguerite could feel them even from where she sat. Saqr raised her hand and dropped one of the strange leaves into the bowl. The fire arched over the offering, forming a second bowl inside the first, and then a soft tendril of smoke wound out, smelling flower-like, a sweet growing plant scent. It was joined by two more tendrils, and all three danced and wound around one another, forming delicate spiraling patterns in the air, each held for less time than a single breath.

It was beautiful, at least if one was fond of smoke and fire instead of sea and wind. Even Marguerite could admit its grace. She watched, leaning forward slightly, to see what the bowl would do next. But she was disappointed. Smoke simply continued to spiral up, forming shapes that must have meant something to Än and Saqr, given the intense way they watched them, but meaning little to Marguerite. The air in the tent was becoming heavy and close, and she dropped her cheek into her palm, falling into a half daze waiting for something exciting to happen.

She started into full wakefulness when the tent entrance shifted, seemingly on its own. No large male shape smelling faintly of horse filled it, but a quick look around the tent told her a guest had entered. One of the foxes had slipped through the opening, its dully gleaming silver coat a near-perfect match for the smoke still winding up from the bowl. It padded up to Saqr, its glistening red eyes fixed on her without any sign of fear, and allowed her to lay a hand on its head. She bent over, and they put their faces so close they were almost touching. Saqr's mouth moved, though Marguerite couldn't hear even the hiss of a whisper, and then the fox barked, once, twice, a high keen more like the shriek of timber on rock than any wolf she had ever heard. Its body tensed, and then it slipped from the tent, smoke seeming to billow from its coat as it went.

"The fox says that it has seen strange things," Saqr said, in a language that Marguerite could understand (courtesy or convenience, she didn't know). She bent back to the fire and gestured, murmuring something low but commanding, in a voice like the first rumbling of thunder.

For a moment, the fire danced as it had all along. Then it died and thick smoke began to billow from the bowl.

There was no sweet plant scent this time. Marguerite burst into a fit of coughing and, hand over her mouth, leaped up and ran for the exit. She cannoned out and spent a few moments gasping and gagging, the wind picking up slightly and pressing against her as though trying to fan the smoke away. She looked up when it seemed her distressed noises were being echoed. Än bent over beside her, also retching, shoulders also heaving. Saqr was not coughing but, looking at her, Marguerite almost wished she had been. She stood still and upright, but the cliffs of her face had crumbled.

Marguerite said nothing at first, even after she had recovered enough to talk. She was starting to find the words, the words that said both what she thought and what she meant without turning her companions against her under normal circumstances. But she had no words yet for this. And, glancing over at Än, also pale, also silent, she wasn't sure there *were* words.

When the silence stretched on, she spoke anyway, because someone had to and she, at least, had a history of being unkind without really meaning to. Perhaps insensitivity would be forgiven in her, as it wouldn't be in someone closer to the situation.

"Bad?" she asked. Just because she had decided to talk didn't mean she was going to say a lot.

"I've never seen anything like this before," Saqr said. Her voice had always been a croak, but it had suited her, the deep booming sound of a toad or a raven, a creature that was meant to speak in croaks. Now it was tinged with an exhaustion that even Marguerite could feel, and each syllable ended in a jagged edge.

"Nothing too bad has happened, really," Än said suddenly. In contrast to Saqr, her voice had gone high and shrill. She was speaking more loudly than Marguerite had ever heard, as if she could shout down their worries if she raised her voice enough. "No one has been hurt. Things are just strange. We'll rest, maybe eat something, and try again."

Though she seemed to be speaking mostly to Saqr, her eyes were fixed on Marguerite. The gold was soft, not gleaming but shining dully, dimmed but still vital. There was a pleading in her face, for what Marguerite didn't know. She responded anyway, because it seemed better to guess and get it wrong than ignore it.

"I'm hungry," she said, more because it seemed safe to agree with Än's last statement than because she wanted food.

She didn't think she had quite gotten it right, but she must have gotten close because Än smiled and some of the tarnish wore off the gold in her eyes.

Saqr sighed. They both started and turned back to her. She still looked unwell, but she was smiling too.

"My granddaughter has some wisdom after all," Saqr said. "You're right. Things are not dire yet. We'll sit and eat. We will sit with the horses while the tent airs out. I haven't shared fruit with Eyas in too long." Nodding to herself, she began to make her way slowly around the rock, the two girls following.

"Happiness can come even in bad circumstances," she added, dropping her voice a little.

Än's shoulders jerked and a flush spread across her face. Marguerite did not respond, less interested in cryptic pronouncements than she was in turning back for a moment to watch the tent. She could no longer see smoke billowing from it. Perhaps the problem had a more prosaic solution. It seemed that the tent was not as waterproof as her own and had not dried from the rain yet; she could see dampness along its edges.

Malik was sitting in the center of the shadow cast by the horses' canopy, Catseye's head resting against his chest as he stroked along the horse's cheek and neck. He rose to greet them, his expression closed off and troubled. He must have seen the distress in their faces (unsurprising, really — if even Marguerite could see it, it would be obvious to a man like him). She had hoped he would be an oasis — he had seemed even-keeled; now his expression darkened to match theirs.

"Something went wrong," he said, not even bothering to make it a question.

Än and Saqr nodded. Something in him seemed to crack and break. Marguerite stepped back. She had seen Malik angry and Malik in over his head and trying to handle it. But she had never, even when he had threatened to strike her, seen him so emotionally raw. There was a look on his face she couldn't categorize, some maelstrom of pain and fear and anger and sorrow. His hands flexed at his sides, helplessly gripping a world that he seemed suddenly not to understand. The horses seemed to feel his distress. Catseye tossed his head and rolled his eyes back into his skull, barely settling when Malik laid a hand on his side.

"What is it?" Saqr asked sharply.

He opened his mouth, closed it, and then twisted his hand in Catseye's mane as if that would stabilize him.

"The water in the sanctuary has gone bad," he said. "I knew I couldn't interrupt a working. I didn't *want* to. I thought you would fix it or at least know why."

Marguerite watched them with morbid curiosity. All three were pale. Än wrapped her arms around her midsection, shaking slightly. Malik, having shared his bad news, turned back to Catseye and murmured to the horse, who pranced nervously in place and kept butting his chest as though asking for comfort. Some of the exhaustion vanished from Saqr's face, to be replaced by grim determination.

"What's wrong with it?" she asked. "Are you sure?"

Malik nodded, Catseye nodding along with his movement. "I'm sure. I went for a wash after we broke our fast. It's — I don't know how to describe it. I've never tasted the like before. It's rancid. It burns your throat when you swallow and sickens your stomach."

Saqr bit her lip, the movement looking more like she was attacking herself than a simple sign of worry. "How much water do we have stored?"

"Two days worth," said Malik. "Perhaps stretching to three, if Marguerite continues her refusal to be sensible and drink enough." He quirked his lips at her, a desiccated shadow of the mocking grins he had so often shot her way.

If she hadn't been so irritated, Marguerite would have been a little bit touched that he was still willing to joke with her.

"Two days isn't much time," Saqr murmured, more to herself than to any of them. "We'll have to decide quickly if it's wiser to stay and try to fix it or if we should seek other water sources."

"That might also be tainted," Än said.

Saqr nodded at her. "You've always been better with water spells. It speaks to you as it never has to me."

Än darted a glance at Marguerite, her face flushing again, before she looked back at Saqr and nodded.

"Fetch a bowl of water. We'll try a variation on a rain scrying. Nothing else has told us why the desert is ill. Perhaps the water will."

Än nodded and hurried away. Saqr patted Malik's arm and then turned toward Marguerite.

"Will you be joining us again?" she asked.

Marguerite, who at some point in the conversation had been approached by Eyas and now had her arms wrapped firmly around the mare's neck, looked at her and made a head movement that was half nod, half shake.

"Will it get smoky again?" she asked. "I didn't like that much."

The old woman made a movement that felt like a denial, which she abruptly cut off.

"Normally I would say no," she said. "But I don't know anymore."

She had seemed in control before, the woman that Än and Malik so clearly admired and deferred to. She looked tired now and out of her depths. The ocean had never defied her, as the desert seemed to be defying Saqr, but she knew how it felt when the world suddenly didn't obey you when it should. It was that, more than any curiosity, that made her nod her head.

They walked back to the big tent together, slowly and carefully. Marguerite did not offer Saqr her arm, but she walked close enough that she was pretty sure she could catch her if she fell (well, slow her fall a little, anyway — Marguerite was realistic about her ability to grapple with another person).

Än was already in the tent when they got there, poking through the little wooden chest of drawers. The big metal bowl stood in the center of the small table, filled nearly to the brim with water. It didn't look rotten. The water was as clear as it had ever been, and she could pick out no unpleasant smell in the air around them. Saqr grabbed her arm in order to lower herself to her place at the table. Marguerite held herself rigid in terror that she would pitch the old woman to the ground. Saqr made it to her seat without mishap, and, because it was water and it was Än's magic and both of those things were a little bit hers, Marguerite made herself comfortable at the end of the table instead of in the tent corner. Both women glanced at her, but neither chased her away.

Än dropped a handful of plants into the bowl and murmured something. Marguerite remembered the last time she had watched Än work with water, the way the surface had dimpled as though under a rainstorm. It remained flat now and still, oddly so considering it must have been disturbed by what Än had dropped in. They all watched it in silence, Marguerite wondering how long they would have to stare at an unreactive bowl.

Her timing was good. The water suddenly shrank in the bowl, pulling away from the rim and dropping to the center, before just as suddenly swelling. It rose above the rim, waves and waves of it, far more than the bowl could possibly hold, spilling across the table until it ran over and soaked into Marguerite's lap. She yelped and Än jumped up.

"Sorry, sorry, I don't know what—" she said.

Saqr cut her off with a raised hand. Her head turned slowly toward Marguerite. Her face was twisted and ugly.

"It was *you,*" she hissed.

Chapter Twenty-One

Marguerite paused her efforts to dab water from her shirt and trousers.

"What was me?" she asked, shoulders drawing in a little. Saqr had been angry when she had seen Caravel, but there was something even worse in her face now. "I didn't ruin your working, I don't even know what you're doing, how could I?"

"Not the working," Saqr hissed. "The desert. We took you in and all this time—" Her voice cut off abruptly, sounding like she was choking.

Marguerite stared at her blankly.

"What are you *talking* about?" she asked, looking to Än for help. She drew back at the look on the other girl's face.

Än had always seemed uncomfortable when she and Saqr clashed or, when the clash was minor, wryly amused. Marguerite didn't understand the look on her face, but it frightened her. Än's eyes were the widest she had ever seen them, and the corners of her mouth were white.

"I should have known when you tamed the wind," Saqr continued. She wasn't shouting. Marguerite (probably) could have dealt with shouting. Her voice came out in a low, continuous snarl, a kettle boiling, a wolf threatening an intruder. "I did know. I saw that you were trouble, that we should never have taken you in. But my grandchildren convinced me that you didn't understand, that you were just *lost* and *scared.* That we should continue to care for you." Her eyes narrowed even more, glittering black specks in her face. "I was wrong about you, girl. You're not full of ice. You're *poison.* And now you've poisoned the desert as well."

Marguerite pushed herself to her feet. It should have been a hard, graceful, defiant movement. She got the defiant part, but her tunic snagged and she stumbled as she rose.

"You think *I* did this? Those weird plants and all that smoke and everything?" She shook her head wildly, wisps of hair pulling loose from her braid and sticking to her face. "You're *insane.*"

She looked again at Än, one hand almost rising from its clenched position at her side to grab at her. Än continued to watch her. Marguerite had seen those eyes once on a rabbit, half torn apart by wolves and still alive.

"Tell her," she demanded. "Tell her I've done nothing."

"She didn't," Än whispered. Her words were defensive, but her voice made it sound more like an accusation. "She *couldn't.*"

Marguerite chose to take them at face value.

"Of course I didn't."

She held Än's eyes. Saqr was the bigger threat. She knew this. But Än — Än had kissed her. If you kissed someone, you should believe they weren't in the process of destroying your home. Än's face twisted under Marguerite's regard.

Some half-formed memory dredged up from the deep, of two people who looked like Marguerite watching her with similar looks on their faces, the last expression she had ever seen from them.

She tore her eyes from Än's face.

"I didn't," she said again, not because she expected them to believe her but because to remain silent was to accept their accusations.

"You'll fix it," Saqr said into the tense silence, her words hard and commanding, unrelenting as the desert sun. "We took you in. We gave you our hospitality when we could have left you to die or killed you ourselves. So you will fix this monstrous thing you have done and perhaps someday you will prove that you deserved our mercy."

Marguerite felt her own mouth twist up. "So this is my *redemption*?" she inquired, ice ringing every syllable. "I repair what I have broken and thereby prove myself a better person?" She sniffed. "No thank you."

"You think this is a storybook?" Saqr snapped. "This isn't about you or some character arc. It's not my job to redeem you. I care only about saving the desert. If I could do it or if Än could, I would throw you to the foxes and be done with you."

"No, I don't think this is a storybook," Marguerite snarled. "Because I don't *have* a character arc because *I didn't do anything.*"

Her shoulders heaved but she wouldn't cry. Not for them. Not for this. She looked again at Än.

"You believe me." She didn't phrase it as a question. But they both knew that it was.

"They told me water was treacherous," Än whispered. "But you seemed to be trying to change..."

She wondered what the desert equivalent of a cliff was and if buzzards were as good to eat as albatross.

The tent opening shifted and then Malik came in, his presence freshening the air like an ocean breeze.

"Is everything okay?" he asked. "I heard yelling."

He smelled good, like horses and leather (and a bit like sweat, which wasn't a nice smell but was at least an honest one). She hadn't realized how tight and cloying the air in the tent was. She turned to him almost blindly and looked up into his face.

"She says I caused this," Marguerite said, feeling her voice pitch upward. "But I didn't. I didn't!" She hated the pleading she knew was in her face. Of all people, it had to be Malik she was pleading for help from (he was the best person to ask, said a part of her mind that had been dormant for a long, long time, a part that knew about people).

"I didn't," she said again and reached out to touch his sleeve. "Don't send me away. I didn't *do* anything."

He put his hand over hers and smiled down at her. It should have felt threatening, to have him hold her in place. But he touched her the way he touched his horses.

"I believe you," he said. He turned to face the women, Saqr raging, Än pale and distressed.

"I do," he addressed them calmly, although she could feel the tension in his arm, in the way his grip was just a touch too tight, although he clearly meant her no harm. "Think about it. Marguerite has a lot of bad points." She found the strength to glare at him. "But she isn't a liar. She doesn't even tell polite social lies. I don't think she knows *how* to be anything but truthful. If she had done this, she wouldn't deny it. She wouldn't think she had to."

His words hung in the air. Then Än's shoulders slumped. "It's true," she said, her voice sounding like her own again, soft and sweet and sure. "She always tells the truth as she sees it, even when what she thinks is really mean."

Malik nodded. Saqr was still hot and furious. "Think about it, Grandmother. If she really had come here as some sort of ... I don't know, deceptive evil spirit, I'm sure she would have been less abrasive and more charming."

"Hey!" Marguerite protested.

He smiled down at her and patted her hand.

"I like you," he said. "So does Än. But you didn't make it easy."

She looked up at him. She put her other hand on top of his.

"I like you too," she said. "Not as much as I like Än and your horse. But you have your good points as well."

He laughed a little, and it cleared out more of the tent's fog. Än shook herself and walked around the table to join them, putting a hand on Marguerite's shoulder. She shrugged it away.

"See?" Malik said to Saqr. "Truthful to a fault."

The old woman looked at the three of them, at the strange tableau they made, the two desert dwellers arranged around the little seawitch.

She folded in on herself.

"You've never argued with me as much in your lives as you have for this girl," she said. And then, "Perhaps you're right. You have many faults, but I've never seen any dishonesty in you." She paused. "I shouldn't have called you poison."

"I've been called worse," said Marguerite. Her hand tightened on Malik's bicep. "Probably."

He was still smiling at her, but there was a weak edge to it now.

"We've all gotten upset," he said. "We'll have a nice cup of tea and feel better." There was command in his voice, although it had a gentleness that Saqr's orders had lacked.

Marguerite shook her head.

"Catseye needs grooming," she said, looking only at Malik, though she could feel Än's heat behind her.

He looked down at her and gave her hand a pat.

"That he does," he said. "You'd better go get him cleaned up at once."

She nodded. It was surprisingly hard to unclench her fingers from the fabric of Malik's sleeve. She looked at him, but she didn't look at the other two as she exited the tent and made her way over to the horses. Catseye and Eyas greeted her immediately, Nahr hanging back until she extended her hand and gave the mare's soft nose a pat. Malik had left his brush kit out. She picked one up and ran it along Catseye's gleaming side, wishing she was stroking a swathe of white instead of black.

She heard footsteps behind her and didn't turn around.

"Hi." Än's voice sounded drained and lifeless.

"Hi," said Marguerite, and ran the brush along Catseye's side again.

The silence lay heavy, as heavy as it had ever lain when the wind had been her steed. Then she heard an intake of breath behind her.

"I'm sorry."

She turned, less because of the words and more because of how wrecked Än sounded. The other girl stood before her, her eyes on the ground, her fists curled against her sides.

"For what?"

That won her Än's eyes. She had seen them brighter, but the gold, though just barely rimming her pupil, was there.

"What do you mean for what?" Än said. "For what happened. For not — for not trusting you. For believing that you caused this. I was just — you're so strange. So alien. So not of the desert. I was scared."

"It's okay," Marguerite said. "I'm used to it."

She had seen a lot of odd expressions on Än's face today. She recognized this one. Än got the same look whenever Marguerite talked about her past.

"That's really sad," Än said. "And it's not okay. Malik stepped up right away. He knew you were telling the truth."

"Malik's not very smart sometimes," Marguerite said. She paused, struck by a thought. "Was that mean? Is that one of the mean things I say?"

Än laughed, a bright, jagged little sound, the bells rusting and splintering away. "Yeah, it is." She sobered, if one could be said to sober from laughter that had very little joy in it. "But it's not okay. Malik was right. I know Malik was right. But I just panicked. I was so scared."

"Of what I can do?" Marguerite asked when Än didn't finish her sentence. It was a familiar enough emotion. Usually she rather enjoyed having her fearsome abilities acknowledged. It didn't feel good now.

"No!" Än said immediately. "I was scared—" There were some things that could only be said under cover of darkness. There were some things so important that they had to be said anyway, even if the sky was bright and wrong. Än turned her head to the ground again. "I was scared that my feelings for you had blinded me to your danger." She took a deep, shuddering breath. "I was scared that I was imagining you were good because I wanted so much to be with you."

Marguerite said nothing to the confession. She stood, feeling very much the pillar of ice she had always imagined herself to be (when had she stopped feeling the ice in her soul with every breath?). Än finally looked at her and then, reaching out slowly, giving Marguerite time to back away, took her hand.

She felt the trickle of water dripping out of the cavern inside her.

"I want to be with you, too," she said. "Even though you were sort of awful back there." Her fingers tightened a little around Än's. She spoke slowly, working each word out before she let it escape into the world. "I think I'm sort of awful sometimes, too. Maybe we can learn how to be less awful together?"

She had never been gracious before. It was sort of a pleasant feeling, actually.

Än smiled. People had been smiling at her a lot lately. This was the first one that felt like a person was grinning at her and not a corpse.

"I'd like that," Än said.

They didn't kiss. She had a feeling that they wouldn't be kissing for quite a while. But she felt lighter. She felt — she felt like there weren't any cliffs in the desert.

"Are you going to come and have a drink?" Än asked, once standing and smiling shyly at each other was starting to feel awkward and not endearing.

She started to shake her head and then rethought the matter. Än trusted her now. Malik always had. And Saqr — Saqr had listened to them, at least. Her throat did feel tight and sore. And it occurred to her for the first time that even going inside for a meal could be a choice.

"Okay," said Marguerite.

It wasn't the most comfortable setting she had ever been in. Malik and Saqr had already finished their tea; all three of them had probably been discussing her while she was with the horses. Malik grinned up at her, his smile genuine, but uncomfortably wide. She had the distinct feeling that she was being reassured. Saqr did not smile and barely met her eyes. She didn't seek the contact. People seemed to seek one another's eyes more than wolves did, but she knew it could still be a challenge, and she was tired of challenging Saqr.

They ate a little with the tea (a particularly potent brew — too many leaves, not enough water, she supposed), and then Saqr announced that she and Än would try one more working before day's end. Tomorrow, they would have to decide if they should leave the sanctuary in search of water. Marguerite didn't wait for an invitation to be issued (or to not be issued). She announced that she would go with Malik. He started but agreed immediately and she forced herself not to look for signs of relief in the women's faces.

Malik didn't say it, but his actions suggested he thought they would be leaving the sanctuary. She helped him begin to bundle up the detritus of the camp, to refresh the wax around the rims of the water jugs and to stretch the horses' legs in preparation for a long journey. The sky darkened on them as they tied the last bundles. There was nothing from the — Än had called them magicians. From the magicians. She supposed she appreciated the lack of accusations.

"Do you want to sleep in my tent again?" Malik asked when it started to get too dark to see the ropes she was knotting. She nodded, grateful for the offer. He offered her a drink and a snack before bed, but she didn't take them. She crawled into his tent and curled up among the leathers and the horse smell.

She had never had trouble sleeping before. Always she had dropped off immediately. She didn't sleep now. She lay in the dark and the mustiness, thinking about the day. Thinking about the rain. Thinking about the poisoned water. Thinking about Saqr's accusations and about the horror in Än's eyes. The sky darkened to pitch black so that she could see nothing in the tent but the pictures in her own mind's eye. It was silent, not even the wind twisting the tent's flaps.

She heard music.

She rose and pushed the tent flap open and walked out onto the sand. It pitched against the soles of her feet, the ripple of it stretching to the horizon.

She could still hear the music. She had heard the melody before. The first melody she had ever heard, a song just for her.

The sand shifted and began to run, swirling around itself. She braced herself, unafraid, watching it churn. Watching it cool. Watching the gold shift to silver. Watching grit spin itself into froth. Watching eddies of sand become eddies of water. Watching the billowing dunes collapse and become crashing waves, the circling birds transformed into schools of fish. Her eyes stung, not the stinging of sand but of salt.

She took a deep breath of good ocean air.

The water rippled and turned once more to sand. She woke.

She could still hear the music, somewhere out in the desert.

She hadn't thought much about her first days in the desert. She hadn't blocked them out exactly, but she hadn't dwelled on them. There had been other worries, other indignities, other pains taking up her thoughts. And then there had been good things, things that blocked the bad things out. She let herself remember now, held each memory up to the light and examined it carefully. She remembered fear, fear wearing a mask called anger and anger wearing a mask called grudging acceptance. She remembered falling. She remembered thirsting.

She remembered a gentle voice, telling her a story about a desert that wasn't hot and dry but cold and dark and pressing.

She remembered a pool of water that had remembered the taste of the ocean.

She remembered an angry girl, standing beside a door that no longer led anywhere and singing a song to drown the world.

"Oh," said Marguerite.

———— «» ————

The camp was quiet when she emerged from the tent. Her dream had gotten that much right. (But she hadn't really been in the camp, had she? She had been somewhere else. She knew that place, or she thought she did.) She didn't need to dress or brush her hair, bless Än and her kindness. She debated packing food or water, but she didn't, somehow, think she would need it. Not as much as they would, anyway. She put on her boots.

She left the tent and climbed to the top of the dune, slipping a little on the sand trickling beneath every step. It had been still in her dream. But the wind played around her a little now, a little more when she hummed to encourage it. When she reached the top of the dune, she sang.

"Will you ride with me once more?" she asked the wind, and before she had even finished, she felt Caravel's head under her palm, as though he had been waiting. Was he always waiting? Or had he known that now was the time she would need him?

She mounted, grateful that a wind horse needed neither tack nor brushing. The quicker she was away, the better. She turned his head out into the desert.

"I thought you were going to stay this time."

She looked back. Än looked tumbled, tired, her eyes drowned out by the shadows under them.

"You ran away last time we hurt you," she said. "I thought this time we had convinced you to stay." Her voice was flat, exhausted. Aching.

"I'm not running away," said Marguerite. "I'm running to. It's different." It was. Funny that she had never noticed that before.

"Where? Why? Why now, of all times?"

She looked down at Än. It was night, so there were things that were okay to say.

"It's calling me," she whispered. "I think Saqr was right. I think I did this."

"What? But you said—"

"I know what I said. I believed it. I really did. But now — something's calling me." She turned back to Caravel, twined a hand in his mane.

"I'm not a good person. I don't think I even was a person for most of my life." She looked back at Än. Some conversations deserved eye contact. "But Saqr was wrong about one thing. This is a story. And it's time I stopped acting like the villain. If I'm the only one who can fix this, I think I should try."

She reached down and offered her hand. Än took it.

"I could go with you."

"I don't think so. It's — it's mine. I don't think you can help, and your family will need you."

Even in the dark, even clouded with exhaustion, even through the blur of tears, the gold shone. Marguerite took a deep breath. Desert air. Mostly, anyway.

"If I don't come back — I didn't really plan this very well. Will you tell Malik that I said thank you? I don't think I ever thanked him for anything. Tell him that, except for the first day, when he was terrible, he was the best man I've ever known." She paused. "Also, pretty much the only man I've ever known. Make sure you tell him that part too."

Än laughed a little and a few drops ran down her cheeks.

"I'll tell him. I promise." She nodded.

"Tell Saqr — she was right, I guess. But that I really wasn't lying. I don't think." She thought again. "Is it lying if you think you're telling the truth?"

Another strangled laugh. "Grandmother's good at that kind of philosophy. She'll sort it out."

Marguerite nodded. "Good. And, um…" She paused. There were words that lovers exchanged when they parted, but none of the things she had read felt like things she could say. Like things that would mean anything, coming from her mouth.

"Be careful," Än whispered. "Try to come back. Please. I think I might be…" She stopped, and Marguerite honestly thought she wouldn't finish the sentence. She did. "I think I might be falling in love with you."

Marguerite let herself have one last look at Än. At the red of her hair, the strength in her form. The gold in her eyes.

"I don't think I'm in love with you," she said. Än flinched, just a little. "I loved the ocean and the rain and the storm and I loved the desert wind. I don't think I know how to love a person. But if I come back from this, I think I'd like to try to learn."

"Okay," said Än. "I can — I can live with that." Her cheeks were soaked and reddening. It would have been romantic to kiss her.

"Cheer up," said Marguerite instead. "I don't know if this will work. You might still need to be strong." She touched her heels to Caravel's sides. He shot forward. Anything Än might have said or not said was lost in the pounding of his hooves.

Chapter Twenty-Two

She was grateful for Caravel. She was always grateful for Caravel, of course. Caravel was the best. But she was particularly grateful that she had a horse who could do his own navigating. She knew where she was going but only in a theoretical sense. She knew where she needed to end up. She didn't have a clue how to get there. Caravel, though. Caravel knew every corner of the desert (did deserts have corners?). She thought of the place she was going and she hummed a little song to him and he went. She trusted him to take her there, as she didn't trust even herself.

They rode hard. Another advantage of a horse that was so much more than a horse. The going was difficult at first, the slick surfaces of the plants turning Caravel's footing as sand never had. But soon they moved beyond the plants, back onto true desert. They galloped most of the time. Though his movements were smooth, she quickly stiffened, and the old familiar pains that she had mostly worked out started shooting through her again. She felt the rubbing of her thighs against his coat, sleek as it was, the striking of her pelvic bone on the mountain ridge of his back, the way her calves trembled with the effort of keeping herself upright. Her back ached, her shoulders bowing as each hoof strike began to feel more like a blow. Her vision blurred with the effort of staring across the horizon.

She didn't slow him, and he didn't slow himself. They continued to gallop, past rolling dunes, past rippling sand, until the only things keeping her upright were the rigidity of her arms on his neck and her horse's determination to keep her aboard.

They galloped as the sun rose, as it beat down on them until it seemed it would flatten them. They galloped as her mouth desiccated, as her throat burned, as the saliva in her mouth turned to brine. They galloped as she regretted not bringing water with her.

They galloped past a great skeleton, its newly uncovered ivory bones gleaming sluggishly, a few dried strips of baleen still hanging from its great mouth, one tiny splinter missing from the top of its skull.

They didn't stop.

They didn't stop because the sanctuary had only two days' worth of water. They didn't stop because the birds and the foxes and all of the creatures that she had only heard about probably didn't even have that.

They galloped until they reached a door on a hill, a door that had once been a door to another world and was now a door to nothing at all, a door that no longer even opened, and only then did she pull Caravel to a stop. It looked the same, still ornate, the patterns still swirling like a wave. Or like a sand dune. Or like the desert wind. She saw that now.

After holding to him so long, she had difficulty unwinding herself from Caravel's back. He had to kneel and pull gently on her shoulder with his teeth before she was able to unclench her tense muscles and roll onto the sand. She licked her dry lips, the brush of her equally dry tongue providing no relief. Should have brought a waterskin. Too late now, and it had seemed a waste at the time. She let herself lie for a moment but only for a moment. If she stayed longer, she wouldn't rise again. Not because of any fear or emotional issues. But she had learned that sore muscles stiffened in that position. So she rolled onto her stomach and slowly, she brought her arms under her body. She pushed upward, shaking, feeling her bones rattle. She got herself sitting and used Caravel's neck as a crutch so she could stand.

She kissed his nose.

Some mad impulse told her to keep him, to bring him with her to this. She quashed it. Some other, deeper instinct told her that he would be no help. That he might be hurt. She couldn't allow that.

She pressed her forehead to his.

"Thank you," she whispered. "For everything."

She stepped back, slow, almost doddering.

"Now *run*."

The wind blew her hair from her face for just a moment. Now that she had been kissed the normal way, she could recognize one when she felt it. Then the wind was gone and the air sat heavy and still.

It occurred to her for the first time that there might be a place between grasping and abandonment, a place that looked a little bit like love.

She turned around.

She had fallen, that first time. She had rolled down the hill in an undignified heap. She had imagined herself making her way down slowly this time, gracefully. She had imagined herself elegant for this.

She didn't roll. There was that. She slid the last few inches, the sand heavy around her, but she didn't roll. She rose to her feet again, thinking that perhaps she had dismissed Caravel early. But she wouldn't risk him. She closed her eyes and breathed. Then she looked.

The tiny hole she had dug had swollen and grown until it was the size of a small lake. A lake with the memory of when it had merely been a seawitch's drinking hole. Waves lapped at the shore. The waters shifted, making patterns in the sunlight. She knew, without testing it, that the waters would be deep. Water was treacherous, after all, and the ocean kept its secrets in a way that the desert did not.

She cupped one hand and lowered it, bringing a palmful of water to her mouth. Salt, of course. She had forgotten the heaviness of salt on her tongue.

She breathed again.

She sang.

There wasn't music in earth the way there was in water. The land did not sing. But there was movement. There was dancing. Ocean and earth danced together, a constant bowing, parting, coming together again. Ocean covered earth and then, when its turn was up, earth thrust it away, until came its time to bow beneath again.

There were some truths that could only come from a lover.

It isn't your time, sang Marguerite. *This isn't your solo. This isn't the bracket in the symphony where you lead.*

The water shifted. The waves rolled, froth spilling across her boots.

The ocean sang back to her, of a desert covered in water, as it had once been, as one day it would be again. It sang of salt in the air. It sang of a wind, running across the waves, catching spray and flicking it across the surface.

(Caravel had loved her voice, which had been shaped by the sea, but she had never sung to him without the taste of the desert in her mouth.)

The ocean sang of rain that didn't hide away, of water that did not betray her. It sang of the drowning of everything she had ever hated. It sang of a place ringing with real music, proper music. It sang of a desert that she didn't need to change herself to fit, that would remake itself to fit her.

(But being the same had hurt, in a way that being different had not.)

It sang her a love song, of seawitch and sea together. It sang of a world made for her.

The ocean sang: *they will believe you were brave and that you failed. They will never know you chose this.*

She looked out across the water. She had missed this horizon. She had missed the sound of water, the way it spoke to her. She had missed the color of it, the gentle grey and blue, so much less harsh than anything she had ever seen in the desert. She missed the darting of fish, the slow arch of whales, the cries of the seabirds. She missed being obeyed.

Sing me a love song, the lapping of the waves whispered. *And make the desert what you want it to be.*

She took a deep breath.

Every song was, at its heart, a love song. She reached inside herself. She touched the hard, gaping hole inside, the hole she had once filled with ice and seawater. She closed her eyes and tightened her grip on what she found inside.

She opened her mouth.

She had never learned to lie in song. But there were things she could find a song in herself about, songs she hadn't realized she was writing. She sang a song about the desert wind, which had allowed itself to be tamed and who had served her faithfully, long after she no longer needed it, until she was ready to let it go. She sang a song about Än, Än who had understood her, who had brought her to a city that sang so she would have the courage to let go of the wind, Än who had kissed her, Än who had doubted her and then repented, Än whose eyes were bright and beautiful. She sang a song about Malik, who had not understood her but who had seen the frightened girl under the ill-tempered witch and tried to be kind to her, Malik who had taught her to ride and to care for horses, Malik who had been told he was cruel and had accepted it and changed. She sang a song about Saqr, Saqr who had ordered the strange lost girl brought to her instead of destroyed, Saqr who had been unafraid to tell her she was wrong and willing to forgive her when she set things right. She sang a song about the desert birds, who loved the wind even more than she did, and a song about the clever little foxes who knew secrets. She sang a song and then another song about horses, about soft noses pressing against her, about warm breath running across her skin, about a mane whipping around her fingers, about powerful legs carrying her over the sand. She sang a song about blossoms after rain, about hidden crevices filling with water, about the patterns that sand made under wind.

She sang until her throat began to burn, until the swelling of it began to choke off her voice, until her mouth was filled with neither dust nor salt but the coppery tang of blood.

She sang one more thing.

She sang, *I'm sorry*.

There could be no anger here. Not between them. Not even after this. The waters stilled and calmed, smoother than she had ever seen as if her song had poured oil overtop of it.

I understand, said the swirl of water on shore.

"Then you'll go?" she whispered, even that tiny slip of air chafing her voice.

For a moment, the rush of water over sand was just water over sand. And then the ocean sang again.

No.

She had no voice left to exclaim, but she forced out a soft, shrieking noise of both betrayal and interrogation.

"Why?"

You woke me up, the ocean sang, and she knew it was true. *You invited me out. You wanted me.*

It sang to her of a vast expanse, just aching to be filled. It sang to her of water, running over the dunes, cascading through the valleys. It sang of exploring the little places that even the wind couldn't touch, of the places that only the steady dripping of water would ever be patient enough to find. It sang to her of rocks it wanted to brush against, as softly as a kiss, as hard as cannon fire. It sang to her of waking to a world just waiting to be discovered and claimed.

She could command it to sleep. It was the ocean and, despite her long absence, she was still a seawitch. She could send it to its rest, and though it would be a fitful one, ever dreaming of that brief moment of freedom, it would go. She had that much power. She could force it back, force it to obey her in this.

But she knew what it felt like to be sent somewhere she didn't wish to go.

There might be another way. If she was clever. If she was desperate. Her throat burned and ached. She had in the past sung for longer but never so desperately or in such harsh conditions. Despite her attempts to save it, the desert had not been kind. Her body was empty. Her windpipe was dry. She could feel that she had torn something deep inside. She would need to rest, to recover it.

"I can fix this," she whispered. And, with the blood running down her throat, she sang one more song.

Outro

The mare's coat was pleasantly cool under her hand, despite the heat of the day. It shifted in the light, a palette of greys from a soft almost white to a stormy grey to a slate so deep it was almost blue. Her mane frothed over her neck and shoulders and over the peak of her head down her forehead. Her hooves, delicate little circles of shell, pink and brown and gleaming and harder than ice, danced across the sand. Her tail floated behind her, a waterfall cascading from her hindquarters onto the sand below. Her eyes were green, the green of bright and growing things.

They walked together, slowly, picking their way carefully, Marguerite stiff and sore, the mare still learning how four legs moved together to cross the sand. Occasionally Marguerite turned her head to brush her lips against the broad shoulder beside her. Although the mare was not yet sweating, her skin tasted vaguely of salt.

She was calm now. She would be wild soon. Marguerite couldn't wait.

She didn't know the path she should walk. There might, perhaps, be some instinct that guided a person home. She didn't think it would help even if she knew how to summon it. Home — home was beside her and yet in front of her at the same time.

She was relieved but not entirely surprised when she saw figures on the horizon. Some part of her had come to accept that Än and Malik would come for her, although the third figure was a surprise. They approached one another slowly. She inspected their faces. They looked, all of them, better. Unsure but better.

Malik moved first, swinging off Catseye and walking up to her without fear. His eyes were on the mare. She would have to get his opinion. Revise her own, as well, she supposed. Caravel, after all, had been downgraded to merely the best *stallion* in the world.

She didn't speak. She waited for him to start.

"Is this going to be a thing?" Malik asked. "You making us think you're dead and then turning up with mysterious horses?"

Marguerite looked up at him and grinned. She swallowed and tried to find the words.

"I don't think so," she said. Her voice felt strange, choked and hurt. It sounded a little like Saqr's, really, a kind of deep-throated croak. But Saqr's voice had suited her, had been a voice of power long accustomed and used. She could feel the waver in her own. "But you never know."

He grinned back at her, but his eyes were troubled. He actually had a rather nice smile. It vanished, suddenly, and his brow wrinkled, a cloud passing over the sun. "Are you okay?"

She shrugged and then nodded, because in the grand scheme of things, the answer was more or less that she was. He accepted it.

"Is this one … you know? Because Caravel was beautiful but that whole thing was a bit of a mess."

"It's okay," she said, her hand continuing to rest on the mare's shoulder. She let herself struggle. Let herself take the time to form the words. Let them go, even half-formed. "It's not her time yet. So it's okay for her to be here with me."

She turned to Saqr. "You were right," she croaked. Hard consonants stuck in her throat. She had to force them out. "I did this. But I think I fixed it."

Saqr nodded. Her smile was nice too. She'd never really smiled at Marguerite, not out of genuine happiness. It deepened the wrinkles in her face but didn't sharpen them and it turned out that her beady, foggy eyes were capable of twinkling.

"You did," she said. "Thank you. For accepting that you did it and for taking responsibility." Her eyes ran over the mare, the green eyes meeting hers calmly.

"I can stay?" Marguerite asked, even though inflections were hard.

Saqr nodded.

"As long as you want."

Än had been hanging back. She stepped up now so that they faced one another. There were things that happened in stories after the story was over, if you'd done everything right. Marguerite leaned forward to kiss her. Än had apparently had the same idea. They bumped noses and then teeth and pulled away blushing.

"I'm glad you're back," Än whispered. "But what did you do?"

Marguerite shrugged. Her fingers tightened in the mare's mane. She had one more thing she had to say before she could rest. It was important. She enunciated clearly.

"I damaged my throat. I don't think I'm ever going to be able to sing the way I used to."

The gold in Än's eyes was so bright, as though she was smelting some of the ache in Marguerite's words.

Marguerite smiled and stroked a hand down the mare's side. "But it's okay. I think — I think it's time I learned how to make desert music."

Än smiled back. It was the first note of a perfect new song, powerful as the ocean, warm as the sun.

Acknowledgments

I can hardly write a whole book about the importance of human connection without acknowledging how many other people contributed to *A Song to Drown the World*, now can I?

Thank you first and foremost to my mom, Denise, who is not only one of my biggest supporters but also my first editor. Nothing I write would be what it is without her. In fact, I'm not sure I'd be a writer at all without her influence.

Thank you to Hooley and Andrea, who were the first people to read *A Song to Drown the World* and the first people to love it. Your encouragement really helped this book to blossom. Thank you to Nora, who didn't read it and thus was able to help me objectively write the pitch. And thank you to my dad, my biggest cheerleader.

Thank you to Brian, my publisher, for believing in me and in this odd little book and for all his assistance getting it out into the wider world. And special thanks to Ella, who did the editing. Not only did you make the book better, you were so incredibly kind and supportive about it.

Thank you to Xena, who inspired most of the best parts of *A Song to Drown the World* and most of the best parts of me. Thank you to Ramses, who wasn't born when it was written and was no help with the edits but would sulk if he didn't make it into the acknowledgments.

Thank you to every editor who accepted one of my short stories into your anthologies and therefore made me believe I could make a go of this writing thing.

I know it's a little bit cheesy, but I always like when I read a book that thanks the readers and so I am going to do it, too. Thank you for looking at this book and deciding to pick it up and thank you for reading this far. I hope that Marguerite's story spoke to you.

About the Author

Rowena Spring writes vivid, magical tales blending the surreal with the intimate. Inspired by the ocean, horses, and a career in science and heritage communication, her work explores connection and transformation. Her debut novel, A Song to Drown the World, showcases her talent for crafting lush, emotionally charged narratives where magic and reality collide.

Need something new to read?

If you liked A Song to Drown the World, you should also consider these other EDGE titles…

The Tongue Trade

by Michael J. Martineck

Discover the Dangerous Power of Words.

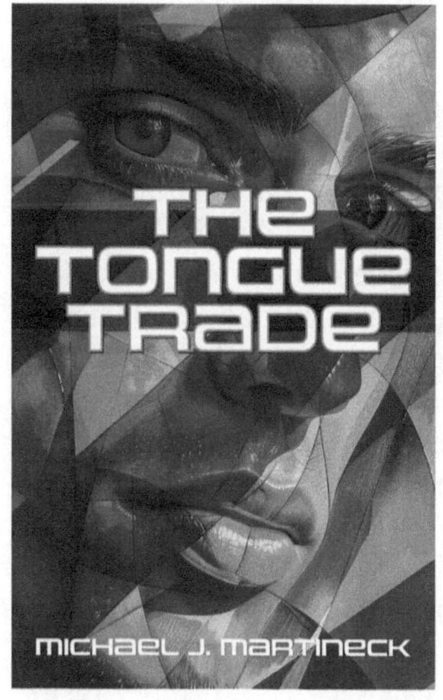

In the not-too-distant future, humanity's ability to communicate has fractured, creating a labyrinth of professional jargons so dense that only specialists like William Kirst, Private Interpreter, can unravel them.

Kirst is a linchpin in a society where understanding is a luxury, and secrets are the norm. His routine existence is shattered when he becomes entangled in a murder investigation, a crime spoken in a language of bullets and blood.

As an interpreter sworn to confidentiality Kirst is bound by an oath that puts his life in jeopardy and his morals in shackles. The more he uncovers, the deeper he's edged into a conspiracy where language, as a weapon and a prison, pushes him closer to a dark truth.

The Tongue Trade is a riveting exploration of language, loyalty, and the lethal power of secrets. It questions the boundaries of ethical duty and the price of silence in a fragmented world.

Where words are the ultimate currency, silence can be lethal.

Pishtaco: Lord of the Lost Inca Gold
by Mark Patton

*An All-Powerful Evil Shaman Wakes to
Protect Lost Inca Gold*

Penelope Augusta Gertrude Farquhar, a woman struggling with schizophrenia, finds herself lost in the Amazon rainforest after a fateful airplane crash. But she's not alone: her voices, now personified as historical figures such as René Descartes, Ada Lovelace, and Ernest Shackleton, accompany her on a quest to find the fabled city of Paititi and destroy the evil shaman Pishtaco, who has amassed the lost Inca gold of Atahualpa.

"Pishtaco: Lord of the Lost Inca Gold" is a thrilling historical fantasy that takes you on a journey through the mystical and mysterious world of the Inca people. Along the way, you'll encounter the pantheon of Inca gods and goddesses, as well as the tribal people of the Amazon rainforest, and learn about their cultures and beliefs. This offbeat adventure is filled with humor, twists and turns, and a unique blend of history and mythology.

Mark Patton's well-researched and engaging writing transports you to another world, while delving into themes of mental health and the nature of reality. "Pishtaco: Lord of the Lost Inca Gold" is a must-read for fans of adventure, history, and mythology.

Shadow Stitcher (An Everland Mystery)

by Misha Handman

Selected as one of the year's most compelling debut novels for Kobo's Emerging Writer Prize, Shadow Stitcher is guaranteed to delight.

This fast paced Noir mystery has a great cast of easily identifiable characters, a plot both easy to follow and intriguing, and an ending that will leave you satisfied.

A former pirate faces mobsters and magic in 1950s Neverland.

Basil Stark isn't the man he once was. A reformed pirate and private detective, he walks the line between criminal and hero, living in the corners of what was once the island of Neverland, its magic slowly fading into the new world of the 1950s. But when a routine missing-persons case turns into a murder investigation, Basil finds himself pulled into a tale of organized crime, murder, unstitched shadows and dangerous espionage. With only a handful of fellow outcasts and a stubborn determination to bring a killer to justice, will he survive the many people who want him dead?

For more EDGE titles and information about upcoming speculative fiction please visit us at:

www.edgewebsite.com

Don't forget to sign-up for our Special Offers

——<<<>>>——